ANI L'DODI

LOVE THAT LASTS

ANA WATERS

For new releases, special promotions, announcements, and ordering information:

www.anawaters.com
linktr.ee/anawaters

For every precious pearl trampled by someone who refused to acknowledge your value. <u>Their</u> mistakes don't determine <u>your</u> worth.

For Hannah and Rena.

"Daughters of Jerusalem, I charge you— if you find my beloved, what will you tell him? Tell him I am faint with love."

— SONG OF SONGS 5:8 NIV

CHAPTER 1

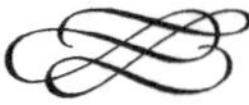

"WHAT IS IT ABOUT PEOPLE BEING IN LOVE THAT makes it so nauseating?" I grumbled around a mouthful of dessert.

My best friend, Lauren Fein, gave me a sideways grin. "Charlotte, if I didn't know you any better, I'd say you sound bitter."

"I prefer to think of myself as sarcastically realistic." I shoved another bite of Parkview Diner cheesecake into my mouth with gusto, and Lauren giggled at my antics.

Laughing now came easily to my dear friend, especially with a 1.25 carat, princess cut engagement ring sparkling on her finger. Regardless of the desiccated state of romance in my own life, I didn't resent a shred of her current happiness. Lauren had survived eight years of unimaginable hell being married to a physically abusive monster and then another two years trying to divorce the psychopath. My own ex-husband used to be best friends with him until Nathan Fein's private perversions became public knowledge in court. Then, it was in Rick's best interest to shun Nathan Fein and pretend they'd never really been friends.

Rick Williams, my wet noodle ex-husband, now wanted to be called *Richard,* and he became even more pedantic after shackling himself to the larger-than-life-with-hair-to-match Stephanie Burgess. She behaved more like Stephanie *Bougie* based on the lifestyle she now shared with my ex-husband, but Lauren gently reminded me those thoughts weren't very pleasing to the Lord. Most of the time I took her advice, but never after my daughters had another traumatizing bout of visitation time with their father and his bottled blonde replacement wife.

"Charlotte," Lauren said, bursting through my morose memories, "you never told me about that guy you met on ChristianFishing.com."

"Turns out it was the same clown who messaged me when I was on LoveJewSchmooze. The one who asked if he could 'take a dip in your waters' because my screen name was *BytheSea98.*"

My friend mimicked a dry heave. "Ew! That guy again?! Is he stalking you across every online dating site, or are you just that lucky?"

"Apparently, I'm just that lucky. I told him to get a better pick up line, the pool is closed, and he was being blocked again."

"Do you ever use that account with LJS anymore? I didn't think you'd be interested in a Jewish dating site because of everything that's happened at Beth Shalom."

"Oh, I still loathe that decrepit cesspool of hypocrisy," I said around another bite, "but I won't find anybody celebrating Chanukah or Passover on a Christian dating site."

Lauren didn't hide her smirk in time, and one of the things I loved was saying things in the most outrageously truthful way possible. Since Richard's funny bone only existed while we were dating, I'd always felt stifled during our fifteen-year marriage.

"Charlotte, whatever happened with that guy you were talking to last year when Grant and I were failing miserably at being platonic coworkers?"

"Former member of Beth Shalom who decided he wanted to be Orthodox Jewish and then recanted his faith in Jesus."

She winced. "Another one of those? Was the guy Jewish, or did he wind up converting?"

"Typical gentile who becomes enamored with all things Jewish and then develops a superiority complex toward mainstream Christianity," I replied. "It wasn't attractive when my ex-husband did it, and it's even less attractive to me now."

"They always wind up overcompensating, don't they?"

"Always, and I don't need a repeat of the hyper-spiritual nonsense I was married to. We both know I'm incapable of being anything other than one hundred percent myself."

She smiled at me. "And you know that I love you for it. There's not a thing I would change about you, Charlotte."

"Oh yeah? Not even that pesky filter I *should* have over my mouth, but it functions more like a broken gate instead? Occasionally, the wind blows and snaps the thing closed when I legitimately need to keep my mouth shut."

She burst into giggles. "No, I love all of that too."

"Well, I'm glad somebody does."

"Jonathan Roseman seems to appreciate it, but you won't give him the time of day."

"Don't start with that again!"

Her eyes twinkled with mischief. "He couldn't stop staring at you when Ruthie and Aaron got married."

"He was officiating his daughter's wedding ceremony. Of

course, he was looking in my direction. I was sitting directly in his line of sight."

"Okay, so what about before the wedding and afterwards? He watched you dance at the reception with a smile on his face. I was totally shipping it."

"I'm the life of the party, what can I say? Besides, he never asked me for a slow dance, so what difference does it make if he was watching me?"

"Maybe he's shy."

"Well, I'm not, so clearly this isn't going to go anywhere."

"He couldn't exactly rizz you up at his daughter's wedding, Charlotte."

"Dancing with me isn't the same thing as rizzing me up."

"But everyone in that room knows you two from Beth Shalom and knows you're both single now. Don't you think they'd be talking if Jonathan suddenly asked you to dance? It would have been distracting for Ruthie's big day."

I rolled my eyes. "If people have nothing better to do at someone's wedding than speculate about the father of the bride, that's their problem, not mine."

"So, you're admitting you're a couple?" she teased.

I stuck my tongue out at her. "Our daughters played together in the temple nursery once upon a time. Who cares? Jonathan and I have known each other for almost twenty years. If he wanted to ask me to dance, he would have."

"Charlotte, you two have only really known each other as the spouse of somebody else. You were married to Rick for most of that time even after Andrea passed away. You haven't interacted as a single man and woman before. Also, you looked stunning that night, and the man could not keep his eyes off of you. Are you telling me you didn't catch him staring *one* time? Grant even asked me about it."

"Probably because you're the one who suggested it in the first place."

"What about Jonathan tracking you down on Instantpics?"

"What about it?"

"Charlotte, how can you not see that Jonathan Roseman is into you? He's always 'liking' your posts and selfies, and he compliments you all the time."

"Yeah, and so do a hundred other guys like Pool Boy who spam my inbox with those idiotic, 'hello dear' messages. Do you know how many phony Keenan Reeves accounts have followed me?"

"Exactly my point! Jonathan is respectful and sincerely complimentary. He's not sending you creeper DMs, and he's putting his admiration out there in public. Why don't you want to admit the obvious?"

I shoved another bite of cheesecake into my mouth so I wouldn't have to answer honestly. There weren't many secrets I kept from Lauren, but Jonathan Roseman was one of them. The kid was too close to the truth, and I didn't want her to know that Jonathan and I had started texting each other six months before his daughter got married to Lauren's old admirer, Aaron Davis.

It was after the first month of messages I realized Jon and I would never have a romantic future. I knew he admired me as a person and as a woman, but we had slipped into a very comfortable friendship. He told me about the women he'd been matched with online, and I asked him for advice regarding some of the bread-crumbing losers I'd been desperate enough to entertain in my lower moments.

I switched the topic to lighter subjects and kept thoughts of Jon at bay. Lauren's upcoming wedding was far more exciting than my disastrous dating life.

I arrived home at my townhouse around 10:30 pm, and both of my girls were scrolling on their phones with the TV blaring in the background.

"Shouldn't you two be in bed? It's a school night."

My oldest, Sophie, spared me a glance from whatever social media app she was posting on. "Man date or friend date?"

"Friend date. I haven't been on a man date in three months."

Lily, my fifteen year-old, eyed me critically. "So, you put on extra makeup and curled your hair for Lauren?"

"Can't I take pride in my appearance without a man having to be involved?"

"Did you post a selfie at least?" she asked. "You look cute tonight."

I grinned back. "Duh."

"And did *he* like it?" Sophie teased, ever the matchmaker and hopeless romantic.

I rolled my eyes and dropped my purse onto the loveseat situated by the front door. "Seriously? Not you guys too."

"Mr. Roseman is *always* liking your pics," she insisted.

"So what? It's a free country. We're friends. I like his photos too. Stop shipping it just because you want Rachel Roseman to be your stepsister."

My oldest pulled a face, her powder blue eyes narrowed into a carbon copy expression of mine. "I think you're lying."

"Excuse me? I have a great number of faults, Sophie Grace, but lying isn't one of them."

"Fine," she groused, "you're hiding something."

I walked into the adjoining kitchen so she wouldn't see the guilty expression on my face.

Both girls trailed on my heels as I pretended to search for something in the refrigerator.

"You just had dessert with Lauren, you're not hungry," Lily said.

I turned my head to see them standing with their arms crossed over their chests in matching fleece pajamas I'd bought them last Chanukah.

Sighing, I closed the fridge door and turned to face them. "What do you want me to say? Jonathan and I are friends. Sometimes we talk. That's it."

My daughters, though only separated by twenty-two months, behaved more like twins. They exchanged a knowing look between them.

"Sometimes?" Lily asked, raising dark brows over the hazel eyes she'd gotten from her father. "You're on your phone every night texting. It can't always be Lauren—especially now that she's engaged."

"Stop interrogating me! Yes, Jon is just a friend. Yes, we talk pretty regularly. He was asking me about a woman he found on SingleMingle last week, so trust me, it is *just friends*."

"Jon?" Sophie cooed. "What happened to *Jonathan*?"

"Less syllables and I'm tired. Leave me alone." I plopped down into a kitchen chair.

The girls promptly surrounded me, one on each side at our breakfast table.

"Would you want it to be more?" Sophie asked. "I mean, Daddy is married to Stephanie, so what are you waiting for?"

Not that I believed my girls wanted me to get a boyfriend as revenge for the stepmother, but I knew they despised their father's new wife. The wondrous Stephanie had provided our blended family with stepbrothers and holy terrors, Braxton and Brayden, and Rick regurgitated all of Stephanie's hyperbolic praise for her boys—at the expense of our daughters. Rick being

Rick, he justified his emotional abuse and neglect by twisting the Bible and claiming, "Stephanie and I are one."

The unfortunate effect was making Scripture abhorrent to our girls, even more than he'd already done by steamrolling them with it when we were married. My own faith walk was a struggle, especially with the hypocrisy of our former congregation, *Beth Shalom*. They treated the new Mrs. Williams like royalty and pretended like the original never existed.

"Bleh, don't even mention her name!" Lily said, exaggerating a gag motion. "I can hear her voice as soon as you say it."

The girls and I fell into a laugh as we all mimicked their stepmother's abrasive, nasal accent straight from New Jersey. "Richard, the soup is so sawlty! Didn't you tell them to make it low sodium?"

The story of Stephanie's histrionics at an upscale Parkview restaurant she'd insisted on for her birthday still brought humor to our house. Stephanie just had no idea my girls played some *Parent Plan* mischief for criticizing the outfits they'd chosen for the event. She'd called their clothes "classless, just like your mother," and my daughters had responded in kind. The tantrum she threw in the restaurant embarrassed Richard—though he still had to publicly defend the shrew—and even the stepbrother terrors snickered at their mother's expense. I supposed it was rather *classless* of me to laugh at the prank, but nobody said I was required to like the woman.

And I didn't.

Sophie continued to eye me suspiciously. "So, you're saying you never thought Mr. Roseman was kind of hot?"

"Ew!" Lily gasped. "Soph, he's like, a hundred years old."

I rolled my eyes. "He's forty-seven. That's hardly ancient. Your dad just turned fifty."

"Close enough," Lily said, still scandalized.

"I'm turning forty-four in a few weeks, does that make me ancient too?"

"That's different!" Lily insisted, always quick to defend me. "You're beautiful and you don't look that old."

I stuck my tongue out at her. "Thanks...I think."

Lily's serious expression didn't alter. "No, Mom, you really do look good. Stephanie wears a hundred pounds of makeup and looks like an old lady. She's three years younger than you, but she looks as old as Daddy."

I smirked. "Well, she does enjoy her frosted eyeshadow and raccoon eyeliner."

Sophie smirked. "I bet she has a coat made out of dalmatians too."

"Okay, okay," I said, holding up my hands. "None of us like Stephanie, but we don't need to bash her like that. I doubt she's murdering puppies."

"Why do we have to be nice?" Lily asked. "She's horrible to us, she's made Daddy even worse, and all she does is shade you."

I inhaled a fortifying breath of self-restraint. Jon would have been proud of me. I didn't feel right venting my real feelings to my girls, but Jon not only let me vent, he sometimes egged me on. I smiled at the memory of a recent conversation.

I looked up to find my girls watching me.

"What?" I asked.

They exchanged a look between them.

"What?" I said more tersely.

"Nothing, Mom," Sophie smirked. "I, uh, need to get to bed. I have a Trig test tomorrow."

I raised an eyebrow. "And that's it?"

My girls had their own silent language, and I realized they were dialoguing about me right in front of me.

"Fess up. Now," I commanded.

Sophie gave a subtle nod to Lily, and she got up too. "Yeah, I think I need to go to bed. I'm sure you have somebody you need to text anyway."

My jaw dropped as they both left the room snickering. I wanted to pick up the phone and text Jon right then, but the absence of their heavy steps upstairs meant they were spying from just outside of the kitchen.

"Go to bed, girls."

"Yes, Mom," they chorused.

"And I'm *not* texting Mr. Roseman."

"Don't you mean, *Jon?*" Sophie sing-songed.

"Upstairs. Now!"

The girls took off giggling, and I waited until I heard their footsteps above my head in their respective bedrooms.

"Too smart for their own good," I muttered and picked up the phone to text my *just friend*.

CHAPTER 2

Just got back, I wrote to Jon. How was your date?

Still on it.

Oof! Sorry, I can TTYL.

No, no, pretend you're having a crisis and need my help. This might be the worst one yet. She has spent the last 30 minutes telling me that Christ did away with the Law and I need to call myself a Christian now.

Ha! Harvey Lebow would die of apoplexy if he heard that.

There's already a bolt of lightning waiting for that chazar for all the lies he's told.

I smirked at Jon's Yiddish pejorative for our old rabbi. Usually, he just let me rant or kept his sentiments more subdued. We had a nice repartee of fire and ice when we discussed our experiences from Beth Shalom.

He sent over another SOS text. *Seriously…I don't know how to end this date without her thinking I'm a complete jerk.*

Does it matter what she thinks? I mean, look at what she's already said to you. Besides, how are you texting me this much on a date anyway? Isn't she mad you're on your phone?

You caught me in the bathroom. I was hiding.

Not a visual I will ever need. Text me after you wash your hands.

He sent me back an eye rolling emoji. *Ha. Ha. I'm hiding out in here, not using the facilities.*

How long have you been in there? She probably thinks you have food poisoning coming out of one end or the other by now.

Just for fun, I sent over a .gif of a projectile vomiting puppet. The movie clip came from a film I'd seen in my early twenties—pre-Richard who would have clutched the pearls at it—and Jon had shocked me when he told me he'd also seen the film and loved it.

After a pause, he finally wrote back, *I literally just laughed out loud. Thank God, nobody else is in here.*

Any time. Go put on your big boy pants and tell Susie Christian you're not giving up your lox and bagels for Easter ham, and then text me when you're free.

He sent me back a .gif of a saluting soldier, and I chuckled. Ten minutes passed with no further messages, so I made my own way upstairs to start my nighttime grooming.

I stared at myself in the mirror, sighing at the sight of my tired eyes. No matter how "young" I looked to my daughters, there was no hiding the effects of time, trauma, or a loveless marriage followed by two years of unsuccessful dating.

Thank God, Rick Williams was no Nathan Fein, but being a petty little piglet instead of a full grown boar didn't change the damage he'd done to my self esteem. My round, pale blue eyes stared back at me in the mirror along with dark circles that no amount of carefully placed concealer could hide. I'd grown into the hooked nose I'd once despised, and I could at least thank Rick's DNA for softening up the version of it shared by both of my daughters. In general, my daughters resembled petite, more finely shaped versions of their "everything's extra with me" mother. Neither of them struggled with their weight like I did, and they each had a pretty good head on their shoulders. I'd made a vow that my girls would never suffer from the mental and emotional torment my own father used on me. It was a huge impetus for my divorce from Rick. His constant criticism of Sophie had led to drastic repercussions. Turning my mind away from that dark season for my girls, I removed the last of my makeup and washed my face.

My phone lit up with a text alert as I slathered on my overnight serum. I exited my tiny bathroom and checked my phone to find a new message from Jon.

Can I call you? I'm in the car driving.

I dialed first and then curled up on the recliner in my bedroom. "Hey," I said warmly.

"Hey," he replied with a smile in his voice. "I hope your night out was better than mine."

"Well, Lauren knows better than to preach replacement theology to me, so I think we're good."

He chuckled, and his tenor voice made for beautiful singing as well as a musical quality when he laughed. "I've been on a few stinkers, but this date might take the cake."

"How did you meet Susie Q anyway?"

"Sitting at Charred Cups with my daughter. Ruthie and I had a coffee date, and I saw Susie Q standing in line. Ruthie caught me watching her and told me to ask her out."

I swallowed down a lump of misplaced jealousy. Even though I'd relegated Jon to the friends only category, there was still a very female part of me that wanted him to find me attractive. Remembering exactly what his late wife looked like only reminded me of the impossible delusion that Jonathan Roseman could find me desirable by comparison. Even back in my twenties, I could never compete with Andrea Roseman's natural beauty and tender heart. Lauren kept insisting she saw interest on Jon's behalf, but I was well aware of my shortcomings. Two years of failed dating had only reinforced that.

"You still there?" he asked.

I cleared my throat. "Yeah, long night. I'm already in my pajamas."

He paused. "Do you need to go to bed? I don't want to keep you up. It is still a school night after all."

I smiled at his droll sense of humor. "All of our girls are in high school and can take the bus. It's just some new wrinkles with *Richard*."

"Ah, good ole Rick." Jon's pronunciation made it seem like he'd rather use another word for my ex-husband. "What is the slime trying to get away with now?"

"Modified winter break for the girls."

"Is he wanting more time or less time with them this year?"

"I told him I was planning to go on vacation and asked if we could switch visitation weeks. He would have the first week of winter break over Christmas, and I would get New Year's."

"So, what's the problem? The girls can basically take care of themselves."

"He's mad that the vacation is for a singles cruise."

"Singles cruise?" he choked. "You never mentioned that before."

"Oh, it was last minute. My boss, Rosaria, is going and her friend canceled. She asked if I wanted to go with her instead, but I can't change the dates."

"Why is Rick giving you a hard time about it? I thought he'd be glad to have you go and save money on future alimony payments."

"You forget that only Rick is allowed to move on and be happy with the *real love of his life*," I said, mocking his nauseating epithet for Stephanie. "I'm apparently supposed to wallow for the rest of my days regretting the divorce and envying her."

Jon laughed. "If Stephanie is truly the love of his life, then I feel sorry for him. Rick's an idiot, and you deserve so much better than how he treated you."

"Wow," I breathed.

"What? It's true, Charlotte."

"Well, you…I just…you've never said it like that before."

"Have I finally rendered you mute? I think there should be an awards ceremony for this momentous occasion. I don't even have a speech prepared."

"I guess you've got on your sassy pants tonight, Mr. Roseman. I like it."

I could hear the smile in his tone. "They are rather sassy tonight, aren't they?"

"What are they made of? Sparkles? Sequins? Satin?"

"Hardly," he deadpanned, "and I doubt they would compare to yours."

I paused, realizing this wasn't the first time it felt like our friendly banter had shifted into something more. "Jon?"

His tone changed from humor to immediate concern. "Everything okay?"

"Were you flirting just now?"

"Flirting?"

"Yeah, you know that thing that people always accuse *me* of doing, even though I'm just a ridiculously charming individual with an extensive vocabulary."

"Can I answer your question by asking *you* a question?" he replied.

I didn't realize I'd been holding my breath until my lungs burned for oxygen. I inhaled deeply and tried for a neutral tone. "I guess, yeah."

"If I *was* flirting, would you be okay with that?"

"I thought we were friends."

"Technically, you're the one who calls us *just friends* and has to mention it in every conversation we have."

"What are you saying? I mean, my girls tease me about you. Lauren teases me about you. They all act like you're interested in me, but I'm just too blind to see it."

The prolonged silence on the phone line spoke volumes, and I faltered.

He released a heavy breath. "Yes, I was flirting with you. I've *been* flirting with you for months, but you either don't see it or ignore it."

"Well, why on earth did you go on a date with Susie Q?"

"Why do you think?" He huffed out a laugh. "The woman I'd actually like to go out with says she only thinks of me as a friend, but she's the one person I want to talk to every night before I go to bed. She's the first person I want to talk to when I wake up in the morning. This wasn't the way I planned to tell you, but yes, Charlotte, I have more than friendly feelings for you. Unfortunately, I don't have much hope you'll ever take me out of the friend zone."

"So, you've been doing what, exactly? Waiting in the wings for me to catch feelings back?"

"Are you saying it's impossible?" he asked, his voice tight. "You're happy to get the emotional lift from our phone calls and texts, but that's it?"

"I never said that! And I thought we were *friends*. Friends do provide an emotional lift to one another. It's why I went out with Lauren tonight. I'm not manipulating you, Jon, and I have never given you reason to think I was stringing you along."

"Well, you're still not answering my question."

"That's because I don't know what to say."

"That's a first."

"Okay, well that was just rude. I'm hanging up now." Irritated, I swiped the phone off. It lit up with a text message a second later.

I'm sorry. That didn't come out the way I meant. I'm nervous, and I'm making a mess of all of this.

Making a mess of what exactly?

My feelings, he wrote. *I'm obviously not handling rejection very well.*

I inhaled and exhaled a deep breath knowing that my response would forever change my future. *Why are you assuming you're being rejected? And please put emphasis on the first syllable of the word 'assume.'*

Are you saying you want to be more than friends? Has something changed?

I paused, my mind traversing over multiple memories with Jonathan Roseman. When I first met him, he was an ebony haired, goateed man in love with his first wife while I was newly married to Rick Williams. I had become friends with Andrea while she was heavily pregnant with their youngest daughter, Rachel, and I had just found out I was pregnant with Sophie. My daughters had worn baby clothes passed down to us from the Roseman girls. Our lives had been intertwined for nearly two decades, just never like this.

Jon's black hair was now predominantly silver, he wore horn rimmed glasses over his perceptive, dark eyes, and I knew his daughters weren't the only females that wanted to call him "Daddy." I'd seen enough thirsty comments on his Instantpics from women of all ages.

Charlotte? he asked, *are you still there?*

I'm here.

You didn't answer my question.

Are you sure? I finally wrote. I caught my reflection in my phone and grimaced.

I'm sure I don't want you going on a singles cruise and falling in love with somebody else. I know you like direct, so how was that?

Pretty direct.

You're still not answering.

But are you SURE?

My phone rang again, and I didn't hesitate to pick it up.

"So, I guess you're not still mad at me," he began.

"I'm not sure what I am at the moment."

"You okay?"

"Stunned is more like it."

"Why are you stunned?" His voice was calming and gentle.

Even though he couldn't see me, I gestured to my mismatched pajamas, hair pulled off my bare face, and curves that my daughters would call *thicc* and Rick called *morbidly obese.* "Jon, I mean, you could have any woman you want. I'm just..."

"You're just what?" he cut me off. "Sensational? Gorgeous? Intimidating?"

I frowned at that last word. "Yeah, I've been called that before."

"You're not intimidating because you're scary or unattractive, Charlotte. You're intimidating because I have to be at the top of my game to keep up with you. You're smart, witty, hilarious, and if I've never said this before it's because I never thought you'd let me. You're beautiful."

I scoffed.

"Let me repeat. You are *stunningly* beautiful."

"Maybe you need a thicker prescription on your glasses."

"Maybe you need to stop deflecting with sarcasm just because your ex was too much of a brain dead imbecile to appreciate the woman he trampled on for fifteen years."

I chuckled. "Okay, I won't disagree with your assessment of Rick."

"Do you think I'm lying about the rest? That it's impossible for a man to find you attractive just because *Richard* is a moron?"

"Look, I come with stretch marks and psychological damage, and contrary to your apparent high opinion of me, men my age do *not* find me all that attractive. They want a cheap hook up, someone young enough to have more kids, or a supermodel. Ironically, it doesn't matter if *they* fell out of the ugly tree and got hit in the face with every branch on the way down."

"Well, I *am* a man your age, and I'm telling you I find you a lot more than just 'attractive.' You're scared, Charlotte, and I want to know why."

"You know I can't compete with Andrea," I said with a long suffering sigh. "You loved that woman with every breath in your body. Maybe if I had never known you two as a couple it wouldn't be so hard, but I'll never be able to live up to that."

After a pause, one where I expected Jon to call off his crush, he finally said, "I'm at your house. Come outside, and let's talk."

CHAPTER 3

"You're what?" I gaped.

"This is a conversation we need to have face to face. We can sit in my car since it's still muggy outside."

"Jon, it's almost eleven! I still have work tomorrow. So do you!"

He sighed. "I'm not letting you off the hook so easily. I think you need to see me look at you when I tell you everything."

"You have never seen me without a full face of makeup. There is no way you're going to give me some sweeping speech while I look like the half-dead crypt keeper."

"I won't force you, but I've never done anything this impulsive in my life. Not even with Andrea," he added.

When I asked Jon if he was ready to see the catfish underneath the makeup contouring, the man had the nerve to tell me to shut up and get my butt outside. Stifling a laugh at this feistier side of him, I threw on a long cardigan and hoped he wouldn't notice the lack of support from my sports bra. I spotted Jon's shiny silver vehicle parked next to my aging sedan.

His interior light was on, and he reached across the center console to open the passenger door of his SUV.

"Hi," I said and wrapped my arms around myself. I met his eyes, watching and waiting to see if he would shrink away in horror.

"I wasn't sure you'd actually do it," he breathed.

"Well, here I am."

We stared at one another as my feet remained glued to the concrete.

"You gonna come in?" He gestured toward the passenger seat.

"Are you sure you want me to? I don't look so great under fluorescent lighting."

He rolled his eyes. "Come on, Charlotte." He patted the seat as if coaxing a timid puppy, and I finally broke into a small laugh.

"Fine." I shoved myself into the car and closed the door behind me.

I took in Jon's outfit and wondered what on earth was wrong with Susie Christian. I normally didn't call middle-aged men "hot," but Jon Roseman was objectively handsome. His burgundy polo set off nicely against his dark glasses, hair and eyes, and it didn't add any pallor to his fair complexion. I realized I was staring when I caught his smile.

"You done ogling?" he teased.

"I approve of the first date outfit. Obviously, I look like death warmed over, so why don't we just get this over with?"

"Please, tell me you don't believe any of that about yourself."

"Well, I do own a mirror, so yes, I do. Being skilled with makeup and hair products doesn't mean I don't know what I look like without them."

"Stop," he said, reaching for my hand.

I pulled mine away. "Stop what? Telling the truth?"

"Stop degrading yourself. Is that your inner monologue? This cruel, unforgiving voice that refuses to see striking eyes and full red lips."

"Well, aren't you Mr. Poetry this evening? You're forgetting the humongous schnozz sitting in between those eyes and lips. Are you planning to write an ode to that also?"

"I think your nose works well for your face. It gives it character."

"Unfortunately, just like the rest of me, it's also plus sized."

"So what, Charlotte? Why do you keep putting yourself down?"

"Your wife was a waif. Your girls are teensy tiny. There is no way you find *this* attractive." I gestured at my bundled up body.

Jonathan let out a growl of frustration, leaned over and cupped my face. "Enough," he said, captivating me with his dark eyes. "You're not ugly. You never *were* ugly. You never *will be* ugly."

"I'm fat."

"You're voluptuous."

"You're delusional."

His eyes dropped to my mouth. "I'm done talking."

My own eyes widened as he leaned forward to press a kiss against my lips. Instead, I laid a hand on his chest before our mouths could connect.

"Seriously?" I asked.

He exhaled a sigh. "You're ruining the moment."

"Are you sure you know what you're doing?"

"I have two children. Yes, I know how to do this."

I laughed. "I wasn't asking if you know about the birds and

the bees, Jon. I'm asking if you're sure you want to do this with *me*."

"Well, I'm not in the car with Susie Q, now am I?"

"No, I suppose not."

"Are you going to let me kiss you, Charlotte?"

"Still deciding."

A low noise rumbled in his throat, and his thumbs brushed against my temples. It was a tender gesture I hadn't experienced from any man in far too long. I allowed myself a moment to savor the sensation and sighed.

I didn't realize he'd leaned in closer until I both heard and felt his whisper against my cheek. "Is that a yes?"

I turned and let my lips answer for me.

All that tension, all that build up, and Jonathan Alexander Roseman was by far the most attractive man I had ever laid eyes —or lips on—in my entire life.

Unfortunately, no unicorns or rainbows were involved in the making of that kiss.

My choir of hallelujah angels yawned in boredom.

It was a *nice* kiss. No feelings of ickiness or I-will-have-to-bleach-this-from-my-memory meeting of the mouths. It just wasn't one of those romance novel kisses where the heroine feels like the most gorgeous, treasured, fairy tale princess desired by her handsome prince.

For all of Jon's passionate declarations regarding my makeup free face, I expected to feel more than the sensation of my mouth pressed against someone else's widowed husband I met eighteen years ago.

He didn't linger long, and Jon pulled back looking confused. When his face tilted back toward mine again, I held out a hand to stop him.

"Please, don't. We have our answer here."

"I thought this would go differently," he murmured, searching my eyes.

"Differently how?"

"Charlotte, you and I just connect. I thought if I kissed you that it would feel *right*. I don't know what I did wrong. That was pretty..."

"Average," I said, filling in the blank for him. I peeled his hands from my face. "I don't think you did anything wrong. You and I just aren't compatible that way."

He sighed. "I told you that I've never done anything like this before, and now I see why. I should probably leave spontaneity up to the professionals."

I exhaled a laugh and leaned back in the passenger seat.

"What?" he asked.

"You know, in every romance I've ever read or watched, after the man professes his feelings, tells the woman she's so beautiful *blah blah*, there's this swelling music and a kiss that transcends reality." Hesitating, I finally added, "That's not exactly what happened with us."

He exhaled a snicker and shook his head. "No, not exactly."

"Look, we do have really good chemistry. We banter well, and I don't have to wonder if I'm going to offend you with my honesty. But I think you just proved that we're better off as friends than anything else."

"It wasn't my best work," he admitted. "I'm a little out of practice."

"I thought it was like riding a bike," I said, nudging his shoulder. "Maybe you just need a better partner."

He held my eyes, his expression serious. "I think I have the right partner."

"Are you talking about a long term partner?" I squeaked.

"Could we...could we try again? Please? I just...I want to see something."

Against my better judgment, I agreed. Although the kiss was better than the first, softer with more promise, I couldn't get past the awkwardness of the situation. As soon as I tried to sink into the kiss and just be in the moment, my brain screamed, *You're kissing Andrea Roseman's husband!* There was also a misplaced familiarity in how Jon held and kissed me—like he was kissing someone else with me as the stand-in.

I turned my face away and cast my gaze to my clasped hands in my lap.

"I don't understand what's going on," he said, frustrated. "I want this with you."

I kept my head bowed.

"Charlotte, what's wrong?"

I met his eyes, silently communicating what I wanted to say.

"I know you're not *her*," he said low. "You're not the first woman I've kissed since Andrea passed, but I didn't expect it to be so difficult. Our friendship has developed so naturally. I guess I assumed this part would flow just as easily."

"How many other women are you making out with anyway?"

He smirked, bringing some of our usual lightness to the conversation. "Tons of them. They have a support group that meets every other Thursday to heal from the trauma."

"And I'm the worst kiss out of all of them. Just my luck."

Jon reached for my hand to reassure me. "I don't think I've ever felt this much pressure before. Maybe that's what it is. There isn't always an Italian opera playing in the background on a first kiss. We just need time."

"Or," I dropped my gaze back to my lap, "you and I really are meant to be *just* friends like I've been saying all along."

"Are you attracted to me, Charlotte?"

My eyes whipped back to his. "Excuse me?"

"You heard me. You talk about yourself like you're a cave troll, but is that to cover for you not being physically attracted to me? Is that what this is about?"

"Jon, you have a legion of admirers on Instantpics. You probably have a thirsty mom fan club worshiping at your silver fox shrine."

"And half of them are bots and spammers trying to catfish me into giving them money. I'm asking what *you* think of me."

"Yes, I think you're attractive," I mumbled. "I'm not blind."

"But you think *I'm* blind in order to be physically attracted to you, right?"

"It's not just that," I said, grudgingly admitting the truth. "There just wasn't any soul in that kiss. It wasn't unpleasant, don't get me wrong. Rick was a wet kisser with halitosis, so you're miles ahead of that."

"Good to know," he deadpanned.

"I just can't think of you like a first date because I've known you for almost half of my life. I wish I could let go and pretend I'm *not* kissing the dad of my daughters' best friend, Rachel, but I can't. I wish I could pretend I'm not kissing Andrea Roseman's husband, but I can't. It's like you expect me to be as familiar and at ease with you in this area just because we're already familiar with one another from Beth Shalom. It makes me wonder if you want *me* or just something that's comfortable."

He stopped to consider my words. "Well, it makes sense. We do come from similar backgrounds. Our kids already know each other. I wouldn't have to explain traditional Judaism, Messianic Judaism, or the kind of religious lifestyle I want to have in a relationship."

"See," I said, whipping out my manicured hand for emphasis, "this is about convenience, not genuine romantic feelings. That's why you kissed me like that."

"No, it isn't," he argued, "but I also can't compete with romance novels and fantasy expectations. I can't change the history we share. I'm not Andrea Roseman's husband anymore. I'm Jon Roseman who never thought he'd be dating again. This is still new to me, but I'm not confused about my feelings for you, Charlotte."

His lips spoke longingly, but all I could remember were those same lips pressed against mine—wishing I was someone else.

I opened the car door and a surge of humidity slapped me out of considering a third kiss. "Jon, I can't just step into her role, kiss you the way she did, and come alongside your life like you're installing a program reboot to the old marriage software. That's not how this works."

"I know you're not my wife."

"Nobody will ever be Andrea," I said softly. "I can't be her. I can only be me."

"I'm not asking you to!"

"But you kissed me like I was her. Like I should know what to do. I felt like I was kissing a robot."

"No...I just...I don't know what the problem is. Don't shut me out. We can talk about this."

"Good night, Jon."

I got out of the car and trotted back to my townhome. Locking the door behind me, I pressed my back to it and tried to process what had just happened. The one man whose opinion I truly valued had kissed me. Actually kissed me.

And it had all the excitement of kissing my brother.

I shuddered at the thought and finally used the back of my hand to remove Jonathan Roseman from my lips.

I replayed the entire scene again, wishing that the kiss had been more than what it was. Passionate, instead of tepid. Searching for *me* rather than simply a repeat of his first wife.

"Bummer," I whispered.

CHAPTER 4

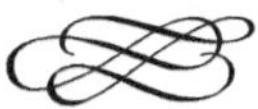

"So, how many ways can I kill a man with *this* one?" I singled out a woodworking tool displayed on a table covered in scary looking instruments of all shapes and sizes.

Luke, my twenty-six-year-old, ginger Viking co-worker laughed. "Oh, are we feeling stabby today, Charlotte? What did your ex do this time? And this one is an insert miter folding bit."

"A who? A what? And a why?"

He grinned at me. "Do you remember when we talked about the different types of jointing?"

I grimaced. "Ugh, yes, but my almost forty-four-year-old brain can't keep up." I began to recite the facts as if from a textbook. "Jointing is how you bring two pieces of wood together. There's apparently a million different ways to do that, and a miter joint is one of them."

"Good," he said. "Blow out some cobwebs in that so-called feeble mind and see what else you remember."

I stuck my tongue out at him. "You're really enjoying this, aren't you?"

He winked at me. "Hearing you beg? Always."

I swatted his tattooed bicep. "Ha, we're not here to discuss your Oedipal fantasies."

"Or yours," he said, nudging me back.

"Fine, I'll give you that one, but only because I'm feeling generous."

He grinned at me. "Happily taken, but my dad is single again if you want me to put in a good word. I would love calling you 'Mom.'"

I laughed and picked up the miter-whatever router bit and studied it. "Maybe I should use this thing on *you* instead. Could we shave off your beard with it?"

"Not until you can tell me how to properly use it first."

"Ugh, fine! A miter is a forty-five degree angle joint. I just don't get why this thing needs to weigh ten pounds to make a puny picture frame."

Luke gently took the tool from my hands, careful not to cut me or himself. With its bizarre, triangular shape sitting atop a cylinder body, he turned the tool as if his hand was the machine holding it in place. "Here's the insert knife," he said, pointing to the rectangular blade screwed to the triangle tool head. "This thing is going to spin at about 18,000 rpm across the grain of the wood."

"To do what?"

"To create the miter fold."

"I thought it was a miter *joint*."

He smiled approvingly. "Good catch! The folding bit is used for a different surface. Jointing is for the edge. This tool is going along the length of the material to cut it into two pieces."

"Why? Couldn't you just use a saw blade or a compression bit if all you're doing is cutting it into separate pieces?"

"See?" he said with a flourish, "you already know more than you think you do."

I waved him off. "Whatever. So, tell me why this triangle doo-hickey insert bit is so special. What the heck is this thing miter-ing anyway?"

"The wood."

I rolled my eyes. "Obviously."

He began to spin the tool again and mimic how it would run in a CNC machine. "See the way the insert knife is angled here? It's going to cut this same, forty-five degree angle on both sides. It will go completely through the material and also create an angled cut at the same time. The sides will mirror each other because of the tool moving in a circular motion as it goes across the surface. When you fold the sides against each other after they're cut, they'll fit together perfectly along the miter because they were cut symmetrically with the same tool at the same time."

"So, is it a miter-*fold* because you're basically folding the pieces together?"

"Yep. Easy peasy."

"And it's considered a *miter* insert bit because you're cutting it just like the jointing style."

"Exactly!" Luke set the tool down and gave me a high five. "See, not so hard, was it?"

I smacked my forehead. "And I only have about a million more parts to learn, right?"

He patted my shoulder reassuringly. "You'll get there, I promise. You've already picked up more than you realize. Besides, I really wouldn't recommend this one for murder anyway."

"What about maiming?"

His sapphire eyes twinkled. "Maybe. Is it more drama with the evil stepmother or something Rick said to the girls?"

I didn't want to mention I had someone else in mind. Jonathan wanted to rehash our kiss, and all I wanted to do was cut it out of my memory. Nevertheless, I found myself impressed with Luke's perceptiveness. "I always forget how much I overshare and how easy you are to talk to. How do you remember all of this stuff anyway?"

"Good memory."

I refocused my attention on the conference table covered in tools. "Anyways, forget I said anything. You don't need to hear about my problems."

The man-bunned Viking nudged me with his shoulder. "You know it's okay to *not* be okay, right?"

"Look, let's just get back to my tutorial. It's easier to update inventory when I know what the heck any of these things do. Miranda still wants those custom miter-whatever bits shipped to Boston Cabinets plus the new product catalog."

He shook his ginger head. "You're deflecting."

"Quit being wise beyond your years or I'll fake flirt with you. Your girlfriend thinks it's hilarious and gave me a few pointers."

On cue, his cheeks pinked. "I didn't realize you guys had teamed up."

"Wanna see the texts?"

"As a matter of fact, I do. Where's your phone? You don't go anywhere without that thing."

He reached around me to grab it off the table, but I moved a hair faster and held it behind my back. He lunged for the phone again, and I spun away from him. I took a few steps backward and shoved it under my bra strap. "Come and get it, Viking!"

He held up his hands in surrender. "Not a chance. All of those Oedipal fantasies are coming from your side, not mine."

I burst out laughing. "Whatever, you walking fetus! Back to work, and no more flirting."

"That's like asking you to stop breathing," he muttered. "Not gonna happen."

Our office manager, Rosaria, poked her head into the conference room. "How does anyone get any work done around here with all of the back and forth between you two?"

"Oh, she does it with Brian, Mac, and Freddy too," Luke quipped, listing off the rest of our machining team. "I'm nothing special."

"Geez, thanks for making me sound like the town bike." I shot him a dirty look, and he had the nerve to shrug. Primly, I pulled the phone out from my shirt and shoved it into my jeans pocket.

Rosaria laughed. "Okay, yeah, fair point. Charlotte, you do like all that banter, but nothing like you and Luke. Not that he's innocent either," she said, throwing a pointed glance his way. "You give as good as you get, kid."

He didn't bother to look up as he rearranged some other tools on the table. "Whatever."

I kicked him in the shin.

"Didn't even hurt." He hid a grin and then sauntered back to his office.

"Kick him harder next time," Rosaria offered. "He can take it."

I chuckled and made my way to my own desk situated in the main lobby of MG Industrial Tooling where I worked as the Sales Coordinator. My main responsibilities included answering phones, greeting customers, and following up on open purchase and sales orders. It wasn't glamorous work, but the same organizational skills belittled by my ex–husband were exactly what endeared me to the company owner, Miranda Gebhardt. Miranda was a five foot, German-born pistol who didn't take guff from anyone, and listening to her fuss (and sometimes cuss) at our German suppliers was both inspiring and terrifying.

Despite our smaller office in the US, our German headquarters located in Our-European-Office-Is-Perpetually-Rude-Because-You're-Just-Stupid-Americans was world renowned. My dear friend, Lauren Fein, had just designed the employee benefits guide for MG's biggest domestic competitor, Geneva Group, courtesy of their insurance broker, Culver Incorporated. While Lauren followed in the tradition of several of her friends working in the marketing department at Culver, I had chosen a different career path during my divorce. MG actually compensated their employees properly, unlike the first job I had following my fourteen year stint as a stay-at-home mom. 7-Square Property Management thought their annual twenty-five cent raise was a king's ransom.

"You two are something else," Rosaria said, leaning against the side of my desk.

"Sip your tea instead of trying to get me to spill mine." I gestured to the glittery pink travel mug in her hands.

My office manager smirked. "I'd quote you the sexual harassment policy from our handbook, but since you and Erik the Red are so entertaining, I normally let it slide."

"He's not harassed, and neither am I."

"The two of you make *me* blush."

"He's a child, Ro. Give me a break. If I can get Rick to stop being such a *Richard* about taking the girls over winter break, I'll be on that singles cruise with you in January. What more do you want from me?"

"Look, all I'm saying is that you better hope his girlfriend doesn't hear the two of you going at it."

"Oh, she has already," I said, opening my weekly purchase report. "Paisley thinks it's hilarious and asks me to text her some highlights. Who do you think gave me all the tips on how to make him blush?"

"More than you already do all on your own?" Ro asked, visibly shocked. "I can't even imagine."

"He's a ginger. The Viking always looks like he's blushing."

"He also told all the guys in the back your ex is a lowlife who never deserved you. I doubt the kid is serious when he's flirting, but I do know that you've been through a lot."

I held up a hand. "Ro, you're pushing too hard. The red-headed man-child and I both enjoy good banter. He was asking my opinion about engagement rings for Paisley, so trust me, there's nothing happening with his old lady coworker."

She sipped her tea again, unconvinced.

"Are we done here?" I clipped. "You know, you have a few POs still missing order confirmations."

Ignoring my attempt to turn the conversation back to a professional one, she added, "For your sake, Viking's sake, and Paisley's sake, I hope one of those guys you talk to online turns out to *not* be a loser. You deserve something real and somebody who can help channel all of that flirty energy for the power of good."

I shook my head. "You don't need to worry about me or the Viking. Go order some paper towels or pens before Miranda gets here."

Rosaria sashayed back to her desk. Luke poked his head out from his office door, and I caught him in my periphery.

"How much did you hear?" I asked, clicking away on my keyboard.

"Enough," he said gruffly. "I didn't think I'd have to worry about gossip in an office full of dudes."

"You'd be surprised," I deadpanned. "You already know about my stint with the real housewives of Hillcrest when I worked at 7-Square."

Luke chuckled. "I don't even want to imagine."

I exhaled my own mirthless laugh. "Trust me, you don't. It was worse than the bullying and mean girl garbage my daughters deal with at school. That to say, don't assume that just because it's guys in the warehouse that they can't be just as catty. Our *male* boss at 7-Square was the worst gossip of them all."

"Does that mean I'll be able to snatch your phone from more appropriate places from now on?"

I finally turned to catch his eye. "You know I'm not really flirting, don't you? I like fun conversations, and yeah, I did get a little carried away earlier. If this is a real issue, we can try to keep things more professional. I don't care what any of the guys in the workshop say about me, but I don't want things to be embarrassing for you. Does Freddy really tease you about me?"

"Yeah, but he just likes giving me a hard time."

"Why? Everyone knows you adore Paisley."

"Doesn't mean I can't appreciate an amazing woman even if it's completely platonic."

I rolled my eyes. "Oh my gosh, you *have* to stop!"

Luke stepped out of his office and towered over me as I remained seated in my chair. "Why is it so impossible to believe that you're a catch?"

I stood up and glared at him despite the nine inch height difference. I couldn't stand to hear the same question posed just twelve hours after Jonathan Roseman had kissed me. "Because your girlfriend should be posing in swimsuit magazines, for one thing, and I'm old enough to be your mother. Plus, my ex replaced me in nanoseconds."

"He didn't replace you with someone *better*, Charlotte. He replaced you with someone who wouldn't call him on his—"

I held up a hand to stop the next word. "Why are you so adamant about this?"

"Because I consider you a friend, and I just want you to see your worth. You deserve to be happy and with someone who really values you."

I smiled at his sincerity before deflecting back with humor. "You sure you don't want to give this Oedipus thing a shot?"

He gently chucked me under the chin. "The right man is out there, and he'll be smart enough to see what I do. He'll also be old enough to do something about it."

"From your mouth to God's ears," I said quietly. "And thanks."

CHAPTER 5

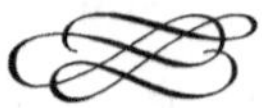

"Tell me again how you convinced me to go," I muttered to Lauren Fein.

We stood inside the foyer of Kyle and Abigail Goldstein's home about to attend home Bible study.

"Come on," she said, nudging my arm. "You'll be fine. You already know Abigail, Jared, and a few others from Beth Shalom."

"Like that's a ringing endorsement. I hate that place."

"I'm aware," she clipped, "but you're missing out on fellowship because you're still mad at what they did to you."

"What about what they did to you and your son? Are you going to tell me you've forgiven Harvey Lebow and the rest of those two-faced lemmings?"

She gave me a patient smile. "This isn't Beth Shalom, and I've told you that a million times. Nobody is here to impress anyone, and nobody has their hands in your wallet. We're just here to worship the Lord and read the Word."

From the next room, I heard the strumming of a guitar and a distinctive tenor voice. I froze dead in my tracks.

"Please, tell me that's not who I think it is."

Lauren's eyes grew wide. "Did I forget to tell you? Jonathan's been leading worship for us with Abigail. Sometimes Taylor Horner joins in too. I'm sure you already knew he plays guitar."

Lauren knew good and well that I had a secret weakness for guitar players. I'd once boasted you could take a complete troll, shove a guitar in his hands, and I'd find him gorgeous. It didn't help that I was already attracted to a man who kissed me like I was his sister. I wondered why Jon had never mentioned leading worship during any of our conversations.

"Did something happen between you two?" Lauren asked, studying me. "You are never this quiet, and you look like you're on the verge of a panic attack."

"I just...yeah, panic attack might be the right word."

"Everything okay?" Grant Kaplan, Lauren's fiancé, asked, coming beside her. He wrapped his arm around her shoulders and drew her close to his chest. "Char, you look like you're going to barf. What's going on?"

Some of my terror subsided. "You know I absolutely hate it when you call me that."

"Which is exactly *why* I call you that," he teased. "You don't need to worry. This is the warmest, kindest group of people I've ever met, and I know they'll make you feel welcome."

"It's not that," Lauren said as we all heard Jon Roseman tuning his guitar.

Grant's brown eyes lit in understanding. "Oh," he drawled. "Is that still a thing?"

"Nothing is a *thing*," I said shrilly. "Lauren, I really want to go. Now."

"I thought I heard some voices out here," Kyle Goldstein said, approaching us. His powder blue eyes were just a shade darker than mine, and his raven hair and beard reminded me of his singing counterpart in the next room.

"Hi, I'm Kyle," he said, extending his hand to me. "If you're a friend of Lauren, I'm guessing you know some version of me and probably everybody else in the next room thanks to all of the *Parkview Chronicles* memoirs." He turned his focus to Lauren. "Can I tell you how proud I am of this girl for getting the guts to publish her own story?"

Grant beamed at his fiancée, and she appropriately blushed.

"Don't oversell it," she said. "I was just obeying God."

I bristled at her modesty. "Laur, you stood up to a psychopath, his slightly less psychotic mother, and an entire congregation of brainwashed zombies who still buy into Harvey Lebow's garbage. You're a hero and an inspiration."

Kyle's eyes widened as an approving smile overtook his face. He was joined by his red headed wife who recognized me instantly from our days together at Beth Shalom.

"Charlotte! Are you really here?" Abigail Goldstein yanked me into a ferocious hug. "Oh my goodness, it's so good to see you!"

Tears stung my eyes, surprising me by how much I longed to feel accepted in a group of believers.

"Girl, you look amazing," she continued, pulling away so she could take in my ensemble.

"I do?"

"Well, when you drop one hundred and seventy pounds of deadweight, it's bound to do wonders for you."

I snickered at her apt description of Rick Williams.

The foyer grew crowded as more members descended upon us to see what had caused all the ruckus. I spotted Jared and

Poppy Levine, and Jared gave me an encouraging smile. Despite his tenure as a Beth Shalom elder, I knew how much he and his wife had done to protect Lauren from her ex. I offered a genuine smile in return.

The second Jon Roseman entered the room, I felt his eyes on me. I looked everywhere but near him, surprised once again when Aaron and Ruthie Davis pulled me into their own hugs and reiterated how happy they were to have me there.

"See," Lauren whispered, tucking her arm into mine, "it's not so bad. Come on and let's get started."

As soon as I entered the Goldstein's family room and located Jonathan's acoustic guitar, I consciously chose to sit as far away from it as possible. Lauren noticed but chose not to comment.

Taylor Horner and Abigail Goldstein sat on either side of Jonathan as they shared the same piece of music situated on a small stand in front of him.

The man known as the mighty Ted Margolin brought the Bible study to order, and his wife, Rebecca, fit every description I'd ever heard or read about her. Her dark hair was highlighted with caramel streaks curling past her shoulders, and when she smiled, it lit up the entire room. She received an adoring look from her husband as he asked her to open the Bible study in prayer. I snuck a glance at Jon to find him already staring at me.

I shifted my gaze quickly, wishing I could run away and hide.

After Rebecca's heartfelt prayer, Ted addressed the room. "We have been very blessed the past few months to have music at our Bible studies. Jonathan said he felt particularly inspired this week, and I'm looking forward to seeing what the Lord put on his heart."

Jon caught my eye before adjusting the guitar in his lap and strumming. I recognized the melody and bowed my head to keep him from seeing the emotion on my face.

He began singing an old Beth Shalom tune straight from *Song of Solomon,* and the second Lauren recognized it, I heard her gasp next to me. *Ani L'Dodi,* or "I Am My Beloved's" in Hebrew, was the swoony song played at practically every Messianic wedding.

Jonathan continued to sing as Abigail and Taylor joined in, and their voices intertwined in beautiful harmony. While a worship song to Jesus as the lover of our souls, something about the waltzing melody had always felt very personal and intimate to me. Once upon a time, it had been my dream to read *Song of Solomon* on my honeymoon with my newlywed husband. Rick had initially humored my request before acting bored and calling it a waste of time. Trampling my heart wasn't even an afterthought.

As Jonathan sang the next verse of the ballad, I felt his eyes on me. Try as I might to resist, I couldn't tear myself away from his dark gaze.

"You are my love, you are my fair one," his tenor voice crooned. "Winter has passed and springtime has come."

The chorus swelled as the entire room sang and beckoned Yeshua to come and dance with us. My own anxiety melted as I felt the presence of the Holy Spirit in a way that had been missing for so long. I couldn't remember the last time I had worshiped God with anybody other than me, myself, or I.

Lauren, God bless her, sang in her own offkey voice, and I didn't dare start singing full voice lest Jonathan Roseman learn one more thing we shared in common. I scanned the room and found everyone enthralled in the song, eyes closed, hands raised or clasped to their hearts.

I'd seen the people of Beth Shalom worship like this, and I knew not everyone in that congregation was as corrupt as its leadership. Some were truly there to honor the Lord. Sadly, they didn't see or realize the deception in the upper ranks. The sight of a room full of people brought back bittersweet memories of my own times of worship as well the pain of being rejected by those same people who claimed to love Jesus.

Jon closed the song as Abigail sang the last strains, beckoning Yeshua to take her hand as the bride to our heavenly bridegroom. I wondered if I even believed in love anymore or if that was just a blessing for *other* people. Better people. People who didn't walk around with bitterness that wouldn't heal and a nose two sizes too big for their face. People who didn't get kissed by an attractive, godly man who wished you were his dead wife instead.

After pausing to soak in the quiet and peace of the moment, Jon strummed in earnest to an old Jewish song that far predated the existence of Beth Shalom.

"*Hinei ma tov u'manayim shevet achim gam yachad.* Behold how good and how pleasant it is for brothers to dwell together," he sang.

I didn't want to be reminded anymore of my former congregation. I didn't want to think about my ex-husband who had developed a massive ego by worshiping in a Messianic synagogue and now looked down his nose at gentile Christians. I didn't want to think about how he'd sneered at my nominal Jewish upbringing as if a few years under Harvey Lebow made him a better practicing "grafted in gentile" than me as a non-observant Jew. My mother was a devout atheist and Rick loved goading her into arguments that always left me stuck in the middle. When they weren't baiting and attacking one another with strawman arguments parroted from podcasts or conspiracy websites, they eventually drew fire on me to pick a side. I put that to a stop when I called out the hypocrisy of both of them for intentionally misquoting the Bible just to win an idiotic fight.

This was also about the time Rick started his bash-your-wife lunches with Nathan Fein and came home tossing around words like *unsubmissive* and *Jezebel spirit* whenever I dared to question his hurtful behavior. He also attacked my girls with his bloviating nonsense, and I warned him about the effects on Sophie, especially. When my daughter threatened her own life, convinced she was unlovable and could never do anything right, I knew it was time to officially end the marriage.

Following that, Rick reached out to Harvey Lebow to have him sic the Beth Shalom women's ministry on me and talk me out of the divorce. After the fourth phone call, I never darkened the doorway of Beth Shalom again. Coincidentally or not, that's also when Stephanie Burgess arrived at the congregation.

As much as I despised the woman for how she treated my girls, I had to thank her for taking Rick off my hands. His initial pigheadedness transformed into more agreeable negotiations as he couldn't wait to be rid of me—and likely needed to save every dime for his new wife's expected lifestyle. Stephanie didn't want my daughters around, so he didn't contest custody or visitation. His ample child support payments allowed him to maintain the money-hungry ex-wife narrative he used at temple, but he still brought home plenty for Stephanie to spend. Beth Shalom had welcomed the new Mrs. Williams instantaneously, and it further alienated me from any current or former members who spoke well of her or Rick.

Snapping back to my current reality, I'd zoned out for the entire Bible study. I wanted to apologize to Lauren, but she and Grant had already gotten up and were schmoozing near the snack table. Movement caught the corner of my eye, and I startled when I realized Jon stood directly in front of me.

"Hi," he said with a smile. "Nice to see you again."

I met his eyes briefly, embarrassed by the childish approach I'd taken in ghosting him all week. I didn't need another reminder of disappointment and unmet expectations for either of us.

Instead, he plopped into the folding chair next to me and scooted closer for privacy. "Are we gonna talk about what happened, or are you going to keep avoiding me?"

"I'm a coward, what can I say?"

He scoffed. "Coward is probably the last word I'd use to describe you."

"Weren't we good as friends?" I asked, facing the handsome, dark eyed, pink elephant in the room. "I liked getting a male perspective on things. I liked knowing I didn't have to measure up to someone else's impossible standard."

He sighed and ran a hand through his thick hair. "I shouldn't have forced that kiss on you. It just wasn't time."

I heaved my own sigh of relief. "You didn't force anything, so relax. We tried something, and it didn't work."

"Agree to disagree, but I won't fight you about it."

"Does that mean you're going to drop it? Do I get my friend Jon back?"

He met and held my gaze. "No, it means I'm going to wait on the Lord to tell me when it's time to pursue something more."

"What is that supposed to mean?"

"Exactly what it sounds like. We're not kids, and I think we just need to give this more time. We both have baggage to sort through."

"No, we're not *kids*," I said, "but we both have them, and my girls have been through enough heartache with their father and that banshee he married."

"Do you think I would be anything like Rick to your girls? I've known them since they were babies."

"True, but we need to be a lot more than just good friends for that kind of a relationship to work. I'm not going to model a passion-free relationship and tell my girls to aspire to it."

He dropped his elbows to his knees and rested his head against his palms. He turned his face toward me and searched my eyes. "We're both pretty practical people. I don't think you're interested in casual dating, and I know that I'm not."

"Does that mean it has to be with each other? Can't we just support one another while navigating the wilds of internet matchmaking and hopefully falling in love again?"

"From everything you've told me, that hasn't been working out so well. My track record with online dating is just as bad."

"So, the next logical step is for *us* to date instead?"

"Charlotte, why do you keep acting like this is such a crazy idea?"

"Because of how everything went in your car," I whispered. I snuck a quick peek around the room just to be sure no one else could hear our conversation. "Maybe it didn't work out because I just don't see you that way."

"That's a lie," he rumbled, scooting even closer to me. "I get that my kissing skills need improvement, but you didn't meet me because you thought our relationship was going to stay platonic. I know it wasn't easy for you to be there makeup free, but it meant a lot that you did it anyway."

"I guess I needed to prove something to myself, and I did."

"And what was that?"

"I can't be an Andrea replacement or fill in."

He expelled a frustrated gust of air. "I know you're not her, Charlotte. I'm out of practice, like I said. Besides, it's not a competition."

"You're right. Because I'll never win."

CHAPTER 6

Jon frowned at me. "Why can't you believe me when I tell you that my interest has nothing to do with my first wife? I loved her. I will always love her. But that doesn't mean my heart is incapable of making room for someone else."

"It doesn't work if you expect me to be just like her."

"But I don't, Charlotte. I like you exactly how you are. You're funny and fun to be around. You make me laugh, you challenge me, and you help me loosen up. I like who I am when I'm around you."

"Oh," I murmured, dumbfounded.

"And I do find you attractive—exactly how you are," he said, his eyes briefly scanning over me. "Those things you like to highlight as faults, I find endearing. I'm not sure why it didn't land that way when we talked, but it's never going to be my intent to reject or belittle you. It's obvious Rick really messed you up."

"I don't think I realized just how much until my mind made counterarguments for every compliment you just gave me."

"Is that why you're so cruel to yourself?"

"I don't know if I'd call it cruel, just brutally honest. Men like you don't go for women like me."

"Men like me?" he asked, surprised. "What does that even mean?"

"Jon, how many times have I told you what an utter sideshow the dating scene is for women my age? The guys I seem to attract are these emotionally stunted men who pretend they're attracted to my strong personality, but what they seem to really want from me is my attention—until they don't anymore. It's all a game to them. Just like the petty little pig I'm ashamed to say I willingly married once upon a time."

"So, let me ask you this again," he said, refusing to release eye contact, "what is it about *me* that makes you think I'm anything like those men or like Rick?"

"Beth Shalom," I answered honestly.

"What about it? I stopped attending during the pandemic. When I lost my job, they lost my tithing checks. When I lost my ministry position, they lost my respect. You know the rest."

"But I saw what it did to my ex. How it changed him. All the legalism and holidays he forced on me and the girls. I know you grew up Jewish, but I didn't. None of the cultural or religious identity meant anything to me until after Rick and I attended Beth Shalom. To be honest, there's a big part of me that doesn't want to celebrate any of the Jewish holidays because it feels like it's a win for him—my gentile ex-husband who thinks he's a better Jew than I am. He takes pride in being better than the Baptists he grew up with, and just being candid, I take pride in being nothing like Rick."

Jon raised both black brows. "Does that mean you need to throw the baby out with the bathwater? What's to stop you from rejecting Jesus because of all the people who mistreated you too?"

"That's different," I said immediately. "I would never do that."

"What do you mean?"

"Because I have my own relationship with the Lord. I know He's real. I know that I don't need Judaism in order to believe in Him or be considered righteous. Beth Shalom acts like it's a sin to hide your Jewish identity. Funny enough, they have no problem hiding *actual* sins like pornography, abuse, and fraud."

Jon sighed and mulled over my words. "You bring up a lot of valid points. I've struggled with this myself since leaving the congregation. I can admit there was a time when I was just as self righteous as Rick. Having visited a few churches, I've been confronted with my own spiritual pride, but it hasn't changed that I still am who I am."

"While I can appreciate that, you grew up religious, and being Jewish means something to you. My mother raised my brothers and me about as secular as you can get. We had a Christmas tree because she liked decorating it, and she knew it would irritate my grandmother."

"So, are you saying you don't want to live any kind of a Jewish lifestyle now? What about your girls? They're half Jewish because of you. Would you deny them the right to know their history and their heritage?"

"What I'm saying is that I'm confused and conflicted. With Rick and Stephanie shoving Messianic Judaism down their throats, the girls want nothing to do with it. Anything religious is now tainted by association. Last year, Rick forgot Sophie's birthday, but he refused to send her an e-gift card because it would be spending money on the Sabbath—not that he wasn't five days late with her gift already. If I push too hard, I'll wind up alienated from my daughters, and the last thing I want is for them to think I'm rejecting them the same way their father does for noncompliance."

Jon shook his head in disgust. "I am so sorry. Rick certainly lives up—or down—to his name. What about a church so they can at least be with other believers?"

"It's just as awkward for us as it is for you. My girls heard the anti-church gospel before they could walk and had it force fed at all of those messianic youth retreats. They can recite the talking points about the Council of Nicea, Russian pogroms, paganism fused with Christmas, Easter, and on. The bigger problem is that we've seen plenty of issues firsthand. The non denominational places are a theater production with lights, smoke machines, and a pre-sermon hype video for the newest 'four part series.' The more established denominations worship their traditions or themselves like Beth Shalom does. They were just as lifeless as that messianic sewer of hypocrisy—minus the slathering of Jewish glitter. I'm sorry, Jon, but jaded would be an understatement."

He sucked in a breath. "That's got to be the most pessimistic viewpoint of Christianity I've ever heard."

"But where's the lie? Don't you think we've tried? Honestly, we could overlook the stylistic differences if either me or my girls were sincerely welcomed into any of these places."

"Why weren't you?"

"Because we *are* Jewish. Because no matter how much we despise the hypocrisy of Harvey Lebow, Beth Shalom, or even their father, we're never going to have a Christmas tree in our house or act like Halloween is suddenly kosher to celebrate. My maiden name is still Weinberg even if it meant nothing to either of my parents."

"What about a traditional synagogue?"

"We tried that too after we left Beth Shalom. The Reform synagogue banned Lily from having a bat mitzvah because a former Beth Shalom member outed me to the rabbi and said that I believe in Jesus. Even if I had sucked it up and had them go through the messianic Sunday school, they didn't see Rick often enough to make it work. I would have had to take Lily on my visitation weekends three times a month."

"And you want nothing to do with Beth Shalom because of how they treated you during your divorce," Jon said, filling in the gaps. "I didn't realize things had been so difficult for you all. I'm sorry, Charlotte."

"I would have done the messianic bat mitzvah for Lily, but she saw how they treated me. She heard the nasty comments when they attended Shabbat services with their father. These former friends of mine trash talked me right in front of the girls, and Rick didn't bother to correct even the most outlandish accusations. More than likely, he spread the rumors himself. Then, there was the day I got a phone call from Liora Fein demanding that I reconcile with Rick. She said I was ruining her own son's marriage by poisoning Lauren against her precious Nathan."

"Liora Fein? The same woman whose degenerate son physically abused his wife and toddler and was addicted to teenage pornography? Liora Fein who covered up her son's toxic marriage and blamed poor Lauren for all of it?"

"That's the one. But the final straw was Tina Fournier."

He grimaced. "You've told me a little about that situation. If it makes you feel any better, I never liked Tina, and neither did Andrea. Even way back when, something always felt off about that woman."

"Well, I guess you're smarter than I am, because we were friends for twelve years before she got some personality transplant overnight. I just can't make it make sense, Jon, and I don't know how to get past the betrayal. How she kicked us out on the street and forced us to go right back to Rick two months after my daughter tried to…"

My voice trailed off at the memory of catching Sophie cutting her arm with a razor. I would never forget the shock and horror of that night, of realizing the damage caused by Rick and his incessant criticism. It probably didn't help that our oldest looked just like me and saw through her father's hypocrisy. When he could no longer break *me,* he had moved onto our firstborn daughter.

I felt Jon's hand on my knee before I registered it with my eyes.

"You okay?" he asked.

I shook my head. "I want my girls to grow up with a real father in their lives. I want them to see how a wife should be treated by a man who says he loves Jesus. I just don't know how I'll ever trust someone again to even try."

He patted my leg and then dropped his hand. "Like I said, that's why I think you need time. I'm willing to give you what you need."

"What if you meet somebody else while you're waiting?"

"What if *you* do?" he countered with a small smile.

"Oh, you mean another bald and bearded cretin who's going to send me empty flattery or waste my time for a week before ghosting me? I think I've had my fill of those, thanks."

Smirking, Jon ran a hand over his silver hair. "Nope, still there. Not shaving my beard, though."

"Very funny."

"What kind of flattery would you prefer so that you know it's not empty?"

I exhaled a short laugh. "Honestly, probably none about my physical appearance."

"Okay, well I think you're a fantastic mother."

"Do you?"

He nodded vigorously. "You forget that I've hung out with your girls while they're spending time with Rachel. They've been through a lot. All of you have. But they're smart, clever, kind, and very perceptive. I know they get all of that from their mother because I've met their father. Total dirtbag."

My chuckle grew to a full laugh. "Okay fine, that is a compliment I can accept."

"Hi guys, I don't mean to interrupt," Jared Levine said as he approached us, "but I wanted to officially welcome Charlotte to Bible study and tell you how glad I am you're here."

Jon and I both turned toward him. "Me?" I asked.

Jared's grin grew. "Yes, *you*. I enjoyed your perspectives in Bible study at Beth Shalom. You made the teachers squirm, and I can't say that I minded even if I didn't fully understand everything that I do now. Most of those guys were so full of themselves anyway."

I shrugged. "Well, questioning lousy teachers is what happens when you read the Bible for yourself."

"Which is what we're doing here," he said quickly. "I saw what happened when you were married to Rick, and I was in some of those leadership meetings. I don't know if this will mean much, but can I just apologize on their behalf and for not standing up for you?"

I fought back hot tears as my voice cracked. "You don't have to do that, Jared. You were pretty brainwashed back then."

"As a fellow *human being*, I knew that instructing leadership to ignore you was cruel. Rick was a pompous weasel, just like

Nathan Fein. Harvey Lebow runs that place like a wrecking ball behind the scenes."

"I appreciate that," I said quietly. "Thank you."

Jared lifted his chin in acknowledgement. Brightening up his tone, he asked, "I guess you two are getting reacquainted?"

"Something like that," Jon murmured. "Charlotte and I go back a few years."

"Oh, I didn't realize," Jared said. "I don't think I saw you talk very much at Aaron and Ruthie's wedding."

"He was the father of the bride and the officiant," I said briskly. "He was a little preoccupied."

Jared held up his hands in innocence. "There's no judgment coming from me. Just an observation. Charlotte, do you think your girls would ever join you here? I think my oldest is about the same age as one of your daughters."

"Oh, how old is Natalie now?"

"She's a senior at Danbury High."

"Sophie is a junior and Lily is a sophomore," I replied. "That might be nice for them."

Jonathan also chimed in. "Rachel, my baby, is a senior this year, and she's good friends with both of Charlotte's girls. Maybe the four of them would like to hang out sometime."

Jared smiled. "I think Natalie would like that a lot. It would be nice for her to have some godly friends to talk to. Our fellowship has plenty of babies, but we're lacking in the teen department."

"Why didn't you bring Rachel with you tonight?" I asked, turning my focus to Jon.

"She's come a few times with Ruthie before I started attending, but school's taking priority. She's got four AP classes this year, and it's been stressful."

Jared's gaze darted between the two of us. "Like I said, I

didn't mean to interrupt, but I really felt like I needed to personally welcome you, Charlotte."

"I appreciate it. Truly."

Jared smiled and then left to join Lauren and Grant who were engaged in a lively conversation with his wife, Poppy.

My smile dimmed as I watched them interact. "I don't think I'm getting out of here any time soon."

"Why's that?"

"Lauren gave me a ride over here so I couldn't bolt."

"Would you be okay if I took you home?"

I hesitated and then narrowed my eyes. "Are you planning a repeat of what happened last week? Did you and Lauren plot all of this?"

"No plotting at all. Scouts honor." He held up his hand in salute.

I exhaled a laugh. "Okay, fine, but don't make me regret it."

CHAPTER 7

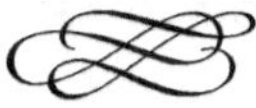

As promised, Jon Roseman was a perfect gentleman driving me home. He kept the topics light and centered around our girls, and it helped me relax.

"Thanks for the ride," I said. "Lauren didn't look too disappointed that I was leaving with you instead of her."

Jon chuckled. "Yeah, that entire room felt like a group of matchmakers." He held my eyes and left his next thoughts unspoken.

I broke eye contact and exhaled a short laugh. "So, you really think I'm buying this whole *just friends* shtick from you? It didn't work so well for Lauren and Grant."

"I beg to differ. They're engaged now. I think things worked out just fine."

I rolled my eyes. "You know what I mean. Are you going to look at me like that every time I see you now?"

"Look at you like what?"

"Like you want to kiss me."

"You already know that I do, Charlotte."

"We've tried that. Twice. Results were less than satis-factory."

"Well, I tend to be of the 'if at first you don't succeed' mindset." He winked at me, and I shook my head and laughed.

"I tend to be of the 'cut your losses and move on' mindset. We're at an impasse, Jon. You think you're going to win me over eventually, and I'm ninety-nine percent sure that if you kissed me again, nothing would be different."

"I already told you that I won't pressure you. I hope that sets your mind at ease."

"I appreciate the sentiment, but knowing that you're wanting something more does put pressure on me."

"How?"

"Maybe it's my old need for people-pleasing, but I feel like I'm disappointing you by not giving you what you want."

"But it's not what *you* want, Charlotte, and I'm more concerned with making sure you're comfortable rather than wearing you down or coercing you into something against your will."

"And because you're *not* bullying me, it makes me feel even *more* pressure to give you what you want because you're being such a gentleman about it. Like I said, old people-pleasing tendencies that I'm still working on."

Jon studied me before smiling. "You have a very interesting way of looking at things. You're also putting yourself in a no-win situation, and that's not what I want for you."

"Oh yeah? So, what is it that you want for me?"

"Ideally, I'd love for you to see yourself the way that I do. I want you to be free from your past and all of the lies you've been told."

I tilted my head to the side. "Not the answer I expected. To be honest, nothing about our friendship has been what I expected."

"Were you expecting another Rick Williams?"

I exhaled a sarcastic chuckle. "I would have blocked you on Instantpics after your first DM if I thought you were anything like *Richard.*"

"Well, then I'm glad I messaged you and even more glad you can see the difference."

"You're way hotter, for one thing."

Jon's jaw fell open before he burst into a full belly laugh.

I gave him a saucy wink and a playful shove. "Who do you think started your silver fox fan club?"

"Does that make you one of my thirsty fangirls?" He paused and then laughed self deprecatingly. "I've heard Rachel use that expression, but I feel like I lose IQ points trying to speak Gen Z slang."

"Oh, my girls won't hesitate to correct me, but that's because they want me to learn it. Female bonding and all of that."

"Lucky you. I just feel like a dinosaur trying to talk to mine."

"And to answer your question, no I'm not 'thirsting' after you. I'm a fan, but definitely not desperate for your attention."

"Desperate? Ouch!"

We both fell into an easy laugh, and his dark eyes sparkled as they held mine.

"Charlotte, I'm glad to know my ego will never get too big hanging around you."

"And maybe we'll get my ego out of the dumpster if I ever start believing half the stuff you say about me."

His expression sobered. "You know I'm not just blowing smoke, right?"

"I know that you believe what you're saying, Jon. Just

because I don't agree with you doesn't mean I think you're being insincere. After everything I've been through, it really does mean a lot coming from a man I actually respect."

He reached over to squeeze my hand. "Whatever does or doesn't happen between us, I want you to know that I genuinely admire your integrity and your honesty. I love that I can trust you to give me your truthful opinion instead of sugar coating things just to avoid confrontation."

"Not that I think you would believe otherwise, but I just want to be clear that even when I'm being brutally honest, it's never my intention to hurt or embarrass you. I'd rather tell you that you've got poppy seeds stuck in your teeth than pretend you use polka dot toothpaste."

"Of course!" he exclaimed. "It's refreshing, Charlotte. I don't have to hide or pretend to be something I'm not. I know that I can be myself around you, and that's a gift that God has given you. I hate that it's been taken advantage of by people like Tina or your ex, but I hope you know that you're safe with me."

"I'm getting there. I think I need to trust myself more than anyone."

We shared a sweet moment of smiles and twinkling eyes before Jon cleared his throat and spoke. "Thank you for talking through all of this with me tonight. You're definitely not a coward. I'd go so far as to call you bold and courageous."

"Are you going to quote *Joshua 1:9* too? I've got that Bible verse on a few bookmarks and coffee mugs in my house."

"I was thinking more like *Proverbs 31:10-11*, but according to you, I'm not allowed to compliment you like that."

"No, you're just not allowed to kiss me. You can toss *Proverbs 31* at me all day long. I've got the entire chapter in Hebrew on a canvas print in my bedroom."

Jon whistled. "I can't imagine that was a gift from Richard."

I blew a raspberry. "No, it was a gift from Lily, actually. That girl is my biggest cheerleader. When she was younger, the only Bible verses she ever wanted to read at night were *Proverbs 31*. She'd get this sneaky little grin on her face every time she asked. She wanted me to know I was a noble wife even if Rick never said it."

His dark eyes glowed. "That's adorable."

"She's an incredible kid. Definitely has the gift of encouragement. Sophie got picked on for being mouthy with her father and a carbon copy of me. Lily was generally just ignored by Rick and his entire side of the family."

"What? Why?"

"Because Sophie was the firstborn and because Lily wasn't a boy. You'd think Helen Williams would have favored Lily over Sophie because she looks like Rick, but Lily's more introverted than her sister and doesn't like the limelight. Helen wants grandkids to show off, not ones that require actual effort. Lily's favorite member of Rick's family is his parents' dog, Evander. He's the only one that pays her any attention."

"I'm so sorry, Charlotte. For all of you. You three deserved to be cherished, not treated like a burden."

"I don't consider it much of a loss, but I know the girls are hurt. Rick got an insta-fam when he married Stephanie, and he's made it pretty clear where his loyalties lie. It hurts my girls, but at least they see their father for what he is. I wasted most of my twenties trying to earn love that never existed from my own father, and I eventually gave up in my thirties. I haven't spoken with him in ten years."

Jon frowned. "How are things with your mom?"

"Things are okay now, but she has a lot of health issues. She lives with my ninety-six-year-old grandmother, so I usually wind up spending time with Bubbe while the girls keep my mom occupied."

"I'm glad you have her."

"Me too. My brothers are another story, specifically my middle brother, Abe. Mom has a blind spot when it comes to him and makes a lot of excuses for his behavior. She doesn't see how much he has in common with my father."

"But things with your youngest brother are okay, right?"

"Yes, things are good with Ben. His wife is the sister I never had but always wanted. We've hashed through a lot. Things with Abe are at no contact. He's one hundred percent team Rick, and he still badmouths me to the rest of the family."

"I don't understand that. You said you guys were close growing up."

"We were. Then Abe got messed up after my parents split. My mother favors him because my father picked on him, but he treats her like dirt. Honestly, he treats everyone like dirt. They walk on eggshells because of his mood swings and make excuses for all of the cruel things he says when he lashes out."

"How and when did he decide to take up Rick's cause against you?"

"Apparently, Nathan Fein wasn't the only person Rick ran to with his made up stories of being emasculated and controlled by me. My brother gobbled up the lies, and it explains why he always shut me down when I talked about being unhappy in the marriage. I really don't know what offense he's using to justify how he treats me now, but when he posted pictures of my girls publicly on FaceSpace and said, 'one day, I'll tell you the truth about your mother,' that was the last straw."

Jon sucked in a breath. "Unbelievable! Did he ever apologize to you for it?"

I rolled my eyes. "According to my mother, he apologized to

Rick for 'disrespecting another man's wife.' Not a peep said to the actual wife, aka his own sister. My mother seems to think that's good enough for her favorite son."

"That's disgusting!"

"Agreed. So, I don't talk to Abe, and my mother can't stand it. That has caused some tension because I refuse to move the boundary or cater to her denial. She's always triangulated the two of us, telling me that poor Abey-Wabey was hurt by something I said or did, and I needed to apologize to him. Those standards never applied in reverse."

"Sounds like he's had some resentment toward you for a while."

"Yeah, I guess you're right." I sighed, putting the puzzle pieces together. "I remember when I finally stood up to my mother and told her that if Abe has a problem with me, then Abe needed to act like a grown man and talk to me about it."

"What did your mother say?"

"Apparently, it's *my* fault my brother came crying to her instead of me, and therefore I needed to reach out to him. I called her out for meddling, told her that we're both adults, and that until *he* can tell me what his problem is, then there isn't a 'problem' as far as I'm concerned. More than likely, my brother just made up something anyway, and he knew that talking to me about it would mean he had nothing to play victim about to everyone else. He'll use my mom for sympathy and helicoptering his problems as easily as he'll tell her off for talking incessantly and alienating him for our dad."

Jon frowned. "That's seriously messed up. I guess it makes sense that he'd listen to Rick. It's *confirmation bias*."

"What's that?"

"It's when you go searching for something that supports

what you already want to believe anyway. Like when the Bible talks about people wanting their ears tickled."

"That sounds about right. I've put up with so much from my brother, but somehow he's always the victim. He would have these hurricane temper tantrums where he'd lash out when you told him 'no.' You had to withstand the storm, and then he would calm down and talk rationally again. He got mad when I stopped taking his abuse. He had messaged me at six in the morning over something asinine, and I finally told him to shut up and let me make my own mistakes. He had been ripping me apart for fifteen minutes, and I'd finally had enough."

"What did he say?"

I snickered. "The pearl clutching would have put Richard Williams to shame. You would have thought I had said a fraction of the intentionally hurtful garbage he was spewing at me."

"Sounds like Abe and Rick are cut from the same cloth—and they've bonded over you as a common enemy. I'm so sorry you had to deal with that, Charlotte. It's such a low betrayal. Your brother clearly had some kind of a grudge against you. Do you know what started it?"

"No clue. I've been there for my brother through his twenties and early thirties, listening to him cry about breakups, about my father rejecting him, or the time he realized he'd blown things for good with the one serious girlfriend he had. Based on my experiences with Rick, Stephanie, and Tina, I would say it's some kind of misplaced jealousy."

"What is your brother jealous of?"

"The fact I did well in school and he dropped out. The fact I didn't screw around with drugs and sex, and he did. The fact I got married and had a family, and he ruined the best relationship he ever had with a girl who probably could have helped him turn his life around. I remember messaging her after they broke up and apologizing for how he had treated her."

Jon sucked in a breath. "Wow. I guess you really liked her."

"I did. Jennie is amazing. Abe never deserved her, and I think he knew it. She loved him anyway, but I guess everything happens for a reason. She's been married for over ten years now, has three kids, and she and I still keep in touch."

"Hm," Jon said, stroking his beard. "Maybe it's revenge then."

"What is?"

"You sided with his ex against him, so Abe sided with Rick against you."

"It could be," I murmured. "I'd never really thought of it that way."

After another lengthy pause, one that had me revisiting several memories of me and my brother with a new set of eyes, I realized Jon had been watching me the entire time. When he didn't say anything, I began to jostle my foot against the floorboard.

"You got somewhere to be?" he laughed.

"Just work in the morning. So do you. I should probably go."

He took hold of my hand. "Thank you for opening up to me. I will keep this all in confidence and also take it to the Lord in prayer."

"I appreciate that. You're a good man, Jon."

He smiled at me, and I was struck by just how handsome he was. "Good night, Charlotte. Sweet dreams."

When Jon Roseman texted me the following morning, I didn't mention that my sweet dreams had included a kiss with him that felt anything but brotherly.

CHAPTER 8

"So, you guys kissed?" Luke breathed, looking unapologetically gossipy.

Rosaria nursed a sequined purple tumbler of tea and pouted. "Does that mean I have to find a new plus one for my cruise?"

I rolled my eyes. "I swear, the two of you are worse than my daughters' high school friends. Remind me not to overshare again."

"Which would also require you to change your entire personality, so it looks like you're stuck with us." Ro smirked and then took another sip of her herbal tea.

Luke, meanwhile, feigned disappointment with an exaggerated frown. "Does that mean I won't get to hear any more of your online dating disaster stories? Those are always the best part of my Monday mornings."

I shot him a dirty look. "Punk."

He grinned back. "You know I'm only teasing."

"Yeah, but you're also completely serious."

He shrugged, not bothering to deny it.

"So, tell me more about this guy you kissed," Ro said.

"We're old friends."

"How old?" Luke asked.

"Old as in his wife passed down baby clothes for Sophie and Lily."

Luke whistled and his eyes widened. "So, what happened with his wife? She wasn't another salty hag like Stephanie, was she?"

I chuckled at his apt description. "Ha! No, Andrea was a very kind and sweet woman. She passed away from cancer ten years ago, and Jon said he didn't have any interest in dating until he realized his youngest was going to be out of the house soon. It was the first time he could focus on something other than raising his girls."

Ro placed a hand over heart and sighed. "That is so unbelievably romantic."

My smile turned sad. "I think he's still in love with her, to be honest. Andrea was pretty amazing."

Ro and Luke exchanged a glance before Luke piped up. "But you said he kissed you."

"He did. And it was like kissing my brother."

"How is that possible?" Ro gasped. "You're the least sisterly woman I know."

"I don't know. I mean the second time was better, but—"

Luke cut me off. "Second time? Excuse me? You kissed your *brother* a second time? I'm not buying it, friend."

"I didn't say he *was* my brother! The first kiss was really not awesome, so we gave it another shot. Unfortunately, it was just..."

"Just what?" Ro breathed, waiting for details like it was *The Bold & the Restless.*

"Like Jon was kissing Andrea instead of me."

"Oh, honey," she cooed, placing a hand on my shoulder.

Luke watched me, and I raised my eyebrows at his strange expression. I wanted to know what was going on in that ginger head of his or if he had any insights to share into the male psyche. Instead, he shook his head and returned back to his office.

Ro patted me on the back. "Well, I'm sorry things didn't work out with this Jon guy, but at least you can still be my plus one in a couple months. We're gonna have so much fun. You never know who we might meet. The love of your life could be on that boat, and you never would have met him without the cruise."

I sighed and shrugged. "Yeah, I guess."

"You really like him, don't you?" she asked quietly. "This Jon guy?"

"What do you mean? We're friends, so obviously I like him."

"You know what I mean. I think you *like* him."

I turned to face my computer monitors. "It doesn't matter what I think. We're not compatible."

"Okay," she drawled, "so we're in deep six denial. Got it. Looks like I'll be sharing a cruise cabin with me, myself, and I."

I whirled back around. "Excuse me?"

"Girl, you've got it *bad* for him."

"What are you talking about? Did you not hear a single word I just said? We tried being more than friends. It failed. Epically."

She tsked and shook her head. "No, honey, you just had a bad first kiss."

"And second kiss," I added.

She waved me off like I hadn't just interrupted her. "Not every first kiss is some magical, Hallmerck moment. Sometimes, it *is* awkward."

"Yeah, if you're fourteen and you've never been kissed before."

"Or," she jumped in, undeterred by my mulish response, "if you're in your forties, you're a little rusty, and you're nervous. I've had plenty of awkward first kisses. Sometimes, it just takes practice."

"And how many of those awkward first kisses worked out for you, Ro?"

"Well, I was with Devon for three years, so we figured some things out along the way. Ultimately, we decided to be friends, but not because we didn't have chemistry in the bedroom. We're just different people."

"Well, I'm not hopping into bed with anybody without a ring and signed paperwork, and the last thing I want is a repeat of Richard."

"Obviously not. Does this Jon guy have bad breath too?"

I snickered. "No, thank God. No death breath you can smell from across the room like old what's-his-face."

She grimaced. "How on earth did you stay married as long as you did if his breath was that bad?"

I chuckled. "The halitosis got worse with age, but he also chewed gum obsessively when we were dating. The funky breath was there, but he always had some kind of mint in his mouth. We didn't do that much making out either. It was a quick courtship and long distance, so that definitely worked in his favor."

"What was so great about Rick Williams that you even married him?" she asked. "I mean, we talk about what a scumbag he is now, but how on earth did someone with as much zest for life as you wind up with someone who has the personality of a moldy toadstool?"

I thought back to those days in my mid-twenties, my own

naivete and desire to get married. The scarcity of available men didn't help. I had been attending a non denominational church for seven years after I'd gotten saved there, but the single men consisted of guys old enough to date my mother or guys young enough for me to babysit. Either way, I was getting hit on by dudes in diapers.

"At the time, Rick was just different," I began, remembering a time when I didn't despise Richard Carl Williams. "I didn't intimidate him like I seemed to do with any other guys my age at church. We met online, and we clicked. We talked on the phone, he laughed at my jokes, and he said he was willing to move to Danbury since he lived in Florida. I think he had been wanting to go to Beth Shalom even before we got together. He was interested in Messianic Judaism long before I was."

"Hm," Ro murmured, leaning a hip against my desk. "Was it love at first sight?"

I exhaled a bitter laugh. "Hardly. He was skinny, not much taller than me, and he didn't have that beard to hide the recessed chin."

She shook her head. "And you somehow still fell in love?"

"Yeah, I guess I did. He treated me better than my family did—not that the bar was all that high. I guess I thought meeting someone who found me attractive and didn't force me to hide my personality meant that I'd have some vindication from all the horrible things I heard from my father and brothers."

"So, he was a replacement father figure?" Ro asked.

"No, I mistakenly gave Rick the role of being my savior. I wanted to be seen and validated and rescued from my family's abuse. It took the pain of seeing the unmasked pig I married and realizing he was *exactly* like my family to finally understand that every single one of them were liars."

She looked thoughtful. "How so?"

"Rick lied about anything and everything. Big or small. If I asked who left dishes in the sink, he either didn't know or tried to blame the girls. Any fights we had about the way he treated me were always my fault. He would look for even one percent I did wrong as if it equated to his ninety-nine. When that tactic stopped working, then it was attacking my 'disrespectful' tone or accusing me of emasculating him."

"So, he gaslighted you?"

"All the time. It wasn't until I watched him do the exact same thing to Sophie that I stopped believing his jerky behavior was a reaction to something I'd done. Sophie was so little, and he would pick on her, deliberately exasperate her, and then play victim when the poor kid finally had enough. It was like looking in a mirror. I still stuck it out for another four years hoping the cretin would change, but his behavior toward me and Sophie just got more antagonistic because we both stood up for ourselves. The breadcrumbs and flowery words on birthday and anniversary cards didn't erase how he treated me like an enemy the rest of the time. I also found out he had been trash talking me with my brothers. The disloyal turd had the gall to play dumb that badmouthing his wife might somehow be detrimental to our marriage."

Ro hissed out a few four letter pejoratives for my ex-husband.

"Exactly," I said with a flourish. "His criticism of me became constant along with his whining whenever I asked him to pull his weight around the house. When I heard him spouting off insults that sounded exactly like the garbage my father and brothers used to say about me, I realized what was happening. I used to ask Rick why my own family treated him so well and me like the heinous daughter-in-law everybody just tolerated. He pretended he didn't know, but it was all a lie. He was feeding them the same narrative they already used against me so they would support *him* instead of me."

"What a creep! And shame on them for disrespecting you like that!"

"Yeah, Richard is no stranger to emotional and psychological abuse. Unfortunately, neither is my family. So, if nothing else, being married to and eventually getting free from the pig also helped me break free from the lies my family taught me. All Rick needed to do was parrot whatever body issues I was already self conscious about, and he knew I would go ahead and beat myself up without him lifting a finger. I hated my weight and my nose growing up because my father shamed me about them all the time. Guess what Rick did?"

"The same thing," Ro breathed, looking at me pityingly. "You are so strong to have survived that, Charlotte. You're one of the most confident women I know. It's inspiring."

I shrugged. "I still struggle with all of those lies, especially with the dried up, dysfunctional dating pool out there, but I've wasted so much of my life trying to please people. It made *me* miserable, and of course, it was never good enough for any of them. So, now I work hard to at least make sure that *I'm* happy. The ogres are content to be miserable so they have an excuse to complain, but I am no longer miserable trying to get them to value what they never appreciated to begin with."

Ro beamed at me. "I'm proud of you. That takes guts to realize all of that and even more courage to act on it."

"Thanks," I said, forcing myself to accept her praise. "I don't know if I see it as quite the big deal you do, but I appreciate the sentiment."

"Charlotte, instead of choosing to be miserable or playing the martyr, you left. You got your girls out of the house from the ungrateful swine you married."

"Yeah, but now he's so wrapped up in his precious Stephanie and the holy terrors, he has no time for his own daughters. I don't want them repeating my mistakes and trying to fill the daddy wound with the first jerk who shows them attention like I did."

Ro smiled affectionately and patted my arm. "I think you're already modeling self respect every time you stand up to Rick. You didn't stay in that awful marriage pretending it was 'for the sake of the kids' just to avoid fear of the unknown or the stigma of divorce."

"I couldn't stay after I saw what it was doing to Sophie. There was no other option, Ro. Don't make me into a hero. I'm just a mom who wants to protect her babies."

"Did *your* mother ever do that with your jerk of a father? How about your jerk of an ex-husband? Give yourself more credit, Charlotte."

I frowned, knowing exactly what my mother had done. She never left my dad. He'd left us. Even before my divorce, she had been Team Rick because Abe was Team Rick up until she didn't see her granddaughters for nearly two years. As my marriage disintegrated, I couldn't deal with her criticism on top of the abuse I already received at home. She just parroted my brother who believed every word of Rick's slander.

"So, tell me again," Ro said, holding my gaze, "why things can't work out with this Jon guy. Is he giving off Richard vibes? Does he have some of that narcissist stink to him?"

Recalling our most recent conversation where Jon told me he wished I could think of myself as highly as he did, I felt a small glimmer of hope.

The problem was that hope was painful.

Hope deferred had already broken me.

CHAPTER 9

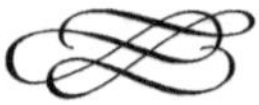

"Rick, come on," I urged five years earlier, "you promised you would stop coming to bed so late so that we could have some alone time."

He barely looked up from his laptop screen. "I just need fifteen more minutes. I told you I'm behind on this work deadline."

"You asked for 'fifteen more minutes' an hour ago. Is this actually for work, or have you been looking at contraband again?"

He glared at me. "You know I haven't looked at anything like that in months."

It also wouldn't be the first time Rick had bald faced lied to me about his pornography struggles. I used to feel crazy thinking God was using cockroaches as a sign, but sure enough, every time I saw one crawling in my house, Rick later confessed he'd been looking at porn. After the eighth or ninth time it happened, I realized it was too often to be a coincidence.

Eventually, my husband grew tired of my "bedtime nagging,"

so he lied about his online activities and swore it was just his demanding boss. I grew suspicious when his avoidant behavior never improved and neither did our love life. I always had to initiate romantic time. The closest Rick came to seduction was a petulant, "Can you help me out?" followed by a begrudging promise to see me satisfied as well.

When I demanded he get professional help or install some kind of computer safeguard for accountability, my errant husband claimed he'd been set free from his addiction.

But the roaches kept coming.

Eventually, whenever I busted Rick lying about looking at porn, he rolled his eyes and snidely asked if I'd seen another cockroach. Belittling me was easier than admitting that even vermin refused to conceal his secrets. I grew wise to the diversion tactic and stopped arguing against his idiotic claim I believed in "divination" rather than trusting my godly authority. Richard the Great aka the patron saint of lying liars forgot I had no problem talking to God myself. I dug in my heels and pushed him to admit the truth, but Rick doubled down on deflecting responsibility. He called me suspicious and controlling while insisting that's why he had to hide things from me.

He lied because *I* was untrustworthy.

Yeah.

I'd given Rick one final ultimatum a year and a half before I filed for divorce. We'd been going twenty rounds about the horrible state of our marriage, hashing through our relationship from the very beginning until its current state. Rick claimed he had felt pressured by me to commit, pressured by me to start a family, and that he'd once upon a time confessed to a coworker he couldn't quite remember the name of that he wasn't ready to be a father.

"You just pushed and pushed, Charlotte. Just like you do now."

"Well, it's not like we can go back in time and return our children. Don't you think it's time to stop resenting me and just enjoy the blessing of having two amazing daughters?"

He wrinkled his nose in distaste.

"Really?" I demanded. "You can't be thankful for the girls?"

"I never said I wasn't thankful, but you can't ask me to just turn off my emotions about what you did to me."

I gaped. "What I *did* to you? I carried and gave birth to two of your children! Don't you think fourteen years is long enough to resent me for something I never even knew you resented until yesterday?"

"You just used me to have kids and be a mom. You don't care about my feelings at all. You do whatever you want and steamroll anyone who gets in your way."

"Rick, it's a miracle we even have the girls considering how often you neglect me. Do you enjoy hearing me beg for sex or something?"

"What? No! Why would you even think that?"

Because of the gleam in his eyes as his mouth said one thing, but the rest of his face looked smugly satisfied.

I exhaled a frustrated breath. "It's not like I tricked you into becoming a father. You told me you wanted to be a dad, remember?"

"I also told you I wanted to wait a year or two before we had kids. You got pregnant a month after we got married!"

"Right," I snapped, "because I totally planned that."

"You could have prevented it."

"Prevented it, how? You refuse to use a condom, you don't want me on birth control, so what is your suggestion other than abstinence? Your computer viewing problems mean that you *do* want to have sex, just not with me apparently. I've seen the smut you look at. None of that is attainable without plastic surgery and poorly acted payment for pizza delivery."

His cheeks pinked. "I didn't realize you had been spying on me."

"You left the web browser open last week when I found you asleep on the couch. You should be thankful I'm the one who saw it instead of the girls."

He clenched his jaw and eyed his laptop as if the computer had betrayed him.

"None of that stuff is real, Rick, and those women don't exist in real life. You can't compare me to that, and it's not fair that you do. I'm set up to fail."

"You call it unattainable," he said with disdain. "I call it laziness." His eyes lingered on my belly and expanded bosom. "You didn't look like this when we got married."

"Because *you're* such a specimen?" I shot back. "Do you think you're so perfect or that I don't overlook your physical imperfections? I love you for who you are, not what you look like. Do I shame you for your bad breath or make you self conscious about it?"

He looked away, gritting his teeth. Despite my penchant for speaking with no filter, we'd worked out a code for my husband needing to handle his halitosis. *You forgot your sunglasses* was an innocuous statement to any bystander, but it was my non-embarrassing way to let him know that a breath mint was needed. Grumbling, he said, "That's different."

"Different, how?"

"Men are visual," he said petulantly, repeating one of Rabbi Lebow's aphorisms. "We need to like what we see."

I surveyed his lean frame, knowing the only reason why his outfit matched was because I did all of Rick Williams' clothes shopping—at his behest. "Are women supposed to be blind? You were borderline scrawny when we got married. The only reason you're not heavier now is because you're not built for it."

"Exactly. Clearly, *you* are."

"Did you carry two children inside of your body?" I hissed.

"No, but I think twelve years is long enough to lose the weight," he replied flippantly. "Your friend, Lauren, bounced back just fine. I doubt she was gorging herself like you do at night. Self control is a fruit of the spirit, you know."

Meanwhile, my fruit of patience had withered into a raisin. "Do you preach those self control sermons to yourself when you're looking at porn?"

"Well, I wouldn't need to look at porn if I had something better to look at in my bed."

My lips pursed. "Is anything *ever* your fault? Must be nice to live responsibility free when you can just blame your vices on me instead of acting like an adult."

"And there you go emasculating me again!" He jumped to his feet. "You're so disrespectful and bitter, Charlotte. Even if you *were* physically attractive, your personality is repulsive. Maybe if you learned what real submissiveness is, we'd have a better marriage. I wouldn't need porn if I had the kind of wife God intended. Lose sixty pounds and get a nose job, and you'll see how much better our marriage can be."

Stunned and wounded into silence, I retreated inside of myself. I had no words for that depth of cruelty.

Rick smirked as if he'd won the battle. "The sooner you learn your place and how God wants our marriage to look, the happier we'll both be. Stop talking to Lauren Fein. Everyone knows she's crazy, and all she does is poison you against me."

I swallowed back a slew of insults about his sinewy shoulders, beady eyes, and body hair in inconvenient places. "I've never been thin. You knew that when you married me. You told me you liked my figure and loved my hugs. Once upon a time, you flew up to Hillcrest monthly to see me. Do you remember any of that?"

His lips flattened. The truth would remain barricaded behind them.

I continued on. "You said you'd never felt a connection with anyone like this before. You said I was the first woman you talked to who was interested in trying out Messianic Judaism. We've been at Beth Shalom for fifteen years even though *I'm* not happy there. Tell me again how I'm the one steamrolling you to always have my way because it sounds like everything has been all about *you*, Rick."

"I would hardly call attending Beth Shalom a sacrifice," he sniffed haughtily. "Would you rather be in some legalistic church or a non denominational dog and pony show?"

"You act like I can't get both at Beth Shalom. Sprinkle a little of that 'Jewish glitter' on everything, and you get the legalism, the dog and pony show, plus a heaping dose of self righteous judgment all in one bite."

His brown eyes narrowed. "You've never really supported me, Charlotte. You just pout when you can't get your way."

"Tell me where you've been willing to compromise on anything, Rick." My ice blue eyes held frozen daggers. "You're always accusing me of your own behavior, and then you play the victim as if it's happening *to* you instead of being perpetrated *by* you."

He rolled his eyes dismissively. "I guess it's time to parrot *the charlatan* again."

"Stop calling her that! Her name is Lauren."

"You should see what her husband says about her," he sneered. "Lauren Fein isn't some all knowing prophet."

"She never claimed to be. Her only crime is posting about narcissistic and toxic behavior on social media. You're just mad that your own behavior gets called out when she does it."

"Ha! I knew it was on purpose! You share our marriage problems with her, and then Lauren pretends it's all her own ideas. I've sent screenshots to Rabbi about what she's saying. Nathan needs to get control of his wife."

Thinking of secrets Lauren had recently shared about Nathan's "control" over her, I shuddered. She had reconciled with her husband following a massive scandal and police investigation of him downloading underage pornography onto the synagogue server. While Nathan Fein put on a show at temple of being a loving husband, I'd seen the bruises on Lauren's arms and a faded bruise on her face when she had disappeared from synagogue for three weeks.

"You're buddy Nathan isn't the saint he pretends to be."

"Ha!" Rick snarled. "He volunteers every second he has to Beth Shalom. He is a good man, and both you and your precious charlatan better learn to start appreciating what you have."

"Or what, Rick?"

"What do you mean?"

"Or *what*, Rick? Are you gonna divorce me? Gonna find a new wife to worship the ground you walk on and act like your feces smell like roses? Just like your breath?"

It was a low blow.

His face went white before it went red.

I knew he wanted to hit me. I saw it on his face. Frozen in place, I silently begged God not to turn me into another Lauren Fein. My mouth had gotten me in plenty of trouble before, but nothing like this.

"Sorry," I said contritely. "I shouldn't have said that."

"Start acting like a loving wife, and I'll start treating you like one," he grit with controlled rage.

I wanted to argue about his selfish, unappreciative, spoiled brat attitude, but I'd crossed a line I never thought I would. Sure, Rick insulted me with ease, but I'd prided myself on never retaliating or berating him the way father had done to me and my mother. I didn't want to become my brother, Abe, who projected his self-loathing out on the rest of the world.

"Rick," I said, reaching out a hand to him, "I'm frustrated with you, but I never should have said that. It was hurtful and mean, and I'm sorry."

His defensive posture eased somewhat. "I appreciate that, Charlotte."

"Can't we try for a new beginning?" I pleaded. "I don't want us to be at each other's throats anymore. I want us to have a marriage our daughters will want to emulate."

"Show me more of this," he said, his tone gentling, "the softer side of you, and I think we'll both be happy."

I placed my hand on his shoulder, willing to work on myself yet again if it meant actual hope for our marriage. "So, you're coming to bed now?"

He patted my hand and then turned back to his computer screen. "Fifteen more minutes."

CHAPTER 10

HEEDLESS OF HOW LOUD HE WAS, RICK FINALLY appeared in our bedroom around two thirty in the morning. Flipping on lights, fumbling around, and banging bathroom cabinets like he was warding off ghosts, I seethed in silence while feigning sleep. He mumbled an apology when he kicked me as he barreled into bed. He fell asleep easily as I lay there, cold from the inside and out. My marriage was dead. The dream of a happily ever after with Richard Carl Williams had flickered its last dying breath. Regardless of how many hoops I jumped through, pounds I lost, or how much I dimmed my inner light, I realized Rick would just move the goalposts and find something new to complain about.

No amount of effort was good enough for my husband because *I* wasn't good enough for him. In truth, no woman would ever be good enough. Rick's perfect woman was an indentured servant whose sole focus was pleasing her master. Pornography provided him with women who obeyed whatever desire he could type into a search bar—and they asked nothing of him in return. For a lazy, entitled man like my husband, porn was a panacea.

I emotionally disengaged from the relationship after that horrible night, and the mourning process for my marriage began. As I formulated my exit strategy, I got back into the workforce knowing I would have to eventually support myself and the girls. Rick assumed it was to have more money to spend, and I didn't bother arguing with him or even responding to his snide comments. His insults were a backhanded way of commending me for getting a job without actually acknowledging my efforts. Instead, he complained that dinner wasn't ready when he arrived home and the house was being neglected. I realized Rick was only happy when he was making everyone else miserable, so I responded with a simple "okay," and went about my business. Only later did I learn he harassed our daughters to pick up the slack since he had no intention of lifting a finger to help.

With my entry level salary, I saved every penny I could in a separate bank account. God helped orchestrate my initial escape by virtue of Rick's willful negligence of our finances. I had always handled our bookkeeping and bills since my husband never took the time to keep our accounting records current. Even after I'd started working, Rick never thought to ask why my paychecks didn't appear in our joint checking account. All that mattered to my husband was assuming he had money in the bank whenever he used our credit cards. As long as he could enjoy his daily macchiatos and bi-monthly bash-your-wife lunches with Nathan Fein, he didn't bother to research anything. I also withdrew cash each time I made a grocery run or trip for household goods to pad my tiny stockpile and get an attorney on retainer.

When I served my husband with divorce papers, he was

shocked. First, that I had saved up the money "behind his back" to hire a lawyer. Second, that I followed through on my threat if he didn't work to repair our marriage. I had grown quiet and withdrawn around him, and Rick praised it as a turn in our relationship because we weren't fighting anymore. In reality, I was no longer fighting *for* the relationship. I was done fighting for my husband's attention, respect, or regard. He still picked fights, but I no longer responded. In doing so, I realized how often my husband had intentionally provoked the arguments he would later claim emasculated him.

"God hates divorce!" he screamed. "How could you do this to me?" He waved the papers in my face, nearly hitting me with them.

"God hates how you treat me, Rick. He hates how you treat our daughters."

"I don't hear them complaining."

"That's because you won't let them say a word you don't approve of. Instead of being able to talk to their father, they take out the pain on themselves instead."

He visibly swallowed, not wanting to admit that his latest bout of shaming resulted in the red scars running across Sophie's left forearm. I'd taken my baby to the hospital and then researched family law attorneys on my phone while they treated her injuries.

"Divorce isn't the answer, Charlotte. You can't just run from our problems."

"I'm not going to spend the rest of my days in a marriage that feels like a prison sentence. You'd rather stay so you have something to complain about to your friends. It has nothing to do with loving me, being loyal to me, or frankly, even liking me. You get a lot more mileage playing the victim than finally ending this charade. Our girls deserve better, and frankly, so do I."

"You just don't want to do the work it takes," he accused. "You're taking the coward's way out."

Old me would have argued with Rick because we both knew the only way I handled confrontation was straight on. The emotionally disengaged, new version of me didn't bat an eyelash at his obvious baiting. Calmly, I replied, "Nothing I do will ever turn me into the mindless robot you want me to be."

Rick denied it all, of course, then doubled down on his victim narrative. Forgetting that I knew the passwords to his social media accounts, I saw his frantic messages to members of our congregation begging them to reason with me, pray against whatever demon was "influencing" me (i.e. attack Lauren too), and to fast and pray that I would come to my senses.

I offered a reasonable divorce settlement so we could end the marriage amicably, but Rick refused to provide child support let alone part with any of our shared belongings. He also knew that my salary at 7-Square Property Management wouldn't cover the cost of a new living situation without his additional finances. By then, he had cleaned out all of our joint accounts. His justification was that since I'd "recklessly spent thousands and thousands" without his knowledge or permission, he needed to move the money *for safekeeping*. What I'd actually done was pay down the credit card balance of his attorney's retainer fee as well as mine. Rick conveniently omitted those details when retelling the baloney sob story to the Beth Shalom faithful. His efforts to keep me trapped in the house with him also included changing his direct deposit bank account so that I had no access to money beyond my meager salary.

At the time, my best friend, Tina Fournier, had presented me with the option of renting her basement to help get me on my feet during the divorce. She knew how frustrated I was living with Rick, and it was clear he wouldn't leave the house. Within a month of moving in with her, however, Tina exposed us all to Covid-19. For reasons unknown, the woman I had loved like a sister began picking ridiculous fights while I was simply fighting to breathe. I asked for space, and Tina went ballistic. Her acts of revenge included locking the basement door to the main house so we couldn't do laundry upstairs. She followed that stunt with scathing text messages to bully me into talking to her. When I advocated for my own health over catering to her bizarre tantrums, we were no longer welcome to stay in her home.

The amount of stress handling my own sickness, researching alternative living situations, and realizing we had no place to go but back to Rick had me wishing I could just meet Jesus and be done with my miserable existence. Depression had as much of a grip on my heart as the virus did, and it squeezed with an unrelenting fist. It was my girls who pulled me through that dark time, physically taking care of me, packing our meager belongings, and reassuring me that living with Daddy couldn't possibly be worse than staying with a heartless monster like Tina.

I still tried finding other housing options, but no homeless shelter would take us while we were contagious with Covid. Section Eight housing was backed up with massive waiting lists, and group home options sounded as controlling and awful as living with Tina. Stuck between the sixth and seventh degrees of hell, I opted for level six, and so back to Rick we went.

In typical petty fashion, Rick tried to prevent me from moving back into the house, insisting that only the girls were welcome. Thank God, my lawyer, Sondra Joyner, read his attorney the riot act. We both legally owned the home, and Rick had no right to deny me access to it. He had also previously agreed to let us come back but then tried to renege on it. Shocking all of us, his bulldog attorney threatened to quit if Rick didn't quit his piggish antics.

With great delight, my future ex-husband relegated me to the guest room while he commandeered the master suite. Now that he was firmly in control, he had no intention of relinquishing his power. He placed paper scraps and other items on top of the master bedroom double doors or just behind them so he could prove I'd *snuck* into the bedroom if any of the items moved. I confirmed with Sondra that he had no right to keep me out of the suite, but I really had no use for the area other than missing my garden tub and bubble baths. To that end, Rick made sure to keep the tub as filthy as possible. He used it as a cleaning depot for his various projects, rinsed the kitchen mop in there, or filled it with odds and ends that accumulated in the bedroom.

The pig was petty indeed.

I begged God to end our marriage and set me and the girls free, especially when I feared Sophie would relapse with her self-harm. Rick's controlling antics only escalated with our return. Worse yet, I saw the influence of Nathan Fein who took great delight in terrorizing his own wife. Lauren could only text me when she knew Nathan was at temple, working, or asleep. The night she called me hiding in the corner of her closet, I genuinely feared my friend wouldn't make it out of her marriage alive.

Then, like Aphrodite rising from the sea—or the coarse woman described in *Proverbs 9:13-18*—Stephanie Burgess arrived at Beth Shalom. Newly single herself, she set her sights on Rick, and the rest was history. He devoured Stephanie's attention as well as her sob stories. Completely missing the irony, he boasted of playing savior to a woman whose ex-husband sounded eerily similar to himself. Initially, I pitied Stephanie and wanted to spare her the pain of my fifteen years of misery, but I heeded the Holy Spirit as he kept directing me back to the first few chapters of *Proverbs*.

Stephanie's influence on Rick was immediate. Gone were the nerd-chic, plaid shirts over t-shirts and jeans. *Richard*, as Stephanie re-dubbed him, now wore turtlenecks and blazers, jackets, jackets, and more jackets. She dressed him in whatever she could find that beefed out his shoulders and gave him the appearance of a sturdier man. More shocking than the costume changes, however, was them purchasing a new home as soon as I refinanced the mortgage and cashed out Rick's equity. The man who had installed a digital lock on the master closet to keep me out of it now couldn't wait to depart for greener pastures.

The still-legally-married Rick Williams shacked up with gotta-trap-a-new-man Stephanie Burgess a month before our own divorce was finalized. I wondered why my husband abandoned the same morals he regularly shoved down the throats of me and my girls, but the Scripture verses I'd been reading about Stephanie landed like a lead weight. Whatever bedroom needs my husband previously sated with pornography were now being met with his new prize. Although thinner than me, Stephanie's grating personality couldn't hide behind the twelve pounds of makeup she wore. Considering everything Rick criticized about me, I wondered what he found attractive about those same traits dialed up to an obnoxious eleven. He flaunted his new relationship with nauseating PDA selfies on social media, and it hurt seeing my husband locked in passionate embraces he'd never given me.

My girls informed me that Stephanie forced Rick to take digestive enzymes to curtail the halitosis. With me, however, he spitefully ate dairy knowing it made his breath smell like he gargled with his own urine. I wondered what was so great about Stephanie that Rick made all these changes for her and only after only a few months of dating.

"I don't get it," I cried to Lauren over a late night phone call. "I stuck with that man for fifteen years, and he refused to give me even a millimeter. With Stephanie-Freaking-Bougie, it's like he got an entire personality transplant. Why wasn't I good enough for him to do that?"

Lauren's response didn't come immediately, and I wondered if Nathan was nearby. Instead, her tone came out thoughtfully like she'd truly pondered the matter.

"I think you answered your own question, Charlotte."

"I did? How?"

"Rick was never loyal to you, and he certainly never respected your loyalty to him."

"Is that supposed to make me feel better? What does that chick have that I don't? Magical lady bits hiding under her tacky miniskirts?"

Lauren burst out laughing. "Honestly, I don't think Rick has really changed."

"So, what's with the new clothes, the enzymes, and parading the *real love of his life* all over FaceSpace and Instantpics?" I asked bitterly. "Either I wasn't good enough, or I wasn't good enough for him to want to change."

"Rick has always been lazy, right?"

"Yeah, and?"

"Do you really think he's suddenly turned over a new leaf for Stephanie? What if the situation is that she controls everything instead? How much easier is his life with a woman who tells him what to do?"

My jaw dropped. "That does not sound anything like the

Rick Williams I was married to. He always accused me of trying to control him. Why on earth would he allow Stephanie to do that if he hates the idea so much?"

"Because what you actually did was demand Rick do the work himself. You made *Rick* responsible for changing Rick. Now, he's got Stephanie to do all the work for him instead. He's still the same lazy slug you married, only now Stephanie is in the driver's seat. I'm sure he's got resentment toward her, but he's just a little boy whose Mommy tells him where to go, what to eat, and how to dress. Personally, I think she's probably controlling Rick the way he always tried to control *you*."

I shook my head, sure there must be something else. "I just can't imagine him letting anyone take over his life like that. He loved his independence. I swear, I think he ate dairy as an excuse to make the halitosis worse and sabotage any hopes of me being romantic—and so he could just go look at porn instead."

"Exactly. What you were asking of your husband required effort and caring on his part. He'd have to prioritize your needs over his wants."

"But now he's prioritizing Stephanie over *all* of his own wants. He barely knows the woman, and he's doing all of this for her. I gave that man fifteen years and two children, and there's no loyalty, no nothing." My voice broke off as I cried.

Lauren tsked. "He acts this way because there's something seriously broken in him, not because there's something defective with *you*."

"Oh yeah?" I sniffled, "So he was just making it up about me being overweight with a huge schnozz?"

"Didn't you once tell me Rick is the king of excuses? He was picking on things you already hate about yourself because those reasons are easier for you to believe than the actual truth."

"Which is what, Lauren? You said I already answered my own question."

"No matter the bogus accusations, Rick knew the truth about you. No matter how horribly he treated you, you would still fight for the relationship, fight for him, and stay loyal."

"I see," I said slowly. "So, Rick didn't care if he hurt me because he assumed I would never leave him—and I'd already tolerated so much disrespect from him already. Stephanie, however, is apparently calling the shots. If the new relationship fails, then Rick has egg on his face instead of being able to keep blaming it all on me."

"Exactly. He needed an excuse to justify looking at porn, and then he got the added bonus of rubbing your face in his own shame to cover for it. Ask me how I know," she said sadly.

"I'm so sorry, kiddo. Here I am wrapped up in my own divorce woes, and you're dealing with a psychopath over there."

"Don't call him that, Charlotte!"

I bit my tongue, knowing Lauren wasn't ready to hear the unfiltered truth. Instead, I made up an excuse about going to bed and prayed God would give me the courage to give my friend the courage to get out of her own nightmare relationship.

CHAPTER 11

Three years later, sitting in my favorite coffee shop near work and staring into space on my lunch break, I realized just how far I'd come since those early days of my divorce. Stephanie had spared me from a hideously drawn out legal battle, but I paid dearly in other ways. Rick couldn't wait to discard me and then crow how he'd found someone so much better. The smug satisfaction he took in acting like he traded up only made me feel like more of an idiot for wasting all those years with him. It was a bitter pill to swallow, wondering why he would treat someone as vile as Stephanie like a queen while he treated me like garbage for the heinous sin of simply trying to please him.

Text messages between us meant to communicate drop off and pick up with the girls always included some comparison and how happy she made him. In one of his more magnanimous texts, Rick said he wished I would one day find equal happiness now that he finally experienced *real love*.

Lucky for him, I had enough self control not to send back a

barfing emoji or a meme of a wooden puppet boy whose nose grew when he told lies. Rick would probably turn it into another insult about my face anyway.

As I swirled my dark roast coffee with no sugar, steamed cream, and cinnamon powder, I saw a familiar face placing an order for a cappuccino.

"Carly!" I called over to the honey blonde woman in her mid thirties.

Mrs. Joe Trautweig turned and caught my eye. "Hi," she said, approaching me. "You're Charlotte, right? I think we met at Aaron and Ruthie's wedding. It was nice seeing you at Bible study on Sunday."

I smiled at her. "That's me! And I promise everything you've heard about me is absolutely true."

She broke into a laugh that sounded like tinkling crystal glasses. I'd read Carly Trautweig's memoirs recently, and while there was an eleven-year age gap with her husband, Joe, you could hardly tell by looking at them. He'd recently shaved off his beard and revealed a baby face underneath. His boyish smile also made him appear much closer in age to his cherubic wife with her wide, aquamarine eyes.

"Where are the twins?" I asked, referring to her children, Ilana and Shai.

"Joe's niece is babysitting while she's home from college, and I'm enjoying a couple hours out of the house."

"I remember those days," I said with a faraway smile, "except my girls are twenty-one months apart."

"How old are they now?"

"Sophie is seventeen and Lily is fifteen."

"You don't look old enough to have kids that big," she said, surveying my makeup and outfit.

"It's amazing what hair dye and contouring can cover up."

She smiled over her cappuccino and shook her head. "I do remember hearing you're pretty forthright about things."

I raised an eyebrow. "Now, there's a word you don't hear every day."

Carly grinned back, and her heart-shaped face couldn't have been more adorable. "My vocabulary is one of the many things my husband says he loves about me."

Just the way she nearly squealed at the phrase *my husband* filled me with a sense of longing. I had never been in love with Rick like that. Not that the pig had given me much to love.

"You okay?" she asked, watching me.

"I just feel like I'm on this never ending road of healing. Like, when am I done? Is there some point where I become a fully completed work and I can stop regretting so many of my choices or people and situations I put up with?"

She mouthed the word "wow," and I wondered why I had overshared with someone I barely knew. I frowned, ready to withdraw behind familiar gates and use work as my excuse to leave.

Instead, I saw intelligence and maturity in Carly's eyes. The turn of her mouth as she considered my words transformed her countenance into a grown woman who had survived her own trauma.

"You and I don't know each other very well," she began, "but the way you talk makes me think that we have some experiences in common. I can definitely relate to putting myself in bad situations and tolerating abusive behavior out of a misplaced sense of obligation."

"You mean with your mother?" I asked. Carly's book depicted the horrors of the raging, religious hypocrite parent who raised her.

She nodded. "There were also friends and even boyfriends

too. I didn't believe I deserved better than how I was treated, so I tolerated the abuse. I always hoped it would get better if I just did more, performed better, and finally did things perfect enough to make them happy."

Tears pricked my eyes thinking of myriad examples with Rick. Every time I advocated for myself, it became a horrible fight and even more abusive than the original issue.

My hurt feelings always translated into me not respecting *Rick's* feelings. How dare I bring up my issues when he was working? When we were eating dinner? When it was after dinner and he needed to relax? When it was before bed and he couldn't have that conversation before going to sleep? When it was a week night and he had to be up for work? When it was the weekend and he just wanted to enjoy his time off from work?

"My feelings never mattered," I murmured.

Carly looked at me sympathetically and patted my hand. "And it's one of the worst feelings in the world when you love someone, they claim they love you back, but their actions show how much they hate and resent you instead."

Her words struck a deep chord within me. "How did you heal from that? How did you make the trauma go away? Do I have to find some amazing man from a book in order to be as happy as you are?"

She laughed and waved me off. "I think you know where the credit belongs, Charlotte. God used my husband to reveal the love He has for me, and I needed to see God working *through* him. I'm still healing from what I survived with my mother and from First United. It's why I'm glad we have the weekly Bible study instead of going to a congregation. I'm honestly not sure if I could ever go to a regular church again."

"That I can definitely relate to," I said. "You grew up going to church with Rebecca's father, right?"

"Yes. My mother was Pastor Bernard Ivy's favorite indentured servant, and I was nothing more than collateral damage for all of the time and money she gave to the church. My mother needed to punish me for not aborting me—hence ruining her life."

I shook my head. "I am so sorry. That's awful."

She exhaled a heavy sigh. "It is. My biological father won't speak with my mother, but he's still keeping tabs on her somehow. He said her health is declining."

"Do you feel like you should be taking care of her?"

"Sometimes," she admitted. "I mean, I took care of the house and cooked meals from the time I was eight. I feel bad for the situation she's in, but even if I wanted my mother to be a part of my life and meet the babies, I don't think she'd want to anyway. All she did was call me an abomination and make me feel guilty for existing."

"That's horrible!" I gasped. "My father is self absorbed, probably a narcissist if you ask Lauren, but I never got treated like that."

"How *did* you get treated, if you don't mind me asking?"

"Like a burden, but also like the family burdens belonged on my shoulders. With my mother, she and I switched roles when I was eleven or twelve. My father was controlling and critical, and my mother still pretends her own failings and negligence aren't that bad because she thinks she's a better person than him. She didn't verbally abuse me like he did, but there's still pain. My mother will come through for me every once in a while, but I feel like it's more about my daughters than me. My father made it clear I wasn't even worth the effort of pretending, but he does with my brothers."

"What? Why?"

"He has completely different standards for them. I went no contact with him almost a decade ago, and it was the best decision for me."

She tsked. "I'm so sorry."

"Well, I've never been called an abomination, so I don't feel right taking any sympathy from you, Carly."

"Why does my lousy childhood negate yours? Do you think your trauma is less valid? The only thing worse than having an absentee father growing up would have been having a father who treated me exactly like my mother did. At least I could pretend what he was like and tell myself that somewhere out there I had a dad who actually wanted me. Adam Zendler isn't perfect by any means, but he has really stepped up."

I smiled at her. "I'm so glad for you, Carly. You deserve that. Do you call him Adam or do you call him 'Dad'?"

"We're both more comfortable with Adam. The babies call him 'Poppa' though, and he eats it up. He dotes on my kids, and I would never deprive him of the opportunity to do that. His other two children want nothing to do with me, and it's put a big strain on his relationship with them. They're not too keen on welcoming the long lost daughter he never knew about until four years ago. There's also some jealousy with his daughter, Tessa, but that's because she's married to my ex-boyfriend."

I gasped. "Small world!"

"Very," she replied with a sardonic expression. "You said you have kids, but since I don't see a ring on your finger, I'm guessing you're no longer married."

"You guessed correctly. I've been divorced for over two years. My ex was practically remarried before he and I were completely *un*-married."

Carly winced. "So, he cheated?"

"Technically, yes. His new wife is one of those blessings in disguise because she helped speed up the divorce. Once Rick had someone new to glom onto, he needed to be rid of me and our girls as quickly as possible. Fighting me about the divorce had nothing to do with loving any of us but about losing the control he had."

"I've heard of men doing that. Are you and your girls okay?"

I shrugged. "They're coping better now. My oldest had some struggles while we were all still living together, but mostly it's just helping my girls process their father's rejection without them internalizing it. They're hurt, obviously, and I have to walk this tightrope of making sure they know it's not something they're doing wrong without outright bashing him. It's not like I can say, 'Well, honey, your father did that because he's a miserable pig and picking on you makes him feel better about himself.'"

Carly's eyes widened at my unfiltered description. "I think I see what you mean about wanting to heal."

My voice hardened. "Why, because I'm bitter and unforgiving? I've heard all those accusations before. People act like I'm supposed to just be 'over' everything that happened, except it's *still* happening."

"What is?"

"Rick berating and intentionally hurting my girls. Now, he's got the blonde barracuda egging on his controlling behavior because she turns everything my girls say or do into some kind of personal attack against her. They both mask their abuse behind twisted Bible verses and hyper spiritual garbage. They use God as their henchman to manipulate and gaslight my children. As a believer in Christ, how could I be anything but appalled and disgusted by that? My girls want nothing to do with any of it thanks to their obnoxious behavior."

Carly shook her head and looked at me pityingly. "I'm the last person to preach against bitterness or forgiveness. It's taken me a long time to get this far, and I know I have plenty more to go. My mother did a lot of those same things. It didn't make me angry toward God, just ashamed of everything I'd done and that He could never love someone like me."

I swallowed, low self esteem and depression always lingering like a shadow to regain footing with my girls and devour them whole. I shook off that thought and retreated behind a wall of sarcasm. "Unfortunately, their father thinks he walks on holy water." Rolling my eyes, I added, "But I'm pretty sure he'd burn if I threw some on him."

Carly paused and then burst out laughing. "That's an incredible visual!"

I shrugged and took another sip of coffee. It was deliciously hot, a hair below liquid magma, and exactly how I liked it. "What can I say? I tell it like it is."

She grinned at me. "I know you're completely serious about everything you're saying, but I love the way you express yourself."

I smiled back. "Not everybody appreciates it, but I'm done pretending to be something that I'm not. In a world of black and white, I choose to be sparkly magenta."

"I love it!" she exclaimed. "I'm so glad you decided to come to Bible study. We have plenty of personality in the room already, but we absolutely have room for yours."

My eyes burned at her heartfelt compliment. No one at Beth Shalom had ever said anything like that, let alone pretended to mean it.

"Thank you," I said, my voice thick.

"I've got to run, but would it be okay if I text you sometime? I can get your number from Lauren if that works."

"I'd like that."

As if on impulse, she reached across the space between us and pulled me into a hug. "Just had a feeling you might need one," she said against my hair.

"More than you know," I whispered and held on for an extra few seconds.

CHAPTER 12

Despite the relative calm and ease of my *just friends* status with Jon Roseman, the steamy dreams persisted. I was thankful he backed off the good morning text messages because there was no way to answer *How did you sleep?* without outright lying. I certainly couldn't blame my flushed cheeks and racing heartbeat as the beginnings of perimenopause.

I threw myself back into the online dating world instead, reviving my profiles with new photos and updating the description about myself. Just like editing a professional profile on Linkedup, maybe my online dating resume just needed some refreshing to find the right match.

I cast the net far and wide, signing up for the trial version of multiple dating websites and copying and pasting my profile info. In addition to the usual bevvy of spammers and sugar daddies on InstantPics and FaceSpace, I now contended with the offerings of EHarmonious, PlentyofFishes, BumbleBee, LoveJewShmooze, ChristiansWhoMingle, SilverSingles, Grown-

UpDating, TruWuv, NerdConnekt, LoveThatLasts, and finally—
on a whim—Cougarville.

I may or may not have imbibed a glass of cabernet when I
originally signed up for the last one. Jon may or may not have
mentioned he had a date with Susie Q the night I partook of
said cabernet. This was back when we were *just friends*, and my
more than friendly feelings weren't waging war with his lackluster kisses.

My new and improved dating profiles also meant a new and
improved screening process for my respective inboxes. First,
there was filtering out the phishing accounts from other nations
who posed as fake military, fake doctors, fake widowers, fake oil
rig workers, fake UN ambassadors, and fake gym rats. I highly
doubted the muscle bound beefcakes had any interest dating a
forty-four-year-old cinnamon roll.

I blew a raspberry as I deleted the daily dozen of "Richard-
Frank.373" and "Har.ry.david_" accounts all posing with ripped
muscles, tattoos, and eons of selfies. For some reason, these
peak male specimens uploaded their nine million photos in one
sitting, just in case you needed to be certain of the date when
the fake account was created online. At least it made my job
easier knowing who to immediately block.

Scouring the latest round of potential matches, I chuckled to
myself. "If you're going to con gullible, lonely women out of
their money, at least put in some effort." I scrolled through one
profile of a very handsome Frenchman who had five other
accounts using the same photos. "Right," I murmured,
"because a man who looks like that in *real* life is going to need
help meeting girls online."

Most of the messages from these phonies began with
sweeping praise of my beauty or some poorly written paragraph
about looking for love. When I called them out or even screen

shotted multiple profiles with identical names or photos, they all claimed someone else hacked their *real* account. With comical indignance, they insisted just how honest they were and most certainly *not* scammers.

After fifteen years with Rick Williams, I had learned only a liar needs to convince you how honest he is.

After the scammers came the dirty old men in their late fifties and up who believed a fat bank account and magic love-making pills made them irresistible to women. No amount of low self esteem would get me to sell my body or soul to the highest bidder. Most of them were also spammers, but a few genuine creeps probably belonged on a registered offender list.

With yet another ill advised glass of cabernet, a message popped up for me on the Cougarville app. I replied and found a very intelligent man on the other end of the screen. Maybe it was the twelve-year age gap that brought my guard down, but he flirted just as heavily as I did. I even employed what Lauren dubbed my "tsunami of charm," sure that it would be too much for him to handle. Instead, the young pup persisted for three weeks and finally asked for a date.

I told myself I couldn't possibly date a man younger than thirty-five, but the plucky, thirty-two-year-old divorce attorney certainly won points for persistence. When I told him I was old enough to be his babysitter, he asked if I would read him a bedtime story. Smirking, I reminded him I had two teenage daughters *he* was old enough to babysit. He responded with a few ideas of how I could pay for services rendered. Amused and impressed, I finally told him my name and learned his name was Sean Bonham.

Charlotte283: It's been fun but you need to find someone closer to your own age. It's never gonna happen.

SeanBonLaywerMon: How do you know if you don't try?

Charlotte283: I'm not dating to have a good time or a hookup. I'd like to eventually find a husband and a stepfather for my daughters. Are you volunteering to permanently handle two teenage girls?

SeanBonLaywerMon: I handle bitter Karens and Chads all day long. Teenagers don't scare me.

Charlotte283: Let me rephrase. You won't just be 'handling' them. You'll be helping to *raise* them. Anyways, this is ridiculous. I'm not going out with you.

SeanBonLaywerMon: Come on! One date.

Charlotte283: Why? So people can ask if you're taking out your mom for her birthday? I don't think so.

SeanBonLaywerMon: I own my own home, Charlotte. Have for six years. I'm not a kid. I wouldn't be on this ridiculous site if I could find any decent women my age. I want to match energy and maturity. We have a connection.

Charlotte283: You do realize that mature women also *look* like mature women, right? All of those Karducci sisters were created by Beverly Hills plastic surgeons and photo filters.

SeanBonLaywerMon: Please refer to my above statement.

Charlotte283: What would you do if I actually called your bluff?

SeanBonLaywerMon: The happy dance.

I burst out laughing. Despite myself, I did blush at such focused and determined attention free from decades of Beth Shalom baggage. Throwing caution to the wind, I figured I could at least learn from the experience and enjoy a free meal. I would not, however, give Sean any unrealistic expectations or lead him on.

Charlotte283: You free tonight?

SeanBonLaywerMon: I knew you'd come around.

Charlotte283: My girls will be home tomorrow. Let's rip the Band-Aid off and end the agony. We both know how this is going to go. As long as you don't mind a heaping dose of disappointment and I told-you-so's, I'll meet up with you.

> SeanBonLaywerMon: Done. You said Parkview Diner is your favorite place, so we can go there. Does 8 pm work for you?

> Charlotte283: I think I have officially lost my mind.

> SeanBonLaywerMon: Nah, maybe just your heart.

Despite my insistence Sean wouldn't find me attractive in real life, I still spent extra time curling my hair into loose waves and applying smokey eyeshadow. I spritzed on my favorite CeCe Chanelle perfume, *Damselle,* and admired myself in my full length mirror.

"Well, round *is* a shape," I murmured. I turned to the side and wondered what some thirty-two-year-old buck would find appealing about my many curves in many places. I layered a black duster over a silver top to cover some problem areas, and I turned to admire how my bootleg jeans clung to my legs. I took a further risk with low-heeled ankle boots as well as my signature ruby red lipstick.

I arrived first at the Parkview Diner, nervously looking around for some blonde man-child who went rock wall climbing on the weekends.

"This is so stupid," I muttered.

"Charlotte?"

I turned and met honey brown eyes and curly hair a shade lighter. Sean was definitely built like an outdoor adventurist, muscular and lean. Instinctively, I sucked in my stomach.

"How are you single?" I blurted out.

"Does that mean I have your approval?" He winked at me

and took in my outfit. "You don't look a day over thirty-five, by the way."

"Oh, so does that mean *you* approve?"

He took a step closer, and my long deprived hormones temporarily forgot the twelve-year age gap. My ego also thrilled at being able to attract such a handsome young man. As superficial as it was—and frankly, as selfish as it was—my poor self esteem needed to stomp out the sound of Rick Williams' voice calling me ugly. Having Sean Bonham stare into my eyes without disdain, revulsion, or wishing I was his first wife was a healing balm.

"See?" he said. "I told you this could work. You just need to give it a chance."

I chuckled and shook my head. "It'll take more than whatever six pack abs are lurking under your shirt to make this work. I'm divorced, not dead, but I'm also not an idiot."

"So, you're really only after my body? Here I thought it was my genius IQ and six figure income you found so appealing." He crossed his arms over this chest like a middle school girl in the locker room. "I feel so objectified!"

This time, I burst into a full laugh. "I never thought I'd meet someone who flirts more than I do."

His amber eyes sparkled. "And here you thought I couldn't keep up."

"How do I know this whole date isn't some TikTak setup and you've got your entourage stashed in a corner ready to film my humiliation?"

"You don't." His teasing smile brought out two dimples.

An image of Sean as a little boy flashed before me, and I cringed at my desperate need for attention. I shook my head and took a step backward. "This was a mistake."

"Nah," he said, ushering me toward the hostess stand. The

warmth of his hand seeped through my thin sweater. "Best decision you've made since divorcing your ex. His loss is my gain tonight."

Sean smiled at the blue-haired hostess who recognized me immediately from all of my dinner and dessert dates with Lauren. Her eyes widened as they darted between the two of us.

"Hi, Jenna," I said, forcing myself to smile. "Table for two."

Recovering, she smiled in approval while Sean looked bemused. He even smelled like a real man instead of the boy I kept telling myself he was.

Loneliness was a powerful drug indeed.

A teen boy announced himself as our server, and I noted he also looked confused by the two of us. Sean seemed oblivious, and I struggled with how desperate I must have looked to the rest of the world.

I mumbled to myself, and he chuckled.

"What?" I asked him.

"Did you just say you're probably going to hell for this?"

"No! I said I'm probably going to *jail* for this. My southern accent gets thicker when I'm upset."

He winked at me. "The accent is cute, just like the rest of you."

Unable to keep myself from flirting back, I dialed the accent up to an eleven. "Flattery won't get you anywhere, sir."

"Yeah, so what will?"

"Excuse me?" My tone dropped immediately to disapproving mom as I realized the fantasy was over. "I already told you I'm not going to—"

He held up a hand to cut me off. "Sorry, not what I meant. What will get you to relax and stop overthinking this? You've already explained your religious beliefs."

Embarrassed at my faux pas, I deflected with humor. "Any chance you could hop into a time machine?"

He pulled a face.

"Look, I agreed to this date, but I already warned you the age gap is too much. I'm sure you're a very good attorney, but you're not going to win this case."

He opened his mouth to argue but froze. Something had captivated his gaze behind me.

He buried his face into his palm. "Please, God, don't let her see me!"

My mouth thinned. "Ex-girlfriend? Or maybe a *current* girlfriend?"

He shook his head. "No, Charlotte. I would never do that to you."

"Okay, so what's the problem?"

"It's an old client. She made my life miserable for eighteen months." Mocking her, he said with an eerily familiar New Jersey accent, *"What do you mean you can't get moah money fah me? How am I supposed to live on only two grand a month fah child support?"*

It was then I heard the braying laugh of Stephanie Burgess-Williams and wanted to crawl into the nearest hole and die. Rick would never let me live down the humiliation. His weaselly snickers joined the new Mrs. Williams. I wondered if they were laughing at me or had potentially set up this entire debacle.

"Do you know her?" Sean asked, watching me.

"I was married to her new husband," I said on a panicked breath. "Get me out of here before they see me. Please!"

CHAPTER 13

UNFORTUNATELY, RICK WILLIAMS still possessed his Charlotte homing device. He must have felt a disturbance in the atmosphere and realized he hadn't criticized me in the past twenty-four hours. I felt his beady eyes on the back of my head before I heard Stephanie's squawking from across the room.

"What is *she* doing heah?" she announced loud enough for Rick and anyone else within a hundred foot radius.

"Did her husband just say *robbing the cradle*?" Sean hissed to me.

"Don't take it personally. If you looked like a cave troll, Rick would still be jealous. I'm supposed to be miserable without him and longing to be Stephanie."

He smirked. "Well, he married Mrs. Robertson, and she would probably take a barely legal lamp post to bed if she could get attention from one. Your ex is no prize."

My jaw dropped. "Did she try something with *you*?"

"Repeatedly, and this was back in my twenties. I asked one

of the partners to put someone else on the case, but Ms. Burgess was apparently very convincing."

"Did she sleep with your boss?" I gaped.

Sean looked like he'd just swallowed his own vomit. "I wouldn't put it past her or him, and that's all I can say on the subject."

"Ew! My girls already think Stephanie makes her coats out of puppies. Don't tell me she's really going to live up to the *Cruellinda* picture we have of her."

"Cruellinda?" he repeated with amusement. "Did you just make her the villain from the *Nine Million Dalmatians* movie?"

"Only because her eyeshadow makes her look twenty years older than me. Also, I don't like the woman, I hate how she treats my children, I hate how she's made my ex even more of a petty little *Richard* than he already was, and quite candidly, I have forgiveness issues I still need to work on."

Sean beamed at me. "You're amazing."

"Oh, she's amazing, is she?" Stephanie demanded, suddenly standing next to our table. "Why are you on a date with my lawyah, Charlotte? You need to get ovah the fact Richard and I are *in love* and stop this obsession you have with me. You're only hurting yahself by holding onto what isn't yours anymoah."

If I had been drinking from the water glass our errant waiter still hadn't brought to the table, I probably would have done a spit take all over her tacky outfit. Instead, I reached for Sean's hand. Let the witch think whatever she wanted.

She glared daggers at me and then at Sean, especially when he pressed a kiss to the inside of my wrist. As he looked at me from under his eyebrows, I realized he wasn't just playing it up for our audience, nor was I unaffected by the special attention.

My wrist was rewarded with a warm breath followed by a more lingering kiss.

Stephanie clutched the pearls—or in this case, a gaudy, costume jewelry pendant—and it became apparent her unwelcome interruption had absolutely nothing to do with the husband she and I shared. She was jealous of the handsome young attorney who rubbed his thumb across my knuckles and skewered my resolve against dating younger men. All of her jealousy accusations faltered as the man she had failed to seduce was actively trying to seduce *me* instead. I felt Rick's glare and met his eyes briefly, seeing pain on his face. I wondered if he was hurt by watching me move on with my life or that his replacement wife had more interest in my date than in him.

"You should be ashamed of yahself," Stephanie sneered. "What kind of an example are you setting for yah children?"

Taking back my hand from Sean, I met her cold, dead eyes. "Look in a mirror before you ever say that again." Gesturing to Rick, I added, "I think your husband is waiting for you to sit down and enjoy the rest of your dinner. Nice to see you, Stephanie."

I turned my focus back to my date, and he looked thoroughly impressed.

"You're incredible," he mouthed.

I smiled back.

Nostrils flared, Stephanie's shrieking grew to higher decibels. "You don't get to tawk to me that way!"

This time, Sean stepped in, using a cajoling tone that had probably been practiced with a plethora of difficult clients. "You're making a scene, Stephanie. I've been begging this wonderful woman to let me take her out for weeks. It's a real date, and I can promise it has absolutely nothing to do with you."

"It doesn't?" she said, her face turning doe-eyed now that she had a scrap of Sean's attention. "But why her?"

"Why *not* her?" he shot back. "She's sensational. And in the interest of not ruining our own date, I think we're going to find somewhere else to eat. Charlotte, are you ready to go?"

Only lightning could have moved me faster as I side-stepped the she-beast and beelined for the front door. I caught the faint sounds of Rick's disapproving tones, and I thanked God I no longer had to live with them anymore. I prayed for the safety of my daughters knowing they would likely pay the price for Stephanie's humiliation. Picking up my phone, I sent a group text to the girls that I had run into their dad and Cruellinda and to brace themselves for impact.

Is he hot at least? Sophie wrote back first.

Sean read the message over my shoulder. "What are you going to tell her?"

"Wanna take a selfie?"

He grinned, and we struck a playful pose and sent it back.

Moooooooom! What the heck?!?!?

What's the prob, kiddo?

How old is he???

Old enough to be your new stepdad, but we're just friends, so don't worry about it. I'll let you know before we decide to elope to Vegas though, k?

MOM!!!!

Love you, and I'll see you tomorrow. I added a winking kiss face and then tossed my phone into my purse.

My stomach rumbled, and I looked away, embarrassed. "Sorry."

"Oh, mine already did that in the restaurant. There's a Lochtie's across the street unless you want something a little more grown up."

"No, Lochtie's is fine. My girls and I love that place."

Sean Bonham and I enjoyed double cheeseburgers and split an order of onion rings and fries. We were joined in the Lochtie's dining room with some members of the active adult community down the road also enjoying '50s style fast food on a Saturday night.

"You have some ketchup on your face," Sean said, reaching across the table to rub his thumb dangerously close to my mouth. He let his hand linger as he cupped my chin.

"It was probably my lipstick. Nice try, Casanova."

He exhaled a self deprecating breath and dropped his hand. "You don't make it easy on a guy, do you?"

I popped a fry into my mouth. "That's probably because you're used to the girls falling all over you, right?"

"But not you," he said, studying me. "Why are you on these dating sites anyway, Charlotte? I saw your profile on Tindering and Bumblebee. It's insane that you're not already with somebody."

"Were you doing research?" I asked with a laugh of surprise.

"I'm a divorce attorney. Of course, I wanted to vet you first. Trust me, I've seen the dregs of humanity in my job. I wouldn't have messaged you if I thought you were anything like the monster we left back at the Diner."

"Well, you obviously discovered I know how to copy and paste. I guess computer literacy is part of your dating criteria?"

"Very funny. Anybody born after 1970 should have some level of computer knowledge."

"I wouldn't overestimate my abilities there, pal. If it weren't for my daughters or my techie ex-husband, I'd probably be using one of those brick cell phones like Zack Slater on *Saved by the School Bell*. I'm a technological T-rex." I mimicked the tiny, useless hands of the feared king of the dinosaurs.

Sean barked out a laugh. He met and held my gaze, and his expression sobered as his eyes delved into mine. "Let me take you on another date, one without any former clients or your ex-husband showing up."

"After what happened tonight, why? I mean, I knew this was probably a bad idea before I even agreed to go out with you, but I had no idea tonight would be a disaster of this magnitude. You seriously can't imagine this going anywhere long term—" my voice trailed off with an uncomfortable laugh as his expression clouded over. "Sean, you deserve the chance to start your own family and build a future, not help me pick up the pieces of my broken one."

"Is there anything I can do to make you reconsider? I promise, my intentions are honorable here." He even placed a hand over his heart.

"I think I'm a challenge for you, and there's some excitement in the hunt. I promise, my life is actually pretty boring, and I've still got trauma I'm processing."

"Don't tell me that scrawny nerd back at the Diner has ruined you for all men. You have so much life and energy in you, Charlotte!"

"Okay, so since you're a divorce attorney," I said, shifting the conversation, "let me ask you something."

"Go for it."

"How many cases have you had where the wife—or even the husband—was clearly abused by their spouse, but a religious group or organization got involved and made things even worse for the victim?"

His face took on a strange look for a half second before

settling back into a pleasant expression. "That's an interesting supposition. Generally hard to prove without some sort of written evidence. Do you have someone specific in mind?"

"No, not any *one* person, per se. Specifically, I'm thinking of toxic evangelical theology where their version of a 'Biblical marriage' tells abused spouses and children to suffer in silence. It shames them for speaking up, or God forbid, getting out and protecting themselves. In my old congregation, women were treated as second class citizens. We were only good enough for childcare and menial labor while the men were the ones on stage in the limelight."

"I'm shocked you attended a place like that given how strong you are."

"I wasn't always like this. The scrawny nerd didn't do damage with his fists, but his words were knives. He also had the synagogue leadership backing him one hundred percent to get me 'under control.' I wasn't good for the corporate image."

"But he married *Stephanie*. How could she be anything other than a sideshow?"

I exhaled a bitter laugh. "Believe it or not, she's just as good at faking the religious facade as they are. From my understanding, the old congregation *loves* her. Not as much Rick does, of course. According to him, she's the great love of his life, and he hopes that I'll find that same kind of love one day."

He rolled his eyes. "She probably wrote those messages herself. There isn't a man out there Stephanie Burgess won't try to manipulate and control. Your ex doesn't stand a chance."

"People used to think that about our relationship too, you know. I was outgoing and charming, and Rick was this wet noodle with no discernible personality. He shamed me for trying to get all the attention."

"And look at what he married," Sean said in disbelief. "I don't get it."

I blinked back tears. I hadn't expected to reveal so much or still have so much pain.

"There is no comparison between you and that walking meme," Sean declared, his upper lip curled in disgust.

I scoffed. "You're only saying that because you want another date."

"I'm saying that because it's true!"

"Look, I'm not upset that Rick chose Stephanie instead of me. It's just realizing how everything he complained about incessantly was just a way to hurt me. Maybe it's wrong of me, but I do take some satisfaction that he married the real life version of the monster he pretended I was. Like cosmic justice."

"Make no mistake about that," Sean vowed. "He's not happy with Stephanie. Her ex-husband looked like he'd been dragged from one end of hell to the other side."

"Poor guy."

"He wasn't that great of a person, so don't feel too bad for him. Very whiny and passive aggressive. He's probably a lot like your ex based on what you've shared."

I chuckled. "You're not wrong about that either. Anyways, this is a lot for a first date—or last date, I guess."

Sean leaned in closer, fully engaged in the conversation. "It's actually good insight for my job. I got into family law because my cousin got screwed with her divorce. She and my niece lived with us when she was getting back on her feet. She was never the same after her ex abandoned them. He didn't want to be married, but he refused to sign the papers—probably to avoid paying child support. Eventually, she took her own life."

"Oh, Sean!" I exclaimed, capturing his hand. "That's terrible!"

His amber eyes looked haunted by the memories. "I changed my focus at law school from corporate to family law and promised my niece I would do everything I could to fight for her and her mother's memory. There was a trust fund my grandparents set up for my cousin and my niece that her dad wanted to steal. My parents hired attorneys and fought for years with him. As soon as I got hired at Browning & Cagle, the first thing I did was take on their case pro-bono and fight his attorney. The lawyer was such a sleaze anyway. Trevor Wormwood. What a name, right?"

My eyes widened. "Oh, I know him!"

"You do? I hope you've never paid him a dime. I try not to throw shade at other attorneys because it's a small circle of us handling cases in the metro area, but the guy is an amoral slime. He makes a total mockery of the Amicable Divorce Attorney network."

"Well, I don't know Trevor personally, but he represented the ex-husband of my best friend, Lauren. She published her memoirs earlier this year, and she mentioned Trevor by name. He got humiliated in court because his client was a lying pig, and it came back to bite him in his behind. I won't say that I'm sorry at all. Rick was best friends with Lauren's ex, and they met regularly for lunch to complain about the two of us. They called us disrespectful and unsubmissive because we wised up to their abusive behavior. Unfortunately, all of their accusations were regularly reinforced from the pulpit."

"Which has us circling back to your original question," Sean noted.

"And that's what I need you to understand about where I'm at right now. I wasn't just getting that *disrespectful* message from my ex. My entire spiritual support system shamed me for wanting better for me and my girls. I lost all of my friends."

He sucked in a pained breath. "I'm so sorry."

"Which is why this will never work between us." I patted his hand maternally.

"What! What do you mean?"

"Sean, I still have so much healing left to do. I can't ask you to help fix what you didn't help break."

CHAPTER 14

Instead of pushing him away, my words landed like a challenge. He straightened his shoulders as if preparing for battle. His tone, however, came out softer. "What else do you think you need to heal from?"

I sighed wearily. "So much of it is turning off the twisted Bible verses and gaslighting I heard weekly at synagogue, daily from my ex-husband, and eventually in my own inner monologue. That's not your problem or any other man's to fix. I think I've been so busy wanting to find love again that I haven't given myself time to process just *how bad* the trauma was."

"I'm assuming that's why you asked me the question you did earlier."

"Basically, yeah."

Sean ran a hand through his fluff of curls. "I don't understand why you would consider yourself a Christian if this is the consistent result you're seeing and have experienced. Christianity can be pretty misogynistic."

"Actually, it isn't misogynistic at all if you read what Jesus said. He elevated women that society called unclean, irredeemable, and beneath its notice. If I had to base my relationship with Jesus on the horrible examples I've seen, I would have given up a long time ago. It's why my daughters both struggle so much now. The banshee and my ex use the Bible to club both of them because my daughters can't be controlled with regular manipulation."

"So, tell me again why you believe."

"Because I've seen God work in my life since I got saved in my early twenties. I was a foul mouthed, rebellious punk on my way to destruction. Jesus got a hold of me one Sunday morning, and I knew I had a savior who loved me even if my father sucked at it. It's been loving Jesus and reading the Bible for myself that's helped me see how the messages preached in the synagogue regarding marriage were total garbage."

Sean inhaled a deep breath as he watched me. "You've really been through a lot."

"More than you know, kiddo."

He frowned. "Don't call me that."

"Sorry," I mumbled. "I should call you Dr. Phillip since you're sitting here listening to all of my drama on our first date."

"I don't mind."

"Well, I have a tendency to overshare and then regret it later. Some people are loose with their bodies. I, unfortunately, tend to be too loose with my lips."

"Part of the divorce lawyer gig is playing unofficial therapist. I'm honored you felt comfortable sharing with me."

I smiled at him. "Do you know that tonight is only the second time I've ever met Stephanie face to face?"

"Lucky you! When was the first?"

I exhaled a laugh. "Rick brought her to a chorus concert for

Sophie. He'd already proposed and needed to rub the engagement in my face."

"How did that go?"

"I mean, it wasn't some kind of a shock. Rick moving in with her before he and I were legally divorced was more a sucker punch than him making an honest woman out of her. I also had no idea Stephanie had her own kids, but she made sure to bring the holy terrors with her to steal attention away from my daughter."

Sean winced. "Oh? They got *worse*?"

"You've met them?" I asked, surprised.

"She brought the boys to the office a few times when she couldn't find a babysitter. I think the receptionist was ready to strangle all of them after they destroyed our lobby."

"I can only imagine. She spoils her boys and lets them get away with murder."

Sean rolled his eyes. "That was her ex-husband's complaint as well. He said nobody could control those boys, and it was due to Stephanie's over indulgence."

"So, how did she wind up with primary custody?" I asked, confused.

"She didn't."

"What!" I gasped. "All Rick does is talk up Braxton and Brayden. The girls mention how often the boys are there when they have visitation with Rick."

"Well, unless she and her ex have reached some new visitation agreement, he has primary physical custody of the boys. It's public record in the court order. I'm not violating any confidentiality by telling you."

"I had no idea," I murmured. "This night has definitely been more educational than I thought it would be. Thanks for answering my question and talking this out with me."

"No problem. I appreciate what you shared. It's a perspective I didn't consider before, and I will keep it in mind going forward."

"On that note, I think it's time to call it a night. You ready to go?" I scooped up trash from our table and piled it on my plastic tray.

"No, but I can't force you to prolong a date I don't think you really wanted anyway."

I stood up and tried to smile encouragingly without being *encouraging*. "Well, it'll definitely make a great break-the-ice story for whatever real date you have next."

Sean stood up with me and gathered my jacket off the chair along with my purse. After I'd dumped out the trash, he stood next to me and held out my duster. I tried to take it from him, but he insisted on helping me put it on. It also gave him a chance to get close to me one more time. I caught another whiff of his cologne and had to remind myself nothing good would come from following my pheromones instead of my brain.

I turned to face him. "Thanks."

"So, can I interest you in a drink somewhere?"

I shook my head. "I believe that's the fast track to Mistake Island, and I did a fifteen year tour of duty there. Gonna have to pass."

He didn't bother to hide his disappointment.

"Sean, you really are a good guy. You're fun and you're funny, and all cards on the table, if you were even five years older, we might be having a different conversation right now."

"No time machine," he said ruefully.

I shrugged. "It is what it is. I did have a really nice time with you, though. Well, after the incident anyway."

He chuckled. "It's not every date you get to experience pure evil."

I burst into a laugh. "Maybe that's a better nickname than *Cruellinda.*"

He watched me with an expression of both longing and regret. When I realized he'd inched closer toward me with my back against the wall, I side stepped him and eased toward the exit.

"Thank you for an unforgettable evening. I'll be praying you meet the right woman for you."

Whatever he wanted to say next remained lodged behind a tight smile as he waved and exited the other side of the restaurant. I inhaled a deep breath, proud of myself for doing the right thing instead of playing footsie with temptation. I had a nudge to check my cell phone and found multiple SOS messages from the girls about an irate Stephanie.

Do you need me to come get you? I asked them on group text.

Mom, she sounds possessed! Sophie wrote.

Possessed? Like in those demon movies I refuse to let you watch no matter how many times you beg me and tell me they're not that scary?

Yes!!!! Lily replied first. *Daddy sounds really mad too. I've never heard them fight like this. I'm scared.*

It's okay, baby, I typed, ready to march over there and perform an exorcism myself.

Can you pray for us, Mom? Sophie asked.

Stunned, I instantly did that, murmuring both in English and in tongues for God to protect my babies from whatever demon had been triggered in their stepmother. The girls rarely asked me for prayer, so I knew it must be serious.

Just prayed. Things any better now? I asked.

Mom, can you please just get us? Lily typed. *I don't feel safe here. She's throwing stuff.*

I looked down at my watch. *I'm over at the Diner. I can be there in twenty minutes. Lil, you've got the ninja skills, so call me on your phone and I'll put myself on mute so I can hear what's going on, but they can't hear me. Soph, start recording on yours.*

Done, Sophie wrote back immediately.

Lily, meanwhile, had already buzzed my phone.

"Mom!" she whispered, panicked.

I could feel her terror on the other end of the line, and my eyes welled with helpless tears. "Go find a place to hide with your sister. I'm on my way."

"We're in Brayden's room. The twins are with their dad tonight, so I don't think they'll check here."

"Where are your father and Stephanie?"

"Still in their room," Sophie said, jumping in on the call. "She's in the bathroom slamming cabinets and throwing stuff. Dad is yelling."

"Okay, stop talking for a second, and let me see if I can hear anything."

The girls became still as church mice while I could pick up the distinct sounds of Mr. and Mrs. Williams and their epic blow out. It reminded me piercingly of knockdown, drag out fights I'd had with Rick, and I fended off a wave of remembered trauma. Stephanie hadn't allowed Rick to suck the life out of her yet, so she fought back much harder than I ever had. The cruelty in her tone when she sniped about his horrible breath sent goosebumps down my arms.

"That's enough," I said, now fully aware that the happily ever after presented by Rick was a house of cards. Even in my ugliest, most frustrated moments, I had never lashed out at him like that. I kept the girls calm while I ran a few red lights getting to Danbury to pick them up.

The blissfully wedded couple were still going at it when I exited my car in their driveway. I texted the girls, and they slipped out a minute later with their school backpacks. I didn't hang up the phone until I laid eyes on my daughters.

"Did you forget anything?" I whispered. "I don't want to have to come back or have dad hold your textbooks or binders hostage."

They shook their heads, both looking wide eyed and terrified. I pulled them close, kissed each of their foreheads, and then hurried to get them in the car.

"Dad's going to be mad that we left without telling him," Lily murmured.

I backed out the driveway as quietly as I could, resisting the urge to peel out. "Don't worry about that. I'm not happy that Stephanie is talking to your father like that, but I've been praying that she wouldn't unleash any of that on the two of you."

"Why is she so evil?" Sophie asked, her eyes watering. "Mom, you never talked to Dad that way, and he was so mean to you!"

I recognized the beginnings of hysteria following the shock of what they'd been forced to listen to all night.

"I don't know, baby."

"She says she loves Jesus, but she sure doesn't act like it," Lily added. "She was cussing so much, Mom."

Sophie repeated some of their stepmother's more colorful insults, and I had to keep my jaw from falling open. Rick Williams had said many horrible things to me during our marriage, but nothing like the venom coming from the great love of his life.

In that moment, the walls of bitterness came crumbling down, replaced with pity instead. My ex-husband wasn't happy at all. Just like Sean said, nobody could be happy being married to someone like Stephanie.

On cue, my phone rang.

"Soph, see who it is," I said to my first born in the passenger seat.

"It's Daddy. Do you want me to pick it up?"

"No, just put him on speaker, please."

"Hello? Charlotte?" he said, sounding panicked. "The girls ran away!"

CHAPTER 15

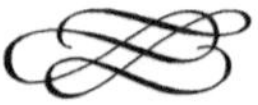

I WANTED TO CORRECT THEIR FATHER, HOPING TO alleviate the fear in his tone, but instead, Rick launched into a series of preposterous lies that all exonerated Stephanie—and de facto himself—from any responsibility. Trying to cover what would be perceived as a lapse in his own parenting, he began his smear campaign against my daughters. All of Stephanie's profanity and soul crushing insults I'd heard with my own ears he falsely attributed to my beautiful girls instead of his hideous wife.

"They were talking back to me and their stepmother the second we got home," he blustered with self righteous indignation. "You really need to get the girls under control, Charlotte. I'm holding you responsible for this!"

Sophie looked stricken, and Lily's eyes were cast down in her lap when I checked my rearview mirror. This was not the way I imagined them seeing their father's manipulations unmasked, but there was nothing to be done for it now.

"Charlotte!" he demanded. "Why aren't you answering me?

Are you still on a date with your boy toy? The least you could do is care more about our daughters rather than fulfilling lustful fantasies. You've already sabotaged my special evening with my wife."

That last comment brought a wave of unexpected laughter. There was nothing left to say to something so obscenely hypocritical and inverted from reality. Just like when we were married, Rick's inability to control me only incensed him further. He began to squawk in a manner similar to his new wife, and I spoke up before he made a bigger fool of himself in front of our children.

"Calm down! The girls are with me, and they're safe."

"What!" he shrieked. "How could you just steal them away from me? You're violating our visitation agreement!"

"They're sitting in the car and heard everything you just said about them. You might want to start apologizing for how you bald-faced lied to cover for your wife's multiple temper tantrums this evening."

His voice came out an octave higher. "What? What are you talking about?"

"The girls put you and Stephanie on speaker while I was driving to get them. They were scared out of their minds. I heard everything. I can't believe you would sit there and try to pin your wife's behavior on *them* and then act like I'm somehow at fault for the lie you just concocted! Why don't you try getting your wife under control instead of blaming everyone else for how terrible she acts?"

As expected, Rick played the role of responsibility teflon. When his posturing and sputtering became accusations of setting him up, I hung up the phone. I could hear Lily sobbing from the backseat, and Sophie sniffled back tears.

"Girls, I'm so sorry," I whispered, pulling into our town-house complex. "This was fifty-seven shades of wrong."

"Why would he do that?" Lily cried. "We were so scared, and he made it sound like that was us! Doesn't he love us?"

I choked on my response, not willing to lie but prayerfully considering my words. Instead, Sophie piped up from the front seat.

"That. Isn't. Love." Her voice quavered as she fought to control her own tears. "Mom, I don't want to see him again. Ever. You have to do something!"

I walked with them in tense silence from the parking lot and opened our front door before I responded. "I don't know what I can do, but I'll send Sondra an email tonight."

"It's not like he wants us there," Sophie said, slamming her backpack down on the foyer floor. "I bet he wishes we didn't even exist."

"Hey, don't say that!" I reached for her arm, but she jerked it away. "Look, you know I don't exactly have the highest opinion of your father, but I remember his face in the hospital when both of you were born. He wasn't always like this."

"Then, I guess a lot has changed in seventeen years," she replied bitterly. "I'm going to my room." She stomped upstairs, leaving me with a crestfallen Lily whose head remained bowed.

"How are you doing?" I asked, approaching her.

My baby didn't respond, but her shaking shoulders told me what I needed to know. My beautiful, sensitive little girl sobbed in my arms, and I just held her.

"You're safe, sweetie," I said against her hair. "You're safe, you are loved, and nobody can hurt you here."

"I was so scared," she whispered.

"I know, baby. I've never heard anything like that in my life."

"Please, don't make me go back!" she begged.

"I can't promise that. Your dad has a legal right to see you."

She finally met my eyes, hurt and betrayed. "Don't you care about me?"

"Of course I do!"

"Then, make it stop, Mom! We hate going there. Why do you make us?"

"It's not that simple. If I withhold you guys from your dad, I get in trouble with the court. We both signed an agreement three years ago."

"We're not property!" she exclaimed. "We have feelings too!"

My heart broke, wishing I had something to offer other than the painful reality of divorce. "Sweetie, the courts don't look at it like that. Since you're underage, I'll get in trouble for keeping you from him."

"Can't you get them to change it? Aren't we old enough to decide if we want to go?"

"All I can do is try, baby, but it's incredibly expensive and there's no guarantee the judge would modify the visitation schedule. It's not like you have to see him that much now anyway."

"Exactly! Why should it be that hard?"

I sighed heavily. "I will talk to my lawyer and see what she says. Just be prepared that it might not be the answer you want."

"It's not fair, Mom!"

"You're right. It's completely unfair, and this entire situation sucks. I wish I could erase it all or make your dad behave better, but I can't change his choices. What happened tonight was scary for all of us. Sophie got the recording, and I'll upload it to my attorney's dropsite tomorrow. We might be able to talk to Family Services and see about getting your dad and Stephanie into some kind of marriage or parenting classes, but I'm not sure there's a whole lot I can do about visitation. I would love to make you all kinds of promises, Lil, but we have to be realistic."

She began to cry again, and I raised her chin gently with my hand. "I will do everything humanly possible to protect you and your sister. That stupid coronavirus didn't stop me, Tina Buffalo-Butt Fournier didn't stop me, and I'm not going to let Cruellinda ruin any chance you have for a decent relationship with your father."

Lily chuckled at the description. "You never let us call her that."

"I've never had the witch interrupt a date I've been on either. Scaring the heck out of you and your sister finally set me over."

"Was the date bad?"

I rolled my eyes and laughed. "Oh, it was epic, kiddo. The guy turned out to be Cruellinda's divorce attorney from Braxton and Braydon's dad."

Her expression immediately brightened as I spilled the tea. "Shut up! Really?"

"Oh yeah, and it gets even better." I wrapped an arm around her shoulders and walked her toward the kitchen table. "She accused me of going out with him because I'm jealous of her and your dad. The truth is that when Sean saw her at the Diner, he looked like he wanted to barf."

"She's such a reptile! Why did Daddy marry her?"

I pulled down a box of hot cocoa from the kitchen cabinet and began fixing Lily's favorite late night drink. Mine would be served in a wine glass. "That, my dear, will probably remain one of life's great mysteries."

We sat in companionable silence sipping our beverages until a soft knock on our front door surprised both of us.

I exchanged a panicked look with my daughter, praying it wasn't Rick. Instead, Sophie's heavy steps come barreling down the staircase to open the door. In walked Rachel Roseman who pulled Sophie into an immediate bear hug. From just beyond her, Jon caught my eye as I moved toward him.

"I didn't want Rachel driving this late at night," he began in an apologetic tone, "and it sounded like an emergency."

"More than you know," I replied.

He looked over my outfit, and his brows creased. "Were you on a date?"

I exhaled a laugh. "Something like that. It's sort of what kick-started the emergency."

Sophie and Rachel disappeared quickly upstairs, and Lily followed. She pressed a kiss on my cheek and thanked me for the hot chocolate.

"You got a few minutes?" I asked him. "I could use a friend."

"Sure. Your girls look traumatized, and that was the impression I got when Rachel begged me to come here. It's okay that she sleeps over, isn't it?"

"I'm thankful she's here. Sophie is not in a great head space right now. Their father and his shrieking high priestess of evil have done more than enough damage to last my girls a lifetime."

Jon raised both eyebrows as he chuckled. "That bad?"

"When I finally have the time to sit down and write my memoirs, this is one hundred percent going in. It's too ridiculous not to include."

"So, you're going to write a book like everyone else at Bible study?"

I grabbed my glass of cabernet and plopped down at the table. I enjoyed another sip before answering Jon's question.

"After the conversation I had with my date this evening, I feel like I have a duty."

"So, you *did* have a date. How'd that go?"

"Total disaster. Stephanie made sure of that. Not that I particularly wanted to go out with the guy, but it solidified a few things for me. Do you want anything to drink?"

"I don't want to put you out."

"No worries. I have water, hot chocolate, tea, or I can make you some coffee."

"Coffee would be great, if it's not too much trouble."

I waved him off as I stood up with my wine glass in hand. "Not at all. How do you take it? Cream? Sugar?"

"I'm pretty basic. Two sugars and some cream."

I took another sip of wine, feeling the tension leave my shoulders as the cabernet snaked its way down to my belly. While I didn't subscribe to the social media glorification of alcohol as a parenting rite, one of the unsung verses in *Proverbs 31* talks about giving wine to those in bitter distress. Being forced to rescue my girls from Rick and the she-beast certainly qualified. Setting down my glass, I measured out coffee into the drip machine and slammed the lid with a little more force than necessary.

"You okay?" Jon asked me.

"No, I'm honestly a wreck. I've had to hold it together for the girls because they were both on the verge of a meltdown, but I think I might finally be having my own." I snatched my wine glass off the counter and plopped down next to him.

"What on earth happened tonight?"

I proceeded to lay it all out for him, not omitting any details. His jaw tightened when I mentioned my date with Sean and that I found him attractive. However, Jon did seem proud that I hadn't acted on any foolish whims. His response to Stephanie's restaurant shenanigans was like listening to black comedy, equal parts humor and horror. It wasn't until I got to the part of my evening that involved Rick's gaslighting that he looked properly aghast.

"And you said he blamed *the girls* for what Stephanie said?"

My empty wine glass sat in front of me, and I resisted the urge to pour another as I already felt sleepy. "Oh, yes he did! Right down to the 'weak chinned shrimp with a whore for an ex-wife,' only he fudged the details and accused the girls of calling Stephanie that instead of what she called me."

"Not that they would be wrong about her," Jon quipped. "I knew that Rick lived with Stephanie before they were married, but I never realized the two of you weren't completely divorced yet when he did."

"Sean said the woman would take a lamp post to bed if it would give her any attention."

Jon clearly didn't like the mention of my date. He was now nursing his second cup of coffee, and I noticed his leg bouncing up and down under the table.

I reached out a hand to stop him, and then we both looked down at my hand on his knee. I pulled it back as if I'd accidentally set it on a hot stove.

"Sorry," I muttered.

"Tell me again why you were out on a date with a kid?"

"He's thirty-two, Jon. It's not like I picked him up at the carpool line when I was dropping the girls off at school."

"Charlotte, you're forty-four."

"And?"

"Could you really see yourself with some guy twelve years younger than you?"

"No! Which is why I told him to go find someone his own age. Anyways, I think you're missing the point. We're not here to talk about my date. I wanted to get your advice on what to do about the visitation issue. You're a dad, so you have a different perspective."

"Well, my situation is very different from yours, and I think it's safe to say that Rick and I are nothing alike."

I lifted my empty glass in salute. "Yes, and it's one of my favorite things about you."

He smirked. "I'm sure."

"Anyways, what were you going to say?"

"Just that you need to pray and seek the Lord on what, if anything, should be done. It's clear that Rick is more concerned about pleasing Stephanie than in taking care of your girls, but I'm not a judge or your lawyer."

"And the courts don't see *people*. They see emotion-free laws and rules, and kids are basically treated like chattel. I don't know if the courts would label what happened tonight as *abuse* since neither of them got violent with each other or against the girls, but the emotional torment is a constant over there. It's just impossible to prove, and honestly, the courts and family services don't care."

"I'm sorry, Charlotte. It's a horrific situation to be in."

"I have to keep reminding myself I only have two and a half years left of this prison sentence with Rick and the Serpentine Wife—assuming I don't choke her to death first."

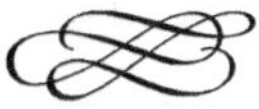

CHAPTER 16

JON LAUGHED. "HOW HAVE YOU NOT RUN OUT OF nicknames yet?"

"Anger and creativity are a pretty dangerous combination, aren't they? Not that it's particularly *Proverbs 31* behavior."

"I think you're allowed to have an off night. This was pretty crazy."

I sighed. "I just feel stuck. Rick won't hesitate to drag me in front of a judge for contempt of court even though he would probably be ecstatic about not having to deal with Stephanie's theatrics when the girls come over. Everything's a competition for that woman, including any drop of attention the girls get from their father. She has to win."

"Can't she see that she already has?" he asked. "Rick made that abundantly clear tonight. What more does she want?"

"There's always something *moah*," I said, mocking her nasal tone. "It will never be enough for her the same way it was never enough for Rick when we were married. She doesn't actually need more, but she does need to keep him constantly working to make her happy. The second he can rest is the second the focus would be on anybody but herself—and she might have to reciprocate some level of effort."

"That's a miserable way to live," he tsked.

"Ask me how I know."

Jon looked at me sympathetically. "I know I've said this before, but I'm so sorry. That must have been a living hell."

"I don't even care about that right now. I just hate how I can't protect my girls from their father or his wife. I hate feeling so powerless and that I have to send my babies in front of a firing squad every three weeks. I feel like I'm failing them, and I'm scared they think I'm failing them too. There are days I wonder if divorcing Rick was all a mistake."

"Why on earth would you think that?"

"Because of *1 Corinthians 7* where it talks about wives not separating from their husbands. Also, where it says that if your husband is content to go on living with you, then you should stay with him to sanctify your kids. Do you know how many Beth Shalom minions quoted me those verses when Rick told them I wanted a divorce?"

"I can only imagine," he murmured. "What did you tell them when they did?"

"I asked if Rick needed to stick his appendage into another female in order for them to admit his emotional abuse and neglect were wrong."

Jon didn't flinch at my colorful choice of words. "Technically, he *did* stick his appendage elsewhere."

"Technically, he did, but I refuse to believe that in the absence of adultery, God is okay with women and children remaining in abusive situations and slowly being tortured to death. You'd wind up praying for the toxic spouse to commit a sin or just keel over and die so you can be free. I don't know if it makes me a heretic for saying that, but after Sophie's stint in the ER, I would have divorced Rick whether or not Stephanie ever came into the picture. My daughter's life mattered more than staying in that lousy marriage."

Jon digested my words. "It's obvious you feel very strongly about this, and I completely understand why. What I don't understand is why you're struggling with the idea of divorce when it's clear how necessary it was for all of you."

"Because as horrible as things were with Rick, I never imagined he would become this *thing* that he is now. What if getting a divorce is why the girls don't want to talk about God and why Rick's heart got hardened even further? What if it's all my fault, and that's why those Bible verses say what they do?" I choked back a sob. "I just don't get it, Jon. What else could I have done? Would things be this terrible if I had stayed instead?"

He laid a comforting hand on my shoulder. "It can't be your fault, Charlotte, because none of what you just said is under your control. Rick refused to stop hurting you or your girls. *That's* why you divorced him. You didn't compel him to act even worse out of spite. He chose to do that. If anything, the threat of losing you three should have motivated him to change his behavior. Instead, he ran right into Stephanie's arms and hasn't looked back. He willingly made those choices. I remember what your girls were like a few years ago, and it's obvious they are so much happier now—even with the wicked stepmother."

My eyes welled up. "Really?"

"Yes! Also, I hear what you're saying about the Bible verses about marriage, but we need to clarify a few things. Rick claims that he *is* a believer, so that's our first problem. The verses you mentioned from chapter seven say if your husband is an *unbeliever,* that you should remain with him. Go back two chapters to *1 Corinthians 5,* and it tells us not to associate with someone who pretends to be a brother in Messiah but acts like Rick does."

"How do you know it says that?"

"Because I prefer reading the Bible in context rather than cherry picking verses."

I stuck my tongue out at him as I wiped my eyes. "Turn off the sarcasm font for a second. What I mean is, how did you connect those two passages together?"

"Because an abusive man is not a true believer. He can label himself whatever he wants, but Scripture is pretty clear." He reached into his pocket and pulled out his cell phone to read directly from his Bible app. *"But I wasn't talking about unbelievers who indulge in sexual sin, or are greedy, or cheat people, or worship idols. You would have to leave this world to avoid people like that. I meant that you are not to associate with anyone who claims to be a believer yet indulges in sexual sin, or is greedy, or worships idols, or is abusive, or is a drunkard, or cheats people. Don't even eat with such people."*

"Wow," I murmured.

"So, if the Bible says we shouldn't break bread with these false brothers, do you really think God wants you to be married to one?"

"But Rick did consent to still live with me. Maybe the girls wouldn't be so set against God or the Bible if I had just stuck it out with him."

Jon's expression looked pained. "He wasn't consenting to live with you, Charlotte. He was consenting to *keep abusing you.* He wouldn't have run off with the shrieking high priestess if he had any real interest in saving your marriage. The way I read these passages, Beth Shalom should have removed Rick and Stephanie from their fellowship rather than freezing *you* out. Once again, they missed the mark by protecting a boot licking fraud rather than protecting their sister in Messiah."

I smirked. "So, I shouldn't be surprised that the corrupt leadership protected their corrupt member who still signs those fat tithing checks instead of a struggling, single mother who calls out hypocrisy in the congregation?"

"People like Harvey Lebow and his ilk use the Bible to control and manipulate, but they're not rightly dividing the Word. Divorce isn't evil in and of itself, especially in a situation like yours. True evil is the way your ex-husband treated you and your girls. True evil was Harvey Lebow blaming you for Rick's behavior instead of holding him and scum like Nathan Fein accountable for their sins."

"Thank you," I said, taking his hand in mine. "You have no idea how much I needed to hear that—especially coming from someone who was happily married."

He looked down at our hands and then into my eyes. "I'm happy to provide you with any sliver of peace I can. Sounds like it was a traumatic evening all around."

I squeezed his hand and then released it. "It's definitely not one I would ever repeat again."

"What about your hot date? Are you planning to repeat that?"

"Who said he was hot?"

"I assumed he was."

I laughed. "Why?"

"Because I can't imagine a thirty-two year-old holding your interest for very long if there wasn't some level of physical attraction."

"Why would you assume that, Jon? Do you think I wouldn't be able to keep up with him otherwise?"

"Other way around. Your brain is lightning quick, and you have enough life experience that I'd doubt you'd tolerate a superficial connection for very long."

"You know, you're making an awful lot of assumptions right now."

"Don't give me another lecture about the first syllable of *assume*. I'm just stating facts, Charlotte."

"Yeah, except I think you would object to me going out with any man who isn't you."

He held my gaze. "You're not wrong about that."

I leaned back in my chair and desperately searched for any other place to rest my eyes. The potency of Jon's stare unraveled any lingering calm I'd gotten from my red wine. "I think you should probably go. It's getting late, and I doubt the girls will be awake much longer."

"So, we're not going to talk about this?" he asked.

"Talk about what? You told me we could be friends and you wouldn't push."

"Well, as your *friend*, I'm still allowed to be concerned you're wasting your time with some kid."

"First of all, he's not a kid. That was absolutely a grown man —just too young for me. Even then, it still took some self control telling him we're not going out again."

Jon didn't hide his relief. "Why did you date him in the first place?"

I swallowed, not wanting to answer that question or explain the timing.

"Charlotte?"

"What does it matter? It's not like you haven't gone on a bunch of dates yourself. Are you gonna tell me you haven't tried dating somebody younger?"

"I have no problem admitting that because I felt like a creep and I'll never do it again. I don't even know half the social media sites or slang they're talking about. It just made me feel even more ancient than I already am."

"So that makes the two of us what, exactly? A couple of T-rexes in good company?"

He grinned and offered a playful wink. "I never said I wanted to be a T-rex. I feel like there should be some other options here."

I smiled at the lighter turn of our conversation. "Oh yeah? So, what dinosaur would you want to be? Are you thinking carnivore, herbivore, or best of both worlds?"

"Can I be the sea monster from the new *Jurassic Planet* movie?"

"The mosasaurus? That thing reminds me of Leviathan from the Bible. No thanks."

He chuckled. "Fair enough. Maybe a triceratops. I could think of some folks I'd like to skewer with a horn or three."

"Like I would ever stop you. Not that Stephanie couldn't use another hole in her face." I held up my hands in apology. "Okay, that wasn't nice."

"No, but it's understandable given what happened tonight."

I smiled back at him. "I appreciate you talking through all of this with me. Lauren's a lot busier now that she's planning a wedding. Thank God, her psycho ex isn't really a part of her life anymore. I wouldn't wish for her story, but that part does make me a little envious. I might believe Rick was actually happy with the fire-breathing monster if he didn't spend so much time making sure to throw it in my face every chance he gets."

"That's because he desperately wants your attention."

"Why? All he did was reject it when we were married."

"Exactly. He has no more power to control how you feel or elevate himself at your expense. Do you really think Stephanie lets him get away with any of the stuff he did to you?"

"Not after what I heard tonight. I mean, I assumed Rick was blinded by whatever magic tricks she performs in the bedroom, but she was so cruel to him. I don't exactly like the man, but I did love him once upon a time—or the version I thought I married and he sometimes pretended to be. Even with all that pain, I would never speak to him the way she did. I don't get it. He worships the ground she walks on, publicly defends the witch no matter how insane she behaves, but she talks to him like he's the scum of the earth."

Gently, Jon responded, "Does any of this sound familiar? I'm sure you could hazard a guess or two why it might be in his best interest to take her side."

"Oh," I murmured. "Yeah, I guess you're right. That's sad."

He raised his brows. "Why do you say that?"

"Because I would never wish a *Rick* for Rick."

"Not even after the stunt he pulled tonight?"

I shook my head. "I know I make plenty of less than flattering comments about him, but all I really want is for him to get things right with the Lord and act like a genuine father to our girls. It makes me sick how he plays at being Wonder Dad with kids who aren't even his."

"You really think Stephanie would allow Rick to treat her precious boys the way he treats your daughters?"

"Definitely not."

"Don't forget that your girls represent *you* when they're over there. No matter what either of those self-involved losers say, you will always be the superior Mrs. Williams. Stephanie is jealous of you because you are a part of Rick's life that she can't touch, and she will never measure up. Every accusation of hers is just projection."

"Hmm," I murmured. "That makes sense."

"You always tell me how Rick thinks you should regret divorcing him. That's just his wounded pride and entitlement. He never thought someone as amazing, forgiving, forbearing, and beautiful as you would finally get fed up with him and leave. He wrongly assumed he could just keep treating you like garbage, you would just keep taking it, and he could string you along with lame promises or keep blaming you for everything wrong in the marriage."

I met Jon's dark eyes, soaking in every word of truth. Whether he kissed me like a brother or not, I desperately needed these words from my brother in Christ. "Thank you."

He smiled as he leaned his face closer. "The reason why Stephanie hates you is because of how much Rick regrets losing you."

"You really think so? He acts like I'm trash."

"The operative word here is *acts*. You left him. And while his self-centered, ridiculous pride won't let him treat you better, he can't stand the fact that you will be loved, appreciated, and respected by someone with the good sense to make sure they never let you go."

CHAPTER 17

"Is that someone *you?*" I asked, realizing I had also tilted my face closer toward Jon's. I inhaled a scent more heady than expensive cologne. It was the aroma of a grown man's attention as he looked at me like something more than the broken discards of Rick Williams.

His voice lowered to a whisper. "I thought you said you didn't want to do this."

"I've also had a rough night and a rather large glass of red wine. I may not be in my right mind right now."

He pulled his face back. "That's not how I want this to happen."

My dreamy haze dissolved, and I jumped up from my seat. "Was this just a game? You finally get what you want, and now you're done?"

His chair scraped against the floor, as he stood a foot away from me. "No! I'm telling you that when the time is right for us, it *will* happen. I don't want you to have any regrets, and I don't want any either."

"Then what was all the schmoozy talk about how I'm so wonderful? Wasn't all of this just a set up from the minute you arrived here with Rachel?"

"I meant every word I said, Charlotte. I'm not manipulating you."

I stared into his eyes, wanting to believe him but also fearing I would foolishly give my heart away again. "How do I know for sure?"

He took my hands in his. "You're going to have to trust me."

"How am I supposed to trust *you*, when I don't even trust myself?"

He reached his hand to cup the side of my face and push a long tendril from my cheek. "I have plenty of flaws, but lying will never be one of them. As for trusting yourself, that's something you're going to have to work out with the Lord."

I shirked both his assertions and his hand. "Only a con man tells you how honest he is."

"No, an honest man who knows you need reassurance that he's not going to hurt you would also tell you the same thing."

"Oh yeah? And how am I supposed to know the difference? You can give me all the swoony looks and speeches you want, Jon, but you kiss me like I'm Andrea. How am I supposed to believe anything you say?"

A growl tore from this throat. "We've already talked about all of this. I don't look at you and see a replacement for my first wife. I just see *you*, Charlotte." He held up a hand to cut off my next statement. "And don't you dare start with the comparisons and putting yourself down. That voice you're hearing doesn't belong to me."

I swallowed, hating just how well he saw my insecurities. It left me feeling exposed and vulnerable.

Vulnerable meant ripe for punishment.

I slid away from him and walked toward the front door. "I think it's time for you to go."

I could feel the frustration radiating from him, and I waited for Jon to lash out. Here was his chance to blame me for an unsuccessful attempt at wooing me, and he'd be partially right.

"What?" he asked.

I raised an eyebrow.

He took a step toward me, and I took one backward.

Sighing, he took a larger step toward me, placed his hands on my hunched shoulders, and gently pushed them down. I half expected him to go in for the kiss he rejected earlier, but he pulled me into a hug instead. My arms remained stiff at my sides, unsure of what to do.

Close to my ear, he whispered, "Breathe, Charlotte. I'm not going to hurt you."

I allowed myself a tiny sip of air.

"Now, again," he said. "Breathe."

My next sip turned into a larger gulp, and it pressed my chest and stomach against his. Instead of jumping in revulsion, Jon commanded another breath and a deeper inhalation. Three more times, he talked me through my breaths, and three more times I anticipated rejection that never came.

Finally, I wrapped my arms around his waist and leaned into his hug and into his strength. As I exhaled, I breathed out eighteen years of trauma from Rick, from Beth Shalom, and from bearing the brunt of helping my emotionally dysregulated children feel loved and safe while I felt unloved and alone.

I cried ugly tears, and Jon continued to hold me as if he had all the time in the world. I eventually motioned for air, my passageways clogged from crying.

I excused myself to the bathroom to blow my nose. Catching

myself in the mirror, I winced at my streaked makeup and red eyes.

He stood in the doorway while I stared at my reflection in disgust.

"Don't do it," he said. "Don't start speaking lies to the woman looking back at you. You're allowed to be less than perfect, Charlotte. You're allowed to be weak, to be hurting, and to rely on someone else instead of always fending for yourself."

"You're gonna make me cry again," I said, my throat closing up. I turned away from the mirror toward him.

He took the tissues from my hands and wiped my face. I could only stare at him in amazement as he placed a kiss on my forehead and rewarded me with a soft smile. "Feel any better now?"

"Why are you doing all of this for me? What did I do to deserve it?"

"Who says you need to *do* anything to be treated with kindness?"

My mouth opened and shut, but no words came out.

"Do you have to do anything to earn Lauren's comfort and support?" he asked.

"No, but this is different."

"Why is it different? I'm your friend too, aren't I?"

"But you're—"

"I'm what, Charlotte?"

"You're a man," I whispered.

Jon glanced down over himself in feigned surprise. "So it would seem. What does that have to do with anything?"

I pulled a face. "Men don't do this."

"Men don't do what? Comfort their friends when they've had a horrible night or have had their heart repeatedly broken for almost two decades?"

"They don't comfort *me*," I said. "Not like this." I hung my head, but Jon brought it back up with his forefinger.

"Has there been *any* man in your life who made you feel safe? Like you deserved to be protected and cared for?"

I shook my head. "I'm a burden. A big fat burden."

"No," Jon said adamantly. "That's the enemy lying to you. You are a *blessing* to the people who know you. The ones who called you a burden were either jealous or mad that you saw through them."

"So, my father, Abe, Rick, Rabbi Lebow?" I asked. "Are you saying all of them were wrong? That there's no possible way I might have been difficult or tough to handle?"

"Why should you need handling?"

"Have you met me?" I quipped.

"Yes, and one of the many things I love about you is the insight you have into people and situations. For anyone with secrets to hide, that would be very scary. For people who desperately need to be seen, like your daughters, it's life changing. Unfortunately, somewhere along the way, you were convinced that your gifts were good enough to be used and taken advantage of, but not good enough to be reciprocated by the same people enjoying the benefits of them."

I sniffled. "And how is it that you think you know me so well?"

"You don't think I saw how Rick treated you all those years at Beth Shalom? You don't think I saw the way Harvey treated you like an annoyance unless he could use you in the children's ministry? Or the way you always lit up a room with your style and personality? Liora Fein would look you up and down in disdain, but the next week, she copied at least one thing you had worn, if not that whole outfit."

My eyes widened, realizing he was telling the truth.

"I've never met your father or brother, Charlotte, but it sounds like they set you up to marry someone just like them. They acted like you weren't good enough, Rick told you weren't good enough, Beth Shalom told you weren't good enough, and you also believed you weren't good enough. There was nobody there to tell you anything different."

"Sometimes my mother did, but I never believed her," I said, finishing his thought. "She doesn't look like me. She's beautiful."

"Look in the mirror again," Jon said, gently turning me around. He stood behind me, a full head taller. "You've got a doppelganger daughter upstairs. If this was her face in the mirror, would you be repeating any of the things you regularly tell yourself?"

"She looks a whole lot better than I do."

He tutted. "That's not what I asked. If this was Miss Sophie's face, would you tell her any of the horrible things you tell yourself? Would you be repeating any of the awful things Rick has said about you, your family has ever said about you, or anything you tell yourself?"

"You already know the answer, Jon."

He met my eyes in the mirror. "But I'm not asking for my benefit. I'm asking for yours. Would you tell your daughter any of those things?" he repeated a third time.

"I see what you're trying to do."

He exhaled a short laugh. "Maybe not, because you're still not cooperating. Let's try it again. Would you say those things to Sophie?"

I realized he wouldn't let the issue go until I relented. "No," I finally replied.

"Okay, so now when you look in the mirror, before you even listen to those old voices in your head, I want you to stop and ask yourself if what you're thinking is something you should ever say—"

"To myself, right?" I asked, cutting him off.

"No, to *your daughter*. I know you love those girls more than life itself. You were willing to start your entire life over to protect them. The problem is, you don't love *yourself* because you've been beat down into believing you don't deserve to be loved. So, for now, look in the mirror and see someone you do believe is worthy to be loved—your child—and then eventually, I hope you will start seeing yourself the same way. Your mother, faults and all, wasn't lying or placating you just because you're her daughter. You *are* beautiful, Charlotte."

I had no words, thoroughly exposed and encouraged all at the same time.

"Mom, are you still awake?" Sophie called from the top of the stairs.

I sidestepped Jon and walked to the base of the staircase in the foyer. "Is everything okay?"

My daughter eyed me critically. "Have you been crying?"

"Yeah, but I'm doing better now."

Jon shuffled toward the front door, and my daughter's eyes narrowed. "Why is Mr. Roseman still here? Have you guys been alone down there this whole time?"

I exhaled a taut breath. "Yes, we have, Soph. Is there a problem? What's going on?"

"Nothing, I just wanted to say I'm sorry for being short with you when we got home. I was upset about Dad and Stephanie, not you."

"I know, baby. No worries. You're forgiven."

"So, you were crying with Mr. Roseman?"

Jon joined me in the small alcove and answered Sophie

before I could. "Yes, I was helping your mom, and now I'm about to go home. Is everything all right?"

Sophie's gaze darted between me and my just friend. "Yeah, thanks for letting Rachel come over so late."

I felt Jon's hand on the middle of my back, but his eyes remained fixed on my daughter at the top of the stairs. "We love your family very much. We're happy to do anything we can to make this situation easier for you guys."

My body sighed into his touch, and my very astute teenager didn't miss a thing. She met my eyes, asking her unspoken question, and I inched away from Jon. "I'll come up to kiss you good night in a minute. I'm just going to say goodbye to Mr. Roseman."

Sophie nodded, and I could have sworn I heard her mutter something about me giving *someone else* a kiss goodnight.

I turned to face Jon. "Thank you for everything."

He leaned in close to my ear. "We'll have our kiss soon enough."

CHAPTER 18

"So," Ginger Viking said on Monday morning, "how did it go with your hottie from Cougarville.com?"

Rosaria held another glittery travel mug of tea, one of many in her collection. This one featured sparkling pumpkins and fall leaves decorating the sides. I could have sworn Ro had a mug for every day of the year plus a matching pair of eyeglasses. "Please, tell me you didn't go through with that," she said.

"Oh, I did," I chuckled, sipping my morning brew of Charred Cups coffee. "The date was…*monumental.*"

"Monumental?" she repeated, eyes wide. "I knew there was something different about you today. Did you guys—?" she gestured with her free hand to finish her inappropriate suggestion.

"Monumental *disaster,*" I corrected with a laugh. "What other kind of dates do I have?"

Luke chuckled. "Of course it was."

Ro studied me. "Girl, you are glowing. I wouldn't call that a disaster. You're holding back info. Did you have to explain the birds and bees to your jailbait date while you were being monu-mentally disaster-ed?"

"Rosaria!" Luke and I gasped in unison.

She wiggled her eyebrows beneath her orange eyewear. "I thought I'd pull a Charlotte and say something outrageous. How'd I do?"

"Coo coo cachoo," Luke sing-songed, joining in our boss's assumption. "There's some part in the *Mrs. Robertson* song about Jesus loves you, right?"

I chuckled. "You are not old enough to even know that refer-ence. Heck, *I'm* not even old enough to know that reference."

"But if the shoe fits," Ro said, her voice trailing off as she fished for details. "Did you hook up with your younger man?"

I scoffed and rolled my eyes. "No, it was the blonde barracuda who tried to rob the cradle. *That* was the monu-mental disaster."

"What!" they both exclaimed.

"Yep. Sean and I went to the Parkview Diner on Saturday night, and sure enough, Richard and Cruellinda were also dining there."

"Cruellinda?" Luke repeated. "You only call her that when she's really done something *really* extra."

"Oh, she more than earned it this weekend."

Ro gestured for me to continue with my tale. "Spill the tea. I'm dying over here."

I smirked. "So, the super short version is that I didn't know my date was actually Stephanie's divorce attorney from her last husband."

"Shut the front door!" she exclaimed.

"It gets worse."

"How is that possible?" Luke asked. "I mean, it's *you*, it's a Monday morning, and you always have dating drama, but I can't imagine how running into that salty hag could get any worse than what I'm imagining. She's already married to your ex. What more does she want?"

"Well, if you can imagine that she tried to *coo coo cachoo* with her divorce attorney once upon a time, you'd be off to a good start. The only person attempting cradle burglary was Miss Bougie herself."

"Stop!" Ro exclaimed, nearly spitting out her drink. "What is wrong with that woman?"

"Too much to list, and that wasn't even the worst part of the evening."

Luke readjusted his man-bun as if mentally preparing himself. "Did she catch you guys going at it or something?"

"Gross! No! I already told you nothing happened. We had barely sat down to dinner, and she spotted us. She caused a huge scene in the restaurant."

"Did Richard join in the fun?" Ro asked.

"No, he just sat there letting his wife humiliate them both. Sean and I left, and then the girls texted me at the end of our date that their stepmother had gone off the deep end."

Luke's face took on immediate concern. The only thing more infamous than Stephanie's attention seeking antics was her temper. "What happened with the girls? Are they okay?"

"They called me in a total panic and said their stepmother was throwing stuff and screaming at their father. They were both terrified. I had them put the argument on speaker phone, and then I drove over and picked them up. They were scared, and frankly, I was scared too. She sounded possessed, and the stuff she said to Rick was just evil. Never, in a million years, would I have ever said any of that to him."

Ro tsked. "Were the girls safe, at least?"

"Yeah, I got them out before Rick had any idea. Then, he

called me and lied about the whole thing. He assumed the girls had run away, so he tried to blame *me* for that, not even knowing they were in the car."

"What the heck!" Luke exclaimed. "Why would he do that?"

"Probably because the barracuda was breathing over his shoulder. Also because whatever the girls do wrong—which for him could be anything and everything—he has to somehow make my fault. Less than 'perfect' is automatically a defect in my parenting rather than him being a controlling, ridiculous hypocrite."

"So, how did he explain Stephanie's behavior? Obviously, that would be why the girls took off."

"Well, that's not the version he wanted me to believe, of course. He accused the girls of verbally abusing him and even misquoted Stephanie to make it sound more authentic. He pretended the toddler tantrum came from our children instead of that psychopath he married."

"But those are his kids!" Luke exclaimed.

Ro answered before I could. "Are you kidding? He knows if he doesn't cover for Cruellinda, she'll make his life hell instead of everyone else's."

I shook my head sadly. "From what I heard, it sounds like she does anyway. All of that garbage about Stephanie being the great love of his life is to protect himself from her wrath—and to make petty digs at me. The truth is that Rick found the female version of himself, only she's about a hundred times worse."

"That's scary," Ro murmured.

"Exactly. The girls don't want to go back to his house, and I'm waiting on an email from my divorce attorney to see if I have to force them. They also got an audio recording of the fight with their stepmother, so Rick can lie all he wants, but it doesn't change reality. Unfortunately, when he accused the girls of calling him all of those awful names, he didn't know he was on speaker in the car. Needless to say, my babies are devastated."

Ro shook her head. "That's awful. I'm so sorry."

"Yeah, that part was the least awesome of the entire debacle."

"Did you tell Rick you recorded the fight?" Luke asked.

"Sure did. And the slime accused me of setting him up and deliberately upsetting his precious wife. Did he care one iota about our children? Nope. Just one more instance of Rick needing to blame his horrible choices on me."

Ro placed a hand on my shoulder. "How are you holding up, Mama Bear?"

I sniffled back tears. "Nothing is ever that man's fault—even when it *is* his fault. I don't blame the girls for never wanting to see him again, but I'm not sure if there's much I can do about it. From my understanding, the kids can choose to stop visitation with the non-custodial parent when they're fourteen, but Rick could take me to court to force them. The flip side is that I'd have to take *him* to court and hope the judge would agree to modify the visitation plan. I'm pretty sure Rick would insist they go to his house out of spite. One of his favorite lines is 'well *you* agreed to this.' Technically, I did, and he's not some career criminal. Sophie and Lily didn't take that news very well."

Ginger Viking looked at me pityingly. "That's definitely a *monumental* way to end your Saturday night. Are the girls okay now?"

I shrugged. "They're coping as best as they can. Sophie took it the hardest. Their friend Rachel spent the night afterwards."

"I'm sure that helped," Luke said sympathetically.

My eagle-eyed office manager, however, had a memory like a steel trap. Her eyes narrowed behind her outrageous orange eyewear. "Okay, so Richard drama aside, you still came in here with a glow. Rachel is the daughter of what's his face, isn't she?"

"Yeah, and?"

"Did you talk to him about any of this? I mean, that's the only other explanation I've got since you said you weren't disaster-ed by the divorce attorney."

"Nobody 'disaster-ed' anything, okay, Ro? Drop it, please."

Luke watched the two of us, his eyebrows raised. "Who is *what's his face*? Charlotte, do you have some other guy you've been hiding from us?"

"Nothing happened with that either," I clipped, shooting my office manager a warning look.

Affecting an English accent, she quipped, "Methinks the lady doth protest too much."

"You would protest too if you were being accused of something that didn't happen."

"What am I missing?" Ginger Viking demanded. "You two know something I don't."

Forcing a nonchalant tone, I playfully swatted his arm "Oh, there's lots of stuff you don't know, kid. Don't stress about it."

He rolled his eyes and pulled a face. "Hardy har, Ancient One."

"Seriously, though. Not a big deal."

Luke remained unconvinced. "Charlotte, you're an open book. And you suck at lying. What are you trying to hide?"

"Who said you were entitled to know my business?" I snapped.

"*You* did, because every Monday is dating drama day!" Ro jumped in. "You're the one who came up with the name!"

Peeved, I said, "You got the drama already. Stephanie is a psychotic hag who continually hurts my children and makes their father act like a complete *Richard*. That's it!"

"Not buying it," Luke said, crossing his beefy arms across his chest.

"If I don't provide more information, are you going to cope, seethe, and mald?" I asked, quoting the Gen Z, online gaming slang the Viking had taught me himself. I jutted my lower lip like I was placating a whining dog.

The six foot puppy glared at me instead. "Don't do that, Charlotte."

"Do what? Give you a dose of your own medicine?"

"I didn't realize we were dishing out bitter acid today." His blue eyes sparkled, ready for battle.

"Why? Would you prefer hemlock? Arsenic? I could always just grab one of the tools from the back and finish you off old school. Which limb would you like to lose first?"

He was about to launch another verbal volley before Rosaria cut us off.

"You two better not even start with that nonsense! I didn't spike my tea today to handle all of this."

"I didn't start it!" Luke protested.

"You spike your tea?" I asked incredulously.

She deliberately took a loud slurp. "I'll never tell."

Luke looked scandalized. "Miranda would never let you do that."

"Chill out, Ginger, I was kidding," she tsked. "You guys only force me to drink after hours, I promise."

I chuckled nervously, hoping we could put the topic of Jon Roseman aside. Going to battle with Luke was harmless and fun banter, and Ro enjoyed it far more than she pretended to protest. I was just thankful the daily back-and-forth with Red

Beard didn't come with all the emotional weight of my conversations with Jon.

I'd never fantasized about being worthy of *Luke's* love and devotion.

However, the current man of the hour wasn't done with me yet. "So, what were you *not* saying before you tried deflecting with insults?"

"Nothing that bears repeating," I hedged.

Ro, traitor that she was, piped up. "She's got the hots for the dad of the friend."

"I do not!"

"Whatever," she said dismissively. "We both know that's why you're not going with me on the cruise."

Luke's head boomeranged back to me, his man bun wobbling. "You're not going on the cruise? I was looking forward to dating disasters on the high seas."

"Nope," Ro replied before I could open my mouth. "She claims it's because Richard won't change the visitation schedule, but I think we all know better."

I shot her the evil eye. "Nothing, and I repeat, *nothing* is happening with Jon Roseman."

"Ooh, so he does have a name," Luke crooned, his expression turning mercenary, "and the fact you're trying to keep it hidden means there's something there."

"And how did you deduce all of that, Detective Ginger Pants?"

He grinned. "Because you wouldn't be this defensive otherwise."

"Maybe I'm tired of having the two of you dissect my life."

"You wouldn't keep sharing every detail if you really were," he responded.

I pursed my lips. "I think I'm all shared out for the day."

"Come on, we're just teasing you," Ro said, taking another sip of tea.

I rose from my chair. "I need to use the ladies room. Please, excuse me."

The playful expressions on their faces dropped, realizing that they had, in fact, pushed me too far.

"Charlotte, I'm sor—" Ro began.

I raised my hand to cut her off. "I can't right now. I need a minute."

"Understood," Luke said, his teasing tone replaced with concern. When we weren't bickering like siblings, we also took an active care in each other's lives like siblings too.

Once I'd locked myself in the bathroom, I took a long look in the mirror. Normally, I stood there and picked apart every flaw or just wished it was a different visage staring back. Of course, all of that just left me feeling hollow, dejected, and defeated.

"What would you tell Sophie?" I said, squaring my shoulders.

An image of her face superimposed over mine in the mirror, and tears leaked down my cheeks. The reflection wasn't ugly at all. She was beautiful.

And she needed to heal.

"Jon, what have you done to me?" I whispered.

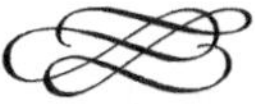

CHAPTER 19

I patched things up with Ro and Luke, and the rest of the work week flew by. With the increased new home construction in our area also came an increased demand in the tooling needed to create them. Those custom kitchens, baths, and closets didn't materialize from vapor—each aspect required a specific cutterhead, profile tool, or saw blade from our catalog. That Thursday alone, we sold more in tooling than my annual salary.

Miranda, who normally worked remotely, stopped by late Friday with a bottle of wine and gift cards for each of us as a thank you for our hard work.

Meanwhile, my attorney confirmed my sinking suspicion that we would not be able to modify Rick's nominal visitation time. Without signs of physical abuse, she said the judge wasn't likely to change the schedule. The girls didn't take the news well and asked if they could stay with Rachel over the weekend. Instead of pushing the issue, I told them I understood their frustration and dropped them off at Jon's house myself. He messaged me with periodic updates, and I was truly thankful for our friendship.

Lauren was enjoying family time with Grant and Ari, and it was strange to be sitting at home all alone in my townhouse with nothing but my thoughts to keep me company. Wasting energy with the spammers and weirdos of the online dating world held no appeal.

Instead, I checked on a couple of upcoming appointments on my calendar app. The property management company where I used to work had just changed office locations, and I realized it was next door to the girls' dentist. Pulling up the map on my phone, I scoped out some of the other tenants occupying the tiny office park.

The name of a church caught my eye. "Grace Abounds," I read aloud. Clicking on their website, I expected to see the usual non-denominational tells—flashy, moving graphics replete with white, Anglo-Saxon Protestant leadership and their picture perfect families, online sermons with promotional videos, and of course, multiple links for financial donations. The Grace Abounds site felt like an encouraging whisper rather than a clanging gong demanding attention. I clicked through the site and read through the "About Us" section:

Grace Abounds is a church of imperfect people worshiping a perfect Savior. We welcome people from all backgrounds, trauma, and previous church experience. We aim to show the love of Christ through service and to help and disciple one another in the faith. Our goal is to facilitate a healthy community that brings the Gospel of Jesus to the world.

My eyes watered as they fell back over the word, "trauma," stunned to see any congregation actually acknowledge what many in my online support groups had documented as their own experience with organized religion. Normally, a promise of being inclusive or welcoming meant turning a blind eye to Biblical sin and presenting a watered down version of Scripture through self help sermons sprinkled with Jesus on top. This was the closest I'd seen to anything remotely resembling my own beliefs or what Lauren assured me her Bible study group also upheld.

Clicking on a link to get more information about the church, I began to fill out the survey questions. "You welcome all kinds of trauma, eh? For once, how about I don't overshare and let's see how you do?" I said, coaching myself through the exercise. "What's the reason for your visit? Let's go with, 'I would just like to be welcomed *as is* along with my children.' Maybe we'll finally get the bare minimum instead of being automatically shunned." I finished typing the rest of my answers and then sent my request off into the great beyond of the internet.

My phone buzzed with a text and photo from Jon. It was all three girls sitting on the couch with movie candy in their laps as they made silly faces for the camera.

Thank you for that, I texted him.

How are you doing?

Okay, I guess. I'm glad the girls are at your house and feel safe around you. I don't take that lightly, you know.

I know, he wrote back.

Have they tried talking to you about any of the nonsense going on with their father?

No, I'm giving them a wide circle. Mostly just observing for now.

Any hot dates this weekend? I mentally smacked my forehead, regretting my words as soon as I'd sent them. Jon's hesitation in responding was enough of an answer that I'd made a blunder.

After what felt like forever but was actually one hundred

eighty seconds, he wrote back, *No.* After another sixty seconds, he added, *You?*

Nobody but me, myself, and I. Found a church online that looks interesting. Might go check it out tomorrow.

Interesting how? Did I ever tell you about the one I visited where the lady got "prophetic words" with snack food?

I chuckled in surprise. *I don't think so. That sounds…different.*

Jon sent back a laughing emoji along with an eye rolling one. *The first week I went, all of her "prophetic words" sounded like TV commercials for the food she gave out to people in the crowd. Like she handed someone a bag of Skattles fruit candy and told the couple how God wanted them to "savor the rainbow" of His goodness.*

Oh my gosh, you're kidding!

Wish I was.

So, what happened? I asked. *Obviously, there's a reason you brought this up.*

Don't ask me why I went back a second time. I had asked for prayer about getting remarried the week before, and the next week, she walked right up to me on the microphone, hands me a big bag of those gummy fish candies, and tells me that God says there are plenty of fish in the sea, but He has a special one picked out. I think I mentioned I had signed up for PlentyofFishes when I asked for prayer. There was a pack of women surrounding me after the service. Ask me if I ever went back after that.

My jaw dropped as I read his message. *You never mentioned any of this before. That is insane! And then to take a personal prayer request like that and blast it out in the middle of the church? That's not prophetic…that's blasphemy! What she did was spill your tea for an entire church to hear. What is wrong with people???*

That was the last time I ever set foot in a church. I got involved with the Margolin Bible Study, and I'm thankful to be there.

Do you think that there are any good churches, Jon? Or is everything just a different flavor of Beth Shalom?

Theoretically, yes, but I haven't found any. Besides, aren't you the one with the jaded opinion of organized religion as a whole?

Yeah, that hasn't changed. Something about this church feels different, though.

I'm intrigued. Can you send me info?

I copied and pasted the link to the church website and gave him a few minutes to peruse the site.

What do you think? I asked. *Any glaring red flags to you?*

So far so good, he wrote. *I think I found the piece that probably caught your attention.* He sent a screenshot of the "About Us" section, and I smiled at his perceptiveness. He followed with, *Do you really think you're going to go?*

As long as it doesn't give off any Beth Shalom vibes, I'm willing to give it a shot.

I'm impressed and I'm proud of you, Charlotte.

I smiled at my phone, picturing his dark eyes. *Thanks. I'm kind of proud of me too.*

He sent back a winking emoji.

Not sure what else to say and not wanting to come up with some lame reason to keep the conversation going, I pretended I needed to go to bed early.

Initially, I planned to putter around the house or maybe find a book to read, but my Bible called out to me from my nightstand. I'd originally purchased it at eighteen years-old, and I'd had the cover rebound after my divorce from Richard. He always mocked how it was falling apart, and I'd retorted that a pristine Bible just shows the owner never reads it.

That had temporarily shut him up.

I flipped my Bible open to *1 John*, particularly fond of chapter four, but feeling a nudge to start from the beginning of the book. As I read through chapter two and got to the section about hating your brother, I felt a pang of conviction. While I harbored no hatred toward my biological brother despite his betrayal, I knew the Lord was challenging me about my attitude toward Stephanie.

"She's *not* a sister in Christ," I said through gritted teeth. "There is zero 'fruit' other than the fact she's bananas."

I felt the Holy Spirit challenge me again about my own attitude. Did I have every right to be angry over what she'd done to my children and to their father? Absolutely! Had I also gone out of my way to share her private business with my coworkers and my children? Also, yes. Did my daughters really need to know about her botched seduction of Sean? Did Ro and Luke? Couldn't I have shared a story of rescuing my daughters without reveling in the disgust I knew they'd show for Stephanie's past indiscretions? They were in my corner already —why did they need every salacious detail?

In truth, if Stephanie had breathed within twenty feet of me, I would have had something sarcastic to say about it. Her mere existence annoyed me.

You hate her, I heard the Holy Spirit say to me.

"Why shouldn't I? There's nothing there to love."

Will hating her change your heart or hers?

I paused, gently, yet utterly laid bare. My mind flashed to an image of a heart covered in metal panels. It was an impenetrable barrier.

You hate her, Charlotte. Confess the burden and release it so your heart can be free.

"Free from what?" I whispered.

Free from becoming just like her if you don't repent.

That last utterance stopped me cold. Hating Stephanie, comparing and elevating myself at her expense was no different than what she did to me. In fact, it made me no better than her. Sure, my actions weren't wrought from insecurity and the selfish disregard of others, but my heart had been hardened by trauma and betrayal all the same. I knew at that moment I stood at a metaphorical crossroads. I could become the monster that hurt me, or I could stop clinging to every offense as a shield. My own pride justified the same behavior I eagerly condemned in Stephanie. I was a hypocrite—and worse yet, I knew I was sinning against God.

"Forgive me, Lord," I murmured, "for holding hatred in my heart. But do I need to *forgive* her? She's not sorry—doubtful she ever will be—and she's just going to do it all over again the next chance she gets. Seventy times seven is when they come to you and repent. We both know she's never going to do that."

Release the burden, Charlotte. Vengeance is mine, not yours. You can't carry this weight.

My mind flashed to the Parable of the Wicked Servant, the one who refused to let his debtor off the hook for a petty amount when he himself owed millions to the king. As much as I wanted to harden myself against all of Stephanie's wrongs, I couldn't do that while talking to Jesus. How much more had I offended Him, sinned against Him, and messed up while fully knowing better? How long had I carried this sin of hatred in my heart while He patiently waited for the moment when I could listen to His gentle rebuke? I also knew that Jesus laid down His life for the entire world—and that included both me *and* Stephanie. Continuing to focus on her sins against me and my daughters didn't erase any of my own unworthiness before the Lord.

"Forgive me," I whispered again. "Jesus, I don't want to be bitter, and I *am* tired from carrying this. So tired," I repeated, my voice breaking. Choking down my pride and self right-eousness, I added, "God, help me forgive Stephanie and let You handle justice. I've judged her and let bitterness take root.

Forgive me, and please wash me clean. I don't want this burden anymore."

As soon as the prayer left my lips, I immediately felt lighter. I prayed aloud in tongues as my heart rejoiced in God's mercy toward me. "Please turn her heart toward you, Jesus," I prayed in earnest. "May she truly know what it means to love and be loved by You."

As I uttered that prayer and several more prayers genuinely asking for Stephanie's good, I felt the comfort of the Holy Spirit. My prayer hadn't erased the damage of what she'd done to me, my daughters, or even my ex-husband, but her behavior would no longer control my emotions. I realized just how much Stephanie had consumed my thought life. No matter how much Rick believed I regretted losing him, my only real regret was that I'd opened the door for Stephanie Burgess to come into our lives.

"Do I need to repent for getting a divorce?" I whispered in prayer. Instead, I was reminded of *1 Corinthians 7* where it says for husbands and wives not to deprive one another of marital relations unless it was for prayer—and at that, to make sure to come back together to avoid temptation.

Answering my own question, I said aloud, "Rick withheld sex on purpose to punish me. He wasn't praying when he was up late at night. He was committing adultery with his computer."

Flipping open my Bible, I turned to the book of *Isaiah*, and my eyes fell upon the following words:

No longer will they call you Deserted, or name your land Desolate. But you will be called Hephzibah, and your land Beulah; for the Lord will take delight in you, and your land will be married. As a young man

marries a young woman, so will your Builder marry you; as a bridegroom
rejoices over his bride, so will your God rejoice over you.

I fought the renewed pangs of betrayal recalling the young woman I'd been who'd had my heart ripped out by the bridegroom who supposedly loved me. "That's not what you designed marriage to be," I said, feeling the weight of shame slip from my shoulders. Jon's words echoed in my head, the reminder that *Rick's* selfish choices had wrought *Rick's* negative consequences. As my mind lingered over my friend and everything he'd done to comfort and encourage me, I felt something bloom in my heart.

"Jon really is a good man," I sniffled, fighting the urge to text him. "I just wish he could see *me* instead of Andrea."

Release the burden, I heard the Lord say again.

"So, it's not meant to be?" I asked.

Release the burden, the Lord repeated without further clarification.

Unsure if that meant releasing any hope for a future with Jon or just the outcome, I closed my eyes and prayed as I felt the Spirit leading me. I asked God to bless Jon with every desire of his heart, to protect my own heart in the process, and to help me to continue healing from Rick's abuse both during and after our marriage.

Emotionally exhausted, I fell asleep and enjoyed my first night of peace in a long time. Praying for Stephanie didn't mean she would choose anything different, but I knew change had begun in my own heart. My options were to remain "right" and miserable or to release the burden and finally heal and be made whole.

And I'd been miserable for long enough.

CHAPTER 20

I ARRIVED AT GRACE ABOUNDS DRESSED CASUALLY IN a swing tank, cardigan, and jeans. My make up was light and so was my heart as I entered the high school gymnasium where the church met. Like so many other church experiences, I anticipated blending in with the crowd and being largely ignored. I picked a row toward the front so I could see without squinting or dragging out my eye glasses for distance.

The room was packed with many young families and their litany of children. The abundance of so many babies provided piercing reminders of my early days at Beth Shalom. As I scanned the room, my eyes did a double take at the silver fox who'd just entered from the back.

His eyes landed on me moments later, and Jon Roseman headed directly toward me.

"Hi!" I exclaimed, standing up to greet him with a side hug. "What are you doing here? Are the girls with you?"

"They were up late watching the six hour *Prideful Prejudice* DVD set Sophie brought over. I left doughnuts for all of them."

"But why are you here?" I asked again, searching his eyes.

"I didn't want you to do this alone. And to be honest, I was intrigued after I did some more research."

I gestured at the empty folding chair next to me. "You're welcome to join me."

He smiled as he slid past me into the row.

"Are you nervous?" he asked.

I shook my head. "Curious more than anything. You?"

"Well, I don't see any suspicious looking ladies holding snack food and a microphone, so I think I'll be okay."

I chuckled as I scanned the room one final time. "So far so good. If I ever decide to work in a church nursery again, I would be up to my eyeballs in babies. Can you believe our kids ever used to be that small?"

Jon's face grew wistful as he took in several families to our immediate left. "Feels like forever ago and just a blink all at the same time."

"I'll see baby and toddler photos of the girls pop on my Face-Space account, and it's like I'm right back there again. I can't believe how much I complained back then. I would trade the attitude and eye rolling for diapers and late night snuggles any day. Life was a lot easier when the girls didn't have an opinion on everything they wear—or what I wear."

Jon laughed and smiled at me. "Speaking of, you look great, by the way. There's definitely something different about you today."

"Oh yeah? It's not the neutral eyeshadow and lip gloss?"

He exhaled a chuckle. "No, not that, but it's a nice look for you. What I meant is that you don't seem so anxious. What happened after we said goodnight on text?"

"Well, I didn't go to bed right away."

"Whatever you did, it has worked wonders. You seem a lot

more peaceful, not so weighed down with some of the things we usually talk about."

I cringed, immediately seeing the angst ridden woman I'd been so for so long. Inhaling a cleansing breath, I thanked God He refused to let me remain that way. "Last night, the Lord held up a mirror. There were things I needed to change, and I finally had the eyes to see them. I guess you could say I had spiritual heart surgery. Not being *weighed down* would be the best way to describe it. The burdens and grievances I've been carrying have been so heavy."

He raised a questioning eyebrow. "Care to elaborate?"

"You probably think I'm talking about Rick, but the one that God really dealt with me about was Stephanie."

"Stephanie?" he repeated, shocked.

"Yeah, I've been so angry and upset about how she's hurt my girls—and even their father—but I didn't see my own ugly in that."

"What do you mean your own ugly? Privately, you've expressed some strong opinions about her, but you've never gone after her the way she's done to you. It's not a coincidence that people at Beth Shalom act like they don't even know you."

"You're right, Jon, but I'm not innocent, no matter how much I thought I was."

He cocked his head to the side and gestured for me to continue.

I took a deep breath, ready to bring my sin into the light and confess it to my brother in Christ. "Any time I heard a bad report about Stephanie or yet another cringey story, I took delight in it. Like it was revenge on Rick for how he treated me and later cheated on me. It was proof that Stephanie *wasn't* better than me—no matter what Rick claimed. This was about my own pride."

Jon held my gaze, studying me before he replied. "That's quite a revelation."

"I know. I'm pretty ashamed of myself."

He reached out to touch my hand. "I don't want you to beat yourself up, Charlotte. We both know Stephanie has gone out of her way to hurt your daughters and alienate them from their father. You were mad for good reason."

"You're right, and I'm not ignoring that. The problem is that I was so busy being 'right' that I didn't see how the *better* option would be Stephanie actually behaving like a good stepmother to my girls. I took satisfaction in her sin—not realizing I was actually happy my girls weren't being treated well. My blindness to that was such a punch to the gut. Yes, I was upset over how Stephanie hurt my daughters, but I also liked being right. My prayers weren't about what would be best for my daughters but about vindication and vengeance. I was angry and self righteous, and I never genuinely prayed for Stephanie's wellbeing or even Rick's. It was more like, 'May they reap everything they've sown' kind of prayers, and then reading a bunch of *Psalms* about judgment for the wicked."

"I see," he murmured. "So, are all of these revelations because Jesus says to love and pray for your enemies?"

"No, it's because all my hatred toward Stephanie and self righteousness in pointing out her mistakes is robbing my girls of a potential blessing. I have never prayed for God to actually *bless* Rick's marriage to Stephanie and make it healthy, or for that matter, for Him to bless Stephanie's relationship with the girls. I've prayed that for Rick before, but I've always viewed Stephanie as the enemy because that's how she's treated me since day one. I spread a lot of stories about her to people I knew would take my side. And while yes, they're true, what does it say about me that I relished humiliating and exposing her to ridicule from others?"

Jon blinked a few times before he muttered a simple, "Wow."

"Wow, what?"

"That's just really impressive."

I slid my hand away from his. "Impressive? Why? It's been so humiliating to see how blind I was to my own sin—and all while I believed I was so much better than her."

His eyes glowed. "It's impressive because you were willing to humble yourself and see your own flaws. It's impressive that you're not making excuses or trying to justify yourself—which you'd be well within your rights to do. Stephanie *has* been horrible to you and your girls. Even to Rick based on what happened last weekend."

"She absolutely has, you're right. The problem is how I've let all the bitterness build up into this giant landfill of offenses that continuously adds more garbage to the heap. Having to carry and constantly process all of that had me on a roller coaster ride to Crazy Town with stops in Depression Depot and the Valley of Overwhelming Defeat. I made myself her judge and jury, and I wanted God to play executioner."

Jon chuckled wryly. "That's one way to put it."

"Last night, the Lord set the options before me. I could either keep being 'right,' or I could finally be free. More than that, I saw I wasn't *right* at all. There were times I believed I loved my girls more than God does."

I shifted my gaze, shamed by that last confession. When I finally looked back up, I realized Jon's eyes never left my face. His dark gaze held compassion and understanding.

"I've struggled with that too," he said softly, "when He took Andrea and left me as a single father. Don't beat yourself up,

Charlotte. It's not something I'm proud of either, but you won't find any judgment from me."

I smiled at him gratefully. "I needed to hear that, thank you."

He smiled back. "So, is that everything, or is there more?"

"Well, like I said, God showed me how I had been more concerned with highlighting Rick and Stephanie's sins than in how it negatively impacts my girls. To see my hypocrisy in judging them—and how I'd even judged God—was an ice bucket to the face. It's been agonizing realizing how badly I've sinned and for how long. To realize how many hours my friends and family have been forced to listen to it. Ugh, it's so embarrassing! Jon, let me be the first to apologize for that."

He waved me off. "No apology needed. I completely understand, but I'm glad you were able to hash through all of this with the Lord. You're glowing right now."

I took his hands in mine as excitement surged through me at all God had done. "This is the freest I've felt since I was in my twenties. I'm not carrying that mountain of every wrong Stephanie or Rick have committed against me or the anxiety of what could be next. Would you believe I prayed for both of them last night, and I truly did pray for their good?"

His smile was one of joy and wonder. "As your friend and someone who has been walking with you through all of this pain, I don't have words for how happy I am for you. You never deserved what happened, and I've prayed for a long time that you would be free from the trauma. I'm in awe of what God has done, and I am one hundred percent rejoicing with you."

Tears stung my eyes at the affection and depth of feeling in his tone. "Thank you for coming today," I whispered.

He squeezed my hands and then released them. "I'm glad I'm here."

It was on the tip of my tongue to ask Jon if he wanted to go out for coffee afterwards, but the shuffling of musicians picking up their instruments captured our attention. A man I assumed was the pastor quieted the crowd and welcomed them to the church. I turned my focus toward the front and sent a quick prayer of thanksgiving that no matter what the service entailed, I had a friend there with me. To my surprise, the pastor didn't ramble on and flatter people for showing up. Harvey Lebow and his entourage had the ear tickling phrases scripted and read weekly by the service leaders. By contrast, this pastor kept his greetings short and invited the worship team to begin playing.

I expected the music to be unfamiliar but hoped I might recognize a song or two. I'd been away from Beth Shalom long enough and had visited plenty of non denominational churches that I'd begun to recognize some of the tunes from my contemporary Christian playlists. Even with the lackluster sermons I'd heard while trying out various churches, the music was usually impactful and well played. Grace Abounds, however, used slower tempo songs that sounded like modern hymns. They contained complex lyrics with choral melodies, and I enjoyed the sound of Jon's beautiful tenor voice harmonizing with them as he read the words off the projector screen. He caught my gaze in his periphery, winked at me, and then continued to sing.

With no drum or electric guitar, I did find myself wishing for a little more of the "oomph" I was used to, but the simple accompaniment forced me to focus on the lyrics rather than just connecting to a musical groove. The words struck deeply, speaking of the cross and the sacrifice of Jesus. In some churches, the gospel message felt like one of shame and an unpayable debt because we were nothing but worthless sinners. In others, the gospel was an ancillary point to the feel good, self help sermons and music designed to hype the crowd. Here, the message of the music had nothing to do with either tearing me down or building me up. In fact, it had nothing to do with *me* at all. It was a message of God's choice to lay down His life for me because He loved me.

As the worship continued, I slowly found the singing voice I'd kept hidden for years. Hearing words of God's unconditional love and acceptance permeated my heart and mind, finding their voice in my response to the music. Back at Beth Shalom, Rick had accused me of trying to draw attention to myself by ad libbing to the songs. For me, it was crying out to the Lord in my own voice along with the worship team. I savored the peace of God and the joy and freedom I felt singing to Him free from condemnation.

For the first time in nearly four years, I wondered if I had finally found a healthy spiritual home for me and my girls. With Jon Roseman beside me, hands raised in worship, it almost felt too good to be true.

CHAPTER 21

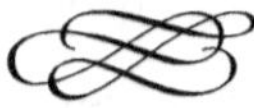

It wasn't until we were invited to sit down that I felt Jon's gaze on me. Turning, I saw admiration and wonder burning in his dark eyes.

"You never told me you could sing," he murmured.

"You never asked."

"You took my breath away."

I chuckled softly. "I wasn't doing it for you."

He grinned back. "I know."

The same pastor from earlier returned to the microphone with a few announcements and then dismissed the children to their classes. At Beth Shalom and other churches, this was also the time that an offering would have been taken. Normally, I'd hear them quote *Malachi 3:10-11* or *Proverbs 3:9-10* and talk about how God's blessing or curse would be on the people for their level of financial giving. While I agreed with the concept of tithes and offerings, the presentation often felt manipulative and shaming. I knew traditional Jews didn't "tithe," and I'd wondered for years if there was more to the Old Testament practice than the modern iteration.

Six months before I'd filed for divorce, Lauren posted a blistering article she'd found on the fallacy of modern "tithing" written by a Catholic priest. The article specifically called out the misused verses from *Malachi* as well as church hypocrisy in claiming to be "not under the law," yet still trying to enforce the Old Testament custom—and incorrectly at that.

Lauren supplemented the article with her own commentary, providing links to *Deuteronomy 14* as well as the entire book of *Malachi* rather than the usual cherry-picked verses. Reading the passages for myself had been eye opening. Thanks to the fear-mongering from the Beth Shalom pulpit, Rick acted superstitious about the entire process. He also ridiculed me for believing anything "the false prophet" had posted. His financial offerings to Beth Shalom resulted in public praise from the bima and private debt on our credit card. When I told my errant husband we needed that money for bills, he scolded my lack of faith in God to provide. He also called me greedy and materialistic, an accusation he would use time and again. Any attempts to show him directly in the Bible only earned me further belittling.

Despite the posturing from Rick, Nathan Fein, and others in the Beth Shalom inner circle, Lauren's article got the temple folks talking. Unfortunately, she paid dearly for it at home. Nathan took out his rage on both her and their three-year old, and she finally got the police involved. I had been proud of her for getting the guts to post the article, and even more proud of her for finally leaving her abusive husband.

The shakeup at Beth Shalom continued as it became clear Harvey Lebow's beloved tithing verses in *Malachi* were intentionally misapplied to the congregation. Read in context, the verses addressed the Levites withholding their priestly tithes to the Lord rather than the lay people refusing to bring offerings to the local storehouse. As synagogue members saw the differentiation between priestly tithes versus the tithes of the general populace, it became clear that God's plan for financial giving was actually *enjoying* that best ten percent of the crops two out of every three years. The storehouse tithe was brought to a literal foodbank in the third year, and from there, the best ten percent brought to Jerusalem by the priests as part of their own tithe to the Lord.

No matter the frequent guilt trips from the pulpit, Biblical tithing had nothing to do with keeping the lights on at Beth Shalom or expanding the community center. Tithes were also never meant to fund Harvey Lebow's pension plan or his IRS-approved "housing allowance" that provided granite kitchen counters and a refinished basement. Somehow, he justified needing that extra money on top of his six figure salary and an already paid-off mortgage. I'd asked my rabbi about it directly, and I received a grudging admission about the home improvements followed by a long-winded speech about the legalities of it.

It didn't change the stench of his behavior even if the IRS rubber stamped it.

Unfortunately, the stories of Beth Shalom financial abuse persisted. Members compared stories regarding the synagogue's hardline stance, and a disturbing picture emerged. Multiple families complained they had been threatened with membership revocation or removal from ministry because their donations had diminished—no matter the circumstances. Truly criminal were the vile phone calls made to people enduring financial hardship both before and after the pandemic. The Beth Shalom leadership had no qualms squeezing money from widows, single mothers, families with special needs children, and most reprehensible of all, members caring for relatives with terminal illnesses.

The financially less fortunate found other houses of worship, and no apologies or explanations were made for the mass exodus.

Drawn back to the present, I anchored myself to Jon's presence while ocean waves of conversation lapped around us. I would have been content to sit and simply take it all in, but families in the rows both behind and in front of us made it a point to introduce themselves and welcome us to the church.

Not surprisingly, they assumed Jon and I were a couple, but he had no problem explaining we were old friends. The pastor we'd seen earlier on the microphone also introduced himself, proving to be just as personable without the spotlight on him. A few minutes later, he returned his lectern to begin the sermon and quiet the crowd.

"What do we do when things don't work out the way we expect them to?" he asked the room at large. "What do we do when God brings us through suffering and grief, through injustice and pain? What do we do with our disappointment and unmet expectations?"

Jon's Adam's apple bobbed as a sheen of moisture covered his eyes.

The pastor continued, "We've been reading the book of *Ecclesiastes* for the past eight weeks, and today, we are going to dive further into chapter six. As I've said already, it's easy to view this book as incredibly pessimistic or even depressing, but the real message can be our deliverance from depression, anxiety, and worry."

I made a keening sound in my throat, desperate to hear more.

Reading from the Bible, he said, *"Whatever exists has already been named, and what humanity is has been known; no one can contend with someone who is stronger. The more the words, the less the meaning, and how does that profit anyone? For who knows what is good for a person in life, during the few and meaningless days they pass through like a shadow? Who can tell them what will happen under the sun after they are gone?"*

The crowd was silent, waiting for the answer.

"Verse ten echoes what we've read in chapter one that there is nothing new under the sun. Put simply, as much as we may think *our* circumstances are different, *our* trials are harder, *our* burdens are heavier, the reality is that someone somewhere has already experienced the same thing. Sometimes it's self pity and sometimes it's pride that tells us we're unique in our sufferings or in the trials we face."

Chuckling, he added, "Now, before anyone throws tomatoes at me or storms out, I want to make it clear that I'm not minimizing anyone's pain or whitewashing trauma. God forbid, I ever make it sound like our suffering isn't real or excruciating as we undergo it. What I *am* saying is that we can take some comfort in knowing that because there *is* nothing new under the sun, we also serve a God who's been handling our kinds of problems long before the days of even Solomon who wrote this. Our souls can find rest as we trust in who God is rather than limiting Him by our own fears and worries. He is more than able to equip and guide us through the twenty-first century version of Biblical problems."

I swallowed my own lump of emotion, silently acknowledging that I'd fully expected the pastor to come at those verses with a smug approach like Harvey Lebow and many others after him. Those places had no real level of interest or care for people beyond what they could provide in free labor and financial donations. Much like 7-Square Property Management, Beth Shalom and many other places I'd visited operated like soulless corporations with an easily replaceable workforce. All that mattered was maintaining the public image and keeping the boss's pockets full.

The pastor continued, "Let's take a look at verse eleven where it says we can't contend with someone stronger than us, and the more words, the less the meaning. I said these passages would help to alleviate some anxiety, so if you're ready for your next, tough-to-swallow pill for this morning, let's talk about the need to control our environment."

I caught Jon's eye in my periphery, and he wore the same look of trepidation. We both knew what Harvey Lebow would say.

"For those of you new to Grace Abounds, please know that we take the Word of God seriously. By that, I mean, we take what the Bible says in light of God's mercy toward us, not as ruthless judgment for every infraction. There is therefore no condemnation for those in Christ Jesus," he quoted from *Romans 8,* "and I'm up here to preach the word to encourage, to exhort, and to bring correction as needed. I see my own sins first before I ever deliver the messages to our church, and I would never suggest anything without first applying it to my own life, marriage, and children."

Jon met my gaze again, surprise evident on his face. My heart rate sped, wondering if after all this time, I might finally be in a house of worship that looked at the Scriptures to guide humans toward holiness rather than toward a self-serving agenda. As the sermon went on, the Lord peeled away layer after layer of trauma and expectation based on my experiences from Beth Shalom. With each note of comparison, I saw how oppressed I'd been as a member there, but also how I'd used defensiveness and a hardened heart to protect myself since I'd left. I wanted to automatically misjudge Grace Abounds rather than have my hopes crushed by one more house of worship turning out to be no better than the one I'd fled.

Focusing back on the sermon, the pastor said, "I came across a blog this week that really helped summarize our very human predicament. Whether it's from fear, pride, trauma, or a misguided belief we can manipulate others—even God—to do our bidding, the Bible is clear. Yes, all of us are free to make choices for our lives and bear the responsibility for those choices. What we are not free to do, however, is to dictate the consequences of our decisions."

He continued, "We mistakenly believe that if we just make all the 'right' decisions that life will be great, heartache free, and manageable. We get frustrated when people and circumstances don't align with our agenda. We get mad at God when we don't see the results we hoped for. I would challenge any of us struggling with that notion to remember that our faith won't grow if it's never tested. All we have to do is look at the heroes of the faith throughout Scripture to see that it rains on the just and unjust alike. The *Psalms* tell us that, 'The righteous suffers many evils, but the Lord rescues him from them all.' How can we say we need a Savior if there's nothing we need to be saved from?"

At the murmur from the crowd, he added, "If it's our own works, our own good choices that spare us from evil, then why would we need Jesus? The shift is subtle, but it can lead us to heartache or even questioning our faith in God if we don't stay grounded. We don't serve a genie, and we don't serve a pagan god. Sometimes, we forget how much we've been forgiven and that we choose to live for God because he died for us. The Bible calls it our 'reasonable service' for what He's saved us from. The problem is when we start believing God owes us something, as if our salvation wasn't already the greatest gift we could receive. Bitterness creeps in when we don't get the things we want. Entitlement says that obedience on our part necessitates God's obedience to what *we* want. If that's the case, then we're attempting to manipulate God by our good deeds rather than serving out of genuine gratitude to Jesus."

As the sermon concluded, the pastor referred to his earlier statement regarding *Ecclesiastes* as an ostensibly pessimistic book. However, the real message of Solomon's writing was to illustrate the underlying truth that our best course of action is trusting the Lord and having faith during the process. If we could recognize how little control we actually had over our children, our spouses, our family members, our coworkers, politicians, and on, we would stop wasting so much time and emotional energy trying to conform it all into our own version of what it should look like. He said if we trust that God is good and His plans are good, then we can find rest for our weary souls as we await resolution for our problems.

I sat in the chair following the sermon utterly in awe of what I'd experienced.

"You okay?" Jon asked.

"I wasn't expecting all that," I murmured. "Wow."

"Do you think you'll be back?"

I met his eyes as mine clouded over in tears. "Jon, I think I'm home."

CHAPTER 22

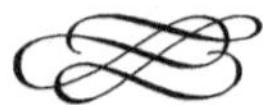

I picked up the girls following church, and I told them about my experiences both at Grace Abounds and also the night before in prayer. They took it all in, not saying much, but also not mocking or questioning what I told them. More than even my prayers for Stephanie and their father, they seemed utterly gobsmacked by my feelings about the church.

"I thought you hated all churches," Lily said as we sat at a patio table outside of Charred Cups. She sipped on a frothy coffee milkshake while I enjoyed my second cup of hot coffee for the day.

"I don't hate all churches," I argued. "We've just had a lot of negative experiences."

Sophie looked at me from beneath her eyebrows. "Mom, you hated every single place we tried. You always had something to complain about." She smirked and then took a sip of her iced strawberry concoction.

I cringed, realizing how my trauma had clouded my perception and made me too unguarded in sharing my opinions. My fixation on being "right" about Beth Shalom had created an entitlement to unleash every negative opinion about the churches we vetted—and my assessments had been merciless and snarky. For all of my complaints how Rick and Stephanie's Bible-thumping turned my girls off to religion, my own sour attitude had only reinforced their reticence. I sighed wearily, ashamed that my self righteousness had made me a hypocrite once again.

"I'm sorry I was so critical, girls. I was hurt by Beth Shalom and careless with my words. I wasn't in a good place, and I'm seeing how I let my pain and my triggers influence you."

"That place sucks, so why are you apologizing?" Sophie asked, tossing her dark hair over her shoulder. "It's not like we wanted to go to any of those other churches either."

I sat aggrieved, watching my daughter mimic my flippant attitude. "I just wish I had been a little more open minded is all I'm saying."

Lily shrugged. "It's okay, Mom. We know you're doing your best."

I smiled back at my biggest cheerleader. "Thanks, sweetie. Turns out that my 'best' still has plenty of room to grow."

"What about the Bible study that Rachel and her dad go to?" Sophie asked. "Is it as bad as Beth Shalom? Rachel says there are some people who used to go there, but not any of the jerks like Tina."

"Would you be interested in going?" I ventured. "I mean, I like Grace Abounds, but it's very different from what we're used to. Then again, that's not necessarily a bad thing."

"Just as long you won't get triggered by going," Lily said. "I don't want you to get hurt again, Mom."

"No, I've been once before, and it was fine. I had a lot on my mind the night I went, so I didn't pay as much attention as I should have. I'd like to give it another try."

Shocking me right down to my low-heeled boots, Sophie said, "Well, then let's try it out."

We arrived about fifteen minutes early for the study, this time hosted at the Margolins' house. The scene was partial bedlam with a plethora of children squawking from one of the bedrooms down the hall. I assumed Natalie Levine, Jared and Poppy's daughter, was wrangling the small children.

"Do you wanna stay with the adults or help out with the babies?" I murmured to my girls.

They exchanged a glance before looking back at me dubiously.

"Are we getting paid to babysit?" Sophie asked.

"No, you're doing it out of the kindness of your heart."

She rolled her eyes. "And our other choice is some boring Bible talk?"

"Why don't you try sounding less entitled right now? I already told you this won't be anything like Beth Shalom, so ease up, okay?"

"We're just nervous," Lily said. "Who else from Beth Shalom goes here? Soph, you said Rachel told you everyone was okay, right?"

I answered before my oldest could. "Jared Levine and his family go here, and you might remember Abigail Goldstein. Rachel is supposed to be here tonight, so that'll be someone your age that you know."

"Does that mean *Jon* will be here?" Sophie asked, her expression turning mischievous. "Maybe you'll have another late night conversation." She batted her lashes and puckered her lips with a loud kissing noise.

Any response besides nonchalance would only earn me

further interrogation, so I kept my face neutral. "Since he texted me twenty minutes ago that they're on their way, I would assume he'll be here tonight too."

Her satisfied smirk fell into a frown. "Oh."

"So again," I asked, "do you want to hang with the grownups and maybe learn something, or do you want to make a new friend with Natalie Levine and play with the cute kids? Natalie's a senior, and I think you would really like her."

"Which one is Rachel doing?" Lily asked.

"Rachel helps with the kids."

The girls communicated silently again before giving me the answer I suspected they would. They sauntered to the back bedroom and I soon heard them laughing along with Natalie. I hoped it would be the beginning of a beautiful friendship.

I kept to the periphery of the dining room as Lauren would be skipping the evening festivities to celebrate her parents' wedding anniversary with Grant. Surveying the scene, it looked like a Food Station fantasy buffet. The table boasted beautifully appointed charcuterie boards, cut vegetables, crackers, and various dips. A tower of red velvet cupcakes would be attacked by me soon enough.

"Hi there," Joe Trautweig, Carly's husband, greeted me as he entered the room.

"Hi," I replied with a small wave.

"Carly told me she ran into you a few weeks ago at Charred Cups."

I lifted an eyebrow. "Is that all she said?"

His green eyes sparkled. "She may have shared a few other things, but nothing that needs to be announced. I don't think I've formally introduced myself, but I'm Joe."

I shook his hand and smiled back. "Nice to meet you. I'm Charlotte, but you obviously already knew that."

"I'm glad you came back to join us. Carly mentioned you used to attend Beth Shalom. Were you there at the same time as Lauren and Jared?"

I nodded. "My ex still goes there along with his new wife."

Joe digested the information before replying. "That sounds like things would be pretty uncomfortable if you decided to go back."

I exhaled a mirthless laugh. "There will be demons throwing snowballs in the seventh circle before I ever step foot in that place again."

Carly caught the tail end of my comment as she arrived with a twin nestled on each hip. She giggled as she approached her husband. "See? I told you she's hilarious."

Joe smiled at his wife. Immediately, his daughter leaned toward him, arms outstretched, and he plucked her from Carly's side. He grinned and snuggled against the wispy blonde hairs at her temple. "Hi, Princess," he murmured.

His daughter, Ilana, sighed contentedly and wrapped her arms around Joe's neck. "I love you, Daddy."

Carly glowed as she watched her husband and her daughter, undoubtedly healing from childhood wounds each time she saw the cycle broken with her own family. Jealous for his mother's attention, her son, Shai, dug his face into Carly's ample bosom.

"That's enough," she cooed as she shifted him. "Mommy's right here, sweetheart."

When Shai began to fuss against her, Carly and Joe both excused themselves to handle their two-year-old twins.

"So, you made it," Jon said from just behind me.

His words skittered along the back of my neck, and I shivered.

"Hi," I said, turning to face him.

I saw the appreciation on Mr. Roseman's face, and I

wondered how long I could pretend I had no interest beyond friendship. Not that I picked the silver threaded, peasant top knowing it complimented my pale skin. Clearly, I'd chosen the blouse for *me* and not because I wanted Jon to look at me exactly like he was just then. I also hadn't chosen a raspberry shade of lipstick or shimmery eyeshadow just because I knew it flattered my complexion against the green blouse. No, I certainly hadn't planned my outfit with Jon Roseman in mind at all.

He took an unconscious step toward me, and I rubbed my hands up and down my arms.

"You cold?" he asked.

"Fine." I strained to make my smile look believable. "Did you guys just arrive?"

"A few minutes ago. I saw you talking to the Trautweigs, and I didn't want to interrupt. Rachel went to help Natalie with the kids."

"Oh good! Sophie and Lily are already back there."

Jon's smile widened. "I'm glad they came with you tonight."

"Nothing short of a miracle."

His eyes crinkled at the sides and I caught his gaze slide over me again. "That color looks amazing on you, by the way."

Refraining from the *Oh, this old thing?* humble brag, my shoulders squared a bit bolder with confidence.

"Thanks for noticing."

"It would be impossible not to, Charlotte, but I think you already knew that."

"Is that so?"

He laughed. "I don't think I've met another woman who understands color the way you do. You know what works and what doesn't, and I've never seen you look anything less than immaculately put together. It's impressive."

I gaped at his compliment, nearly reminding him of that one time he *had* seen me at less than perfect. Then again, reminding him of our lackluster kiss would remove that hungry look as if I was a red velvet cupcake he couldn't wait to devour. Blushing, I turned my gaze anywhere but his dark eyes.

"What? No quippy comeback?" he teased.

"You'd be blushing too if I looked at you the way you're looking at me right now."

"I doubt what I'd be doing is blushing." He lowered his voice and then lowered his gaze to my mouth.

I took a step backward as the passion and longing in my dreams began to feel too real. What if it was just another epic fail?

Before I could say anything, Ted Margolin called the Bible study to order from the next room.

Jon walked close beside me, nudging me with his shoulder. "Will I get to sit next to you twice in one day?"

I could only stare at the flirty iteration of Jon Roseman as if he and I had switched personalities. "What's gotten into you? You weren't acting like this at church this morning."

"What can I say? I'm just happy to see you." He gestured toward a loveseat that would have just enough room for the two of us. "Care to join me?"

"I'm going to sit over there," I replied, needing the physical space from him. I knew that sitting side by side on a cozy little sofa would keep me utterly distracted all night long. As it was, I already felt ready to leap out of my own skin.

"Suit yourself." He plopped down on the couch without a care in the world.

Not even my deliberately worn blouse could provide enough armor to withstand his flirtatious energy. I wasn't sure what to do with this alternate version of Jon or why he'd changed so much from the man who told a room full of strangers at Grace Abounds we were *just friends*. My thoughts turned morose as I wondered if he would just treat me like Andrea again if I finally gave in.

I frowned and flipped my Bible open in my lap. It wasn't until I heard his voice rise in a chuckle with an accompanying female that I dared to glance his way.

My stomach dropped as I beheld a thin blonde join him on the settee with a shy smile on her face. Quickly searching her left hand, I realized she was as single as her sofa mate. She seemed timid, but Jon didn't hesitate to share his Bible with her as the evening progressed. Once again robbed of my ability to focus, my internal anxiety proceeded to beat me up for bringing my girls to a function where I was now even more eager to flee.

After everyone had been dismissed to grab snacks, I caught the happy couple chatting in my periphery near the desserts. Those luscious red velvet cupcakes suddenly looked like lead balls as Jon offered one to his new bestie.

"Good. Thanks for saving me the calories," I muttered. "Guess we really are *just friends* after all. That didn't take long."

CHAPTER 23

I WENT OFF IN SEARCH OF MY GIRLS, SURE I'D FIND them overwhelmed or anxious to leave. I entered the kid playroom filled with children of all ages and sizes. Each family was represented from Margolin, Goldstein, Horner, Levine, and Trautweig. Carly had remained with the teen girls, consoling Shai who apparently couldn't stand to be parted from his mother.

My girls looked content as they watched an animated Veggie Tunes movie we'd kept on a constant loop when they were little. The new generation of children looked equally as enthralled with Barry the Tomato and Rob the Cucumber. Sophie and Lily both sat with a child in their laps and looked up at me as I entered the room.

"Ready to go?" I asked.

"Just a few more minutes?" Lily begged. She cuddled three-year-old Max Margolin close to her heart as the little boy had fallen asleep in her arms.

The sight was adorable, and there was no way I could say no

to my baby while she held onto another baby. It made me instantly flash forward to a time when she might hold her own child one day. Blinking back tears, I replied, "Sure."

Rachel Roseman was caught up in a building block masterpiece aided by high schooler Ryan Levine who helped wrangle the Goldstein and Horner boys. Meanwhile, head baby-sitter Natalie Levine was surrounded by the Margolin girls playing hairdresser with her long curls.

My firstborn sang along to the *Brenda Manatee* song with Ilana Trautweig in her lap. The cozy scene made me realize it would be my girls dragging me back to Bible study next week. Silently, I promised the Lord I would actually pay attention. Jon and his slender friend could plan their happily ever after together, and I could ask for safe travels on my singles cruise with my boss. There had to be at least one man on the ship with a chubby girl fetish.

Instead, the silver fox approached from behind and stood close enough to send goosebumps down my spine. He extended his arm in front of me with a red velvet cupcake in hand. Talking softly near my ear, he said, "I seem to recall this being your favorite flavor."

The low purr in his voice made my toes curl, and I buried my attraction behind a mantle of sarcasm. "I thought you were already sharing desserts with someone else tonight. I certainly don't need her leftovers."

"What are you talking about?"

I glared at him over my shoulder. "Don't play dumb."

"Who's playing at anything?"

"Certainly not me," I said coolly, turning my attention back to my girls.

Jon tugged on my shirt sleeve. "Why are you acting like this?"

"I'm not acting like anything."

"Now, who's playing dumb?" he shot back.

I spun around to give him my full attention. His eyebrows raised at my scowl. With Rick, I had gotten good at hiding my emotions. With Jon, I couldn't hide anything.

His teasing smirk disappeared. "What's wrong, Charlotte?"

"Nothing."

"No, something is obviously very wrong."

"Why would anything be wrong just because I don't want your stupid cupcake?"

His lips flattened. "Wanna try to tell me again how you're not mad?"

"So, I'm not allowed to have emotions you don't approve of? Okay, *Richard.*"

Jon's grip changed from a gentle pull on my sleeve to a firm grasp on my forearm. "We need to talk."

"Why bother? Is this really about some cupcake? Fine, I'll take it." I yanked my arm away and snatched the offending dessert. "Did your new friend not want to ruin her girlish figure? Mine was ruined a while ago anyway."

He raised an eyebrow. "You sound jealous. Is that what this is about?"

"Like I ever stood a chance."

"Charlotte," he said, drawing out the sound of my name. "Please, just talk to me."

Huffing, I pushed his hand away and gestured for him to join me in the hallway. At least I could endure my humiliation in private. I sat the cupcake down on a hall table and faced him.

"Why are you tormenting me?" I hissed. "What point do you need to prove?"

"Tormenting you?" he repeated in shock.

"Yes! One second you're acting all concerned and protective.

Then, we're just friends to everyone at church. You show up tonight acting like Don Juan, but then you get yourself a new plaything during Bible study and bring me her leftovers." I gestured to my formerly favorite flavor of cupcake mocking me from where it sat.

"Are you talking about Allie?"

"Allie?" I asked. "So that's her name? Did you get her number too?"

"I don't understand what the problem is. Why are you acting like this?"

I sniffled back tears and simply shook my head. Whatever feelings Jon pretended to have for me were either as shallow as a toddler swimming pool or easily transferred to a more receptive vessel. What other explanation could there be?

We stood in tense silence where I refused to answer his question or meet his eyes. Finally, he spoke up. "Allie's been to Bible study a few times. She's a friend of Lauren's. I'm surprised she's never mentioned it to you."

"Well, Lauren has a habit of trying to fix you up with her friends of hers," I said bitterly. "Since she knew I wasn't interested in you like that, she must have moved right down the list of eligible women. How kind of her to provide you with some matchmaking assistance."

He frowned. "You're being really unfair to a friend who absolutely adores you. That's not what happened at all."

"Oh really? How else do you explain what happened tonight? Have you always been a player, or was I just too blind to see it?"

"A player?" he choked. "Charlotte, what has gotten into you? This isn't like you at all."

"I could ask you the same thing. Was I even your first choice tonight, or were you just waiting for *Allie* to show up?"

He looked nonplussed. "I went to church this morning to see *you* and support *you*. I invited *you* to sit with me on the couch—which you declined, I might add."

Interrupting his next point, I exclaimed, "Exactly! And when you couldn't get what you wanted from me, you had a backup ready to go."

"Charlotte," he entreated. "You can't be serious."

The tilt of his head and disbelieving tone reminded me too much of Richard's gaslighting. I hardened my protective shell yet again. "Blondie was practically in your lap the whole night sharing your Bible, and she looks even younger than Sean. Did she tell you what she wants for Christmas and promise to be a good girl? Does she get a candy cane from one of your elves?"

He looked like he was holding back a laugh. "Are you sure you're not jealous?"

"I don't care whose chimney you visit, Mr. Roseman, just leave me out of it."

This time, he did exhale a chuckle at my choice of words. "For the record, I've never had a Christmas tree in my home, so I'm not about to start playing Santa Claus now."

I rolled my eyes. "You know what I mean. And I thought you said dating younger women made you feel like a creep. Was that a lie too? You don't want anyone to go out with me, but it's fine for you to cozy up to whomever you feel like, right?"

"Has Lauren told you anything about Allie? I think it might help clear up some assumptions. You do remember when you told me about the first syllable of that word, right? I'm surprised you can't see your own hypocrisy."

His insouciant tone made me want to slap him. Whatever peace and freedom I'd experienced the night before in prayer and that morning at Grace Abounds had evaporated.

"Do me a favor, and spare me the details of how you met your next wife and toyed with my emotions until you did."

Jon sobered immediately. "That's enough."

"Well, that's certainly one thing we can agree on. It's been *more* than enough, especially after this morning at church."

"Charlotte, would you just let me explain instead of jumping to conclusions?"

"Why don't you start by wiping that nasty little smile off your face every time I get upset? Is hurting me funny to you?"

"Of course not! Why would you ever think that?"

"Because of how you're acting."

"And how am I acting?"

"You're making fun of me!" My exasperation finally gave way, and my voice broke. "I'm just a big joke to you."

Jon stepped closer, a muscle clenching in his jaw. "You know that's not true."

"Oh yeah? Right now, I don't know who you are. Certainly, not the man who flattered me this morning at church and then moved on to greener pastures just a few hours later."

"Charlotte, I—" he reached a hand to touch my face, but I jerked away.

"Don't even think about it! In fact, don't call me, don't text me, and you can shove that cupcake and all your fake flirting right up—"

He muffled my final thought with a searing kiss. His hands cupped my face like a man who knew exactly what he wanted, and the press of his lips had nothing to do with Andrea Roseman or Allie-whoever.

This was a kiss just for me.

He hungrily sought my mouth in an embrace that refused to be satiated. Better than any speech, Jon's lips finally communicated what I needed to hear. The rasp of his beard and the scent of his cologne flooded my senses, and I grabbed fistfuls of his shirt collar.

There was no uncertainty in the possessive way Jon held me and erased every petulant accusation I'd thrown at him. He dropped one arm to wrap it around my waist and press us even closer together. If Jon Roseman had a point to prove, so did I. My hands released his shirt to dive into his thick hair, reveling in the silky feel against my fingers. His grip around me strengthened like iron.

Whether it lasted seconds or minutes, I was utterly lost. I had never been kissed so thoroughly in my life. At the approaching sound of adults coming to collect their children, he tugged me into a hallway bathroom and closed the door behind him.

"We can't!" I exclaimed. My arm flailed lamely in front of me as I fought to catch my breath. "Everyone will know—especially our daughters. My lipstick is all over you."

"Just shush for a second." He recaptured my cheeks in his palms and stared into my eyes. His chest heaved in heavy breaths, his pupils dilated. "I probably shouldn't have done that here or now, but I suppose it's better to ask for forgiveness than for permission."

"I never said you could kiss me."

His gaze darted toward my lips. "I kinda feel like you did. And I meant forgiveness from the Margolins."

"Oh."

"Also, I think you owe *me* an apology. There was a lot of ugly you just accused me of. None of which was true."

"You're right, I'm sorry," I murmured.

"Maybe because you've been in denial about how you feel about me?" he prodded.

I blushed. "I guess I didn't like seeing you with Allie."

"You *guess*? You accused me of being Santa Claus with shady intentions."

"Okay, fine, I didn't like it at all."

"You also owe me an apology for assuming I would just replace you with someone else. You've been pushing me away and acting like the feelings I have for you aren't genuine. I've prayed for a lot of patience and understanding, but that *did* hurt. You know me better than that."

Seeing my own blindness and temper tantrum through his eyes, I cringed in shame.

I tried to look away, but Jon tilted my chin back up to face him. "No more hiding, Charlotte."

"You're right, and I'm so sorry. I was wrong. I didn't realize how much. I guess, it was just that tone you took. Like you were making fun of me."

He looked contrite. "You're very funny even when you're angry, and I didn't clue in just how upset you were. It was kind of adorable, actually."

"It still hurt," I said quietly. "You don't know what it's like to have someone treat your feelings like a joke."

"I'm sorry," he replied immediately. "You're right. I won't do that again. I should have taken you seriously, and I'm sorry that I didn't."

I sniffled back tears. "Thanks."

"So, we're good?" he asked.

I nodded.

His eyes locked with mine, and I felt the pull as his mouth angled toward mine again. A keening sound resonated in my throat.

"But there is one thing I'm *not* apologizing for," he said close to my ear, "and that's kissing you. Because I'd do it all over again. And I think you would too."

CHAPTER 24

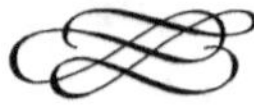

"Tell me it isn't true," he said, leaning back to stare into my eyes.

"I can't."

"You can't do what?"

"I can't tell you it isn't true. People write books about the kiss you just gave me. I was completely wrong about you and me."

His smile turned wolfish. "So, I guess you approved of this one?"

Not bothering with words. I pulled his face down and let my mouth answer a different way. Within seconds, he had me wrapped securely in his arms as he retook the lead in our passionate duel. Somewhere between his groans and my whimpers, I realized it wasn't Rick Williams who had ruined me for all other men—it was Jon Roseman and his very unbrotherly kisses. My steamy dreams couldn't touch the real life combustion between the two of us.

We parted, both of us panting, and he rested his forehead

against mine. "I know you're not Andrea," he said low. "I'm not thinking about anyone else."

"Message received," I exhaled.

He peeled our faces apart so he could meet my eyes as he made his next declaration. "My past is in the past. That was a different life. You are part of the life I want to have now. Can you finally believe me?"

I reached up to touch his face. I had to make sure I wasn't dreaming. I smiled as I noted the bright pink lipstick now staining his lips and around his mouth.

"You're a mess," I laughed.

"Still worth it." He leaned in for a soft kiss before pressing me close to him, my head resting against his chest. His heartbeat thundered against my ear. "I promise, there isn't anybody else, Charlotte. Do you believe me now?"

"I believe you," I whispered.

"So, are you ready to start this new adventure together?"

"Is that what we're calling it?"

"What else would you call it?"

"Better than anything I've ever dreamed," I blurted out.

He chuckled, and the sound rumbled beneath my ear. "You've been dreaming about this, Charlotte? I thought you wanted us to be just friends."

"I don't kiss my *just friends* like that."

"I should hope not!"

I giggled like one of my teenage daughters and laid my hand over his heart. "Is all of this really for me?"

His pulse quickened, and I had my answer. With his breath warm against my neck, he asked, "Do you need me to show you again? I never took you for a slow learner."

"I might need extra tutoring."

A sound of pure pleasure thrummed in his throat. "Then, I

guess we better start right away. You're going to have to commit several nights a week."

"Of course! I don't want to fail this class."

"I promise to devote as much time as you need. Hours and hours and *hours*," he added with a suggestive lilt.

I exhaled a laugh, feeling like I might just float out of the room.

Instead, a loud knock on the bathroom door sent both of us crashing down to earth. Jon pushed me behind him to shield me from whoever had interrupted our high school worthy make out session.

"Hey! Is someone in there?" Natalie Levine called. "I've got a kid who's gonna be sick."

"Just a second," I yelped. Gesturing frantically, I motioned for Jon to hide behind the opaque shower curtain while I struggled to concoct a valid reason for my lipstick being so obscenely smeared. I flushed the commode and then grabbed some toilet paper to wet it against my swollen mouth.

"Just stay in there!" I hissed to Jon. "You can't come out the same time I do."

"Am I supposed to just wait in the shower while some kid does their business?"

"Your girls were little once. It's fine."

"I feel like this could be illegal."

"You'll feel a lot worse if anybody sees your face right now. I'll meet you at the food table in ten minutes."

While the shower curtain rustled shut, I opened the bathroom door with what felt like the most obvious, caught-in-the-act smile ever.

"Hi!" I said brightly.

Natalie's eyes widened along with those of seven-year-old Eva Margolin. "Um, Mrs. Williams, are you okay?" Her eyes lingered too long on my ruined lipstick, and I turned away, feigning interest in the soap dispenser.

"Just peachy," I lied. "I hope everything is okay with your little friend."

"My tummy hurts," Eva moaned.

"Oh, I'm so sorry, sweetie, let me just get out of—"

With perfectly directed aim, the little cherub upended whatever had upset her stomach all over my pants and shoes.

"Oh!" Natalie shrieked. "I'll get her mom and dad." She rushed from the space, yelling for Rebecca and Ted.

"Run. Now!" I barked at the shower curtain.

Jon popped out, and Eva screamed before she let loose another round of tummy trouble. Like a master painter, she covered any previous spots she'd missed on my clothing or the floor.

"Face it, we're not getting out of this alive," Jon laughed. He grabbed a bath towel and handed it to me. Hunching down in front of Eva, he said, "Hey, sweetheart, I'm sorry I scared you. Can you walk with me to the potty?"

She eyed him dubiously, specifically the fuchsia lipstick decorating his mouth. Her eyes narrowed as she swung her gaze to my own lips painted the same hue.

"Here, I've got you," I said, jumping in between Jon and Eva. I scooped up the little girl toward the toilet and ignored the sickness dripping on both of us. "Jon, why don't you wash up while I take care of Little Miss?"

He took in my soiled appearance with palpable shock, but then he caught my meaning. He rubbed at his mouth with handfuls of soapy water while Eva wretched again. I kept her curls off her face while she finally hit payload in the commode rather than covering any more of me or the bathroom. The sound of her distressed parents wasn't far behind.

"Sweetie, what hap—?" Rebecca Margolin skidded to a stop as she took in the sight of Jon at the sink while I stood next to vomiting Eva. My all-day lipstick wasn't going anywhere from Jon's face without makeup remover, and I knew we both looked guilty as sin. I tossed Rebecca another towel which she promptly used to cover the mess at the doorway.

"There's some baby wipes in Max's room," she said to my *just friend*. "It'll help with the um..." she gestured toward her mouth, and Jon took her meaning. He sent me an apologetic look before scurrying off.

"Mommy!" Eva wailed.

I shifted backward so Rebecca could comfort her daughter.

"The shower head is detachable," she said to me. "You can hose off your pants in there. If you need to borrow a pair to get home, I'm sure I have something that will fit. We're probably close to the same size."

I kept the self-deprecating commentary to myself, thankful for her discretion. I'd worry about my pants later. In the meantime, I removed my shoes and took up Jon's hiding place.

With the shower head blast-cleaning my pants, I only heard the muffled sounds of Rebecca talking to her husband as he entered the bathroom. The shower curtain pulled back further, and Ted Margolin eyed me hosing off my fully-clothed ankles and feet. "What happened before my daughter decided to decorate you with her dinner?"

"What do you mean?"

"I passed Jon Roseman in the hallway. I don't recall him wearing that particular shade of lipstick when he disappeared a little while ago."

Wide-eyed, I whispered, "I'm so sorry."

"I'm Ted, by the way. I don't think we've officially met."

I cringed further, utterly humiliated. "I'm probably never

going to darken the doorway of your home again, so no worries."

"Your, er... *friend* looked rather pleased with himself, so as long as you guys can save it for before or after the study, we'd be more than happy to have you join us again. Jon's been a great addition to our group. Seeing how fond he is of you, I'm sure you will be as well."

"Why are you being so gracious about this?"

His gaze drifted over my slacks decimated from the knees down. "It's the least I can do after Eva ruined your outfit. We can run your clothes in the dryer if you want and let you borrow something in the meantime."

"I offered already," Rebecca called over her shoulder. She had her daughter perched on the bathroom counter as she rinsed off her legs and feet in the sink. "Charlotte, do you want to borrow a pair of pajama pants?"

I turned off the shower and began squeezing the water from my rinsed bottoms. "I appreciate the offer, but I'd doubt they'd fit."

"They're my pregnancy sweats. They'd fit an elephant, and you are far from that, my friend."

"Debatable," I muttered.

She pulled a face. "I hope you don't really mean that."

I sighed. "Sorry, I do appreciate the offer and for being so understanding about this debacle. I promise, it will never happen again."

With perfect comedic timing, Jon reappeared in the doorway. "Oh, I have no doubt it will happen, just not quite like this."

The Margolins shared a surprised laugh. Meanwhile, Jon sent me a smoldering look I felt all the way to my soaking wet socks.

Much to my surprise, Rebecca's maternity pajamas fit

comfortably, so much so she said I could keep them. My daughters were dumbfounded by my new apparel, asking too many questions I wasn't ready to answer—like why my hair was so messy, why I was flushed, and how my normally perfect lipstick got so smudged. Thankfully, they didn't see Jon with pink lips that not even the baby wipes could fully unstain.

We arrived back home with my defiled dress pants crumpled in a grocery bag. Pulling back the double doors in our kitchen concealing our washer and dryer, I dumped my clothes into the washing machine along with some other towels waiting to be laundered.

"You gonna tell us what happened?" Sophie asked, munching on a red velvet cupcake.

"Where did you find that?" I asked. "I thought they cleaned up all the food by the time I got you girls to leave."

"It was sitting on a table in the hallway. So random." She munched another eager bite. "What were you doing in the bathroom for so long anyway?"

"Eva Margolin got food poisoning, and she puked all over the bathroom and me. I had to hose off my pants." Hoping that ended the conversation, I dumped in laundry detergent and started the wash.

"Before that," Lily asked. "You and Mr. Roseman left the room, and then it must have been at least twenty minutes before Natalie took Eva to the bathroom. I didn't see him after you guys left."

"Oh, maybe he wasn't feeling well either."

My girls eyed me like they both knew I was lying. I had never been very good at it.

"Mom," Sophie said, eyeing me critically, "what happened to your lipstick?"

"What do you mean?" I pretended to straighten up all the laundry supplies on the shelves above the machines.

Kitchen chairs scraped across the floor, and I knew my girls weren't far behind. They flanked me on either side.

"Mom," Sophie began again, "what happened with Mr. Roseman?"

As the girls proceeded to stare into my soul, memories of the best kiss in recorded history caused a blush I knew I couldn't hide.

"Did you guys—?" Sophie sputtered.

"Yes, we did, okay? You got a problem with that?"

Lily looked horrified while my oldest seemed very satisfied with herself.

"About time," she muttered. "You have no idea how long I've been shipping this."

Lily's reaction was almost comedic. "Weren't you supposed to be learning about God instead of kissing Mr. Roseman? Mo-om! Ew! That's so cringe!"

I avoided their prying eyes and tried for an indifferent tone. "The kiss happened afterward. I didn't go to Bible study to make out with Mr. Roseman."

"Wait, you *made out* with him?" Sophie gasped.

Ripping off the bandage, I said, "Yep. Sure did."

"Was it good?"

I chuckled as she clasped her hands over her heart like it was a live action romcom. "It was more than good, sweetie, but it shouldn't have happened at the Margolins' house. That part was wrong. I already promised Ted and Rebecca we won't do that again."

"So what, you just couldn't control yourselves?" she persisted. "Was it like a movie kiss? PG-13 or rated R?"

"Ay yo!" Lily exclaimed. "That's sus! I don't want to hear this!"

I burst out laughing at the dramatics usually shown by her older sister. "No, it wasn't *sus*, Lil. I don't think you've even used that word since middle school."

"Still sus," she insisted, crossing her arms over her chest.

The looks on my daughters' faces could not have been more polar opposite of one another—just like their personalities. Sobering my expression, I said, "Look, it definitely shouldn't have happened at Bible study, but I won't tell you I'm sorry that I kissed Mr. Roseman. I'm not sorry at all."

CHAPTER 25

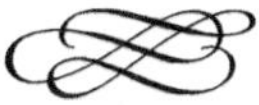

"Honey, it was the *best* kiss I've ever had in my life."

"Including Dad?" Lily asked.

No matter the pain both girls had from their father, I also knew that rejecting Rick meant rejecting half of their DNA. Choosing my words more carefully this time, I replied, "The time with your father was a different part of my life. Jon was the best kiss I've had since I've gotten divorced."

Sophie leaned in to give me a hug. "Then, I'm happy for you, Mom. You deserve this."

I greedily held on to my firstborn. Hugs were still commonplace between me and my girls, just not as frequent with our busy lives. She kissed my cheek and smiled at me. "I like how you smile every time you say his name. It's cute."

I blushed, not even aware of it. "Thanks, baby."

Sophie turned and whipped out her phone as she thundered upstairs. I assumed it was to text her BFF and compare my story with whatever version Rachel got from her father regarding his berry stained lips and mustache.

Lily remained in the kitchen with me, but she looked pensive and sad.

"What's wrong, beautiful?"

She sniffled back tears. "It's really over, isn't it?"

"What is?"

"You and Dad getting back together."

Stunned, I replied, "Honey, that was never going to happen—even if he divorced Stephanie and said he wanted to be married again."

"Oh."

"Weren't you just telling me last week about how you never want to go to his house again? I don't understand where all of this is coming from. Your sister seems happy about me and Jon."

"She likes all of that mushy romance stuff."

"And you don't?"

"I guess...I don't know," she said, cutting herself off.

I put an arm around her shoulders. "What's wrong?"

"I just thought that maybe you and Dad could work things out, and we could be a real family again."

My heart broke at the wistful, little girl sound of her voice. "You've never said anything like that before, sweetie. You and your sister begged me to divorce your father for a long time. Do you remember that?"

"No, I just knew you were really unhappy."

"Are you saying you were okay with him?" I asked skeptically. "Even after what happened with your sister?"

She shrugged. "Sophie argues with Dad about everything. As long as I don't talk too much, things are fine. He likes to talk more anyway. It's not a big deal."

The heartbreaking confession of her words, of what she didn't yet have eyes to see, tore at my soul. My precious girl deserved so much more than walking on eggshells and dimming her light just to receive bare minimum treatment.

I paused, realizing my response to Lily's admission was far different than it would have been a week earlier. Replacing my usual outrage and acrimony was an overwhelming grief instead. I saw Lily's pain as uniquely her own rather than filtering it through the self righteous need to deem myself the "better parent." The situation had nothing to do with me and my feud with her father.

"I'm sorry, sweetheart. I wish things could be different than what they are, but we've all made choices we can't take back."

"Are you sure?" she asked, her brown eyes pleading with me.

I gave her a sympathetic smile. "I'm sure, baby. I don't think your dad will be getting another divorce."

"I wish he would!" she exclaimed with uncharacteristic emotion. "He was never like this when you guys were married."

I didn't want to argue the point or relate details of her father's abusive behavior behind closed doors. Instead, I let my introvert share her feelings, commended her for doing so, and then assured her I'd take everything to the Lord in prayer.

Lily went upstairs, and I puttered around on my phone to emotionally decompress from the evening. By the time I made it upstairs, the girls were both asleep, probably worn out from their adventures in babysitting. I handled my bedtime routine and crawled into bed. Not two seconds after I'd set my phone aside for the night, it buzzed with a text message from Jon.

I've already gotten the third degree from Rachel, he wrote. *She enlisted her sister for reinforcements. How are you holding up over there?*

I chuckled as I replied. *More surprised than anything else.*

His response was immediate. *Surprised, how?*

Sophie is treating this like one of her Regency era romances.

Jon sent back a winking emoji. *That sounds about right. What about your baby girl?*

She's taking it much harder than I expected.

My phone rang a moment later. "Sorry, I just wanted to hear your voice," he said in a rush. "I'll probably go to bed dreaming about it. Well, that and other incredible things you do with your lips."

I audibly gasped, properly scandalized, flattered, and blushing.

"Are you still there?" he laughed.

I cleared my throat. "You caught me off guard, Mr. Sassy Pants. Usually, I'm the one making the outrageous comments."

"I know," he responded gleefully. "You've been a good influence."

My blush deepened. "Do you really mean that?"

"Of course! I like who I am when I'm around you."

"I'm not so sure I feel the same."

His mirth died instantly. "What do you mean?"

"I get all insecure…and jealous. And scared," I tacked on.

"Scared of *me*?"

"Kind of."

"Charlotte, why are you scared of me? I would never want to hurt you."

I exhaled a heavy sigh, searching for the courage to say what needed to be said.

Concerned, he asked, "You believe me, don't you?"

"I'm scared you'll wake up and see the 'real me,' aka a broken, struggling mess and either run off scared or realize that you can do so much better."

When he didn't immediately respond, my stomach dropped.

Swallowing back tears, I quickly added, "Look, I know you're not Rick or a monster like him. That's not what I meant. You were really supportive the night everything hit the fan with him and Stephanie, and I will never forget how you encouraged me."

"So, why are you scared of me?" he asked quietly.

"I've spent my entire life being *too much* for everyone. That was Tina's excuse when her personality completely changed after we moved in. She went from calling me her best friend to treating me like some ungrateful burden in a matter of weeks. I'm scared I'll eventually be too much for you too."

Jon surprised me when emotion choked his voice as well. "Do you see yourself the way Rick does?"

I did a double take. My gut reaction was to deny it, but I wondered if Jon saw something I couldn't. "What do you mean?"

"You said you're scared I'll see you the way Rick does, but you also said you don't believe I *am* like Rick. I think there's a part of you that believes the way he sees is the way you actually are—which is why you fight so hard to prove him wrong. You're at war with yourself, and it has more to do with Rick's opinion of you than being afraid of mine."

"You're right," I moaned, thoroughly exposed and humiliated. "What do I have to offer you besides dealing with trauma you didn't create?"

I heard the smile in his voice. "You have many wonderful things to offer, and it's why I haven't given up on you or a future with you."

"But why isn't it too much?" I demanded through my tears. "Why aren't you scared of me or the work it's going to take? You were so happy with Andrea, Jon. You guys made marriage look easy. Honestly, I was jealous of you two."

"I didn't know that," he murmured.

"And the way you revered her memory for so long..." my

voice trailed off as a montage of memories flooded my mind. "You have no idea how I longed for just a drop of that kind of love or devotion from Rick. All I got for my efforts were heartache and rejection."

"Why are you telling me all of this?"

"Because I can't comprehend how a man who adored his first wife the way you did could possibly feel that way about *me* —the person Rick Williams treated like utter trash. I can't make it make sense."

"Ah," he said slowly. "Well, if you're open to hearing it, I think I can shed some light on the situation."

"Okay," I mumbled.

"First, let's be clear that your ex-husband does not hold the gold standard by which you should measure your self worth. I know you would never suggest your girls do that."

"Of course not."

"Good. That being said, you also had a very different type of relationship with Rick than they do. He was your husband and knew you intimately. He knew how to hurt you better than anyone."

"Yes," I whispered.

"So, you need to remember that the same man who lies to your daughters about who *they* are is the same man who lied to you for fifteen years about who *you* are. We both know he's lying about Stephanie too. There's no truth in that man at all."

"You're right, Jon. You're absolutely right."

"The problem is all the lies have become ingrained in your mind. You're going to have to dig them out. The good news in all this is how you're actively struggling to do just that."

"Why is that good news instead of a pathetic show of how messed up I am? How do I not know better by now?"

Warm and smooth like honey, he said, "You're a fighter,

Charlotte. No matter how beat down, how angry, or how defeated you feel, there's still that part of you that will get back up and fight because that's just who you are. That's the woman I kissed tonight. Even though you seemed convinced I could somehow replace you, you still fought for your own worth. Rick's lies are there, but you're fighting to be free. You should be commended for the work you're doing to heal and realize your incredible value. The only thing that's been *too much* are the lies and burdens put on your shoulders by people who needed to deal with their own demons instead."

"Are you sure?"

I could hear the tears in his voice. "Yes, my love."

"Your *what*?" I breathed.

"We'll get to that later," he said gruffly. "I just want you to see that your struggle is because you're *healing*, not because you're stuck."

"What about all the horrible things I said to you earlier tonight?"

"I thought I made my feelings for you pretty clear."

I pulled a face. "But I still said them, Jon."

"You did," he conceded, "but given what you thought was happening, I can understand why you were hurt and confused."

"I assumed the worst about you."

"You also assumed the worst about yourself. Trust me, I don't think I'm 'settling' for you, Charlotte."

"But Allie is thin, and young, and—"

"And she's not you," he cut me off. "She's not curvy, hilarious, fearless, and looks into my soul every time I have the privilege of staring into her eyes. I don't know any other woman with such lovely, discerning eyes the color of icicles in the moonlight."

Unable to help myself, I asked, "Did you just come up with that?"

"Actually no," he laughed. "I've been hanging onto it for a while. Too corny?"

"Not at all! No one has ever complimented me that way."

"This is just the first of many. It's time you see yourself the way you are, and I'm gladly volunteering for the job. Unlike some other people in this world, I know better than to throw away a diamond."

CHAPTER 26

"WHAT HAPPENED TO YOU THIS WEEKEND?" Ro took a sip of tea from a Parkview Ranger travel mug. Barely five minutes into the new work week, my office manager was ready for her *other* Monday morning tea.

"When did you suddenly become a fan of baseball?"

She shrugged. "When I started dating the Production Manager from Hillcrest Custom Furniture. He kept coming by our booth at the Woodworking Fair pretending he needed help with his edgebander machine. Apparently, he also wanted my number."

I smirked. "Does that mean you're not going on the singles cruise either?"

"Ha, I knew it!" she exclaimed.

"You knew what?"

"Something happened between you and the silver fox, didn't it?" She searched my face for any telltale signs.

"Why do you assume every bit of news in my life involves a man?"

Luke barreled through the front door as I posed my rhetorical question. Shaking his ginger man-bun still damp from a post-workout shower, he said, "Don't start the Monday Dating Disasters without me! I need my coffee first."

I rolled my eyes. "Didn't we have a discussion about boundaries last week?"

He threw his lunch into the fridge and filled a paper cup from the office coffee carafe. Gesturing with his free hand he said, "Okay, I'm ready. What's going on with your silver fox friend who I absolutely did not stalk on social media and who Paisley absolutely did not say is giving total Daddy vibes?"

"You stalked him?" I gaped.

He smiled shamelessly. "Yep, this weekend. I gotta protect my friends, don't I?"

Both touched and horrified, I shook my head. "You guys are awful."

Ro grinned and took another sip of tea. "You're stalling, Williams. Spill it."

I tapped my chin for dramatic effect. "I don't know how much I want to share. I mean, this is all pretty personal."

"Personal?" my coworkers repeated in unison.

"You know I don't just kiss and tell." I swiveled in my chair and waited expectantly for the outcry.

"Oh, you totally kiss and tell, you liar!" Ro shouted. "That's always our favorite part!"

I chuckled and sipped from my own coffee cup.

"Did Daddy finally figure out what he was doing?" Luke crooned.

"Ew, don't call him that! I get it's a Gen Z thing, but it's still weird. I will never call that man 'Daddy' unless it's in reference to one of his daughters."

Rosaria rolled her eyes at Luke. "Your generation has issues."

"Like yours doesn't."

"Anyways," I said, clearing my throat, "yes, we did kiss. Yes, it was a toe curling, roll your eyes in the back of your head, choir of angels singing from heaven type of a kiss, and hopefully, not the last one."

Luke squealed louder than Ro, and she nearly spit out her tea.

Chuckling at the sight, I added, "Also, I prayed to release the anger and bitterness I've had against Stephanie, and I think I have a possible church home for me and the girls."

"Hold up! A who, a what, and a *why*?" my office manager squeaked.

I re-crossed my jean clad legs with an extra measure of sass. "Yeah, it was a pretty eventful weekend."

"How on earth did any of that happen?" Luke said, mouth agape. "Stephanie is evil incarnate."

I cringed at his description, convicted by how mercilessly I'd painted her. "She's not evil incarnate. A lot of what she does is evil—and I'm not discounting that. What I didn't see, unfortunately, was my own hypocrisy."

"Explain," Ro said, motioning with her hand, "because this I've gotta hear."

"I judged Stephanie for tearing me down to elevate herself. This weekend, I realized I do the same thing, and I'm not any better."

"I disagree. You *are* objectively better," she retorted.

"Am I, though? I was devastated by Rick's betrayal and the cruel things he's said since our divorce. I wanted to prove I'm better than her. It was about validating my wounded ego and pride."

Luke rubbed his goatee, his brow furrowed. "Honestly, that sounds like Rick using both of you like puppets. He pits all of you against each other to take the focus off what a total loser he is."

"I never thought of it that way," I murmured.

"He wants to be the bone caught in between two dogs fighting over him."

"Hey!" Ro objected.

He waved her off. "I didn't mean it like that. I'm just saying that Stephanie's extra-ness might be Rick's fault."

"How is that even possible?" I asked. "She was no saint before they were married. You can ask her old divorce attorney or her ex-husband."

"Think about it," Ro said, jumping onto Luke's train of thought. "Rick manipulated your insecurities. He convinced you all of his faults and failures were somehow *your* fault for not being good enough. Do you think the leopard suddenly changed his spots? That he's not manipulating Stephanie the same way?"

"Why would he do that?" I asked. "He talks up Stephanie like she's a thousand times better than me. She's alienated him from our girls, but he always blames me for that. Why would he intentionally provoke his wife in ways that hurt their marriage or makes his relationship with our daughters even worse? That would be *Rick* creating the situation he's constantly complaining about."

As the words slipped from my mouth, I saw the unhappy truth. Despite his woebegone persona, Rick Williams was no more the pitiful victim of Stephanie Burgess than he was of my own anger toward him.

"Wow," I said, tears stinging my eyes. "Just wow."

"What's wrong?" Ro asked.

"He's so sick!" I spat. "Evil!"

"Whoa, what happened?" Luke asked.

I sifted through memories of Rick's despicable treatment of the girls and me. Analyzing his deranged phone call following his fight with Stephanie, I realized I had put the blame on entirely the wrong person.

"This is all Rick," I said. "He's antagonizing Stephanie exactly like he did to me. She doesn't have the self control to behave like an adult, and I have no doubt he's deliberately driving her crazy. Same tactics, different wife. He makes it look like she rules the roost so he can keep the whiny victim role. He'll even get the backing of Beth Shalom to tell Stephanie she needs to submit to her godly authority."

Ro's eyes widened behind her burgundy framed glasses. They matched perfectly with her Rangers travel mug. "So, he lets Wife Number Two be the bad guy while Wife Number One runs around in circles trying to figure out what he sees in the cheap replacement."

"Unreal," I muttered. "I knew there was no way he could be happy when Stephanie is literally everything he ever said he hated about me—other than not being as heavy."

"You're not that heavy," Ro said, "and you know how to dress your body. Right, Luke?"

He held up his hands in surrender. "I respectfully refuse to answer the question."

I chuckled softly. "It's fine, I get what you're saying."

"Has Rick *ever* cared about your kids being collateral damage?" Ro asked. "To Stephanie, he can just blame the girls for their reaction to her antics. To the girls, he does that 'oneness' garbage so they blame Stephanie for him being a jerk. They come home upset, and now you're mad too. As long as you're blaming Stephanie, the girls blame Stephanie, and

Stephanie blames the three of you, guess who's *not* being blamed for creating all the chaos and strife?"

Luke's mouth formed a large "oh" shape before his eyes narrowed. Forgetting he was in the presence of two women old enough to be his mother, Ginger Viking unleashed a diatribe of four letter nouns, verbs, and adjectives straight from a loading dock.

"And to think I actually felt sorry for him," I said tearfully. "Even after everything he's put me through. I'm an idiot!"

"You were an emotionally battered wife," Ro countered. "You're also one of the biggest hearted people I know."

"But how could I let him manipulate me like that? How could I have fallen for it?"

Ro leaned over and pulled me into a hug. "That man is a snake, and he's your real enemy more than Stephanie Bougie ever was. She believes she's your enemy because of all the lies Rick has told her and the emotional abuse he's probably doing to her too."

"But what about their fight?" I sniffled and wiped the tears from my cheeks. "I heard the stuff she said to him, guys. It was cruel."

"What kind of stuff was he saying back?" Luke replied.

"I couldn't hear it. All I got was Stephanie sounding like a lunatic."

"But you know Rick," Ro said. "When you guys fought, did he scream at you, or did he calmly hit you with low blows designed to make you lose your ever loving mind?"

"The latter," I said immediately. "He was so good at pretending to be completely calm. Oh man, now I see why God had me pray for her."

"Why?"

"Because she needs to be free from Rick's lies even more

than I did. Stephanie is already unstable, and Rick is standing there with kerosene and a match waiting for her to light herself on fire."

Luke raised two ginger eyebrows. "To do what?"

"To prove that he can. Because he thinks it's fun to poke and poke at you until you finally lose your composure. Then, he clutches the pearls and points to your reaction instead of how he pushed you to the edge. My brother Abe used to do that when we were in elementary school, and my mother always bought it. I remember his sick little smile when he'd do it. Honestly, I don't think all that much has changed for Abe. I just stopped tolerating it in my life."

Ro sipped her tea while I continued to spill mine. "So, now what?" she asked. "You gonna say something to Stephanie?"

I shook my head. "No, I have to show her different."

"Why, so that she knows you're not the she-devil Rick pretends you are?" Luke asked.

"No, it has nothing to do with proving myself anymore. Rick parades Stephanie at Beth Shalom pretending they're both something they're not. That congregation isn't healthy, and whatever her actual relationship with Jesus looks like, Stephanie won't find any real accountability for herself or Rick there. All they care about are Rick's tithing checks and keeping him happy so he signs them."

"So, what are you going to do?" Ro asked again.

"I'm going to talk to my girls about Stephanie in a very different light."

"How will you do that without implicating their father?"

"I have no idea. I need to pray about that and figure out a strategy. I have unwittingly fed into Rick's sick game by trashing Stephanie and letting my girls do the same."

"Hey," Luke interjected, "don't blame yourself for that.

Stephanie has said and done some unbelievably cruel things, and the girls are right to be hurt by it. Even if Rick is manipulating things behind the scenes, she still chooses to act that way toward two innocent kids. It's not her fault her husband is a dirtbag manipulating her insecurities, but it *is* her fault for taking it out on his children."

"What a mess," I sighed. "Truly, what a disgusting mess."

Ro placed a hand on my shoulder. "I know you'll figure this out. I'm already amazed by the changes I can see from Friday to today. Whatever it is that you're doing, keep doing it."

Taking her advice to heart, I cried out to Jesus for help. I didn't have the power to set anybody free, open blind eyes, or speak to souls that had been hardened by trauma and lies. I just knew that if God could change my own heart literally overnight, the seemingly impossible task of my girls having a healthy relationship with their stepmother wasn't too hard for Him.

My prayers for Rick weren't nearly so charitable, and I knew I had some heavy duty healing in front of me.

CHAPTER 27

Jon and I sat in facing leather chairs as we savored some Charred Cups coffee. Though I generally abstained from caffeine so late in the day, any excuse to meet up with my former *just friend* who also happened to be the best kisser in recorded history felt like a win. Since I was missing dinner with my babies, I had Indian food delivered to the house and asked the girls to save me some *manchurian gobi*. Sophie assumed I wanted extra kissing time with Jon, and that seemed like a better reason to give her than needing his emotional support. Either way, the magical lips of Jon Roseman would be involved.

"That was quite a revelation you had today," he said, following my summation of events. "It all makes sense, even if it's an emotional crime scene." He took a large gulp of coffee. "I want you to know I completely believe you."

"So, I don't sound crazy or paranoid for believing the worst about Rick?"

Jon shook his head. "Honestly, the only part I'm struggling

with is how he could juggle so many moving parts. How did he keep his stories straight and remember which version he told to which person?"

"That part I can answer. It's not so much about Rick's ability to lie but his ability to manipulate people, women specifically."

"Manipulate women? What do you mean?"

"Believe it or not, Rick is pretty perceptive and has a high emotional IQ. Unfortunately, he's also narcissistic, so using people, hurting people, or even deriving pleasure from his petty little revenges are the norm. Our children are not excluded from this."

Jon's eyes widened. "Do you think he enjoys hurting your girls?"

"I think he enjoys punishing them because he can't control how they perceive him anymore. Having the power to create negative consequences or instigate an emotional reaction helps him assume that 'control' he needs to have. He's also lazy and entitled, so if the girls say or do something that inconveniences him, Rick will retaliate for that too."

"Retaliate for an inconvenience? Isn't self sacrifice part of Parenting 101?"

My eyes filled with tears. "Jon, you know I'm not making this up."

"I know you're not, but it's cruel beyond comprehension. How can a parent be that ridiculously selfish toward their own children?"

"The problem is that everything is about Rick. You're not supposed to need anything from him, but he expects you to center your world around him. When reality inevitably happens, that's when he starts the verbal abuse about how *ungrateful* you are. In his mind, anything above bare minimum effort means we should fall on our knees groveling because he deigned to give us his precious scraps. Calling out his hypocrisy earns more insults and accusations. He can't lose control, so he finds some way to bully you back into submission."

"Because you asked him to change an already hurtful behavior? How does he justify doing that?"

"He'll fabricate some previously unknown offense and pretend he was scared to speak up all this time, but now," I gasped dramatically and mimicked Rick's theatrical hand gestures, "he can no longer remain silent about it—meaning that he just made it up. Other times, he references an actual event, but he twists and omits key details to frame himself as the victim. You did the behavior to him *first*, so now he's just giving you a taste of your own medicine. Press him for details, and he crumbles. Since the lies never add up, he'll attack your tone of voice in confronting him or accuse you of malicious intent. He has the mentality of a seven year-old."

"Just when I thought I couldn't like him any less," Jon deadpanned. "I hope you and your girls don't buy into those lies anymore."

"We're still unpacking things we didn't realize we were believing. You've gotten a taste of that already."

He gave me an admiring smile rather than the weary sigh I feared. "But you *are* breaking free, Charlotte. I see the differences every time I talk to you, and it's encouraging."

I smiled back. "Thank you. I am very blessed with good friends who speak Scripture to me even if I'm acting like a toddler while hearing it."

"Good thing you're a cute toddler." He winked at me and took another sip of coffee.

Laughing, I stuck my tongue out at him and pulled a preschool aged, Sophie face.

His eyes crinkled in humor. "I love this part of your personality. I've been so focused on raising Ruthie and Rachel, I forgot how to have fun."

"You were also grieving," I replied, my smile fading. "You don't need to beat yourself up over that."

"Oh, I'm not," he said quickly. "I intended that solely as a compliment to you."

"Thank you." I offered a smile and drank deeply from my coffee cup. We sat in a comfortable silence for a minute before Jon asked his next question.

"Have you figured out how Rick was able to fool you for so long about Stephanie and vice versa?"

"At the end of the day, it's about everyone begging Rick to take their side while he's the one manipulating the conflict. He plays off the complaints of his disgruntled female harem and encourages the negative narrative we have about each other. None of us realized he was orchestrating everything."

Jon shook his head in disgust. "He's a pig. In every sense of the word."

"I'll never regret having my daughters, but I look at Rick and wonder what on earth I was thinking when I married him. Meanwhile, I'm supposed to figure out what to do with the impotent rage and frustration. I have to communicate regarding the girls without wanting to claw his face off."

"Do you want the real solution?" he asked.

"As opposed to what?"

"As opposed to an answer that will make you feel better in the short term but won't help deal with all the injustice of everything that's happened."

I re-crossed my legs and took a swig of coffee. "Hit me."

"When both of you are standing before Jesus, you'll have to give an account for everything you've done. So will Rick."

"Okay," I drawled.

"You know that your judgment has been paid for by Yeshua's death on the cross. Your sins, your bad choices, all the mistakes you've made. The reality is that you're no more righteous standing before God than he is. Yeshua died for the sins of both of you."

"How is this supposed to make me feel better? I actually feel worse now."

"Because Yeshua is coming back to this planet to bring justice. *His* justice. What you've experienced so far has been the broken 'justice' of this world. Right now, it seems like Rick is getting away with his abuse of you and your girls—even Stephanie. Ultimately, he will have to stand before Jesus and explain why his wife and daughters deserved less than bare minimum effort. He will have to stand and explain why he bludgeoned your daughters with the Bible while never applying those standards to himself. Whatever justice you could have conjured in your own mind will be nothing compared to what God does. You may even find yourself saying, 'I wanted justice, but not *that* much' when you see how the Lord makes things right."

"Hmm," I murmured.

"When God's justice comes, you know you're taken care of because of your faith in Jesus. We can't say the same for Rick. Since God spared you from the same hell Rick will receive if he doesn't repent, you can start praying he receives the same *mercy* you've also received. It gets the focus off of Rick, off everything he's done, and it gets it back on Jesus."

I exhaled a weary sigh. "You're right, Jon."

"Keep your eyes on the Lord instead of what's going on around you," he said. "You'll feel overwhelmed by your own powerlessness and the weight of Rick's behavior if you keep focusing on it. *Colossians 3* says to set our minds on things above, not on things of the earth."

"I thought that was in reference to material wealth versus heavenly reward."

"Well, try thinking of it in terms of heavenly justice instead of earthly justice. You can't change Rick's heart or mind, and he has so much hatred toward you that he wouldn't have ears to hear from you no matter how sincere you were in delivering the message. If you keep your eyes on the Lord, on how *big* He is, how *good* He's been to you, it'll help you keep the right perspective about everything else."

I sniffled back tears. "So, does that mean I ignore everything Rick does to hurt me or the girls since I'm unrighteous too? Well, gosh gee, how can I complain when I said a bad word yesterday after I stubbed my toe? We're totally equal, right?"

Jon took hold of my hand. "I told you it was tough love, Charlotte. None of us are righteous. Not you, not me, not Rick, not Stephanie. I'm not saying you don't deserve justice. The *Psalms* are full of King David crying out for it against his enemies. I just want you to think about what actual justice means in terms of eternity. You said you don't want to carry this weight anymore. I'm showing you the only way you'll ever be free from it. You have to give it over to Jesus. Not only because yes, you've also sinned, but because vengeance belongs to the Lord. Because God *is* good. Because, yes, Rick is how he is, but you aren't sharing a bed with him anymore. You're receiving child support and alimony. You have a roof over your head, a job and coworkers you love, food on your table, and a friend who adores you and wants you to see the amazing woman you truly are. You *are* being blessed despite the Rick shenanigans."

"You adore me?" I repeated quietly.

His dark eyes sparkled. "I have for a long time, Charlotte. You are God's blessing to *me*."

Tears fell freely down my cheeks. Jon brushed one away with his thumb and cupped my chin. He set down his coffee to cradle my face with both hands.

"Everything about you is beautiful."

I tried to turn away, but he wouldn't let me.

"From the crown of your head to the souls of your feet, outside, inside, and everywhere in between."

I smiled through my tears. "Andrea said you used to pray that over your girls when they were babies. That God would bless them all over. I thought it was the sweetest thing ever. Rick never did anything like that."

"I'm sorry to hear that."

I searched his eyes. "Why are you saying that kind of blessing over *me*?"

"Because you're precious to me, Charlotte, just like my daughters."

My shoulders shook and the tears flowed without restraint. Jon released my face to pull me into a standing hug. I sobbed quietly against him as he ran his hands up and down my back.

"Charlotte," he said against my hair. "Don't lose sight of all the blessings in your life just because you're not seeing justice as quickly as you want. The Lord isn't turning a blind eye to what's been done, and He wants to see you and your girls healed even more than you want it for yourselves."

I pulled back to stare into his eyes. "I don't deserve you."

He tsked. "Other way around. My life has so much color and humor in it, thanks to you. The way you're so open about your struggles and also open to correction speaks to your heart and your willingness to be vulnerable. It's beautiful."

I rested a newly manicured hand on his cheek. "I suppose I

have better things to do with these nails than claw off Rick's face, hmm?"

He gently tugged my hand away to study it. "How about we leave justice to God and spare this lovely nail polish? What color is this anyway? Bubble gum glitter? Think of your manicure if nothing else." His light tone helped ease the pain of seeing my own self righteousness while hyper fixating on Rick's failings.

I stared down at my fingers held in Jon's hand and wiggled them "I think you're right. Blood and sparkles don't mesh well together."

He brought the back of my hand to his lips. "They are very lovely hands, by the way."

I grinned and lowered my voice to a sultry pitch. "All the better to run through your silver hair, my dear."

His grip moved from my wrist to my upper arm as he stepped within kissing range. "How soon can you start?"

My saucy response died in my throat as I locked eyes with Tina Fournier, now Tina Madison, across the room. Her eyes lasered from me to Jon as she stood frozen in the Charred Cups entryway.

Jon turned to see what caught my attention and frowned. "You okay?"

I hadn't seen Tina since the day we'd moved out of her basement four years earlier. She'd made it a point to avoid me when I'd gone back to her house to retrieve the remainder of my belongings. Instead, she'd sniped at me via text so she could insult me uninterrupted. The three times I went back, she always had some new complaint. I'd kept my responses to single words, not wanting to engage her and stunned by how relentlessly cruel she'd become.

"I can't deal with this right now," I murmured in panic. "Jon, I can't deal with this on top of everything else. I can't."

"Just breathe," he soothed, drawing me close. "I'm not going anywhere, and that witch won't be allowed to say anything to you."

I met his gaze and tried to anchor myself in those dark depths. "Is she gone yet?"

"No, unfortunately. She's also got her phone out and is very unsubtly taking pictures of the two of us."

"Why? Neither of us go to Beth Shalom, and we're both single now. We're not doing anything wrong."

"Exactly," he said, pushing a tendril of hair off my face. "Don't forget that being happy is the best revenge."

"I don't need revenge. I just want peace. Help me, please!"

He gave an encouraging smile and squeezed my hand. "You're not alone, and she can't hurt you anymore. Looks like she's just waiting for her order. She'll probably leave us alone if she knows what's good for her."

As Jon predicted, Tina opted to avoid a potential public spectacle. However, knowing Tina as long as I had, she did her best work behind closed doors anyway. When she pretended to be your friend, you couldn't ask for a better listener or cheerleader. When your back was turned, she was telling someone else your confidential problems and acting like your life would be so much easier if you just did whatever *she* thought was best.

Tina, of course, was never wrong.

I shuddered as the memories began to fill my mind.

CHAPTER 28

FOUR YEARS EARLIER, MY GIRLS AND I WERE CAUGHT in the throes of pandemic hysteria and lockdown. We had been forced to quarantine in Tina's basement for two weeks after her younger son came home from college with Covid. Tina called the virus a media hoax until she had gotten ill herself. Despite the bad flu symptoms, her tests remained negative. The girls and I were all healthy, but virus exposure mandates kept us stuck in the basement "dungeon" ordering online groceries and dinner. With the washer and dryer located two floors above us, we wound up washing clothes in the bathroom sink and ordering replacement undergarments.

Tina decided to lift the quarantine ban three days before the recommended seclusion ended—mostly because she was bored and wanted me and the girls upstairs to keep her company. Paxton had returned to school, and she claimed we were out of the woods. The girls and I stuck to protocol before leaving the actual house, but just a day after we'd earned our freedom, Tina's illness relapsed along with a positive Covid test. It only took two days for me to develop symptoms mirroring hers. Overnight, I was bedridden with chest tightness, a horrible cough, irritable bowels, and a fatigue I had never experienced before or since.

Sophie and Lily nursed me through the illness, and I thanked God for preserving their health. Miraculously, they had zero symptoms of the virus even though they tested positive. It was on my third day that Tina began hounding me with text messages. I wondered if it was the virus clouding my perception, but it seemed like another entity had taken over the body of my best friend. I kept telling her I would talk to her when I felt better, but that wasn't good enough.

You're stonewalling me, Charlotte, and you're just doing it to make me spin in circles and get upset.

Dumbfounded, I replied, *What are you talking about?*

You've been ignoring me the last few days. I would never treat you like that!

I've barely been able to stay awake. I'm not checking my phone other than to see the time. I'm not ignoring you.

Don't play dumb. I know you're doing this on purpose to get back at me.

I frowned, realizing Tina inadvertently admitted culpability in neglecting our friendship—but only by accusing me of her own behavior.

Tina had met her boyfriend, George Madison, three months before I moved into her house, and their relationship progressed quickly. Pre-boyfriend, we texted at all hours, met up for coffee or brunch as often as possible, and we supported each other through the trials of life. As soon as George entered the picture, Tina canceled plans or would even cut me off mid-sentence if it meant taking a phone call or text from George. The friend I supported through her first husband's passing and subsequent rebellion from her sons became a ghost. When I told Tina I had filed for divorce, she temporarily reverted back to the attentive friend of old, but that didn't last long.

At my best friend's urging, I uprooted my daughters forty-five minutes away from Rick to move into her home during my divorce proceedings. Tina promised I would live in a house with genuine emotional support rather than constant criticism, and she called it an honor to provide a sanctuary away from Rick. She'd heard all my laments about his controlling behavior and my fear of Sophie regressing into self harm. Tina even went so far as to offer herself as a second mother figure to my girls since their grandmother wasn't currently in the picture.

The first week after we moved in, she did show me around to her favorite spots. She also made sure to tell everyone about my *desperate situation* before placing a hand to her heart and repeating the same story of how she just *had* to help us. By the third or fourth recitation, something felt off. Tina's grand display also meant having three people downstairs who could hear all the activity going on above our heads on the main floor. That included late night visits from George despite the holier-than-thou image Tina maintained while unironically critiquing the morality of everyone else around her.

Days before our first quarantine, I'd gently confronted Tina about the contradiction. She said she was "ironing it out with the Lord" and not to worry. She claimed she was scared to get remarried and to share her freedom and her first husband's assets with a new man. I asked why she would share her body with someone she didn't think was worthy to share the rest.

That lone question sparked my best friend's transformation into my worst enemy.

Before that, Tina seemed to play dumb if George was *really* interested in her and wanted me to recount every little detail of their courtship. She claimed it was just her insecurities, but I wondered why she needed me to repeat it so often.

"But are you sure?" she'd purr. "Charlotte, I told him I don't believe in sex before marriage, but what if he decides to dump me?"

"Didn't you tell me he's a Christian, Tina?"

"Well, he says he believes in God, but he had some bad experiences at church. He said he would try out Beth Shalom since he knows how much it means to me."

"So, why do you keep doubting his intentions? George told you he's looking for a forever relationship. I doubt he'd be wasting your time if he didn't think that could happen with you. The guy texts you morning, noon, and night."

"I don't know!" she'd cry with a childish smirk, almost like she was testing me. "I just get so scared. I was with David for twenty-three years before he died. I don't even remember what dating was like. How can I *really* know that he's serious?"

At this point, Tina would sniffle back a tear or two, the same tear she'd been sniffling for the last three years since her husband had passed. According to Tina, it hadn't been a very loving marriage, but it proved to be a lucrative one still paying dividends. Even though she already owned an SUV, Tina purchased a sporty coupe worth double my salary at 7-Square. She bragged incessantly how she paid cash for the car and how George fawned all over the bells and whistles when they went driving together. She'd watch me expectantly, as if waiting for me to do the same. Instead, I suppressed the urge to roll my eyes and then changed the subject back to her next date with George. Tina gushed about that for a while too, then she'd take on a pitying tone and ask when I thought Rick might start paying me child support.

"I hope nothing happens to *your* car," she'd say with heavy condescension, "because you could never afford to fix it."

That fateful, Covid-riddened day, Tina stopped pretending to be my friend altogether.

You're just jealous of me and George having a healthy sexual relationship because Rick didn't want to do his duty. That's why you've been giving me the silent treatment. Go ahead and admit it. You're coveting what you never had.

All I told you was that I couldn't talk yesterday because I'm sick and I feel horrible.

Oh, please! We both know you're sitting there judging me.

Tina, how many times have you used Scripture to talk about my anger or attitude toward Rick? I was being a friend and using the Bible to help YOU too. You can't change what it says about sex before marriage just because of your own fears. You're acting like God will eventually see your side of things and change His mind. With all the stuff you post on Face-Space about the Bible and sexual immorality, I was surprised to find out you were sleeping together. It's still a sin whether it's a homosexual or heterosexual relationship.

God understands that I have needs.

I exhaled a frustrated sigh. *Tina, there is no way God told you it's okay for you to sleep with George before you're married. That would either make Him a liar or the Bible a lie.*

Now, you're just trying to make me doubt what I heard from God. You don't get to tell me what He said to me. You weren't there!

*Do you really think His Word applies to everybody *but* you? I don't think what you heard is the Holy Spirit. I think you heard what you wanted to hear.*

How dare you! She huffed. *I never thought you'd be so overcritical just like your husband. You've never talked to me this way before.*

I was losing control of my temper, wondering why Tina kept deflecting instead of embracing the same truth she'd given her oldest son when he came out as bisexual a year earlier. She'd sent me screenshots of her messages to him, and nothing in my address had been as confrontational or shaming as what she'd sent to her own child.

My eyelids drooped, my emotional energy already spent. *Look, maybe this isn't the best time to talk about this.*

Don't you try to weasel your way out of this, Charlotte Williams! You pretend you're joking when you say I live in the 'penthouse' and you're in the 'dungeon,' and I'm starting to see the real reason you're so down on me and George. I tell you I have to leave early from one little brunch, and you act like I'm always choosing him over you.

Tina, I'd been begging you for three weeks to go out with me for brunch because you promised we would when I first moved in. You were thirty minutes late before we ever left, and then you ducked out forty minutes after we sat down because George called. I'm confused why you're compromising Biblical standards for a man you barely know. I'm hurt by how you've been treating me when we've been friends for twelve years.

How I've been treating you?! She fumed along with angry emojis. *I take time out of my busy weekend and the only free time George has to spend it with YOU, but it's just not enough for my needy little friend, is it? How selfish can you be??? You also haven't paid me a dime of rent. Don't think I've forgotten about that. I'm not running a charity house.*

I bit back the caustic reply I wanted to give her. Instead, I tried to stick with facts. *You told me I didn't need to pay until I got on my feet with the girls. We've barely been here for a month. When do you want me to pay you, and how much?*

Ignoring me, her rant continued. *As if you could afford it! And I see the way you look at my car and then smirk when I talk about how blessed I am. I can't help it that I got an extra $75,000 from David's estate. Why shouldn't I have nice things?*

Who's saying you shouldn't? I'm glad you got all the extra features you wanted. I've just never been a big car person, so it's not something I'm impressed with. I'm not going to apologize for that.

Ha! I knew it! You ARE jealous!

My frustration rose as she continued to twist my words. *All I said was I don't care about cars.*

Whatever. You can't fool me. You're jealous that I have a boyfriend, a beautiful home, and money. You're jealous that you're poor and I'm not, and you're acting like a child with this ridiculous silent treatment you've been giving me.

Exasperated and physically exhausted, I offered a desperate prayer for God to intervene. Tina knew I was stuck in bed. She was the one who got me sick through her own carelessness! She knew all about my horrible marriage, my financial hardship, and my longing for emotional companionship. With a sinking feeling in the pit of my stomach, I realized my best friend capitalized on my personal struggles to prove she was better than me.

And she was furious that I didn't agree with her.

When I confided my difficulties in helping my girls deal with the divorce and their father's behavior, Tina bragged how her boys simply adored her first husband. She accused me of coddling Sophie and Lily, but she made excuses for the verbal abuse she received regularly from her oldest son and distance from her youngest. I also knew she bought them off with electronics and cash to keep them coming back. She'd complained for years how that's all they wanted from her.

All of that, I kept behind my lips and from my fingers on my cell phone. Instead, I went for the path of least resistance.

Both of us are still recovering from Covid. The stress doesn't help, and I'm having trouble breathing right now. You said your oxygen levels were not so great either. I don't think this is the best time for a conversation.

Well, that's the first intelligent thing you've said all day. I also can't taste or smell either. You're lucky the version you got isn't as bad as mine. We will talk later, and you better deal with that attitude you've been giving me.

Tired and defeated, I sent back a thumbs up emoji so she would know I wasn't ignoring her even though that's exactly what I wanted to do.

She replied immediately. *I don't know who this bitter person is pretending to be my Charlotte, but you better start showing some gratitude for everything I've done for you. I'm the only thing keeping you off the streets and away from your ex.*

Appalled at her cruelty, I had nothing left to say. I sent screenshots to Lauren who was equally horrified by Tina's behavior. I had to know I wasn't crazy, and Lauren provided the validation I needed. I never received a text following Tina's tirade, and I left the matter alone thinking she just needed time to cool off.

After four days of cryptic radio silence, my current landlord and former best friend pushed a printed letter underneath the basement door. She demanded we leave her house by the end of the month.

This is still my house, and I no longer want you or your children in it.

Hand trembling, Tina's note crumbled in my hand and I collapsed to the floor.

CHAPTER 29

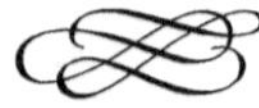

"She's gone," Jon said, bringing me back to the present.

My body sighed into his. "Thank God."

He searched my eyes. "Are you okay?"

"Honestly, no. And we can add Tina Fournier to the list of people I need to release to Jesus. Part of me wants to see her reap every horrible thing she did to me, and the other part wants to see her transform back into the woman she used to be. I miss our friendship, Jon. I miss all the good times, the laughs, and the times we prayed together. Was all of that fake? Do I sound crazy for even wondering that?"

He smiled down at me, and his hand skimmed the side of my face. "You're amazing."

"I'm a mess is what I am."

"You're processing the trauma and injustice done to you and your children. That doesn't make you unworthy to be loved or cared for."

"But it makes being a part of my life challenging and time-consuming."

"Rejecting you because of that would be selfish and cruel—like what Tina did."

I shook my head. "She didn't reject me for having hardship, Jon. She thought I was ignoring her and sort of lost her mind. She became a completely different person, and for whatever reason, she hasn't changed back."

He released a heavy sigh. "Think about what you just said. She *lost her mind* because you wouldn't give her attention. That's not normal behavior. It's selfish beyond logic or reason."

"Why is it selfish to not want to be ignored? She was all alone upstairs."

"Why was that your responsibility to fix?"

"I'm not saying it was my responsibility. I just feel bad for her situation."

"And where was Tina's compassion for *your* situation?" he growled. "We're talking about a grown woman who threw a tantrum because the illness *she* gave you made it physically impossible for you to answer your phone. Her behavior was despicable, and there is no way to rationalize or justify what she did."

"Look, I don't think—"

He cut me off, "Tina didn't become a different person because of a text message. That would be legitimately insane, which is why you're struggling so much with it."

Frustrated, I shot back, "Well, then what happened? What am I missing?"

"The mask finally came off. The person you see now is the person she's always been. The friend you miss never actually existed."

I scoffed. "You're making her sound like Rick."

Jon gave me a flippant look as if I'd just proved his point.

"You can't be serious," I replied.

"Don't you think it's strange Tina is so supportive of Rick and Stephanie on social media and also at Beth Shalom? Wasn't she supposed to be *your* best friend who hated the way your husband treated you?"

I swallowed down that bitter pill of truth. "I just thought she was getting back at me by doing that," I mumbled.

"Because that makes it okay?" Jon asked incredulously. "A woman in her early fifties displaying the maturity of an eight year-old who decides they're not your best friend anymore?! Charlotte, I love your big, beautiful heart, but Tina Fournier doesn't deserve it."

"What if you're wrong? What if part of this really *is* my fault?"

He inhaled a deep breath, clearly struggling for patience. With a calmer tone, he asked, "You said Tina was already acting strangely when you moved in, right?"

"Yeah," I drawled.

"Have you considered that maybe Tina didn't expect you to take her up on her offer?"

"What? Why?"

"Crowing to others about how she 'saved' you from Rick is very different from the reality of sharing her home with three extra people. Tina had to actually make sacrifices rather than just play at being savior."

"She did complain a lot," I admitted.

"You also said she ditched you any chance she could for George."

"She did. It made me feel like dirt every time she did it."

Jon craned his neck as if trying to guide me in the right direction. "Can you see how that was intentional?"

My eyes widened. "Why would she want me to feel that way?"

"Because she really is no different than Rick. Gloating about that stupid car was a way to make you feel inferior and hopefully as jealous of her as she was of you."

"What did she have to be jealous of? The woman had everything!" I fought back hot tears. "What could I possibly have that would make her be as cruel as what you're saying?"

He offered a sad smile. "I'm not sure you'll believe me if I sing praises about your beauty or your character, but I have no doubt Tina was jealous of your relationship with your girls, if nothing else."

"All she did was boast how her boys loved their father."

"Exactly," he said with a flourish. "You told me Tina's relationship with them is toxic and abusive."

"It is! I've seen it firsthand and also via text. She sent me the screenshots."

"So, what better way to overcompensate than to take credit for a husband who isn't here to contradict anything she's saying? Rick's failure as a parent doesn't automatically make *you* a failure, Charlotte. That's what Tina needed you to believe. She, however, *did* fail, and she took out her frustration on you."

"She failed? How? Tina and those boys have everything they could ever want."

"It's just optics. You have what truly matters."

"I do?"

"Yes! For every material possession Tina believes makes her better than you, the one thing she probably wants more than anything is the way your girls took care of you during Covid. Tina had nobody, like you said. No amount of money in the world can replace kindness and care—especially from the children we've poured our lives into. It's the one thing Tina couldn't buy, despite her best efforts to do exactly that. Materially, you had nothing compared to all of her wealth, but you were blessed with Sophie and Lily. On top of that, none of the hardships you've endured have stolen your humor, your faith in God, or the generosity of spirit that's inherent to who you are. As far as Tina goes, most people don't even like the *fake* personality she uses, let alone the real one."

"Hey!" I objected. "I'm not an idiot, Jon. Yes, she rubbed a lot of people the wrong way, but she wasn't always like that, you know. She could be a lot of fun, and she has done a lot of nice things for me over the years."

"Okay, fair point. Obviously, she wasn't *all bad* with you, or you wouldn't have been friends with her in the first place. I'm not saying you're stupid, Charlotte. I'm saying Tina is that manipulative. Who wouldn't enjoy spending time with you? And yes, I'm sure Tina rewarded your good behavior by acting like a good friend. It doesn't mean she wasn't using you the entire time. Anyone can fake being nice. Even charming. Nobody fakes being self centered."

I frowned.

He continued with his truth bombs. "The second you prioritized yourself over Tina's selfish demands, she blamed you for her intentional cruelty. Sound familiar?"

My jaw fell open. "Jon, please don't tell me I turned away from one narcissist only to take comfort in the arms of another! I couldn't have been *that* stupid, could I? Maybe we're missing something. Covid can mess with your brain."

"You were married to Rick longer than you were friends with Tina. She doesn't deserve the benefit of the doubt or your sympathy any more than he does. And don't think she won't answer to God for what she's done. None of this was an accident."

My shoulders slumped, finally admitting defeat.

Jon placed his hands on my arms and stared directly into my eyes. "I want you to hear from my own lips that you are *not* too much for me. The only way I can prove I'm not going anywhere is over time, and that's not a problem. You already consume plenty of my thoughts whether I'm physically with you or not. It's a blessing, Charlotte, not a burden."

"Are you sure?"

"You earned my respect when I saw how you persevered with Rick despite how pedantic he was, even in public. That doubled when you stood up to him and the Beth Shalom leadership to protect your girls. Helping Lauren get free from Nathan while withstanding the slander from both him and Rick is nothing short of courageous. You did what was right because it was *right*. Walking alongside you in this healing journey is an honor."

"What about all the anger and bitterness?" I countered. "I didn't realize how bad it was until a week ago. Shouldn't I be 'over' some of this stuff by now?"

"You used anger to survive. Rick hasn't stopped attacking you—even after marrying Stephanie—and your anger has been a shield to protect your heart from his betrayal. It's helped you to function through the unimaginable, but you're not in survival mode anymore. You and your girls are safe now, and it's time to get free from the past and its hold on you."

"If I'm so safe, then why am I still angry? Why am I still getting twisted into knots about Rick or having panic attacks at the sight of Tina?"

With those deep brown eyes, Jon continued to stare into my soul. The warmth in his voice smoothed my frayed nerves. "Anger kept you numb from the pain because it focused your attention on the wrongdoings of others. God is uncovering the trauma lying underneath."

"I see."

"As agonizing as it will be walking through the bad memories and grieving the past, God is ultimately using this for your good. Anger will hide trauma for a season, but it will poison you if left unchecked. As you're getting set free, you're going to experience *all* the negative feelings, but I promise to support you every step of the way."

I smiled at him. "Thank you. Honestly, you feel too good to be true."

He returned my smile and gestured for me to join him back in our seats. "The feeling is mutual. I didn't think I would ever feel these emotions again."

"Which emotions?"

"Passion. Protectiveness. Lo—Longing."

I knew that wasn't the "L" word Jon initially meant, but I didn't force the issue. I was not going to be repeating it back to him. Too much, too soon, and too easy. All of it felt way too easy. Every major blessing in my life seemed like I'd worked my tail off to earn it or suffered endlessly to keep it. Jon Roseman freely offering himself seemed more fairy tale than anything resembling my forty-four years on planet earth.

And I wasn't ready to wake up from the real life dream come true.

CHAPTER 30

"Jon?" I asked.

"Hmm?"

"Would you kiss me?"

He smiled. "Any particular reason?"

"Just want to make sure I'm not imagining the way you look at me or everything you said tonight."

"I promise, this is very real." He anchored his hand at the base of my neck with this thumb stroking my cheek. "See? Real as real can be."

I turned my face toward his palm and kissed it. "Oh yeah?"

"Never thought I'd be jealous of my hand," he rumbled, tipping my chin toward him and capturing my mouth with his own.

Our kiss wasn't overly long, yet every touch revealed the depth of his emotions. Jon blanketed me in both protection and possessiveness, branding my heart in the process. Not until a barista cleared her throat did I realize they needed to close the coffee shop. Jon escorted me to his SUV, and we blithely chatted on the way home.

He walked me to my front door, and I noticed all the lights were on in the family room.

"That's weird. The girls should be in bed by now." I jingled the keys in the deadbolt and unlocked the door.

"Here, I'll come with you." He reached beside me to pull the handle open.

Perched on the edge of the sofa, Sophie clacked loudly on her laptop with a scowl on her face. Lily sat on the adjoining loveseat, quiet and withdrawn. Neither of them paid much attention as Jon and I entered the room.

Trying for a light tone, I said, "What heinous offense has the internet committed this time? I'm surprised you're both still up."

When they didn't reply, my apprehension grew.

"Lil?" I asked, turning to my baby. "Why do you look like you've seen a ghost?"

Wordlessly, she pointed to the laptop on the coffee table. Sophie took a break from typing to rub tears from her eyes. She noted my presence and switched browser tabs from an online chat to whatever offending content had upset her and her sister. She stood abruptly and gestured for me to see for myself. Jon sidled next to me as we both searched for signs of digital carnage.

Before us sat Stephanie's FaceSpace page, and to no one's surprise, she was wrapped in Rick's amorous embrace. Skimming the picture caption, I suppressed the urge to remark about their wedded bliss. I scanned the photo once more, wondering why this particular display of affection caused so much distress. Then, my eyes traveled down to the comment section.

I sucked air as if I'd been punched in the gut. Jon's harsh intake of breath followed mine.

"Tell me it isn't true," I said weakly.

Jon's tone dripped with contempt. "Wish I could."

Stunned and horrified, I re-read the photo comment.

> Tina Madison: Loooove this picture! Introducing you guys was one of the greatest privileges of my life. God had a perfect plan, especially with all the suffering you two endured to be together (Jer. 29:11). *Some people* are only happy when they're making life miserable for others. Keep smiling and keep the pics coming! I love how in love you are! #couplegoals #truelove #secondchances

A whoosh of adrenaline surged to my extremities and left me trembling in its aftermath. "She *introduced* them? Rick and I weren't even legally divorced yet! How can she sit there and praise their adultery like it was God ordained?"

"The same way she pretends God blessed her fornication with George," Jon spat. The anger in his voice caused Lily's eyes to bulge.

Whispering, I asked, "Are you okay?"

"Are *you*?" he hissed. "Do you see what she's done?"

"I see it. I still can't believe it."

"How does Tina know Stephanie?" Sophie demanded. "Why would she fix up Cruellinda with Dad? I thought she wanted to *help* us. You know, until she became a total—"

"Language!" I chastised.

"What? It's not like it isn't true."

Jon shrugged. "She's got a point."

"Not helping," I said through clenched teeth.

"But *why?*" Lily asked, her eyes brimming with tears. "Daddy didn't even want to move out until he met Stephanie. Tina ruined our family on purpose. I thought she was your best friend, Mom."

"Oh, baby," I breathed, coming to her side. "Don't give Tina too much credit. Our family was broken long before your father left us. There have been bad choices made all around, including my own."

"But you and Dad could have gotten back together!" She glared at the computer screen. "Tina said she loved us like the daughters she never had. Why would she be happy about what Stephanie's done to our dad? To us?"

"Because Tina's a backstabbing liar, that's why!" Sophie raged. "Look what she said about Mom. Who do you think *some people* are? She's made comments on other pics too. This one is just from tonight."

"Soph, how did you find out about any of this?" I asked. "You said Stephanie blocked you guys on all of her socials, and I know neither of you are friends with Tina on FaceSpace.

Jon held up his phone. "Ruth sent me the screenshot and several more. I think we have our answer."

"But how did you two get it?" I asked again. "I didn't think you texted Ruthie."

Lily spoke up. "Ruthie sent screenshots to Rachel, and then Rachel sent it to us. We were chatting on Wussup, and then Rachel told us to hang on a second because her sister was texting her. Tina's comment showed up in Ruthie's newsfeed. I guess they're friends on FaceSpace."

"Well, that's about to change," Jon muttered, furiously texting his oldest daughter.

"Mom, do you get it?" Sophie said.

"Get what, honey? That Tina and Stephanie are best friends apparently?"

"No!" she shrieked. "They've been working together this whole time!"

"I don't think so," Jon cut in, looking up from his phone and making meaningful eye contact with each of us. "Stephanie's being manipulated against you girls by Tina. The witch is playing games to get revenge on your mom."

Ever my champion, Lily shook with a surprising display of emotion. "What do you mean *revenge*? We thought our mom was going to *die* because of her!"

Sophie followed Lily's outburst with a chilling wish for Tina's demise, including every symptom I'd experienced with Covid. Daring me or Jon to correct her, she glared at us.

"Do you believe me now?" he whispered close to my ear. "Please, tell me you're not still blaming yourself for how she treated you."

My voice broke at the same time as my heart. Denial had kept me numb from the pain, but the agony of Tina's betrayal was too much to ignore. "She knows what Rick did to me, Jon. She sat on the phone with me for *years* listening to me cry about it. Why would she encourage both of them to hurt me in the worst ways possible?"

A muscle ticked in his jaw. "There are no words for this level of cruelty. At least, nothing I can say in front of your daughters."

"How can she pretend they're all the victims of *my* abuse instead of the other way around? Do they coexist in Upside Down World together? This is insane!" I beat my finger against the laptop screen before exhaling in revulsion.

Jon's eyes narrowed as he re-read the public declaration of treachery. "I think this is who Tina was texting when she photographed us tonight. She probably sent those photos right to Stephanie. Who knows? Maybe she even told her to post this steaming pile of vomit."

"Wait, did you see Tina?" Sophie asked. "When?"

"Jon and I were at Charred Cups, and she walked in. She took pictures of us hugging."

"That's so weird! Why would Stephanie or Tina care about your love life? Stephanie's completely obsessed with Dad anyway. When his perfect little Cruellinda isn't yelling, she's got her claws all over him."

"Don't call your stepmother that!" Pain and frustration over-flowed, and I felt ready to split in half. Jon laid a hand on my arm, and I sent him a grateful look. Remorseful, I said, "Sorry, Soph. I just…don't call her that, okay?"

"I'll call her whatever I want! She deserves it!"

With a soothing tone, Jon said, "Both of you need to save your anger for the right person. I'm not saying your stepmother is innocent, but I'm concerned she's being riled up against you."

"She's *not* innocent, no matter how much you and Mom suddenly think so," Sophie spat.

"I never claimed she was innocent," I replied.

"Well, then stop acting like it! She does all this gooey love garbage with Dad just to rub it in how he chose her over us. She'll make out with him right in front of us too. Oh, *Richard*," she crooned, imitating Stephanie's accent with accompanying kissing sounds.

Jon looked appalled, and he visibly swallowed before daring to speak. I silently praised his restraint in withholding his true sentiments. Instead, he redirected focus for my daughters. "I believe everything you're saying, Sophie. I also think Tina's meddling is adding fuel to the fire. Based on some of these

FaceSpace posts, it looks like they discuss your mom on a regular basis."

Both girls scanned the comment again.

"I don't get it," Lily said. "What did you ever do to Tina to make her act like this?"

"Absolutely nothing," I admitted. "I did nothing other than tell her 'no' just *one* time. That was my heinous offense."

Jon tsked. "Yeah, you're a real monster, Charlotte. How dare you get sick with the virus *Tina* gave you and then be unavailable for her latest round of emotional abuse and belittling? How selfish of you."

"Jon," I warned.

"No, seriously," he said. "There is no defense for this sick, sadistic, *deliberate* behavior." He gestured emphatically at the computer screen. "This woman was *never* your friend. She used you until it no longer suited her. Now, she's working double time to trash your reputation in case you ever tell your side of the story. The harpy has the added bonus of manipulating Stephanie to hurt you and the girls at close range."

Sophie and Lily watched me, waiting to see what I would do.

I read the caption again, my eyes lingering on the words, *some people.* "What on earth is Tina even talking about? When she was sisterhood president at Beth Shalom, people complained about her all the time. Nobody could stand her condescending attitude and rudeness. I said she had a lot going on with David's death and dealing with her boys. I even told Tina how I *defended* her when she came crying to me about the gossip. And this is the thanks I get? She intentionally destroys my family and then tries to make it *my* fault she did it?"

My knees buckled, and I cried out. Jon caught me before I hit the floor and eased me onto the sofa. A scream of anger, anguish, and horror shredded my throat. Lily jumped out of her skin and burst into tears.

"Mom! Stop it!" Sophie yelled. "You're scaring her!"

Lost in my own grief, I hit the pillows on the couch, the cushions, and even my own legs. The only sounds I could make were half sobs and wails. Somewhere in my periphery, I was aware of Sophie comforting her little sister. Jon, meanwhile, gave me enough space to vent my anger but still remain close if I needed him.

As the vengeful screams subsided, my hysterics began. In all my rage against Rick and Stephanie for what they'd done to my girls, I'd never once suspected my *best friend* could have intentionally manufactured so much pain for everyone involved.

My girls were at constant odds with their stepmother—and there was Tina, blaming me for everything *she* coached Stephanie into doing. Who needed Rick to exacerbate hostilities when Tina's forked tongue planted its malicious pearls under the guise of friendship?

Undoubtedly, she also poked at the paper thin skin of Mrs. Williams. With Stephanie's penchant for complaining and victimhood, Tina had to know every gushing social media post was simply overcompensation for an unhappy marriage. The fawning commentary, however, reinforced the prison bars of public perception. Compounding the problem, I knew Rick also demanded Stephanie maintain appearances—that became clear as I realized he held the camera in all of their smooching selfies.

What a fool I'd been wondering why he'd 'changed' for her and not me! Rick Williams was still the same selfish slug who blamed his faults on anyone but himself. My daughters could attest to that. Meanwhile, I'd spun around in anguished circles wondering why my husband lavished Stephanie with all of the affection he punished me by withholding.

Seeing the photo for what it was, I grieved at their blindness and my own. No matter how many sugary pictures either of them posted, Rick couldn't escape the truth. Only misery made him happy, and he needed someone he could scapegoat for his sins. Unfortunately for him, he married a woman equally adept at deflecting responsibility.

In that respect, he had genuinely met his match.

Enter Tina Fournier once again, all too eager to incite retribution against me for The Williams Family 2.0 marital woes. It also offered the perfect smokescreen for her puppetry. Every natural and negative response I had to the mistreatment of my daughters served as "proof" of Tina's accusations about me. Rick and Stephanie could now unite over a common enemy —and all while shirking blame for their own vile behavior.

I shuddered at the demonic level of cruelty and deception. Forcing my eyes above as Jon had recently encouraged me, I saw my saving grace was Tina's hubris. God had orchestrated the events of that evening, and there was a reason He wanted everyone's actions exposed.

I thought back to when I'd read *Proverbs 9* for months on end, always assuming Stephanie was the coarse woman in the text. As God removed the veil, I saw how the evil, despicable woman leading the innocent toward their own demise was the best friend I'd once entrusted with my entire heart.

I joined my babies on the sofa and mourned the betrayal with them as Jon did his best to comfort us all.

CHAPTER 31

After that night, I saw Tina's face everywhere. Even with her profile blocked on social media, she appeared on my FaceSpace memories or suggested contacts when updating my Linkedup profile. I had logged in to post an MG Tooling ad for an upcoming trade show and got blindsided instead. The sidebar on the bottom right of my homepage overflowed with potential professional connections reading like a who's who of former synagogue friends.

Staring at Tina's face framed in an "Open to Work" banner, I wondered if she'd blown through all of David's money. I couldn't remember what George did for a living, but her boys had always been a heavy financial burden. Regardless, Tina looking for work surprised me even more than her use of countless photo filters de-aging her back to puberty.

I clicked the "remove" button and watched her dissolve into the internet ether. "Good riddance," I muttered.

Next on my list were several women I hadn't thought of in years. It saddened me to realize I'd once cherished seeing these faces weekly. Now, they just brought grief and bitter-sweet memories. These were supposed to be godly women, and only God Himself could say if they truly were. Either they were manipulated and deceived by the wolf in the pulpit, or they acted as willing participants in his myriad abuses of Scripture.

For over a decade at Beth Shalom, I had poured my heart out and prayed with these women at services, at retreats, and at messianic conferences. We'd shared in life events, baby and wedding showers, kid birthday parties, and on. It seemed like a lifetime ago, but the memories burst forth like a flood.

"And now they're all strangers that I used to know," I said, wiping a tear from my eye. Most of the familiar faces looked the same, but I would never view them the same way again. The majority abandoned me after I walked away from Rick and the congregation. The rest simply faded into oblivion. Like the cult it was, as soon as I left Beth Shalom, I ceased to exist.

Even before my departure, several ladies deliberately shunned me when Harvey Lebow enlisted their families for synagogue leadership. It happened too many times to be an accident or just a friendship drifting apart. What became painfully obvious was how they all sold their souls, their marriages, and their children to move into those upper ranks. The women became uppity and cliquey while the men were effectively neutered. Despite the heavily patriarchal views preached from the bima, the husbands served as brainless lackeys or babysitters while the women volunteered whenever the doors were open. Harvey Lebow commanded quite an army of indentured female servants to keep the temple social calendar running. Men were "the head of the household," so long as they allowed their wives to be commanded by the never ending to-do lists of their beloved rabbi. Apparently, one of those commands included giving me the cut direct with their noses in the air—sometimes quite literally.

Rick defended Beth Shalom no matter what, and he accused me of holding onto unforgiveness whenever I brought it up. Even with example after example, somehow it was always my fault. Thank God, I'd never counted Andrea Roseman among the throng of synagogue sycophants. I'd always appreciated her encouragement during those early years when I wondered what I was doing wrong to keep being treated that way.

After clicking through a few profiles, I received an instant message from Elisha Castle, a woman I'd served alongside on the women's monthly breakfast committee. She used to lament the superficiality of Beth Shalom until she got promoted to the invite-only, intercessory prayer team. Then, she became a hard-core apologist whenever I brought up issues in the congregation. Things eventually soured, and I confronted her about the way she'd ghosted our friendship. Her response was to completely ignore me and then post on FaceSpace how she was "being attacked by Satan." Rolling my eyes at the memory, I opened her message out of sheer morbid curiosity.

> Castle_Elisha: Oh my gosh, I didn't even know you were on here, Charlotte!!!! I heard you've been seeing Jon Roseman. How exciting! Do you think you guys would ever come back to Beth Shalom? We miss him on the bima. The cantoring just isn't the same :(Anyways, I hope you're doing well.

"Wow," I exhaled. "Thanks for tacking on the well wishes after pumping me for gossip first. Did Tina send out a group text or just put it on the sisterhood email chain? And no, *Elizabeth*—who changed your name to Elisha so you could try to sound more Jewish—it'll be a frosty day in Hades before you see my face at that dump again."

Rosaria walked into the office and caught me typing and deleting a reply. The scowl on my face must have said it all.

"All right, what did the cretin do this time? Or is it that two-faced, backstabbing, money grubbing, wicked witch of Cordele?"

"I guess you don't like Tina that much either, huh?"

"Girl, I already hated her for giving you Covid and kicking you onto the streets. She should be glad I don't practice voodoo. I promise, she'd be in a lot of pain right now."

I smirked as I continued to pound away on my keyboard. "Leave vengeance for God, Ro. I promise, He's got it covered."

"How do you figure that?"

"Because I can't think of an example in Scripture where God didn't first expose a sin before rendering judgment for it."

She shrugged. "I guess I'll have to take your word for it."

"Besides, this has nothing to do with Rick or Tina. Apparently, it's a Beth Shalom reunion on Linkedup, and I was not ready for it. I just got a DM from some synagogue flunky who thinks I'm too stupid to remember how she publicly shamed me before shunning me altogether. It was devastating at the time, but for her, it was probably just another Tuesday."

"Run that by me again," Ro said, looking over the rim of her glasses. "I haven't even had my Earl Gray yet."

I re-read the message just to be sure I wasn't filtering anything through the lens of old offenses. My mouth flattened as the words hit exactly the same. "Apparently, gossip has already gotten back to Beth Shalom that Jon and I are dating. The entire women's ministry is showing up on my Linkedup feed."

"Which means they've been trolling your socials."

"Exactly. We have no plans to announce our relationship on social media, so the only way they could know is from Tina's adventures in voyeurism last week. This delightful little message is from a former friend who informed me, 'you don't know what friendship really is,' when I called her out for ignoring me. Of course, she still expected me to drop everything the second *she* had a crisis. All she cares about now is confirming the rumors and seeing if Jon will come back to Beth Shalom. These people shredded my reputation without a second thought, but they really think I'd ever encourage anybody to go there. It's insane. They're all insane!"

"No kidding. I see where Rick gets it."

"He was like that before. Beth Shalom is a mecca for entitled narcissists and a factory for minting new ones. Elizabeth was the latter. Once upon a time, she actually had a personality. Now, she's just like all the rest—using and abusing people as long as it can somehow serve the Beth Shalom machine. It is a textbook cult, and I will die on this hill."

Ro's eyebrows shot up. "Look, you don't need to convince me of anything. Any place that would reject you and choose Stephanie is already highly sus."

Collecting steam and just needing to vent, I said, "They all pretend to be so moral and righteous until you point out the flaws in their precious idol. They treat people horribly who don't fit the mold. It's like all the worst parts of middle school. If they can't find a use for you in the congregation, then they have no use for you as a person. God forbid you don't reflect well on the corporate image, and they'll freeze you out socially so you leave or get in line. You're always on the outside looking in just wanting to be seen. Some of the disaffected people linger on hoping they can be the change they want to see. Others think they'll miss some miraculous transformation if they finally get the courage to leave. I'll admit to doing that for a while. Eventually, it just became too much."

"So, what happened?"

"I tried to help those who remained. I validated what they'd shared with me in confidence, but I never told anybody to leave the congregation or go against a spouse who wanted to stay. I supported them and encouraged them to seek the Lord above anything else. Ultimately, it would have to be their decision, but they knew I was a friend no matter what."

"Did any of them leave?"

"A few did, but I realized a lot of them would rather complain and play self righteous martyr. They refuse to speak up and be rejected by the ruling class. When I asked why they were complaining but not actually *doing* anything, it was a bunch of denial and gaslighting about their previous concerns. They couldn't admit they'd sacrificed their families and years of their lives for a lie. It wasn't a pretty realization for me either, but anything was better than the bottomless pit of Beth Shalom volunteering and financial giving." I pulled away from my keyboard and silently reconsidered my response to Elisha. "I don't know why I'm even bothering. It's not like any of these so-called women of God are going to apologize for treating me and my girls like garbage. They enjoy their tiny scraps of perceived power far too much."

"Exactly," Ro called over her shoulder, depositing her belongings into her office. She emerged with her travel mug *du jour,* a beach themed container with glittery turquoise waves, authentic sand, and tiny pearls and starfish layered in between. Not to be outdone, she wore pearlescent plastic frames and starfish earrings.

"Are you planning another vacation?" I asked, eager to change the subject. "Or are you auditioning for the next live-action mermaid movie? I hope they do that quirky one from Australia with the two girls who ended up on *The Original Vampires*. I think it was called *H20: Water Needed*."

She curled her upper lip and exhaled a laugh. "Very funny. No vampires, mermaids, or hybrid werewolves will be involved in this, thank you very much. Things cooled off with Ronnie, and the cruise is nonrefundable. I'm trying to psych myself up into going."

"Bummer! That didn't last very long."

"We had nothing to talk about other than tool holders, saw blades, and insert knives. That got old real fast. I think he was using me to get a discount anyway."

"What a pig!"

"Exactly."

"Well, I'm glad you're moving on, Ro. You can definitely do better than that. Have you found another plus one to go with you?"

"Looks like I'm gonna have to meet him on the boat. If I have any of your luck, hopefully he'll be half as good a kisser as your silver fox." She winked at me and wiggled her eyebrows.

I laughed. "Well, I hope you get your toe curling kisses too."

"Is everything cool after the meltdown with you and the girls the other night? That was probably tough for him to see you all like that. It takes a strong man not to run from a room of overwrought females."

"You forget he has two daughters."

"I forget nothing, babe. I've got three sisters, and my dad couldn't handle any of it."

"Well, when you put it like that, then yeah, Jon is pretty amazing. Too good to be true, honestly. Every time I start to complain I'm too much, he tells me to shut up."

She frowned. "That is *not* okay."

"Ha! You didn't let me finish. He shuts me up with those magical lips of his." I flashed an unapologetic grin. "The man kisses me senseless. I might have even complained a time or two just to get some extra smooches."

She cracked up laughing. "That sounds more like you, Charlotte. You had me worried for a second there. Enjoy every single one of those kisses!"

"Oh, trust me, I do! Jon's been so supportive and understanding. Unfortunately, the girls are a mess, and I'm not sure what to do. At this point, I'm praying for the words to say because nothing I've tried so far has been very helpful."

"What about counseling?"

"We tried last year, but we didn't get very far. Sophie is just angry, and Lily holds everything in. I know they confide in Jon's daughter, Rachel, but she's a friend not a trained therapist. Plus, she'd never violate their confidence to me or her dad."

"I'm sorry, Charlotte. I hope you can figure something out soon."

"Me too."

"In the meantime, leave this synagogue chick alone. Give her all the attention she deserves—aka *none*—and focus on enjoying your new man and helping your girls heal. Also, how you're going to ruin Tina Madison's life."

"You had me up until the last one, Ro."

"All I'm saying is that we've got a room full of show tooling, and I know how to dispose of a body. I've listened to enough *Real Crime* podcasts. You wanna tear her up with carbide blades, high speed steel knives, or diamond tips?"

"Ro!" I exclaimed.

"I'm enlisting as tribute," Luke called from his office. "I still have connections at *The Home Store* who can get us lyme to dissolve the bodies plus shovels and giant garbage bags. Paisley just listened to this really gruesome podcast the other night. She'd probably help too."

I burst into laughter. "You guys are amazing, but there will be no murder and no covering up of dead bodies. Ro, we are not living out some fantasy you have from *The Original Vampires*. Knock it off."

"Party pooper," she muttered.

CHAPTER 32

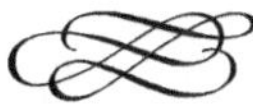

"Thanks for coming over," I said, snuggling into Jon's chest as we sat side by side on my sofa. "I don't want to leave the girls alone right now. Sophie is a raging fireball, and Lily is walking around on eggshells thinking she's going to set off her sister on a rant or me into another crying jag. This entire week has just been one giant trauma trigger."

He pulled me closer for a hug and kissed the top of my head. "Stephanie drama aside, what else has you triggered? How many other Beth Shalom women messaged you this week?"

"So far, just Elisha. I chose not to respond, and she hasn't pushed the issue. Unfortunately, you can't block anyone on Linkedup, and I don't have grounds to report them as spam other than how I can't stand their smarmy hypocrisy."

"What happened to all that love and forgiveness you were preaching after a couple weeks at Grace Abounds?"

I smirked. "Apparently, I have a lot more anger and trauma to process before I even get to all that. I didn't realize how much of this has been buried and festering below the surface."

"Well, you've had a lot going on dealing with your divorce, with Rick and Stephanie, and then helping your girls emotionally regulate while you've been ignoring your own needs."

I frowned. "Yeah, and trying to fill those emotional needs with dating app trolls certainly didn't help. I think my lowest point was agreeing to go out with the divorce attorney."

"Have you heard from him since your date?"

"No, and that's probably for the best. The last time I went on Cougarville, his profile had been deleted. Hopefully, Sean either found somebody or he's taking time off."

"You're pretty tough to get over, Charlotte." Jon put a finger to my lips before I could rebut his comment. "Don't even mention your ex's name. Tonight, we are here to enjoy ourselves and ignore the rest of the world outside your front door. It's a Saturday night, and I'm with my girlfriend. My daughter is upstairs hanging out with both of yours, and I can hear them giggling. I have no complaints."

"Girlfriend," I murmured, repeating his words. "Feels so weird being in my forties and calling myself that."

He turned to meet my gaze. "Would you prefer something else?"

"No, I mean it's accurate. It's just weird. I feel like a teenager again."

"That's because we were making out pretty hot and heavy earlier." He stared down at my mouth like he wanted another round.

I laughed and playfully swatted his midsection. "I had no idea I'd be the one blowing all the hot air about romance, and you'd be the one putting your money where your mouth is."

"I happen to like your mouth." His voice lowered to a near growl, and the hungry look in his eyes made me blush. With a ravenous smile, he asked, "Am I allowed to put *more* money where your mouth is?"

I burrowed myself under the fleece blanket covering both of us. Our legs were outstretched and tangled together on the coffee table. I tried to shift away, but Jon pinned my feet in between his ankles.

"Don't tell me you're getting shy on me now, Charlotte."

"Shy? No. Stunned? Yes. The word *insatiable* comes to mind, and I'm still reeling."

"Are you complaining? The woman who once accused me of kissing you like I'm your brother?"

"I never said it was *just* like kissing my brother. Besides, you've more than proven yourself, sir." I pulled at my feet again, but he held them firmly in place.

"Ah, ah, ah," he teased. "Where do you think you're going?"

"You won't let me escape, will you?"

"Not on purpose."

"Who knew I was dating the big bad wolf?"

His laugh rumbled under my ear as he released my ankles to pull my entire body closer to him. "You're irresistible, what can I say?" Grinning down at me, he said, "Did you bring a picnic basket? The big bad wolf is hungry." He growled for comedic effect, and I shrieked in laughter. Leaning in for what should have been a quick kiss, I slid my fingers into his hair. Jon's second growl came from a place of passion, and I finally put a hand to his chest to slow down our burning pace. The desire for every intimacy denied to me during my marriage was not a fire needing to be kindled. Spontaneous combustion felt imminent.

With sore lips and heavy lids, I asked, "Why do I suddenly feel like a forty-four-year-old virgin who just happens to have two kids? Nobody has ever looked at me or talked to me the way you do."

"You sure don't kiss like a forty-four year old virgin. Not that I'm complaining." He pressed his lips against mine softly and then smiled down at me. "As much as I'm enjoying this, I think it's a good idea to cool it down. We have some necessary steps to handle first. By the way, what's your ring size?"

I pulled the fleece completely over my head. "Gah! Stop it! This is supposed to happen in romance novels, not real life."

Jon chuckled and slid down so that we met eye to eye under the blanket. Using a comical, evil villain tone, he taunted, "You can run, but you can't hide. I'll make you mine, Charlotte!"

I gasped in delight and decided to tickle him as revenge. It quickly escalated into a silly fight that brought our three daughters stampeding down the stairs. By the time they discovered us, I was laid perpendicular across Jon's lap in the fetal position. I laughed and squealed as tears ran down my cheeks.

"Uh, what is going on?" Rachel Roseman asked. "You guys okay?"

Lily's face scrunched in distress, "Mom, is Mr. Roseman hurting you?"

I glanced into Jon's dark eyes as he held back a laugh. Clearing my throat, I straightened myself and my sweatshirt, both of which had gone askew, and sat up.

"Just a tickle fight that got out of hand. No biggie."

My oldest daughter smirked. "Tickle fight? Is that what you guys are calling it?"

"Sophie!" I gasped.

She laughed, and it was a welcome sound to my ears. "I'm just kidding. But um, what happened to Mr. Roseman's hair?"

Jon's silver mane sat in mad scientist disarray thanks to static electricity from the blanket and our tickling activities.

I stifled a giggle beneath my palm. "This is quite a look for you."

"Do I even want to know?" he deadpanned.

Rachel had already snapped a photo and walked over to show her father. "This should totally be a meme, Dad."

Jon barked a laugh at the fabulously unflattering picture. "Let's put it on our Chanukah cards this year. Bubbe will love it."

"Is *Bubbe* what your girls call your mom?" I asked him.

He nodded. "Amazing lady. I think you'll love her and vice versa."

Sophie's eyebrows raised in pleasant surprise while the scowl on Lily's face darkened.

"What's wrong, baby?" I asked her.

"Are you guys seriously gonna get married, or are you just messing around because you're both lonely?"

"Ay yo!" Rachel objected. "That's my dad!"

"Yeah, and he's all over *my* mom."

"She doesn't seem to be complaining," Rachel shot back.

"You just want a new mom. It's not my fault yours died."

"Hey!" Jon exclaimed while his baby cried out in pain. "Not okay, Lily!" He stood to his feet and smoothed his hair to regain some dignity.

Angry tears spilled from her eyes. "You are *not* my dad, so stop trying to act like it. You ruined everything!" She stomped upstairs leaving a shellshocked Rachel, a wide-eyed Sophie, and me and Jon in utter disbelief.

"What just happened?" I murmured.

"She's been talking to Dad," Sophie said quietly.

"What do you mean she's been talking to him? Neither one of you has asked to go back to his house since Stephanie went full *kaiju* on him."

"Check the phone records, Mom. She's been talking to him

every night after we saw the FaceSpace photos with Stephanie. He said he was tricked."

"What do you mean? Your dad is holding the camera in all those selfies. Nobody tricked him into posing with his wife. He's probably the one who told her to post them on social media in the first place."

She shook her head. "No, Dad says he had no idea Tina fixed him up with Stephanie. He thinks you and Tina set him up to make the divorce go faster and so you could get custody and child support. He told Lily he's hiring a lawyer to get us back."

"What!" I shrieked, leaping from the couch. "That's insane! Your sister can't possibly believe any of this, can she? I would never do that to your father, and I certainly never would have encouraged him to be with Stephanie!"

"That's what I said," Sophie retorted with a long-suffering eye roll. "I don't think Lily believes you would do that, but he's really mad about Stephanie and Tina."

"Your father chose that relationship, no matter what Tina's involvement may have been. Nobody forced him into dating Stephanie or moving in with her before we signed our divorce papers. He's the one calling her the love of his life and rubbing his marriage in everyone's face for the last three years."

"Well, yeah, and Dad says *everything* is a set up whenever he gets caught doing something wrong…but this is different."

"Different, how?" Jon demanded. "He's still blaming your mother for his selfish choices. Sounds like business as usual to me."

I placed a restraining hand on his arm. "He's still her father," I pleaded.

He lifted his chin to silently acknowledge my request. Turning back to Sophie, he softened his tone. "When was the last time your dad said he was sorry for anything he's done to you, your sister, or your mother? Is he apologizing for all of that now?"

She swallowed before answering. "Well, Lily said Dad was crying a lot on the phone, but I don't know if he said the word *sorry*. He doesn't really do that, even if he knows he messed up. He said he made a huge mistake and wants his wife back, so I don't know if that counts as an apology."

"I am *not* his wife—!"

"She is *not* his wife!" Jon and I said at the same time.

Sophie rolled her eyes and harrumphed as if repeating herself to toddlers. "Look, I know. I'm happy for you guys. You're definitely #couplegoals and whatever else Tina lied and said about Dad and Stephanie instead. Lily wants our family back together, and Dad knows that. Honestly, I think he's just playing her because he's jealous of Mr. Roseman. She said he asked her a bunch of questions about you guys, but she didn't know anything. He got mad and made her cry. It's like he wants her to be his little spy or something."

Keeping the profanity I wanted to say gritted behind my teeth, I managed to calmly ask, "Why is our relationship any of his business?"

"Probably because you guys aren't posting everything all over FaceSpace and Instantpics like he is. I don't think he believed you would find somebody else."

"He can't seriously think I'm pining away for him, can he? I'm the one who filed for divorce, and he was the one who couldn't wait to abandon us for greener pastures."

My oldest shrugged.

"How did you find out about all of this anyway, Soph? Did Lily tell you, or did you overhear something?"

"Lily, told me, but she also told me not to tell. It didn't feel right, but I didn't know how to tell you. Please, don't be mad at her."

"Thank you for letting us know," Jon said sincerely. "We need to protect your sister and your mom from whatever your dad is trying to do here. By all accounts, he's blissfully in love with your stepmother, so maybe Lily misunderstood or just heard what she wanted to hear."

Sophie shook her head. "Lily said this is one hundred percent a secret, but Dad is going to leave Stephanie. I think there's some other stuff going on, but either she won't tell me what he said or Dad didn't give her the details. All I know is that it doesn't sound good."

"Something isn't adding up, Soph. Your father knows I will never go back to what our marriage used to look like. I wasn't happy, and I know he wasn't either."

"He just wants what he can't have anymore," Jon said, his dark eyes blazing as they met mine. "It has nothing to do with love and everything to do with jealousy. He can't stand to see your mother happy and loved when he used to have her begging for any scrap of his attention."

Rachel and Sophie wore matching shocked expressions but for entirely different reasons.

"You're in love?" Rachel whispered, her gaze darting between the two of us.

"Dad made you *beg* for attention?" Sophie demanded.

Jon stepped away from his daughter to hold my hand and address both of our girls as a united front. "Yes and yes. I am in love with this woman beside me. I've loved and respected Charlotte for a long time, and Sophie, the way your father treated your mother was criminal."

"You love me?" I mouthed, staring wide-eyed at him.

He winked back at me. "I do." He squeezed my hand, and

his declaration held notes of how he'd say it under a Jewish wedding canopy too.

Jon's eyes shifted to his daughter who looked dumbstruck. "Rach, are you okay?"

She nodded, continuing to stare at the two of us. "I just never thought you'd get over what happened to Mom. All I've ever wanted is to see you happy like you are in those old pictures. I've hated the idea of going away to school next year and leaving you all by yourself."

Tears filled my eyes as Jon released my hand to embrace his daughter.

In the meantime, I walked over to Sophie and pulled her into a hug.

"Do you love him too?" she said just loud enough for me to hear.

"I've loved him as a brother and a friend for a long time."

"Yeah, but are you in love with Mr. Roseman?"

I felt his gaze as Jon watched me intently along with his baby girl. I caught his eye, and his heart cried out to mine from inside those dark depths.

Jon Roseman was nothing like Rick Williams, and I knew that in my soul.

It was time to face my fears.

"I love you," I said, beaming at him, "and I am absolutely crazy about you too."

From the top of the stairs, Lily let out a muffled shriek of anguish and slammed her bedroom door.

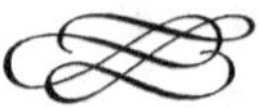

CHAPTER 33

CHARLOTTE, WE NEED TO TALK, RICK TEXTED ME OVER THE Family Wizard Messaging app. *When can I call you? It's important.*

You can message me here. Unless you are bleeding, dying, or stuck in a ditch, I would rather communicate in writing.

After a five minute pause where I assumed my noncompliance had resulted in the sullen, silent treatment, Rick surprised me by writing back. *I'm worried about Lily. Do you know why she's suddenly ignoring me? She's been making more of an effort to reach out to me, and I don't want anything to negatively influence our father-daughter relationship. She needs *both* parents in her life.*

The audacity of that man! Rick could no longer pump intel from a well that had gone dry, so he wanted to manipulate *me* into re-establishing the connection. As I'd already apprised my daughter, my relationship with Jon was none of her father's business beyond the fact we were dating. Lily still wrestled with wanting her nuclear family back together, and it took a while for her to see how Rick's request for intimate details was completely inappropriate. I understood her natural longing for reconciliation, but facilitating a romantic relationship was not a burden meant for her shoulders. Moreover, no amount of duplicity on his part—or hers—would aid the cause.

Lily asked if things would be different if Jon and I had simply remained friends. Matter-of-factly, I reminded her of Rick's choice to start his new life with Stephanie before our own marriage was over. He had already been romantically unavailable for three years regardless of Jon's role as friend or boyfriend. When Lily protested by using her father's latest tales of woe, I had to painfully restate the obvious. Rick was very much still married to her stepmother, and I would never jump into an adulterous relationship and reciprocate old sins upon Stephanie.

Lily could at least agree that two wrongs did not make a right.

Returning back to the present conversation, I typed and deleted a harsher response before finally settling on, *Lily is doing okay, and your concern is noted. What would help the most is for you to stop filling her head with the idea of you and I getting back together or that you're leaving your new wife to make that happen. I assure you, it won't work.*

I'm simply trying to open up dialogue, Charlotte. I would hope you'd be mature enough to handle a good faith conversation for the sake of our children and for their future.

What you're doing is causing confusion for our youngest daughter, and it needs to stop. For three years, you've done nothing but flaunt your new marriage in our collective faces. You've made it quite clear how you feel your new wife is an upgrade over the first one.

I never used those words, Charlotte. You're twisting things. If you would just talk to me, you would see how your jealousy and bitterness are what's really hurting our girls. What they need to see is a Mom and Dad who are able to show one another grace and forgiveness. We all make mistakes—including you. I hope you can show me the same graciousness I've displayed toward you over the years. It's what God would want from both of us.

I inhaled deeply through my nose and out through my mouth, pushed to the edge of my patience. I remembered all too well how much Rick loved provoking me. Throwing God into the mix of his entitled demands typically caused explosive disagreements—and here was Richard Carl Williams back to his gaslighting tricks. My ex-husband absolutely wanted me back. The *old* me whose emotions he could toy with to feel powerful and in control.

"Not anymore," I muttered. Older, wiser, and emotionally disengaged, the desire to repudiate his drivel died a quick death. Rick already knew he was lying. Why waste my precious energy trying to convince a liar that his accusations were, in fact, nothing but lies?

"Blessed are the peacemakers," I said, "because I refuse to feed into your drama."

Whatever issues are happening in your current marriage, our fifteen year-old does not need to hear about your adult problems. I sincerely hope you and Stephanie are able to work them out.

He didn't respond after that, and I enjoyed the reprieve. Rick would come slithering back with new ridiculous demands soon enough.

He always did.

I filled in Ro and Luke later that morning, and they responded as expected. Ro hissed out threats to stick pins into a Rick effigy, and Ginger Viking let loose his colorful vocabulary on the subject. In the meantime, another message popped up on Linkedup, and I wondered if there was some cosmic "Kick Me" sign sitting on my back. The hits just kept coming.

Castle_Elisha: Sorry to bother you again, but do you know what's going on with Stephanie and Tina? I thought they were best friends, but now they're flaming each other on FaceSpace. It's gotten pretty ugly, and nobody knows what to say. I was hoping you might have some advice or insight into the situation.

Charlotte Williams: I thought my silence would be enough of a message, but it looks like I'm going to have to be more direct. STOP messaging me. We are *not* friends. According to you, I don't even know what friendship is. Whatever is happening between Stephanie and Tina is none of my business, and shame on you for fishing for gossip. Mind your own business and pray for them instead!

Castle_Elisha: Your name came up, which is why I asked. I thought you'd want to know what they're saying about you.

Charlotte Williams: Well, I don't. Bye.

Undeterred, Elisha sent FaceSpace screenshots. I scanned them briefly, but the vitriol spewed between the fire-breathing monsters exceeded my tolerance for their brand of poison. Instead, I saved the screenshots and then uploaded them to the online dropbox for my attorney. We would have them on file if Rick persisted with revised custody and visitation, but I wouldn't have to give either woman any undue attention in the meantime.

I tried to focus on work, but the situation gnawed at me. It seemed too coincidental for both Rick and Elisha to message me on the same morning about the same subject. I texted Jon, and he told me to keep my eyes glued on Jesus. He reminded me this was their monkeys, their circus, and inevitably, they'd just scapegoat me for their narcissistic behavior anyway.

Gifted as a blessing in disguise, a malfunction with the MG Tooling database caused a glitch that deleted data for any assigned customer ID containing less than five digits. The task of manually updating the thousand or so accounts fell into my lap. Thankfully, it was a simple matter of double clicking a data entry field, allowing it to auto-populate, and then re-saving the customer information. The relatively brainless task kept me focused on something other than the muck of Rick and Stephanie's marital woes.

I received additional text message alerts from Rick, and I decided to temporarily ignore them. His badgering had nothing to do with the safety and welfare of my girls, and I needed additional time with Jesus to gird up my patience. Silently, I prayed at my desk and echoed the sentiments of Asaph, the Biblical psalmist, commanding his soul to chill out. The peace of God was the only way to navigate across the stormy waves of chaos.

I eked through the rest of my work day and finally ventured a peek at Rick's messages once I'd settled into the parking lot outside of my townhouse.

He had sent me four more texts, each about ten minutes apart, then seemed to give up around lunchtime. I was about to open the first one when my phone rang.

"Mom, are you home?" Lily asked.

"Yeah, I just pulled up. What's going on?"

"Can you come in?"

"Everything okay? Where's your sister?"

"She's at Rachel's. They um, didn't want me there."

My heart broke for her. Lily had done it to herself, but Rachel and Sophie were still angry about her outburst regarding Andrea Roseman. Sophie couldn't understand Lily's desire for a unified family, and despite Jon's best efforts to encourage his own daughter toward forgiveness, Lily had deeply offended her.

I turned off my phone and walked into the house. No sooner had I dropped my purse on the couch than Lily ran into my arms and buried her face against my chest.

"Oh, baby," I cooed, smoothing her hair as she sobbed. "It's okay. It's going to be okay."

She shook her head against me. "I'm so stupid, Mom. I have no friends. I'm a loser. It would be better if I was dead!"

I pulled back and held her gently by the shoulders. "No, ma'am! You are *not* a loser. You are an incredible, amazing, wonderful person, and this world needs you. Your family needs you. Your sister and I need you."

"Sophie says I'm an idiot. She said she wished Rachel was her sister instead of me."

I sucked in a harsh breath. "She shouldn't have said that, Lil. It was wrong, and I will talk to her about that. You're not an idiot. You have a big heart, and it's not wrong to want to see your parents in a loving relationship. Unfortunately, that's just not possible for your dad and me. No matter what he's telling you, that's not the kind of marriage we had or I think we could ever have together."

"Do you love Dad?"

I shook my head. "Not like that. Not anymore. Jesus says we're supposed to love everyone because He does, and that's as far as it goes. I don't hate your dad, and I don't even hate Stephanie, but he chose to marry someone else. That is the marriage he needs to fix. Even if he regrets the decision now, trying to get back together with me won't solve the problems they have—just like marrying Stephanie didn't change the issues he had in his relationship with me. It is what it is."

"Why can't you help him, Mom?"

"Because it's not my job to fix your father's mistakes. He's an adult, and he knows what the Bible says about the work he needs to do. Asking me to 'help' also means that if something doesn't turn out right, I'm now partially at fault. It's your father who's responsible for cleaning his own messes, not me."

"That just seems mean."

I cupped the side of her face. "It's the most loving thing I can do for him, baby."

She scowled. "How is it *loving* to refuse to help someone?"

"Because I tried for fifteen years to help your dad, and it blew up in my face. He liked to complain and make excuses, and it was easier for him to blame me for why he wouldn't even try. I had to stop helping him because it wasn't doing any good."

"Well, it sounds like he wants your help now."

I sighed heavily, knowing I had to canvas an emotional minefield. "Lily, when you ask me for help with homework, is it my job to *help* you or to do the work for you?"

She pulled a face. "This is different."

"No, it actually isn't. If I did the work for you, you would never learn what you need to know for class. Instead, you'd just fall even further behind. Your teacher would keep giving you new assignments, and now you'd need me even more to give you all the answers. You might even start to believe you can't do it on your own. Instead of learning, making mistakes but growing from them, you'd be failing tests in school because you didn't do the work. It might even be tempting to blame me for why you failed as if it was my job to give you all the right answers instead of *your* responsibility to learn the material. Make sense?"

She nodded slowly. "Yeah, I guess. So, loving me is forcing me to learn the lessons on my own."

"Exactly. I do want you and your sister to have a healthy relationship with your dad. I want you to feel comfortable being yourselves around him and not walking on eggshells either because he's going to be overly critical or because Stephanie will throw a fit about something. Unfortunately, the homework they need to do in their own hearts is not something I can do for them. They've both blamed me, you, and your sister long enough. Me reconciling with Dad wouldn't fix any of that. You and Sophie still walked on eggshells when we were married, and I was miserable living like that. I won't do it ever again."

"Are you saying you didn't do anything wrong and it's all just Dad?"

"No, not at all!"

"Well, is there something you could have done better, or are you just making it all Dad's fault the way he acts like it's all yours?"

I met and held her eyes. I *had* done my homework with Jesus, and painful to admit, I was hardly innocent myself. "I had a part to play too, Lil. I was hurt by your dad's behavior, and I let it build up in my heart. There were a lot of times I was unkind to him, impatient, or got frustrated easily. Toward the end, I just didn't care anymore. He got into a small accident with my car, and since he said he was fine, I asked what happened to my car. He was hurt because he thought I cared more about the car than I did about him. Mostly, I was irritated that he dented it and acted like it was no big deal. I was hurt, and so I lashed out at him. It was wrong, and I've had to look at my own heart and all the anger. God has helped me forgive your father and also repent to Jesus for what I've done. That being said, just because I've worked on healing doesn't mean I want to get back together with him."

She pulled away from my tender grasp. "Because you're in love with Mr. Roseman now?"

"No, baby. Because your father and I never had a healthy relationship. He chose to make a new life with Stephanie rather than work on the relationship he and I had, and it is what it is. I had to grow and heal, and I've found someone who loves me, loves you girls, and who I genuinely respect and admire. Everyone has moved on with their lives."

She sniffled and shook her head.

"Baby, it's gonna be okay."

"You don't know that. What if you marry Mr. Roseman and it's even worse than when you were married to Dad? What if Rachel hates me forever and then Sophie wants to be Rachel's sister instead of mine?"

I offered a gentle smile. "Lil, you're getting upset over things that haven't even happened. I don't know what will happen if I marry Mr. Roseman or your friendship with Rachel, but I know for a fact your sister would never treat you that way. She loves you and has since the moment I told her you were in my belly. Don't doubt that."

Lily's eyes filled with tears and spilled over, and I silently prayed as I held her. While she was upstairs getting ready for bed, I shot Jon a text and asked him to send Sophie home and also speak to both girls about their relationship with Lily.

I couldn't fault my baby for her big heart, but it didn't excuse willfully blinding herself to the truth. To that end, I begged God for His grace toward all three of our daughters.

CHAPTER 34

RICK CONTINUED TO PESTER ME INTO THE WEEKEND, and I skimmed and promptly ignored his whiny texts. Lily worked things out with her sister and their best friend, and it helped steer her loyalties away from her father's shenanigans. Meanwhile, I continued to pray and brace myself for the imminent bombshell coming from the Williams Marriage 2.0. For Rick to come crawling back—or his wounded ego version where I should be the one groveling in gratitude for the opportunity—it meant we were due for an implosion.

To my utter horror, Sean Bonham's warning came crashing back after Elisha sent another round of screenshots. Before me sat the real reason for Rick wanting to restore his broken family, and I seethed at his egregious act of fraud. My lazy ex-husband could more easily repair something he'd stomped on and discarded rather than a nuclear disaster.

> Tina Madison: There can be nothing worse than loving and trusting someone like a sister only to realize they were never really your friend. The betrayal is something I would never wish on my worst enemy.

I set down my coffee so I wouldn't foam at the mouth. I knew the post had to be about Stephanie, but it landed like a ridiculous insult to injury. Piqued, I forced myself to continue on while muttering words like *lying cow* and other less savory sentiments. I vowed I'd repent of my bad attitude once I'd finished with Tina's exercise in shameless hypocrisy.

> When someone deliberately harms your children, better an upper millstone be tied around their neck. Vengeance might be God's, but I won't be silent about the trauma done to my son. I don't care how many years it's been, nothing will wipe away your stain on him, you godless Jezebel!

I covered my mouth in disbelief. Thinking aloud, I said, "Both of Tina's boys are in their twenties now. How long ago did this happen? Did Stephanie mess around with Paxton or with Colt?"

Colton Fournier, Tina's firstborn son, claimed he was nonbinary, queer, and a host of other names and adjectives after first coming out as bisexual that Tina dismissively referred to as the "part of the Alphabet People Cult." Admittedly, I didn't know much about the latest wave of sexual identification, only that Colton's androgynous style drove his mother batty. Tina was smothering and opinionated on her good days, and her son resented it. The text messages between them read like petty school children on the playground.

By contrast, younger son Paxton came off as more of a loner, quiet and completely closed off emotionally. Whereas Colt wanted to be the life of the party, Paxton preferred lingering in the shadows. He didn't strike me as the kind of young buck to fall into bed with his mother's friend, but I could also envision Pax being easy pickings for someone as manipulative as Stephanie. Loneliness was a powerful drug, and I knew all too well the mistakes I'd made in more desperate moments.

I shuddered at the mental image of either scenario, but the hateful social media posts suddenly made sense. The "We Hate Charlotte Club" had officially disbanded. Rick, Stephanie, and Tina were three heads of the same monster, a metaphorical *Ghidorah* of Japanese film lore. With each neck a different dragon head, they were now attacking each other for survival.

"I wonder what bothers Tina more," I murmured, "that Stephanie seduced one of her sons or that the woman she used to seduce *my* husband was actually manipulating *her* instead. Oh, those poor boys!"

Despite the public display of Mama Bear claws, Tina's unhealthy obsession with her children had little to do with love. Her sons were an extension and reflection of herself, and she'd said as much over the years. Likewise, her little pet Stephanie was supposed to be a convenient puppet, not a free thinking agent with her own desires.

Frowning, I opened the next few screenshots containing Stephanie's rebuttal in the court of public opinion. Tina had responded with a passive aggressive meme minutes later. Tit for tat, Stephanie posted a meme of her own.

> Stephanie (Burgess) Williams: Hopefully, people realize that not everything you read on the internet is true. *Some people* play the victim while spreading their venom.

> Tina Madison: Liars beware: the truth always wins.

> Stephanie (Burgess) Williams: Only a liar has to convince you how honest they are.

"Ug, this is so disgusting! Both of you are liars!" I rubbed my eyes and wished I could bleach their words from my brain. I sent the screenshots to Jon and warned him to find a private place to view the heinous information.

In the interim, Ginger Viking approached with his usual coffee and paused to scan the contents of my computer screens. The coffee in his mouth promptly sprayed across my desk.

"Gross!" I yelled, jumping to my feet. "Go get a paper towel."

"Does that mean what I think it does?" he gaped, wiping his mouth with the back of his hand.

"Clean your coffee off my desk and then we'll figure out what's going on with the spilled tea," I replied.

Luke rushed into our galley style kitchenette and returned with cleaning materials.

Elisha had sent a few other screenshots, but it all read like more of the same. Rick distancing himself from Stephanie pointed to Tina's accusations being true, but I also wondered if he was just mad at being manipulated. He certainly hadn't improved in how he treated me and the girls. His only "change of heart" was in who he felt could best serve his selfish needs.

Luke read over my shoulder and reacted in gasps and grunts before meeting my eyes.

"Are you as confused as I am?" I asked. "I mean, it's not like I wasn't already warned about Stephanie, but Tina is such a two faced liar. This whole thing is more toxic than a Brittany Spires concert at Chernobyl."

He shook his head in disgust. "Buffalo Butt has two boys, right?"

I nodded. "Yeah, and if what Tina's saying is true, I don't know which one Stephanie messed around with. Also, I don't know how long the two of them were friends. This could have happened years ago, possibly when someone was underage."

"Do you really think Stephanie would have slept with a teenager?"

"I don't know. Given how old the boys are, this happened a while ago. Possibly when Stephanie was still married to her first husband."

"So, multiple crimes here?"

I shrugged. "Looks like. This must have taken place before David passed, but Tina never mentioned Stephanie in the twelve years she and I were supposedly best friends. Something just isn't right."

Luke studied my ex-husband's new wife with his upper lip curled in disgust. "I can understand how Stephanie bagged a guy like Rick since he likes strong women he can hide behind. I have a harder time believing either of Tina's sons would be interested in her. Then again, never underestimate a man with a free opportunity." He folded his beefy arms across his chest before turning away.

As Luke went back to the kitchen for a replacement coffee, my mind continued to whirl. I realized how in my efforts to clear my heart of bitterness, I had turned Stephanie into the victim of Rick and Tina's machinations. I recalled the longing glances Stephanie had bestowed on Sean and her brazen jealousy despite being on a date with the husband she'd stolen from me. Transforming Stephanie into the unwitting victim was my way of making her sins easier to forgive. Unfortunately, it was a foolish endeavor. Likewise, for all of Tina's sins against me, I would never wish harm against her children as revenge for what she'd done to mine. The Fournier boys weren't responsible for their mother's cruelty.

Lifting my eyes upward, I asked the Lord to reveal the truth and help me and my girls stay clean from the mudslinging. I eked through the rest of the week, and Jon brought me to church the following Sunday. Part of me hoped I'd see the answer written in big letters on the projector screen.

Instead, my unrest lingered as peace slipped through my fingers like sand.

"Charlotte, you have to stop," Jon said, placing his hand on my knee as it jittered up and down. "Not your circus, remember? Did you hear any of the sermon today?"

"I just can't make it make sense."

"Why does it matter? You're not getting back together with Rick, you're not friends with Tina, and Lily finally accepted things can't go back to how they were."

"But I still want to know."

"Why? What difference does it make? I don't think the answer would improve your opinion of any of the people involved. Be thankful they're tearing down each other instead of you, for once."

I sighed heavily. "I don't want them tearing down anybody. I would rather they all sincerely repent and get their lives right with Jesus."

His face held a sad smile. "I love that you want that for

them, but it will take a literal act of God for that to happen. It doesn't mean it can't, but for Rick and Tina especially, they have such a warped view of Jesus."

"What if Stephanie messing around with Colton is why he's so sexually confused now? What if that's why Paxton is so quiet? The kid definitely seems traumatized."

"You have to stop," Jon said more forcefully. "This is not your fight, and these are not your sons. You also don't know if Tina is making this whole thing up. It wouldn't be the first reputation she's ruined with outrageous lies."

"Jon, there's no way she'd publicly tar and feather Stephanie for harming her kids if it was made up. Colton, at least, would call out his mother for doing that."

"Look, here's what we *do* know. Tina set up Stephanie and Rick. We don't know if Stephanie knew about your connection with Tina, but obviously, she was all in favor of the match-making. Rick, from what we can gather, had no idea about any of it. Not that it makes him innocent of adultery and aban-donment—only that he didn't know he was being manipulated as revenge against you by Tina. Rick thought marrying Stephanie was his *own* brilliant idea to get back at you. Now, he's got egg on his face for being the dupe of both women and being tied to Stephanie's scandal. He looks like a complete fool."

"That's because he *is* a fool," I said, "and I don't mean that as an insult either. According to *Proverbs,* that's exactly what he is. It grieves me for my girls and also as his ex-wife. Sure, I've had moments of wanting to see Rick exposed and humiliated after what he did to my reputation, but I never envisioned something like this."

Jon looked thoughtful. "Do you remember the conversation we had about God's justice versus yours?"

"Oh," I murmured. "You told me that God's version would be much more thorough than anything I could imagine."

"Exactly. Tina and Stephanie aren't the innocent victims any more than Rick. They all hurt and betrayed you and your children. They've slandered you to anyone who might believe their garbage, and all while making a mockery of the Lord in the process. Nothing that's been hidden will remain in the dark forever, and all I can pray is that your vindication will finally shine forth."

"I don't need vindication at their expense, Jon. I just want to be emotionally divorced from the three of them. I want my heart to be healed, and I don't want their stupid behavior to affect me anymore."

He put his arm around me and pulled me into his chest. Kissing the top of my head, he said, "And I love you even more for it. You are absolutely owed vengeance, and I love that you don't even want it. That speaks to how much healing has already happened in your heart, Charlotte. It's inspiring. I remember the conversations we used to have about all three of these people. Tina got mercy she didn't deserve from you, and Stephanie and Rick were a huge source of anger and bitterness. You've come so far, and I am unbelievably proud of you."

I laid my palm flat against his heart and sighed into the warmth of his body. "Thank you."

"So, I guess it's official," a familiar voice said from behind us.

Jon and I both rose to see Elisha Castle in the flesh.

"What are you doing here?" I gaped. "Are you stalking me now?"

She let out a trilling little laugh. "Someone told me you were going here, and I wanted to check it out for myself."

"How is Charlotte's life any of your business?" Jon growled.

"And you know how Beth Shalom feels about members in high profile ministry positions attending other houses of worship. Can't have a house divided, remember?"

"Josh and I left Beth Shalom."

"What do you mean you left?" I repeated. "You stopped being my friend because I dared to point out flaws in the synagogue. Did you finally stop making excuses for all their corruption and abuse?"

A sheepish look crossed her face. "Yeah, about that…I'm sorry, Charlotte. You were right to call me out for what I said to you all those years ago. I just didn't know how to handle being on the prayer team and then hearing the negative stuff you said about Beth Shalom."

"It wasn't *negative stuff*, Elisha. They were valid concerns, and they turned out to be true. You can ask Lauren Fein yourself. Beth Shalom kept her pig ex-husband on leadership despite everything he did to harm her and their son. They covered for the underage porn he downloaded onto the synagogue servers, and there you were, shunning Lauren along with the rest of that hotbed of hypocrisy."

She glanced down at her designer ballet flats.

"If you came here looking for gossip, you won't find any," Jon added. "We have nothing to share about our relationship or what's going on with the Williams' marriage or with Tina."

"No, but I do," she finally said.

CHAPTER 35

"What could you possibly know?" I demanded. "Why send me all those screenshots? You're the one who asked *me* for information, remember?"

"I did. And then I had a conversation with my son because he's still friends with Paxton Fournier. It changed everything for us."

Jon and I exchanged a glance, bracing ourselves for the worst.

"I don't think Paxton was lying when he talked to Aiden," she began, inhaling a deep breath. "It's Tina and Stephanie who are both misrepresenting the situation, but about completely different parts of it."

"So, what *did* happen?" I asked.

"There was never any sexual misconduct between Stephanie and the Fournier boys. Tina's post makes it sound that way, and it's why Paxton reached out to Aiden. For Stephanie to clear the record still paints herself in a horrible light, and Tina knows that. Rick is caught in the middle because defending Stephanie against Tina's accusations means he has to defend what Stephanie *actually* did, and there's no way he can do that. I'm not even sure he knew about anything until the scandal blew up on social media. Everybody knows Stephanie's got a big mouth and an even bigger personality, so I've been genuinely surprised how she kept this a secret for so long."

"Explain," Jon said tersely, "and stop with the cryptic answers. We're not here for gossip or speculation, Elisha."

"Stephanie had an affair with *David* Fournier, not either of his sons. They worked in the office together, and the relationship went on for several years. Eventually, they got caught. It's the real reason Stephanie's first husband filed for divorce. I can't say for certain, but I feel like she gave him primary physical custody of their boys to keep it out of the divorce paperwork and becoming public record. Of course, Stephanie has a very different version of things, but after what Paxton shared, this made the most sense."

"Oh," I breathed.

"Did that Sean guy ever mention an affair?" Jon asked me.

"He just said she seemed desperate for male attention however she could get it. I can't say I'm surprised, but I also understand why he couldn't come right out and tell me. If adultery isn't mentioned in the divorce decree, there's no way he could have shared that without violating her attorney-client privilege."

Elisha looked confused, but I didn't feel like explaining my connection to Stephanie's former divorce attorney.

Re-focusing the conversation, I asked, "How did Paxton know about the affair with his father or Stephanie's divorce details?"

"David and Stephanie became careless at the end of their relationship. This wasn't long before David passed either. From my understanding, Stephanie attended the funeral with some of their coworkers. That's how she first befriended Tina."

"And nobody thought to mention it to David's *wife*?" I asked incredulously.

"I have no idea."

"So, what *do* you know?" Jon asked her.

"Look, this is all second hand from my son. Aiden says Paxton walked in on his father and Stephanie together while he was in high school. That's *the stain* Tina is talking about on FaceSpace. I don't think she had any idea David was unfaithful, let alone with someone she considered a close friend."

"So, that's why Pax is so quiet," I murmured. "That must have been horrible for him—and then to keep it a secret all this time! Tina bragged constantly about the bond between the boys and their father, but I can't imagine Pax remaining *this* loyal, especially after David was gone. There has to be some other explanation."

Jon's eyes narrowed. "This is all pretty delicate intel, Elisha. Do you really expect us to believe your son is now privy to this type of information?"

She didn't flinch at the accusation. "Like I said, the boys have been friends for a long time, and I think Pax finally got tired of carrying the burden. He saw the FaceSpace post where Tina took credit for Rick and Stephanie's marriage, and he knew had to tell his mother the truth. I don't think he realized Tina knew Stephanie at all or that Rick had married her immediately after the divorce. Pax says Stephanie swore him to secrecy at the funeral and told him nothing good would come of his mother or brother finding out about the affair. She said his father would want to rest in peace knowing he still had their respect."

I gasped in disgust. "That self serving snake!"

Elisha placed a hand on my arm and met my eyes. "Just so

you know, Paxton stuck up for you. He told Tina what she did was wrong by kicking you and the girls out with Covid. He feels really guilty for getting you guys sick."

I waved off Paxton's culpability even though he couldn't see my reaction. "It's not his fault, and I never blamed him for it. Tina was careless, not Pax. Water under the bridge."

Jon took control of the conversation. "So, that's it? Paxton saw the photo comments and finally told Tina about his father's relationship with Stephanie?"

"No, there's more. Pax hated how his mother crowed about splitting apart Charlotte's marriage, and he couldn't believe how Stephanie had gotten away with fooling everyone. Tina's behavior was wrong, but she had no idea just *how* wrong. She didn't know Stephanie had fractured her own family first."

"Tina never had a happy marriage," I corrected. "At least not to hear her version of it. More like a business partnership."

"I didn't know about any of that, but obviously there wasn't much hope for turning it around if David was sleeping with someone else. His cancer progressed quickly, and that's when he got sloppy at hiding the affair—they both knew his time was short. The day Pax discovered them, Stephanie had taken David to his oncology appointment. I think Tina was busy with something at Beth Shalom. He said David explained the situation and begged him not to tell his mother. His father apologized for not being more discreet, but not for the affair itself."

"And you found out all of this from your son?" Jon asked her again.

Elisha swallowed and nodded. "Yeah. Pax reached out to Aiden after he confessed to his mother. He knew she wouldn't be happy about it, but since his dad is gone and both Tina and Stephanie are remarried, he thought his mom could handle it."

"Clearly not," I deadpanned. "Tina loves her secrets, but to be played like this would have set her over. I've gotten a taste of her wrath, and it's scary, to say the least. I can't even imagine what she said to Pax. I saw what she texted Colton about being queer, and it was absolutely horrifying."

Elisha's expression was grim. "Aiden saw the text messages she sent Pax, but he wouldn't show me. It sounds like what you're describing though. All he really said was that she'd lost her mind and Pax was struggling with wanting to kill himself."

"That's horrible!" I gasped. "Poor Pax!"

"That's why he reached out to Aiden. He was having suicidal thoughts, and he needed to talk to somebody who would understand. With Tina, we all know she can be vicious and downright cruel, so it was appalling but not a surprise for any of us. I think Rabbi is even scared of her."

Jon blew a raspberry. "More like your rabbi can't be bothered since Tina only bullies *women* in the congregation. He's never had much regard for them anyway. Tina's probably saving him the trouble of doing it himself."

Elisha frowned but acceded his point with a nod. "Yeah... you're probably right. I can't deny it anymore."

"This is so awful!" I cried, my heart full of pity for Tina's youngest son. "Pax is a good kid. He doesn't deserve any of that."

To my surprise, Elisha was not finished. "Josh and I went to Rabbi because we didn't feel right about how the situation was being handled. Tina is on sisterhood leadership, and Stephanie got moved onto the intercessory team a few months ago. The drama isn't good for anyone, and it's causing division because people are choosing sides."

"Is this why you asked me what was going on?" I said to her.

"Initially, yes. Aiden was acting funny too. All I could see were the accusations going back and forth on FaceSpace. I think

I made a comment about it at dinner one night, and that's when Aiden told us everything. He's worried about Pax. There's been so much tension at temple because of it, and Stephanie shares vindictive things about Tina in our prayer meetings. She pretends it's a general prayer need regarding spiritual warfare or a Jezebel spirit influencing the congregation, but nobody's fooled."

Jon rolled his eyes. "Are we still in middle school? Sheesh!"

"What did Harvey say when you brought this to him?" I asked.

"Harvey?"

"Yeah. Your rabbi has a first name. I refuse to call him by his self-appointed title anymore. Thirty years ago, he took a couple seminary classes and called himself 'Rabbi.' It's an open secret for all of the boomer generation leaders in Messianic Judaism. If you've wondered why Harvey's Hebrew pronunciation is atrocious and he can't read from the Torah, that's why. He knows almost nothing about Judaism other than playing at the appearance of it."

She winced. "Yeah, I guess that makes more sense."

"So, what did he say when you confronted him?" Jon asked.

"He told us to mind our own business and let him handle it."

"Ah, so do nothing?" he spat.

She shook her head vehemently. "No! Rabbi called a meeting with Josh there and a few other men and had a sit down with Rick only."

"Weird," I murmured.

"He told Rick to get his wife under control and that it was an embarrassment to the congregation. Josh was stunned. Rabbi basically told Rick, 'Your ex-wife caused a lot of drama around here, but at least we could keep her in line. Fix it, or we'll demote both of you from being *shammashim*.'"

My mouth sagged as my arms fell lifeless at my sides. Apparently, my ex-husband had a use for me besides being his emotional punching bag. He'd rather suffer another divorce and reconcile with the wife he hated instead of forfeiting his lofty position at Beth Shalom.

Jon's eyes burned bright in anger. "I always think my opinion of Rick can't sink any lower, but he still manages to exceed my expectations."

I turned back to Elisha. "Is that everything, or is there more?"

"You were right to call me out for being a horrible friend," she said contritely, "What I posted on FaceSpace about Satan attacking me..." her voice trailed off.

"Yes?" I demanded when she didn't finish. "Did your precious rabbi put you up to it?"

She nodded. "He told me to distance myself from you because bad company corrupts good character. He also told me not to say anything to you directly because it would make your *tendencies* even worse. He said you would eventually catch on when people stopped listening to your gossip and complaints. He told me to pray for God to soften your heart."

I swallowed that bitter pill of information while I could hear Jon's teeth grinding.

"That fraud has harmed more lives than I can count," he glowered.

Elisha met my eyes. "I am so sorry for what I said and did to you, Charlotte. It was wrong, and I'm embarrassed by how long it took me to realize it. I knew Rick and Stephanie got together fast, but I had no idea Tina was behind everything. You guys were best friends, and Tina made it seem like you betrayed *her*.

All three of them have said horrible things about you, and combined with what Rabbi...er Harvey warned me about you, it seemed crazy that all of these people would be intentionally lying."

"Except for what you knew about my character back when we were still friends," I said pointedly. "Before you sold your soul to Beth Shalom and stuck your head in the ground about everything wrong in that place."

Tears filled her brown eyes. "You're right. And I have to live with the shame of what I've done. I found out you've been coming to this church, and I needed to tell you everything in person. You never deserved what I did to you or what anybody else in Beth Shalom leadership has done. It was wrong. *I* was wrong."

"Did Harvey tell you to shun me after you got promoted to the prayer team, or only after I called you out about our friendship? Things got weird before you ghosted me."

"What do you mean?"

"Exactly what I said. Was it some sort of unspoken rule at Beth Shalom that once you move into the inner circle, you can't be friends with Charlotte Williams anymore? It certainly felt that way."

"Honestly? Yes and no. You questioned things, and you got other people asking questions too. Rabbi didn't like that. He said you were unsubmissive to your husband, unsubmissive to his leadership, and a bad influence. He never told us outright to reject you, but it was basically understood. I can see now that it was cowardly and deliberately hurtful. He used us to punish you for seeing what we couldn't."

I inhaled and exhaled deeply, grateful to be validated, but gutted by the revelation. All I ever wanted was an explanation for the disparity between what was preached in the congregation versus the poor treatment of its members. Instead, I was treated like a pariah for shining a light on it.

Lost in thought, I didn't immediately register the feel of warm, comforting hands running up and down my arms. "Thanks," I murmured, meeting Jon's concerned gaze.

"They never deserved you," he said fervently. "None of them. Not Rick, not Beth Shalom, and certainly not that witch who pretended to be your friend."

I turned my attention back to Elisha. "Is that everything?"

"Tina and George are getting divorced, but you probably already knew that."

My eyes widened, floored that the revelations weren't over yet. "Are you sure?"

She nodded. "I don't think he's been happy for a while. Paxton told Aiden about it. He likes George, and I think he felt sorry for him being married to his mom. I'm not sure how the scandal with Stephanie and David plays into all of that, but I don't think George agrees with how she's treating Pax."

"She'll probably blame that on Stephanie too," I mused aloud.

"What a mess," Jon exhaled. "What a complete mess."

CHAPTER 36

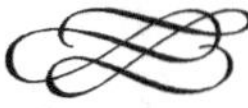

"I don't even know how to process this," I said, staggering backwards into Jon's awaiting arms. "Here I was working on forgiveness toward the three of them—Stephanie especially—and it turns out she's just as guilty as the other two." I tilted my head to meet his eyes. "They all used each other, didn't they?"

He cupped the side of my face as his expression softened. "Your husband and best friend thought they had the perfect revenge against you. Stephanie proved to be the wild card nobody saw coming. Rick and Tina assumed they would manipulate her like they do to everyone else, and Stephanie thought she'd fooled everybody once again."

Elisha cleared her throat, reminding us of her presence. "I just wanted you to know the truth, Charlotte. I felt like you deserved that much. I don't agree with how Rabbi or Tina have handled things, and you helped me to understand why, even though it's hard to hear. If Tina had just told the truth about

Stephanie and David, it would have been enough. Now, this thing is snowballing out of control. It's like they can't help themselves from making it worse."

"Have you never met a narcissist?" I asked. "Let alone a wounded one?"

She scoffed. "Everybody throws that word around these days."

"How about Leviathan?" Jon offered. "People are fond of using that demon name too, but it's real, and we have all encountered it one way or another."

She looked nonplussed. "Never heard of it."

He replied, "It's mentioned in the books of *Job, Isaiah,* and *Psalms.* Think of a twisty water dragon that gets people spinning in circles with its lies. In this case, it's false religion, or what *2 Timothy 3:5* calls, 'maintaining the outer form of religion but denying its power.'"

"Isn't that just Satan anyway? Why get so specific with the demon?" she asked.

I arched an eyebrow. "This coming from the same person who once believed every woman Harvey Lebow doesn't like has a Jezebel spirit? Is it really that far-fetched, Elisha?"

She pursed her lips. "I'm just saying that I've never heard of it."

"Trust me, you know it when you stare into its eyes. With Tina, you could feel her calculating and assessing you, always smugly satisfied like she knew something you didn't. With Rick, I saw it more in our family photos. Dead eyes, but also this perpetual undercurrent of seething. His face looked like a mask with a hateful glare staring at you from behind it."

She shuddered. "That sounds like a horror movie."

"If you've been in a relationship with someone manifesting it, you'll feel like you're living in one. Ask me how I know."

Adding to my defense, Jon said, "The things I've seen Harvey say and do behind closed doors are such a stark contrast to the warm and friendly persona he uses with visitors. He treats members of that congregation like batteries powering his Beth Shalom kingdom. I've seen firsthand how he throws away those 'dead batteries' once he has no more use for them. Literally and figuratively, he discards people who either burn out or don't tow the company line."

"So, you think *all* of those people have this demon?" Elisha sputtered. "Couldn't it be some misunderstanding or even just sin?"

"Oh, it's definitely sin," Jon responded quickly, "but think about the level of cruelty and total disregard for people. Think about the amount of cunning it takes to live their double lives. Most evil of all, they know they're harming innocent people. They relish in their deceit and the element of surprise. They want complete destruction of anyone they deem their enemy. Who does that sound like to you? How could it be anything other than demonic?"

She frowned heavily.

He continued, "How could anyone who has truly experienced the love and grace of Jesus willingly cause suffering to others when it's our Messiah who says how we treat people will show if we really belong to Him? You've read *Matthew 25*, I'm sure."

Her eyes widened and she stammered to give voice to her thoughts.

I left Jon's protective embrace to offer comfort. "I didn't come by this revelation overnight, and I've taken it to the Lord so many times. Even as the victim in all this, that didn't make me sin-free. Repenting and cleaning my own heart helped reveal so much of this. Our battle isn't against flesh and blood, remember?"

She slowly nodded. "I feel like a bomb has gone off in my face. I'm reeling."

"Welcome to the club," Jon quipped. "There's been no shortage of surprises today."

My breath caught, instantly reminded of the surety I felt the night Tina publicly announced her own betrayal. Her hubris had been her downfall, and God allowed the trap Tina set for me to ensure her own destruction. Awed, I said, "And to think, all of this is because Jon and I decided to meet for coffee four weeks ago. If Tina hadn't been there, hadn't seen us, who knows if she would have felt the need to spoil our relationship by boasting how she'd hurt me."

"Pride comes before the fall," Jon quoted from *Proverbs*.

Quoting the same book, I replied, "Whoever digs a pit will fall into it; if someone rolls a stone, it will roll back on them."

Elisha seemed to shake off the stupor of our conversation and begged off. I couldn't blame her as Jon and I had equal amounts of difficult information to chew and digest. We didn't stay much longer at church, and when he took me home, I planned to give the girls a more high-level version of events. Instead, I noticed a car parked behind mine in the cul-de-sac. Jon had picked me up and taken me to church, so I had left my car at home. As we approached, I realized my girls had an unwanted visitor in the house.

"This day just keeps on getting better," Jon muttered, recognizing Rick Williams' flashy new vehicle. "Is he allowed to just show up to see the girls?"

I fought against the churning anxiety in my gut. "It's not like I have a restraining order, but he's never done this before.

Elisha knew we would be at Grace Abounds, and if *she* knew about it, I'm concerned Rick did too."

Jon pulled into one of the visitor parking spaces, and we walked briskly back to my townhouse.

I opened the front door with little preamble, and Rick's eyes widened as if caught with his hand in the cookie jar. Surprise gave way to sullen jealousy as Jon quickly filled the space behind me.

"What is he doing here?" my ex-husband blurted out.

"Funny, I could ask you the same thing," I retorted. "Girls, did you invite your father to come over?"

Sophie's gaze shifted to her sister, and Lily's head bent in shame.

"Do you have a problem with me being here?" Rick sneered, nose in the air. The catlike gleam in his eye set off warning bells. Even a negative reaction would be "proof" to my ex-husband that I still had feelings for him. Regardless of whether those feelings were disgust and loathing, he would somehow still internalize it as *she wants me back*.

Forcing out a sigh of boredom rather than exasperation, I replied, "I have a problem with you being in my home unannounced. Just like I'm sure you'd have a problem if you arrived home to find me having tea and scones with Stephanie."

He barked out a mocking laugh at that thought. He'd worked too hard to make us all hate each other to think it could happen.

I tried to keep my voice calm. "Lily, did you invite your dad over?"

"Yeah," she whispered.

He jumped to his feet, wagging his finger. "See! I *was* invited. Is there a reason why our daughter needs to hide something like that from you? The courts don't look kindly on parental alien-ation, you know."

"She didn't hide anything," Sophie interrupted. "Mom had her phone turned off at church. Quit trying to start a fight, Dad."

His eyes lasered to our oldest as he exhaled what sounded like a hiss. "Don't you take that disrespectful tone of voice with me, Sophie Grace! Your mother may allow—"

"That's enough!" Jon roared, posturing himself to defend both me and Sophie. "This isn't your house, and you don't make the rules here."

Rick looked Jon over with obvious disdain. "And you think you do?"

"No, *I* do," I snapped. "Whether Lily invited you here or not, you will not disrespect me in my own home."

He rolled his eyes. "Typical. Nothing's changed about you."

At this point, I smiled wide, shocking the smirk right off his face. So much *had* changed in my heart, and even with Jon Roseman poised to do battle like my knight in shining armor, I felt the spiritual fruit of all the homework I'd done in my heart.

"Rick, if you'd like to continue this conversation with *Lily* or even resume visitation of her spending the night, that's fine with me. However, I would prefer you not stop by my home without talking to *me* first, rather than our daughter. Lily, you're free to go with your dad, but for future reference, please don't invite him over without me being home."

She met my eyes from beneath her lashes, perhaps looking for the vengeful response her father would have given in the same situation. Instead, I smiled at her encouragingly. "It's okay, baby. It's an honest mistake."

Rick cleared his throat. "Well, uh, I have some other things to do today, so I won't be able to change my plans simply to make it more convenient for you, Charlotte."

"If you have time to talk to our daughter in my living room, I don't see why you'd have a problem talking to her five minutes up the road at Dinky's Donuts. Lily's always loved the chocolate glazed ones. If the plan was to ambush *me* by being here, I'm not going to apologize for disappointing you."

Guilt flashed for a split second before he covered it with his pompous peacock persona. "Of course, you'd have to make it all about *you*, wouldn't you?"

"You are in my home, Rick, so yes, it *is* about me right now. I'm providing a solution to the current problem. Since you came here to see our daughter, you've got several options. You can see her at your own home when you take her there, you can take her to some location close by, or we can end the current visit. Either way, you will not be staying here any longer."

Completely ignoring me, his eyes swept over our tiny great room and into the kitchen. "It's a nice place, Charlotte."

A low snarl rumbled in Jon's throat, and I knew it was self control from the Holy Spirit that kept him from fighting in a more primitive manner.

I moved to stand in front of Rick and block his eyeline and forward progress. "You need to leave my house. Now."

"What are you gonna do? Have your boyfriend beat me up?"

"No, I'll just call the police and you can explain to them why you refuse to leave. Sophie's got her phone out, and she's been recording. I've asked you multiple times to go, and you're refusing."

"I was invited here!"

"Not by the owner of this home. Consider the invitation revoked."

"Just stop!" Lily cried, jumping to her feet. "Dad, let's just go, okay?"

"Your mother needs to understand she doesn't get to boss me around," he sniffed indignantly. "No wonder you girls act this way when this is what she models for you."

The lid on my temper rattled, and I knew this was exactly what Rick wanted. He would just keep pushing until I finally cracked. What he didn't know was that it would only take one word from me, and Jon would drag my ex-husband outside like yesterday's trash.

Rick would also deliberately traumatize my baby girl in the process.

"This conversation is over," I clipped. "You can either leave now, or you can explain to the police why you're refusing to go. Sophie, go ahead and start dialing."

"You wouldn't dare!"

Instead, our oldest daughter proved to be every bit as brave as I knew she could be without Rick's constant smothering. I couldn't rebuke his domineering behavior under his own roof, but my house offered protection for both of us. As Sophie began speaking to the dispatcher, her father made quite a spectacle of leaving—without Lily. She stood by wordlessly while he forgot her existence. His seething eyes were all for me, and I could hear the remembered insults as they echoed in my subconscious.

After the front door slammed shut, Sophie stayed on the phone long enough to ask if I wanted the police to drive by our home and ensure Rick had truly left the premises. Lily broke down sobbing, and it was Jon who comforted her. I assumed she would reject him, but she gripped the front of his shirt and cried tears of an utterly broken heart.

"I'm so stupid!" she moaned. "He never even wanted to see me."

Jon held her tightly, letting her vent while also speaking comforting words of all the things he admired about her.

My heart squeezed as tears coursed down my own cheeks.

Before me was the father figure my girls had been missing and the most perfect representation of God's love to all three of us. I wrapped my arms around Jon and Lily. Sophie joined us in our first hug as the new family I hoped we'd become.

CHAPTER 37

I WASN'T SURPRISED BY THE SCATHING EMAIL I received from Rick on the Family Wizard app. The threats his lawyer sent to Sondra Joyner, my old divorce attorney, did raise some concern, but the video we uploaded courtesy of Sophie's phone helped quiet the promise of legal proceedings. His attorney suddenly stopped responding to Sondra's emails.

Jon's response to Lily changed her previous apprehension toward him, and I loved watching them form their own bond independent of me. However, it broke my heart watching her last shred of hope die about her father. No matter how much any of us wished Rick would choose a relationship with his daughters over his own stupid pride, Lily had to accept his choice to remain a self absorbed jerk. This time, there was no Stephanie to blame for his callous disregard. The grief made my beautiful little introvert even more withdrawn, and Jon and I both prayed she would come to know the loving arms of her Heavenly Father as we did our best to display His love toward her.

Jon and Rachel spent more time at our house, and with Jon and I laughing and preparing meals together, it gave promise to what our blended family could become. We alternated between his house and mine for movie nights, and the girls loved their sleepovers. Occasionally, Jon would submit to mani/pedi treatment from the girls, and I saw both of my daughters flourish with a father figure who didn't ridicule the request or turn it into some hyper spiritual lecture about gender roles.

Three weeks after my run-in with Elisha Castle, I sat at the car dealership scrolling on my phone as a routine oil change had escalated into a two-tire replacement along with rear brake pads. Jon had taken our girls to see the mega hit *Barbara Doll* movie, and I was wearing my "Kentastic" sweatshirt while I waited.

My phone rang with a number I didn't recognize, and I assumed it was the dealership with an update on my sedan.

"Hello?" I answered.

"Charlotte? This is Tina."

I blanked, not sure what to say.

"I didn't know if you still had my number in your phone."

"No, I don't." I tensed, waiting for her to unleash verbal abuse and accusations. Instead, supernatural peace flooded my senses. I exhaled slowly, buoyed by God's presence.

"Well," she huffed, "I know it's been a while, but I wanted to check and see how you're doing. Once upon a time, you were one of my closest friends."

"That's not why you called."

"Excuse me?" she gasped.

"You didn't call because you miss me. I know what this is about."

"Well, that's some greeting after everything I've done for you."

"I have no interest in revisiting everything you've *done* for me. Tina. You didn't snap photos of me and Jon Roseman at Charred Cups and then share them with Stephanie and whoever else at Beth Shalom because you 'miss me.'"

"How did you—?"

"And you didn't comment on Stephanie's FaceSpace photo or brag about setting her up with Rick—*while he and I were still married*—because you 'miss me.' I suppose I should give you credit for helping speed up my divorce, but I will never be grateful for what you did to my girls. The reason you're calling is because you want to play the victim about Stephanie the same way you and she have played the victim about *me* for the last three years."

She choked and blustered, clearly not expecting to be called out. Finally, she cried, "She betrayed me, Charlotte. The same way she betrayed you and Rick. I thought you, of all people, would understand what that's like. She hurt my *children*."

I refused to be baited either by misplaced empathy or Tina's galling hypocrisy. "You reaping what you deliberately sowed into *my* family is none of my business or concern. I can't even call it justice because I would never wish that type of ill on you or your boys."

"So, you don't care what that whore has done?" she shrilled.

"Oh, I care very much what she's done to Rick and my girls, but you blasting all over social media that Stephanie sexually assaulted your son rather than having an affair with their adult father is reprehensible, even for you. Clearly, your goal is to trash Stephanie's reputation, but people at Beth Shalom are more likely to believe the truth about David and Stephanie rather than this insane lie you've got going."

"Who told you that?" she hissed.

"Am I wrong?"

"Who told you that!" she demanded again.

"Your son, Tina. He told me himself."

Her self righteous anger died a quick death. "When did you talk to Pax?"

"About a week ago. He told me about the affair and the promise his father forced him to make. He also told me what you're posting online about Stephanie isn't true."

She quickly doubled down on her lie. "There's no way you talked to Pax. No one in my family would ever associate with the likes of you."

And yet you're the one who called me looking for sympathy you don't deserve, I wanted to say. Instead, I indulged in a heavy roll of the eyes but kept my tone neutral. "Pax found me on social media and wanted to apologize for giving us Covid and for how you treated us afterwards. I told him none of that was his fault."

"Well," she huffed, "he did come home sick with the virus. My taste buds still aren't the same, but it's nice to see you're not holding a grudge against him. He was only a child."

"There was no need for Pax to feel guilty since he's not the one who got lonely and told me and the girls it was safe to come upstairs even when it wasn't. It wasn't Pax who called the CDC regulations a government hoax to manipulate the presidential election. It also wasn't Pax who threw a temper tantrum because I didn't answer *one* text message and then deliberately made me and my girls homeless. *You* did that."

She scoffed. "That's not how it happened."

Ignoring her, I continued, "I do have to thank you, though, for what you posted on FaceSpace about Rick's marriage. The girls and I have been blaming the wrong person for Stephanie's hyper sensitivity and why she feels so threatened by the three of us. She was your revenge ticket against me, only she wound up playing *you* instead. I'm sure that was a bitter pill to swallow."

"How dare you—!"

"Oh, and thanks for the opportunity to explain my side to Pax instead of the twisted version you've been using to make yourself the victim. We had him over for dinner last week with Jon and Rachel Roseman. Your son is bright, funny, and an incredibly sensitive young man who didn't deserve those text messages you sent him. If you could just get out of your own way, Tina, the two of you might have a real relationship."

"You...you had dinner with him?" she croaked. "He won't talk to me."

"We did. It was a lovely evening, and he helped Jon out on the grill."

Emotion clogged her voice. "He used to love doing that with David."

"Well, maybe you should start by apologizing to Pax instead of attacking him for telling you the truth about his father and Stephanie. Your son loves you, but all of this ridiculous behavior pushes him away."

And just like that, my open window to speak into Tina Fournier's life vanished. Her inner demon awoke and realized she might get free from its clutches. I felt a shift in the conversation as the invisible wall came crashing down around her heart.

"Don't you dare tell me how to be a mother to my child!" she fumed.

"Goodbye, Tina. I wish you well and hope you can make peace with both of your boys."

"No! We're not done—!"

I cut her off by hanging up and immediately blocking her number. Several voicemail notifications appeared, and I assumed it was Tina leaving evidence I would be uploading to Sondra's website later that day.

I texted Jon about what happened and also shot Pax a heads up message about his mother. Jealousy and the fear of exposure meant she'd be blowing up his phone soon enough. Tina needed to control the narrative, and she could no longer manipulate me into compliance. Jon asked if I was all right, and Pax surprised me by asking if he could join me and my family at church the next day. Shocked, I told them both yes and waited to see what God had in store.

We made quite an eclectic group that Sunday. Jon sat next to his lookalike daughter, and my two girls sat to her left. I sat on the other side of Jon, and then twenty-five year-old Paxton Fournier occupied the spot on my right. Tall, handsome, with dirty blonde hair and bright blue eyes, Pax turned heads as soon as he walked in the room. My girls both agreed he was very good looking but also "ancient" according to their high school standards. Thankfully, Pax also viewed them like younger sisters rather than an underage love match. He and Sophie shared similar personalities, and I liked seeing the two of them draw each other out of their respective shells.

"Thanks for letting me come with you," he said.

I turned to face him and smiled back. "Of course! You know you're always welcome to join us."

"Is this place different from Beth Shalom?"

"Night and day. Grace Abounds is very understated."

His eyes took on an understanding light, and I nodded in encouragement. The pomp and circumstance of Beth Shalom held no appeal for either of us.

A familiar blonde appeared, and I cringed at the misplaced jealousy I'd once felt toward her. She'd done nothing to earn my ire other than trigger my own insecurities.

"Allie!" Jon called, rising from his seat. "What are you doing here?"

She blushed and smiled. "Lauren mentioned that you've been coming here, and it's easier than Sunday nights with my daughter. Bella's in first grade now, and we can't stay out that late."

I glanced at Pax and he was utterly transfixed. Every trait of Allie's that once had me feeling inadequate clearly captivated the youngest Fournier boy. She looked like a real-life Barbara Doll, and Pax would have made a perfect Kent. With a daughter in elementary school and a world-weariness I'd never noticed before, I wondered how old Allie actually was.

"Would you like to join us?" Jon asked, gesturing next to Pax.

"Oh," she murmured, finally noticing him and startling at the intense blue gaze meeting her. "I, um…"

"Mama," a petulant voice called. Tugging on Allie's dress impatiently, her tow-headed daughter wore a fearsome scowl. She looked nothing like her mother save for the matching hair color. Her eyes were a deep brown and her skin more olive toned than her mother's fair complexion.

"This is Bella," Allie said sheepishly.

I noticed she didn't make eye contact with Pax, but he continued to drink her in as if memorizing every detail about her.

"We'd be happy to make room for both of you," her admirer said, realizing there was only one open seat beside him rather than two.

Allie smiled gratefully. "That's so sweet, but you don't have to go to any trouble on my account. Bella has a tough time sitting still, so I was just going to sit in the back. I couldn't get a babysitter, and her dad…" her voice cut off, and she pressed her lips together. I recognized the look on her face instantly, both the signs of trauma and also the fear of not being believed. I wondered if Bella's father was like my ex-husband or Lauren's. Either way, Paxton had his work cut out for him if he intended to pursue her.

"Girls, can you scoot down one?" I called over to my daughters.

They looked up from whatever video had them laughing at Rachel's phone, and then my teenage matchmaker quickly assessed the situation. Sophie's eyes darted from shy Allie with her head bowed, then lovestruck Pax with his heart about to burst from his chest, and finally, to Little Miss Bella who clearly wanted to be the sole focus of her mother's regard. Sophie's gaze met mine, and with a quick raise of my eyebrows, I confirmed her suspicions.

"Come on, guys, scoot," she commanded. The girls moved over, and then Jon and I shifted seats to make room for our new friends.

I shot Jon a side-eyed glance, and he responded with a quelling look.

"Let God handle it," he muttered. "If it's meant to be, He won't need your help."

CHAPTER 38

PAX DECLINED OUR INVITATION TO ATTEND THE Margolin evening Bible study, and I wondered if that had to do with Allie also not being there. While disappointed I couldn't watch the real life romance novel play out before me, I did finally lay eyes on my dear friend and the future Mrs. Grant Kaplan after what felt like months of ships passing in the night.

"Charlotte!" Lauren exclaimed, wrapping me in a bear hug. "Tell me everything! I'm so sorry I've been MIA. With Ari in public school and planning the wedding with Grant, everything has just been crazy. You know I want you to be my maid of honor, right?"

I laughed as we parted. "Maid, matron, tomato, to-mahto. Nothing would make me happier than watching you start a *real* marriage with a man who genuinely loves and respects you. You deserve nothing less."

Tears filled her amber eyes. "Thank you. And truly, I am sorry for flaking out. I know I haven't been a great friend lately. I'm ecstatic for you and Jon, and I wish I could have been there to celebrate with you—especially after I heard about him wearing your lipstick at Bible study. Too bad I couldn't have seen it firsthand."

A loud laugh escaped my mouth before I covered it quickly with my hand. "You heard about that?" I whispered.

She winked at me. "You forget I work with the mighty Margolin. He had a few questions at the office for me."

"Oh man! I wanted to call you and tell you everything, and then life happened over here too. I think I also owe you an apology."

She waved me off. "No worries, girl. After all the dating disasters, I just assumed you were keeping this one close to the vest."

I shook my head. "Nope, just negligence and busyness. Which is also why I'm not about to be a hypocrite with you being caught up in all things wedding. Your life and your son's life will be changing dramatically in just a couple of months. I know you want to spend as much time as possible with the dreamboat, love of your life. "

She blushed and swatted at my arm. "I have never called Grant anything like that."

I grinned shamelessly. "You don't have to, youngin'. It's written all over that doe-eyed look of adoration you give the man any time he enters the room—or you know, breathes and exists. That is love with a capital 'L,' my friend."

Her mouth dropped in shock before her blushed deepened.

"You know you missed me," I teased.

She laughed and broke into an ear splitting grin. "Yes, I have! I still can't believe you thought I'd fix up Jon with Allie," she said with a lowered voice. "She's not here tonight, is she? That could be a little awkward."

"No, but we saw her this morning."

"Oh, so she went to church? She told me she might, but she was having an issue getting a sitter for Bella. How did that go? Was it weird?"

"Totally fine. She and Bella sat next to Pax Fournier."

Lauren nearly choked on her own spit. "Did you just say *Fournier*? As in the son of that horrible woman I refuse to name? As in the son of that selfish, fifty-year-old spoiled brat who rubbed your nose in her dead husband's money and then gaslighted you for not being as impressed with herself as she is? *That* Paxton Fournier?"

"The very one."

She gestured wildly with her hand as words failed her. "How…when…how much have I missed, Charlotte?!"

I chuckled good-naturedly. "Do you want the long version or the short, because I've barely scratched the surface of all the secrets and double-crosses of the 'We Hate Charlotte' Ghidorah monster."

"The *what*?"

"Ghidorah is a three-headed dragon from all those Golizzard movies. Technically, it's a kaiju."

"You know I don't speak sci-fi or comic book. I'm completely lost."

I exhaled a chuckle at her wide-eyed expression. "A kaiju is a Japanese movie monster. The Ghidorah has three heads that all breathe fire. Basically, it's a big scary dragon that fights off the nuclear fire-blasts from Golizzard. I just assigned each head a name—Stephanie, Rick, and Tina."

"Ah," she replied, "that makes sense. And you said those three have all turned on each other, right?"

"So it seems, but all three of them are also lying one way or another, so who knows?"

"For now, just give me the abridged version, and I promise I'll meet you later this week for cheesecake for the full story."

"It also involves Elisha Castle, if you can believe it."

Visibly stunned, Lauren said, "Elisha? What does she have to do with any of this?"

"More than you know. I wouldn't be surprised to find her and Josh showing up to Bible study one night."

Her mouth pursed as if she'd sucked on a lemon.

"Yeah, you're having the same reaction I did when she first reached out to me on Linkedup. It's amazing what supernatural eye surgery can do for a person's ability to see the truth."

Both of Lauren's eyebrows raised high on her forehead. "Is that right? The same Elisha Castle who had the Beth Shalom prayer team interceding for poor wittle Nathan Fein against his Jezebel ex-wife? How evil of me to tattle to the police because my husband bruised me and son repeatedly," she spat.

I sighed in disgust. "Yeah, that one."

"I guess I still have some healing left to do," she mused. "I didn't expect to have that much of a reaction. I'm not sure I could see her face to face without giving a piece of my mind."

"Trust me, Elisha already got an earful from me. She finally saw the evil of the Beth Shalom machine unmasked. I hate that's what it takes for any of these blind sheep to wake up—like God forbid they actually *believe* an abuse victim rather than make excuses for the obscene behavior—but she and Josh aren't blind anymore, that's for sure."

"How do you know they're not spying for Harvey Lebow? We've had a few of those show up here," she said, referring to Jackson Howe who had infiltrated the group five years earlier.

"Elisha says they left the synagogue. Her son, Aiden, is friends with Pax, which is how I found out about any of this."

"Small world," Lauren tsked. "How are you holding up? This

has to be a lot of information to process on top of Rick's shenanigans."

"No joke! I've got my hands full these days, but in a good way. Definitely a welcome change of pace from all the Stephanie bashing I used to do."

"A *good* way? Do tell!"

I smiled. "Jon is over almost every night, or the girls and I are at his place. It's a jam packed schedule for all of us."

"Are you guys already playing house?" she asked with a mischievous twinkle in her eye. "That didn't take very long."

"Something like that. No co-ed sleepovers, obviously."

She gestured to my left hand. "When is he gonna put a ring on it? I'm shocked you're not racing to the altar to start those co-ed sleepovers you mentioned. Didn't you once refer to yourself as a shiny red sports car that's been locked up in the garage?"

Now, it was my turn to blush.

"So, the conversation *has* come up," she purred. "Interesting. I never thought I'd be the one getting *you* all flustered, Charlotte. Usually, it's always the other way around."

"Well, a lot has happened since the last time we talked. Some days, it feels too good to be true. I never thought someone as good looking as Jon would ever go for someone like me."

"Excuse me? Why *wouldn't* he go for someone exactly like you?"

"Look, we both know I have emotional damage. I didn't realize just how far Rick had shoved my self esteem into the toilet until Jon called me out on it. It's been a process, but the man says he loves me and he thinks I'm beautiful—and I believe him."

Her amber eyes glowed. "I'm so happy for you, Charlotte!

You deserve so much better than all those losers you kept finding online. Anything is an improvement over your ex, but I didn't want to see you settle. Scarcity, or even just the perception of it, can start making a moldy loaf of white bread look like a Thanksgiving feast."

I chuckled at the old memories. "There was definitely a time when I wondered if my only options were a buffet of unhealed, unresolved Mommy issue having, breadcrumbing bozos who acted like I should be grateful they lowered themselves to grace my plus sized presence. I'm glad I was wrong."

"Bravo for persevering through all of that," she laughed, "and I will always be grateful to God I didn't have to endure the dating scene post-divorce."

"Well, I don't have any hot coworkers like you did, so God had to provide a man somewhere else."

"Nope, just hot divorce attorneys," she quipped, sticking her tongue out at me. "I finally got around to looking at the picture you sent me of your online friend. How on earth did you resist the charms of SeanBonLawyerMon? Those DMs were pretty swoony."

I rolled my eyes and laughed. "Because I only *joke* about the Oedipal romance fantasies. I have no desire to be with a man I could have birthed or babysat twenty years ago."

Lauren burst into laughter.

"No, seriously," I said, gaining steam, "it's not like I even have the older woman mystique. I was married to *Richard*, for goodness sake. Every time Jon kisses me, I'm reminded how little I actually know about genuine romance or anything else that happens behind closed doors. Trust me, I am all talk."

She fluttered her lashes playfully. "Are you saying *you* need a birds and bees conversation?"

"Ha, no! I'm just saying that these young studs on

Cougarville thought I had something to teach them, and other than writing a paper check or how to cook rice on the stove, there's not much there. Besides, what the heck do I have in common with someone who says 'bussin' and 'rizz'?"

Lauren doubled over in giggles, and I simply smiled and enjoyed making her laugh. Waving a hand dramatically, I added, "Not that Sean even talked like that, but it was still weird. Things worked out the way they were supposed to for me and Jon, and I genuinely hope Sean can find someone his own age. He's a nice guy, but he's not a Christian, and the twelve-year age gap was more than I could handle."

"Not a Christian," she repeated. "That's a far cry from my friend who wanted any future beau to celebrate Jewish holidays with her."

"Well, like I said, a lot has happened."

"Not that God didn't take care of that for you too," she said with a satisfied smirk.

I allowed my friend the freedom to gloat at her matchmaking. I had never been happier in my life. "Yes, it's nice that Jon already knows and celebrates the Jewish holidays. I've wanted my girls to experience this apart from all the hyper spiritual garbage and legalism from Rick. All of a sudden, everything's fun and exciting instead of boring for them. Meanwhile, I no longer feel like an abject failure teaching them anything about their heritage."

"Are they more open to being Jewish now?"

"Honestly, Laur, every step of my relationship with Jon has brought me closer to Jesus, not Judaism. Not that it isn't important, but the healing God has done in my heart has been through Jon encouraging me—or even rebuking me—from Scripture. We pray together. Thanks to Jon and now Grace Abounds, I feel like I'm really learning about the power of what

Jesus did for me on the cross. The Jewish holidays have always been an expression of my faith, but understanding God's love for me has been a game changer."

Her eyebrows raised once again. "What's made this different from what you were already taught? I know you used to go to church once upon a time."

"That church talked about God in the general sense of Him loving me, but the overall focus was self improvement with His help. At Beth Shalom, it was Yeshua *plus* serving, or Yeshua *plus* the Jewish identity. It was never just about Jesus being enough. Harvey Lebow certainly never taught how much God loves me by dying for me. It was always about what *I* owed God and needed to repay by volunteering as my 'reasonable service.'"

My friend smiled at me in wonder. "I am so proud of you, Charlotte. As much as I'd love to give the credit to Jon, I know this is because of the hard work *you've* done."

"Let's not pretend that I had any magical revelations apart from the Holy Spirit. I got myself into a whole bunch of sin and bitterness left to my own devices. Glory belongs to God, not me."

"I'm not saying God doesn't deserve credit. I'm just telling you not to discount the work I know you've also put in."

"Laur, you have no idea how many temper tantrums I've thrown or all the ways I bashed or judged Stephanie, Rick, and Tina the same way they've done to me."

"But you didn't give up on God, and He never gave up on you," she quickly amended. "I see the changes, and not just the weight you've lost."

I glanced down at my midsection, most aware of *those* changes. As I'd released the burden of Rick, Stephanie, and Tina, the physical weight of their betrayal also melted away. Jon and I danced together to online workout videos, and what had started as initial embarrassment and self consciousness on my part quickly became a mutual goal of being there for our children—and future grandchildren. Ruthie had just announced her early pregnancy with her husband, Aaron.

"I love seeing how happy you are," Lauren said, beaming at me. "I told you last year at Aaron's wedding that Jon's had his eyes on you. You can't hide that kind of admiration."

"Well, now he's got his lips on me too, so it's a win for everyone."

She shook her head with a laugh. "Promise me you'll never change. Jon doesn't make you temper this part of your personality, does he?"

"Not at all! Turns out he's got a pretty sassy side himself. For all the years that Rick neglected me and our marriage, God provided a man who will definitely restore the years the locusts have eaten." I gave a saucy wink, and we both broke into slumber party worthy giggles.

Lauren pulled me into another hug. "Oh! I'm just so happy for you! You deserve every shred of this happiness, my friend."

With tears smarting in my eyes, I hugged her back.

CHAPTER 39

As the fall season kicked into high-gear, I found myself growing wistful regarding the Jewish High Holidays. The local synagogues charged for tickets to attend those special services, and that also meant becoming a member. After Lily's attempted bat mitzvah and being outed as a believer in Jesus, I feared one rabbi would send out a spiritual APB to all the other local rabbis in the area. *Apostate! Abort Mission! Do not let her in!*

Unfortunately, that left me with the annual dilemma of wanting to be with my people yet counting the cost of following my Jewish Messiah. Even Poppy and Jared Levine's connections at the Reform synagogue, *Beth Tefillah,* couldn't sneak me in the doors as they were only permitted because of Poppy's mother. I faced an impossible scenario, told by many that I needed to sacrifice one for the other.

I refused to relinquish either.

Jesus Christ of Nazareth, *Yeshua HaMashiach,* had set me free from sin, from hatred toward my ex-husband, and was progressively healing the compounded layers of trauma from my marriage. To deny Him by claiming it was to *worship* Him felt like the utmost in both hypocrisy and betrayal. Yet to abandon the Jewish, Biblically mandated holidays in favor of Christian ones—often rooted in paganism and marred by modern commercialism—I couldn't do either.

Some eighteen years earlier, that tension had created the perfect spot for Beth Shalom to offer itself as a best of both worlds congregation. Every member of the Messianic synagogue learned to recite the talking points of how you didn't have to stop being Jewish in order to believe in Jesus. Weekly, the service leader read from *Matthew 5:17-19* where Jesus says He didn't come to do away with the Law but to fulfill it. As a congregation, we were lauded for worshiping on *Shabbat,* or the Jewish Sabbath, rather than Sunday. With condescension oozing from his lips, Harvey Lebow made light of our poor, uneducated Christian brethren and their *manmade* holidays and pagan traditions—as if we didn't have any in Judaism.

Admittedly, I bought into the idea that Beth Shalom was the closest modern equivalent to how the disciples worshiped in the first century. There was no church back then, no traditions beyond the Jewish holidays Jesus Himself celebrated. Added to that, *keeping Torah* was one of the few ways I could actually please my husband.

After I left Beth Shalom and attended churches of every other flavor and denomination, I realized *all* of the congregations tried to pass themselves off as worshiping as close to the Bible as possible. By tickling the ears and egos of the members, it circumvented most of them from checking the Scriptures or even digging into extra-Biblical resources to find out where their religious traditions originated.

At the Messianic synagogue, the members spoke passionately about the Jewishness of Yeshua, yet they hesitated in sharing the actual *gospel* of Jesus Christ crucified for the sins of the world and raised from the dead. The Beth Shalom version of evangelism meant inviting people to services and leaving the salvation message to Harvey Lebow's sermons.

Flung back to the present, I sought the Lord on how I could reconcile my conflicting desires. The previous year, I'd tried watching traditional Jewish services online, but nothing compared to physically standing in a room full of worshipers chanting ancient prayers like *Avinu Malkeinu* or the *Aleinu*. Beth Shalom's siren song of "no tickets" beckoned me, so I took it to the Lord in prayer, begging for clarity to understand my longing. While Harvey Lebow boasted how he didn't charge tickets to attend *his* High Holiday services, I knew firsthand he demanded a much higher price for his "free" religious circus.

You don't need Beth Shalom in order to praise Me in Hebrew, I felt the Holy Spirit say.

"But I want to be with my brothers and sisters for the holidays…even if they're my brethren in the flesh and not the Spirit." Saying the words aloud, I felt guilty, knowing that Scripture taught the opposite of what I'd confessed. "I'm sorry, Lord. I just don't know what to do. Why do I feel this way?"

Pray for them, Charlotte. I gave you the same desire I gave Paul to see all of Israel saved. Paul praised me in a jail cell. You can praise me on your sofa.

So I sang.

"*Aleinu l'shabe'ach la'adon hakol. Latet gedulah l'yotzer beresheet…*" I continued on, feeling the presence of the Lord with me. As I chanted the Hebrew liturgy of bending my knee and bowing before the Lord, I did so. Loudly and giving free reign for my alto voice, I belted my favorite part, "*Bayom ha hu, bayom ha hu, yiyeh Adonai echad. U'shmo, u'shmo-o-o, u'shmo e'chad.*"

Pressing my hands to my heart, I sighed into the heavy peace permeating my family room. While I had found the abridged Hebrew prayer and English translation on a Reform Jewish website, I wasn't fond of the license they took in translating it. Even with my basic understanding of Hebrew, something felt off. Searching through multiple websites and online translators, I pieced together the prayer in English and the final stanza in my Hebrew concordance directly from *Zechariah 14:9*:

It is our duty to praise the Master of everything, to give glory to the Author of Creation. He has not made us like the families of the earth or our portion like theirs, or made our destiny like all of theirs. And so we kneel, bend the knee and bow, and then stand before the King, the King of all kings, the Holy One, Blessed is He. We declare that the Lord will be King over the whole earth, and on that day the Lord will be the only One and His Name the only One.

Smiling to myself, I added, "And every knee shall bow and every tongue confess that Yeshua is Lord."

"Amen," Jon said, watching me from the bottom of my staircase.

Startled, I asked, "How long have you been standing there?"

He grinned. "Well, I was upstairs with our girls getting another manicure," he held out his purple painted nails, "and then I heard this heavenly voice singing. My cantor never sang like that growing up. He certainly wasn't as beautiful."

I blushed. "I think you're confusing me with someone else. Maybe that handsome guy in the mirror who could be a professional singer."

"Oh no, you're definitely the Hebrew singing angel I heard. Too bad Harvey is such a chauvinist he'd never allow a woman to chant Hebrew from the bima. You would have brought people to tears. *I* still have chills." He gestured to his forearms covered in goosebumps. "What prompted you to sing the *Aleinu*? It was stunning."

I motioned for him to join me on the couch. "I was praying and asking the Lord about going to synagogue for High Holidays."

"Which synagogue did you have in mind?" His dark brows raised above his glasses. "I know you won't go to Beth Shalom, and we don't have tickets for anywhere else. Were you thinking of the *Chabad*?"

"No, I went for *Rosh HaShanah* two years ago. They rush through all of the prayers, and I don't like how they separate the men from the women. I know it's an Orthodox thing, just not my cup of tea. It felt lifeless and like I was on the outside looking in. I don't think I'd want to go back again."

He shrugged. "Fair enough."

Sighing heavily, I said, "I just miss the feeling of being gathered with an entire congregation for the holidays. I miss the palpable presence of God, the anticipation of a new year, and just feeling connected with our people globally in Spirit. Even with that bully preaching in the pulpit, I miss Beth Shalom. Or I guess I miss the friends I *thought* I had once upon a time." I lowered my face in shame. "I know, I know. I sound like a battered wife remembering the good times."

His hand came quickly under my chin to lift my head and meet my eyes. "So, maybe the place wasn't *all* bad, hmm?"

My eyes widened in shock. "You're not saying we should go back, are you? Jon, I'm already confused enough!"

He chuckled but kept his gaze level with mine. "I'm not telling you I think we should go back. We both have some very strong opinions about what we experienced at Beth Shalom and the denomination as a whole. But maybe we should stop demonizing the place and the people. Not *every* person at Beth Shalom is rotten, and not *every* Messianic synagogue is as corrupt. I did get saved there twenty-six years ago."

"Maybe," I mumbled.

His eyes shifted to the scratch paper on the coffee table with my Hebrew translation. "What's this?"

"The Charlotte version of the *Aleinu*."

"You love questioning the establishment, don't you?"

"Have you met me?" I deadpanned.

He leaned in for a soft kiss. "Met *and* fell in love."

I kissed him back.

Jon pulled away to dig his fingers into my hair and rest his forehead against mine. "I'm proud of you, you know."

"Why's that?"

"I love your tenacity and intelligence. I love how you see beyond the surface and listen to that gut instinct telling you to keep digging. I love that you *don't* just go along with things for the sake of tradition or not making waves. I don't think you could just follow along even if you wanted to. You have this innate sense of right and wrong, what some might call discernment, and I am very thankful to have you in my life."

I smiled back at him. "So, what are we going to do about the holidays, Jon?"

"Why don't we have them here? I chanted the high holiday liturgy for years, and we can do the entire service if you want."

My eyes welled with tears, touched by his thoughtfulness. "Are you sure? You don't have to if you don't want to."

"Clearly, this is very important to you, and honestly, it is for me too. We don't need to make a big production out of it, but it could be both nostalgic *and* new for our girls. Also, based on what I heard as I was coming down the stairs, we are going to share the cantorial duties. You are more than capable of both carrying a tune and conveying the gravitas of these prayers."

And that's what we did.

We started with the Biblical Feast of Trumpets and modern Jewish New Year, *Rosh HaShanah*. I prepared traditional fare of cut apples and honey, symbolic of wishing for a "sweet new year" and also a honey cake. To commemorate the feast, Jon blew the *shofar*, or ram's horn, explaining to the girls about the different shofar blasts and their significance.

The first blast called *tekiah*, was a long, loud blast calling people to attention. The next, *shevarim*, came as three broken blows, almost mimicking the sound of wailing. The third, *teruah*, resounded as nine staccato blasts serving as a wakeup call to the new year and for spiritual attentiveness to God. Finally, there was the *tekiah gedolah*, or "big" tekiah, which was a longer, sustained blast done at the end of the Rosh Hashanah service.

From the time of the Feast of Trumpets was a ten day period leading up to the Day of Atonement, or *Yom Kippur*. Those ten Days of Awe, or the *Yamim Nora'im*, were meant to be a time of reflection and making things right with those we had wronged and also those who had wronged us. I prayed at length about the former Ghidorah monster, realizing that behind the wretched behavior were three broken people who desperately needed healing. Even as I caught myself having mock conversations where I held them accountable or simply unloaded on them, I felt hollow afterwards. Eventually, my prayers became, "Okay, God, what do I need to change so You can get glory from this?"

For *Yom Kippur*, Jon and I both took off work, and the girls wanted to stay home from school and participate with us. Customary for the holiday, all of us fasted, and we took turns reading and chanting through the liturgy. Going through the *Al Cheit,* or *For the Sins* confession, I actively kept my thoughts focused on my own sins rather than trying to point a finger at Rick, Stephanie, or Tina. Each line of the traditional prayer was confession after confession of how I'd sinned against God, and it helped redirect my focus from my own self righteousness. It also filled me with gratitude how my Savior had died to cleanse me and set me free of every sin we read aloud. My scarlet sins had been made white as snow.

Jon strummed his guitar and sang a traditional Hebrew lullaby from Scripture, *Hodu L'Adonai,* and I closed my eyes as the words permeated my entire being.

"Give thanks to the Lord for He is good, and His love forever endures," all of our daughters also sang along.

Tears fell freely down my face as my spirit leapt in thanksgiving toward my Savior. "Thank you," I murmured brokenly. "Thank you, Jesus."

CHAPTER 40

OUR JAM-PACKED JEWISH HOLIDAY SEASON continued with the week-long Festival of Booths, or *Sukkot,* following five days after Yom Kippur. God ordained the holiday in remembrance of the forty years the children of Israel spent wandering the desert living in those same booths, yet their clothes and shoes never wore out. Per the instructions in *Leviticus 23* and based on our own research, Jon assembled the makeshift, holiday hut, called a *sukkah,* in his backyard.

I teased him for not purchasing supplies from The Home Store to jerry rig a structure out of 2x4" lumber, but Jon found a sukkah kit online and put it together with the help of his son-in-law, Aaron. Once the base structure stood tall, they attached the fabric sides that could also be pulled back like curtains. The girls and I were then commandeered to beautify the sukkah, and they jubilantly went to task like it was the Christmas tree they'd always wanted as children.

As if answering their prayer for childhood wish fulfillment, the big box stores unveiled their winter holiday decorations in early September. We found a wide selection of luminaires perfect for the sukkah. Giggling and crowing over their work, Sophie and Lily covered Jon's sukkah in strings of white lights and wrapped them around each of the corner pillars. We also purchased LED crystal globes to hang from the center roof beam and provide nighttime overhead lighting. The addition of summer garden decor conveniently now on clearance also allowed for adornment for the surrounding landscape.

While Sophie, Lily, and Rachel hung up the lights, Ruthie and Aaron arrived with bags of groceries from Joey's Real Food. Along with the ingredients for Andrea Roseman's chocolate chip pumpkin loaf, Ruthie provided an assortment of summer gourds and mini pumpkins to use for decoration. The newlyweds got to baking in the kitchen, and Jon and I joined the girls in adding a touch of freshness to our harvest themed hut. We strung up the gourds with twine and hung them amongst the beams and lights on the lattice roof.

Sukkot had not been a holiday I grew up celebrating, but as a member of Beth Shalom, it became one of my favorites. The congregation constructed a large sukkah with bamboo and lattice walls. Inside were ground lights illuminating the structure and hay bales for people to sit. The thatched roof with palm fronds followed in accord with the tradition to see the stars through the ceiling, and the synagogue children made paper decorations during their weekly Bible study class. Each year, I had made it a point to sit in the sukkah, either with the girls or even by myself, and soak in the history and wonder of honoring God's command dating back to Moses. The presence of the Lord always felt a little bit closer within the walls of a sukkah.

With its clear symbolism of the Jewish wedding canopy, I always wished Rick and I could have gotten married in one or even renewed our vows during the festival. He belittled the idea, and with each passing year, my hope for our marriage died along with the dream. Years later, he held his own wedding ceremony with Stephanie Burgess inside the Beth Shalom sukkah. Creating new memories with Jon and our girls was a wonderful balm to what had become an annual sting each time the holiday rolled around.

Beyond the Biblical command to celebrate the holiday, I had to admit that Beth Shalom had done right by its members by correlating the ancient holiday to the end of days. In addition to the Mosaic Scriptures regarding the holiday, we also read from *Zechariah 14:16-19* where it describes a post-apocalyptic peace and the Messiah reigning in Jerusalem. The passage describes how native born Jews and all the surrounding nations will go up together to the Holy City and celebrate the Feast of Booths. With Sukkot as one of the *shalosh regalim,* or three pilgrimage feasts where Jews are commanded to travel to Jerusalem to honor the Lord, this version in *Zechariah* speaks of a time when *all* nations will come to worship God that way. It was verses like these where Harvey Lebow proudly proclaimed, "See? In the end times, *everyone* will be practicing Messianic Judaism!" It made a great selling point as the congregation ooh'd and ahh'd over the sukkah structure on the front lawn of the synagogue.

Back then, I truly believed all of the "Biblical Judaism" we practiced at Beth Shalom aligned perfectly with Scripture. Years removed, I simply prayed for grace to honor the Lord as best I could. My heart's motivation no longer centered on practicing the most *perfect* form of worship but in expressing my love to God with a thankful heart. The result was freedom from comparison to others and peace that my Heavenly Father was pleased with my efforts.

Biblically, the command was for all native born Israelites to live and sleep in their own sukkah for the duration of the holiday. In Israel and in more Orthodox circles, many Jews did exactly that. Since Jon and I were not legally or spiritually ready for our co-ed sleepovers, we instead partook of the tradition to eat and fellowship under the open roofed dwelling. Jon pulled out a picnic table and chairs from his garage, and the girls and I supplied a vinyl tablecloth and other weather-safe decor to create an inviting atmosphere. We used the extra pumpkins and squash as paperweights as fall winds proved unpredictable for our tablecloth. During the first full weekend of Sukkot, Jon invited our entire Bible study group to join us for a potluck dinner that Saturday night. Pax Fournier was happy to help Jon grill again, perhaps even more so with the addition of Allie Sanders and Bella to our party. I didn't think it was coincidental, but Jon lovingly told me to stay out of it.

With the decorations and food tables set up outside, the Roseman home transformed into a sylvan paradise. Joining the star-of-the-show sukkah, fairy lights draped the covered patio. We'd also staked the backyard with stained glass lights illuminating a pathway to the sukkah and additional outdoor seating. At the rear of the property, the wooded area and cicadas offered their music to the ethereal festivities.

Part of the Sukkot commemoration meant waving a *lulav* and *etrog* as a prayer for God's favor on the harvest rains for the upcoming season, collectively called the *arba'ah minim,* or four species. The four plants were meant to symbolize the different parts of Israel's terrain—mountain, river, desert, and farmland. The *lulav* portion was a collection of three different species of plants, all native to Israel, and then bound together. The center of the lulav was a closed, date palm frond with myrtle on one side and willow on the other. The three were assembled as a long wand, bound together in a woven holster also made from palm fronds. The fruit of the holiday, the *etrog*, was a yellow citron, most closely resembling a giant lemon. Jon had ordered his lulav and etrog set from a Conservative synagogue near Parkview, and he placed them on the table in his sukkah as more of a show and tell for the children than for ceremonial usage.

While Beth Shalom gladly partook of the Jewish tradition and prayer for waving the lulav and etrog in six different directions—the four directions of the compass plus upward and downward—the more we researched the practice, the more leery we became of it. The Torah did specifically enumerate the plant species to use during the Feast, and we were happy to comply. However, the use of those plants for religious ceremony differed amongst the ancient rabbis. The Jewish children's book I'd once used with my daughters likened the lulav to a rain stick, and further research led to roots in Jewish mysticism. Jon and I ultimately decided to recite the traditional blessing for the lulav minus any potentially dodgy practices. We could hardly eschew Christian holidays for their pagan origins while making excuses to tolerate the Jewish ones.

Swathed in the aroma of charcoal and roasted food as conversation swirled around me, I inhaled deeply of the idyllic atmosphere. I glanced at the stars above and released a sigh of pure contentment. Jon sidled up to me and wrapped his arm across my shoulders.

"*Hag Sukkot Sameach*," he said near my ear.

"And a Happy Sukkot back to you," I replied.

His eyes swept over the yard and our gathering of friends. "This looks absolutely amazing. Sukkot is supposed to be about hospitality and welcoming our invited—and even unexpected—guests. I can say without a doubt that tonight is a smashing success. I couldn't have done this without you or your girls, Charlotte."

I leaned into him and wrapped my arms around his waist. Jon responded by pulling me even tighter against him and kissing the top of my head.

"It's a fairytale," I whispered, thinking more of the man next to me than the twinkling lights engulfing us on all sides.

"Speaking of unexpected guests," he said, his arms dropping from me as his voice hardened. "Is Lauren going to be okay with this?"

I watched as Josh and Elisha Castle entered the backyard area along with their son. Twenty-five-year-old Aiden Castle beelined toward Pax, and they embraced warmly. Pax gestured toward Allie as she blew bubbles with Bella, and a strange look crossed Aiden's face when he took in the object of his friend's affections.

"Oh, I smell trouble," I murmured.

"Quit writing a romance novel and keep an eye on your friend," Jon lightly scolded.

"Grant's here, so I'm not worried about anything happening with the Castles."

"Actually, Grant is busy with Ted and Jared, and Lauren just walked right up to Elisha. She doesn't look happy, Charlotte."

My gaze shifted to the confrontation, and sure enough, my tiny friend was lighting into both of them. Attuned to his fiancée, Grant heard Lauren's raised voice, and he stalked across the yard to join her.

"Should I run interference?" Jon asked.

"I don't think Lauren needs your help, but this is still your house. I wonder who invited them."

Answering my question, Ted Margolin joined the fray, and he seemed apologetic as he clearly tried to broker some kind of truce. Josh Castle stood wide eyed while Elisha's eyes shone with tears.

"What do you think she said to them?" Jon asked me, taking hold of my hand.

"Probably an ice bucket of truth about the pain they caused her and Ari," I replied as we reached the edge of the kerfuffle.

"Jon, I apologize," Ted said, looking directly at us. "The Castles contacted me about attending Bible study this week, and I mentioned we would be at your house celebrating Sukkot. I didn't realize there would be an issue with anybody else."

In all my years of walking with Lauren Fein through her hellacious marriage and divorce, I had never seen her look so angry. Freedom from Nathan's abuse and finding real love had certainly strengthened her backbone.

"Are you okay?" I whispered to her.

She sent me an accusing glare as if I might have known but didn't tell her.

"Calm down," I shot back. "I had no idea."

"Isn't this whole holiday season about forgiveness and new beginnings?" Grant asked in a soothing tone.

Coming from anyone else, Lauren might have literally taken their head off based on the feral look in her eyes. Instead, her shoulders stiffened before slumping down.

"I promise, we didn't come here to cause trouble," Elisha said, holding up her hands in innocence. "We just wanted to fellowship with other Jewish believers. The churches around here don't have a clue about Sukkot."

"Don't you start that Messianic garbage here," Lauren growled. "None of us Beth Shalom survivors are here to ride the spiritual superiority train. And so help me, if you're here to spy for Harvey Lebow like your little buddy, Jackson—"

"Whoa, whoa, whoa," Ted said, turning sharply toward my

friend. "Lauren, I've never seen you like this. I think we should take this conversation inside and have a private discussion."

Like the prince she deserved, Grant fought for his true love. "First, I'd like to know what happened to make my fiancée this upset. Obviously, there's some history here."

"Which we should probably discuss without an audience," Ted said through gritted teeth.

"But this is *my* house," Jon interrupted, "and I'm on Lauren's side. Elisha came to Grace Abounds to tell us the truth about some mutual *friends* of ours, but I know firsthand there's a big apology owed to Lauren for what she was put through at Beth Shalom. I caught wind of the directives coming from the top down regarding her ex-husband."

Ted's eyes widened before they narrowed on our unexpected guests. "I see."

CHAPTER 41

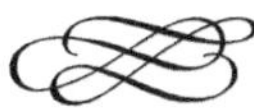

GATHERED AROUND JON'S DINING ROOM TABLE, Lauren laid out the facts for the Castles, Ted and Rebecca Margolin, Grant, Jon, and me. Also included in the group were more former members of Beth Shalom—Abigail Goldstein and Jared Levine representing their respective families. I knew most of Lauren's story even beyond her published memoirs, but it was the secrets shared by the Castles that shocked the entire room.

"Wait a second!" Lauren exclaimed. "Are you guys saying that Harvey and the other leaders told you *I* had the porn addiction?" She glared daggers at Elisha. "And you actually *believed* it?"

"You weren't there to defend yourself," she replied lamely. "Nathan had everyone fooled with his pitiful husband routine. Honestly, the guy comes off like a total nerd who wouldn't know how to hurt a fly. Sometimes, he does act arrogant, but usually, he seems so clueless and sheltered by his parents. His mother does so much for him—like he doesn't even know how to be an adult."

"He's lazy and manipulative, not incompetent," Lauren retorted. "All you'd have to do is check public records to find multiple police reports of physical abuse against me and my son or even the testimony from our child support hearing eighteen months ago."

Elisha looked nonplussed. "I'm sorry," she mumbled. "I didn't even think to do that. At the time, I couldn't understand why anyone would want to leave Beth Shalom because we loved it so much there."

Abigail Goldstein snorted in disbelief, but Jared Levine shot her a warning look. "Listen, we all drank the Kool-juice at one time or another. When you're in leadership like the Castles were, they groom you to feel special and a step above the regular members. Abigail, when you were on the worship team, I'm sure it wasn't much different."

Grudgingly, she admitted his point with pursed lips and a quick head bob.

The Castles looked relieved and remorseful. At least someone in the room could understand their plight.

Josh Castle put his arm around his wife. "They always do a good job of making the people who left seem like they had something wrong with them. I'm ashamed to admit that I believed it. We were never treated poorly, so it didn't occur to me to think otherwise."

I glanced at Grant, amazed he hadn't leapt from his chair to defend Lauren. Instead, he held her left hand bedecked with his diamond promise to love and cherish her. My own heart warmed, realizing he understood her need for comfort more than baring his fangs.

Elisha Castle held up her hands in self defense. "We didn't

know Nathan like any of you did. This was back when his parents still attended the synagogue. We didn't have a reason to suspect that Rabbi…er Harvey, would tell all these people to lie and cover up for Nathan. That *all* of those people would knowingly spread slander about Lauren instead. Not that anybody is perfect, but we never thought Harvey could do something so horrible."

Before Lauren could jump all over Elisha, Josh added, "After what I witnessed him do to Rick, I know you guys are telling the truth. It lined up with everything Pax told Aiden afterwards. I promise, we believe you now."

"But you still assumed the absolute worst about *me* and *my* character," Lauren cried.

"I know, and all I can do is keep apologizing," Elisha said, agonized. "We assumed these were all godly people—imperfect like anyone else—but not the kind to maliciously hurt someone. Lauren, when you posted that article on FaceSpace about tithing, you were opposing core beliefs of the synagogue. You know what sticklers they are about it. Rick Williams called you the *false prophet*, and with all of the other stories, I guess it just all made sense."

"Because Rick is some model of godly behavior himself," Jon sneered. "Everyone pretends they didn't know he was shacked up with Stephanie before they got married, let alone that he was sleeping with her before his divorce from Charlotte was done."

"We actually *didn't* know that," Josh murmured. "I mean, we knew the relationship happened quickly, but they didn't share all of that information. None of us thought to ask. Didn't seem like it was our place."

"But believing all these atrocious rumors about Charlotte and Lauren were perfectly fine?" Jon pressed.

"We talked about this already," Elisha replied tersely. "I said I was sorry."

"Not to me, you didn't," Lauren snapped.

Agitated, Josh said, "What do you want from us? My wife and I made a huge mistake and believed the wrong people. We were deceived, and by definition, that means you don't know you're believing lies. I promise, it was never our intent to hurt anybody." His brown eyes shifted from Lauren and then to the rest of the former Beth Shalom members.

"So, you did what you were told," Ted said with controlled anger. Since he worked together with Lauren, I knew he viewed her as a kid sister. Grant Kaplan might have been the only other man alive more protective of my friend. Harshly, Ted added, "Did you even stop to consider there might be two sides to the story? Why would you automatically believe the worst about a godly young woman who's been walking with the Lord since she was ten years old, but you didn't think to question all the holy rollers? What made them so special that you took their word without bothering to even think for yourselves?"

"It's not like that!" Elisha protested. "Do you have any idea how hard it would be to think our spiritual leader had us intercede in the throne room of God knowing he fed us a pack of lies to pray about?"

"I do," Rebecca Margolin chimed in. "My father was a corrupt pastor who grew more brazen each year. He bald-faced lied all the time and routinely did it in God's Name or by twisting Scripture. He fooled people for over thirty years because they bought into his persona. When he needed to play the victim, he knew how to manipulate the church to go to war —even if his own family members were the casualties. He weaponized that entire congregation against me, and nobody batted an eyelash. The reality of his actual intentions were too cruel and evil to compute. Nobody wants to believe the man or woman leading their church is a wolf in sheep's clothing, let alone all the ways they've been fooled and manipulated by them."

Turning back to the Castles, Jon asked, "What were you told about why I left there? Or Abigail or Jared for that matter? They told you Lauren was some porn-addicted adulterer and Charlotte was a Jezebel with authority issues. What bogus excuses did the two of you believe about why *I* left after two decades of serving? Why didn't you stop and question anything?"

"We did!" Josh argued. "That's why we're here now."

"No, you're here because Pax Fournier called your son, and the corruption of Beth Shalom finally landed in your own home," he corrected. "Whatever lies were spewed about Abigail, about Jared, about me—let alone Charlotte and Lauren—didn't give you a moment's hesitation. How could it be possible that Beth Shalom was *never* wrong? Was 'maintaining a Jewish identity' so important that you buried your heads in the sand about the very obvious issues in that place?"

"Don't answer that," Lauren interrupted, though with significantly less ire than before. All eyes turned to her as she had started the entire brouhaha with her outburst. "My parents struggled with this issue, and it cost us our relationship for a while. The brainwashing is real. I shouldn't be surprised they slandered me so badly, but it still hurts knowing everything I suffered and that people actually believed it."

"Well, we *are* sorry," Josh said. "So, let me apologize to you on behalf of me and my wife for believing the lies."

Lauren nodded and swallowed back tears. "Thank you," she murmured.

"Worshiping my so-called *Jewish identity* almost cost me my family too," Jared Levine said. "I was so fixated on proving how

Jewish I was, I couldn't see my own sin or hypocrisy. I hurt my wife and my children, all while thinking I was *better* than them. Poppy wanted nothing to do with Jesus because of how obnoxious I was. It's a miracle she ever forgave me."

Resolutely, Jon said, "This all starts from the top down. Harvey Lebow was a Jewish kid who got saved in the early 1970s and got rejected for it by his parents. He and the rest of these first generation, boomer messianic leaders lost the forest from the trees with the Jewish identity shtick. The problem is they're raising disciples as obnoxious as they are, or they're causing people to turn away from Jesus altogether. The only people I know from twenty-five years ago who are still involved in Messianic Judaism are on the payroll somehow. Everyone else is floundering on their own, has gone back to traditional Judaism, or like us, found a community of believers in a church or fellowship group."

Josh and Elisha clearly looked frustrated, and I could see we were getting nowhere. Emotions were high, and so many of us had wounds from religious trauma. I found myself in the unusual spot of quiet introspection rather than sharing my unfiltered opinions.

"Listen, can we stop and pray?" I asked. "I don't mean for Harvey Lebow's imminent destruction or imprisonment either." I shot a meaningful glance to each member of the Beth Shalom walking wounded. "Before Paul got saved, he had believers thrown in jail and even killed. The community in Jerusalem was wary of welcoming him because his reputation preceded him. They were right to be cautious and allow him the chance to prove himself, but our situation isn't that severe. It took courage for Jon and Elisha to come tonight, especially with the rest of us here. We don't need to beat them over the head with our collective PTSD."

"Beth Shalom murdered your reputation," Jon thundered. "Don't you care?"

"Do I care that a bunch of lying abusers made sure I'll never go back to a place that brought me so much pain and confusion anyway? Nope! You and I prayed about this exact topic a few weeks ago. Kind of feels like a blessing in disguise." Turning to the group, I added, "I've really struggled this High Holiday season wanting to be with other people who celebrate them. At one of my lower points, I even considered going back to Beth Shalom."

Lauren and Grant, who'd heard many of my rants regarding our old congregation, sat slack jawed. Jon came to stand behind me and placed his hands on my shoulders. He whispered an apology in my ear before addressing the room.

"I guess it's time for us to put our hurt feelings aside and focus on why we're all gathered here. Charlotte and I wanted to commemorate the Jewish holidays with our daughters. It has nothing to do with the Messianic talking points but about us wanting to connect spiritually with the worldwide Jewish community. Most importantly, we want to celebrate Jesus in all of this."

I grasped his hand on my shoulder and spoke from the heart. "To be perfectly clear, none of this religious ceremony compares to the privilege of knowing Jesus. Yeshua died for us and sent His Spirit to guide us and live in our hearts because we could never keep all the Torah on our own. So, as Jon said, while we want to be connected with our people, if we don't keep Jesus at the center of our worship, then we're missing the point."

The Castles nodded, and the rest of the room gave their approval as well.

Jon smiled down at me. "We have these appointed feasts as a copy and shadow of God's ultimate redemption plan. We see

Yeshua in Sukkot and the concept of *Immanuel* or 'God dwelling with us' when we're in the sukkah. Likewise, the parallels between Rosh HaShanah and Yom Kippur with *Revelation 20* are jaw dropping. It all points to Jesus, and God help me if I ever lose sight of that again or make an idol out of my Jewishness. Charlotte's the one who called me out on that."

"One day at a time," I said, with a wink and a grin.

The mighty Margolin took a deep breath before addressing our group. "I think we've neglected the rest of our friends outside long enough. If no one has any objections to the Castles joining us, I think we should welcome our guests and work together toward healing from the past. I don't expect anything to be instantaneous, but we can't heal if we refuse to let go of our grievances. That's what the Ten Days of Awe are supposed to be about."

Lauren looked dubiously at Josh and Elisha before nodding her head to acquiesce to Ted's request. She slipped outside with Grant, and as the room emptied, Jon and I were left alone with the Castles.

"Thank you," Elisha said, taking my hand in hers. "You didn't have to say any of that, but you did. You kept this from becoming World War III."

"Keeping my heart right with Jesus is more important than being right in my own eyes," I replied, squeezing her hand and then releasing it.

Jon added, "We have plenty of food, so please, help yourselves. Also, I'm sorry for being harsh with both of you." He slipped his arm around me as a show of solidarity. "I'm very protective of this amazing woman, but I can see where I jumped all over you. I apologize."

"Apology accepted," Josh said, shaking his hand.

I smiled briefly at Elisha and then watched them exit

through the sliding glass doors in Jon's kitchen out to the backyard.

"What a night," I sighed, slumping down in a dining room chair.

"You were amazing," Jon replied, joining me on a neighboring seat.

"Oh yeah?"

"You got the focus back where it needed to be—which is on the Lord. Charlotte Williams, who used to be labeled as a loose cannon and needs to be 'handled,' is the one who invited Jesus into the conversation to prevent a complete disaster."

I chuckled, "God is funny like that, isn't He?"

Jon smiled back. "Think you could handle a little more excitement?"

I rolled my eyes. "I'm not sure. You're not expecting anyone else from Beth Shalom to show up, are you?"

Wordlessly, he produced a square, velvet box from his pocket. Shifting from his chair down to the floor on his knees, he scooted toward me and held my eyes captive. I sat frozen in place as my heart pounded in my ears.

Finding my voice, I whispered, "Are you serious?"

His wolfish grin appeared. "I was just thinking of something else we could celebrate tonight. Got a minute? Because I need to ask you a very important question."

EPILOGUE

EIGHTEEN MONTHS LATER, RO'S TAN HAD LONG FADED from her singles cruise along with any hope of finding a significant other. Her official stance was that the only male she needed in her life was her German shepherd. Luke had proposed to Paisley during her grad school spring break, and Lauren had just celebrated her one year anniversary that February. Pax hovered protectively over Allie and Bella at church, although Allie either remained oblivious or used her daughter as a distraction. As Elisha predicted, Tina and George Madison went their separate ways, but Rick had changed his tune about Stephanie. Their toxic, over the top marriage was back on the menu.

After Jon's Sukkot proposal, we both agreed to give ourselves a long engagement and let the girls adjust to the idea. I figured news would travel back to the Beth Shalom hive once I told Rick. Not to be outdone, his wife suddenly sported a fancier diamond on her wedding finger. Hours after Jon and I made our relationship public on social media, Stephanie and

Rick flooded the internet with gushy pictures about their dream marriage.

Tina Fournier no longer found those posts inspirational.

Jon and I continued to attend Grace Abounds and eventually became members of the church. Other than myself, nobody was more shocked by the decision than my dear friend, Lauren, who often reminded me of my previous thoughts regarding organized religion.

"What makes this church so different?" she'd asked me over cheesecake at the Parkview Diner.

"It just *is*, Laur. They take the Bible seriously, and I don't mean their own interpretation of it and then condemning anyone who doesn't fit the congregational mold. Jon and I spent four hours at dinner getting to know one of the elders and his wife."

"Four *hours*?" she choked.

I nodded. "Yeah, we talked Bible from soup to nuts. At one point, the elder asked if we thought we were better because we're Jewish believers in Jesus. It wasn't accusatory, just curious."

"What did you tell him?"

"We told him absolutely not! Yes, we're passionate about who we are, but it's because we want to worship the Lord *through* our God-given, Biblical identity rather than worshiping *ourselves* because of that God-given, Biblical identity."

"Can I just say how proud I am of you?" my friend beamed.

I grinned back.

"Also, that ring is stunning."

I flexed my fingers to enjoy the emerald cut diamond reflecting every beam of light in the room.

"Charlotte?" an unexpected, male voice called.

My jaw dropped as I beheld Stephanie's ex divorce attorney,

Sean Bonham, in the flesh. I must have been blinded to how attractive he was when we had our date because that more vulnerable version of myself should have been a sitting duck. Instead, I silently thanked God for protecting me. I stood up and greeted him with a side hug.

"Who's the lucky guy?" He glanced down at my engagement ring.

"An old friend who became something more," I replied coyly.

Sean powered through with a smile. "If you're happy, then I'm happy for you. You deserve the best."

"Thank you. I hope you find what you're looking for, Sean. You're a great guy and deserve to be happy too."

At that moment, the third member of our cheesecake date arrived with her daughter, Bella, in tow.

Just like Pax Fournier, Sean's reaction to Allie was instantaneous. I had a feeling SeanBonLawyerMon would heal from his Cougar crush even faster than expected. Lauren shot me a side eyed glance, and I winked at her.

Muttering, I said, "Here we go again. I hope Allie's ready."

ACKNOWLEDGMENTS

For Vicky. Thank you for embracing my "sparkle girl" personality and teaching me how to use CNC tooling responsibly rather than simply wondering why all of those bits and blades look like instruments of torture.

Kasea, the absolute best sister I could ask for. My brother married the most amazing woman on the planet, and I selfishly get to benefit.

Mike, thanks for marrying Kasea. Also, I'm so proud of the man you are, the man you're growing into, and that no matter how many times I bring up the fact I used to help change your diapers, you still have more silver hair than me.

To my church family who welcomed me and my family exactly "as is," and provided a spiritual home for us to grow and rest.

For my beautiful babies who are growing up waaay too fast, but I'm not sorry we left potty training behind. You three bring so much light and joy to my life. I thank God every day for the privilege of being your mother. Also, stop calling me *cringe*.

To Jesus, the Lover of my soul, who patiently waited for me to see how my value has never been in what I can do to "repay" Him, but in finally knowing He's already paid my debts.

EXCERPT FROM ESHET HAYIL: MORE THAN BEAUTY

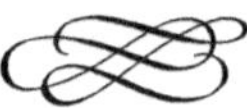

IT WAS ANOTHER SUNDAY AT GRACE ABOUNDS Church. Another Sunday with the same man purposefully seating himself to my left. Another Sunday where I wasn't going to catch feelings for him. Another Sunday where there was nothing I could do besides grit my teeth and tell myself beauty truly *was* a curse.

Maybe if I dyed my blonde hair to black, drowned in baggy clothes, or feigned a limp, Paxton Fournier would find somewhere else to sit. I'd hoped in vain he'd show interest in any of the single girls his own age. Goodness knows they didn't hide their interest in *him*. I already felt older than my thirty-two years as a divorced single mother, but none of that seemed to intimidate my six years younger admirer.

All the usual suspects filled our row of folding chairs within the gymnasium of Lion of Judah Christian School—where Grace Abounds rented their meeting space. First, there was Pax's self-appointed matchmaker, forty-something Charlotte Williams, and her slightly older, forty-something fiancé, Jon Roseman.

Next were Charlotte's teen daughters, Sophie and Lily. Jon had two daughters of his own, one who was married and one who was in her first year of college. Sometimes the extra girls joined us, sometimes they didn't, but it never changed my weekly seat. Charlotte and Jon had adopted Paxton like a surrogate son, and Charlotte did everything in her power to manufacture opportunities for him to talk to me.

Every week, I tried to sneak in the back, and every week Pax's well-intentioned and *very determined* friends invited me to their row. Whether I had my daughter, Bella, with me or not, they always made sure to have those one or two seats reserved. I could've fought harder and held my boundary, especially with my tantrum prone child who didn't like sharing Mommy with anyone, but having *any* friends who wanted me around was better than the alternative of having no friends at all.

My brow wrinkled, and I struggled to focus on that morning's sermon.

"You okay?" Pax whispered.

"Fine," I mumbled.

Of course, he'd been watching me.

His hooded blue eyes continued to search my face, and I shrunk inside myself. My personal struggles were none of Pax's business. The pre-divorced version of me might have savored every dollop of attention from an attractive younger man, but that naive girl no longer existed. Unfortunately, the more I kept up my walls, the more Pax seemed patiently determined to see them lowered.

Across the aisle, I caught Charlotte's inquisitive glance, probably cataloging our every move. I considered her a casual acquaintance, mostly because she was the best friend of Lauren Kaplan. It was Lauren, three years earlier, who had looked me directly in the eyes and invited me to her Bible study home group. She'd offered a version of Christianity I'd never experienced from my ex-husband. Some of the home group members also attended Grace Abounds Church, and after visiting both gatherings, I found I preferred a larger crowd where I could slip in and out. Unfortunately, I had the full attention of Pax and his helpers since he regularly attended both meetings.

I'd asked Charlotte a few questions to find out about Pax, initially to be sure his interest was in *me* and not Bella. While he seemed harmless enough, I would never allow my own childhood trauma to be visited upon my daughter. Charlotte was happy to provide details, undoubtedly to encourage any interest she perceived on my part.

According to Charlotte, Pax was a complete teddy bear—with a monster for a mother and a deceased father who was no angel either. That's also when I'd learned he was much younger than how he carried himself. If he'd acted like every other guy his age, Pax would have been easier to ignore. Instead, it was his maturity that led Charlotte to helping him obtain an inside sales job at her company, MG Industrial Tooling. Even with my second-grade bodyguard, Charlotte still assumed I was younger than my thirty-two years, and she'd mentioned how Pax was the same age as another Gen Z coworker of hers. I was ashamed of just how little I'd accomplished in life, so I didn't bother correcting her assumption.

A salaried sales job with bonuses and room to grow was a far cry from my own job as a front desk assistant at Bella's elementary school. I'd gladly taken the job to remain close to my daughter during her father's visitation weeks and to have my vacation time coincide with hers. After the divorce, it became obvious Brett had demanded the fifty-fifty shared custody to reduce child support, not because he wanted to work on their relationship. According to Bella, he usually left her to her own devices—which literally meant some sort of screen to keep her occupied and needing anything from him. To counteract his emotional neglect, I made sure Bella and I had lunch dates at school during his scheduled weeks. Every sacrifice was worth it for my high-strung baby girl, but as my emotional energy regularly wore thin, I wondered how different life would be if I'd chosen someone other than Brett Sanders to be her father.

That particular Sunday, my semi-feral little protector was with her dad, so I had no shield to hide behind. I didn't have to turn to know Pax's searching blue eyes were a few shades lighter than mine. His fashionably styled hair drew attention to a handsome face that could have been attracted to any other single female in that church. Anyone besides me.

"Are you sure you're okay?" he asked again.

I inched my body away. "I said I'm *fine.*"

He adjusted his own posture and sat straighter in the chair. The movement captured the interest of both Charlotte and Jon. Charlotte's fiancé, unlike most men I encountered, felt "safe" even before she'd laid claim to him a year earlier. Jon didn't look at me like an object but like a daughter. *That* kind of attention I welcomed with ease.

After the service, Charlotte and her girls surrounded me while Jon drew Pax into a private conversation. I could have sworn I saw a subtle nod and a wink in my direction. I mouthed the word "thank you," and Jon offered a smile before pulling Pax's arm—and attention—far away from me.

I felt the stare of someone else, and so did Charlotte, because she turned her focus toward a man behind us.

"Sean!" she exclaimed, breaking into a large smile. "What are you doing here?"

From just beyond her, a golden haired, golden eyed man

approached. His gaze met mine, and a shock of both attraction and vague recognition coursed through me. I knew I'd seen him somewhere before, and the feeling intensified as he stood beside Charlotte. Beaming, she yanked him into a brief, enthusiastic embrace.

"Nice to see you too," he laughed.

Eyes bright, she asked, "What brings you to Grace Abounds?"

"You invited me, remember? I decided to take you up on your offer."

Meanwhile, Charlotte's daughters looked absolutely gobsmacked, especially her youngest, Lily. Surely, her interest should have been in Pax who was demonstrably closer in age, but the self assurance in Sean's demeanor couldn't be taught. I glanced at Charlotte's friend and found his eyes were already on me. The nudge in my gut grew to a steady roar as his tailored ensemble reminded me eerily of Brett. I raised an eyebrow in irritation when Sean's direct stare didn't waver.

Oblivious, Charlotte swept her arm grandly to introduce us to her friend. "Sean Bonham, these are my girls Sophie and Lily, and this is—"

"Allison Sanders," he said before she could finish.

My raised eyebrows matched my heightened irritation. Having *one* church admirer was already one too many. "Do I know you? Is that why you keep looking at me like that?"

Color seeped into Sean's face as all four of us watched and waited for a response that never came. Finally breaking eye contact, he rubbed the back of his neck.

Charlotte's eyes flickered back to me, and she broke the tense silence. "Allison," she murmured, repeating my full name. "Sean, I didn't realize you'd already met."

I shot him a Bella-worthy glare. "Neither did I."

Finding his voice, Sean said, "I apologize for the outburst. We haven't been formally introduced, but we belonged to the same neighborhood HOA at one point. I didn't realize you go by *Allie*. I've seen you a few times around the block...and in my office."

Charlotte's eyes grew large, and it was clear she knew something I didn't. "Girls, can you come here for a minute? I need to ask Jon a question."

Lily continued to stare open-mouthed until her older sister, Sophie, yanked on the back of her shirt. Blushing, she scurried toward her mother.

Sean took a step closer and lowered his voice. "I live in Old Towne Hills, and I still see your ex on the golf course."

"How do you know he's my ex?"

"Well, I would assume he's your ex since I used to see the two of you walking around the neighborhood with your daughter. He has a new woman with him now. It's been a few years, hasn't it?"

I pressed my lips together, not wanting to be reminded how Brett's "stupid mistake that only happened *one* time" became his immediate live-in girlfriend after I moved out. I should have hated Alexis for what she'd done, but I mostly pitied her. She was the same age I had been when Brett Sanders swept me off my feet twelve years earlier. It also meant she would have to become a shadow of herself to keep him happy. I'd seen no evidence that Brett's controlling and entitled behavior had undergone any transformation. To Alexis' credit, Bella said she was nice enough, just preoccupied with her health and fitness social media persona.

Setting those thoughts aside, I studied Sean. He was handsome. Ridiculously so. I'd have to be blind, dead, or in denial to miss it. However, Charlotte's reaction to how he said he knew my name renewed the disquiet I felt.

"What do you mean you've seen me at your office?" I asked. "What do you do for a living? Whatever it is, you're obviously doing well if you live in Old Towne by yourself." I glanced at his bare wedding finger.

Sean hesitated before exhaling a self-conscious chuckle. My brows drew together as the self-assured armor showed some vulnerability. "I'm a family law attorney," he began.

"Meaning what, exactly? Wills and estates, or…" my voice trailed off as I had a sinking suspicion it was something much closer to home.

"I specialize in contested divorce cases," he said, filling in the blank. "I saw you in my office a while ago. Your attorney is one of my colleagues, and she came to me looking for advice regarding your divorce settlement."

My mouth formed an "oh" as I searched his eyes for any signs of a lie. "I didn't realize Maria had talked to anyone else about my case. Even if you're another attorney at her firm, isn't that supposed to be privileged information?"

"Like I said, she was looking for some insight. Maria was just trying to do right by you. I promise, she's one of the good ones."

"And what does that make you?"

Sean paused, his amber eyes assessing me. "You don't think I'm one of the good ones?"

"I don't even know you."

"Maybe you ought to give me a chance before you prejudge me."

I rose to the challenge, channeling some of the fearlessness that oozed from every pore of my child. "How would you feel if some complete stranger walked up to you and announced they know your name and your private business?"

He surprised me by smiling. "Charlotte's planning to publish her memoirs soon. My name made it into her book along with our catastrophe of a first date. A whole bunch of complete strangers are about to know *my* personal business if it makes you feel any better."

I couldn't hide my surprise. "You and Charlotte went out?"

"We did."

"Do you have some kind of older woman fetish? Like a cougar hunter or something?"

"She's not *that* much older," he groused.

I glanced at my mid forty-ish friend, trying to imagine the two of them together.

Sean waved a hand to regain my attention. "It's ancient history. Charlotte gave me some food for thought, and I wanted to visit her church since she speaks so highly of it. Given her past experience with organized religion, anything that meets *her* approval has to be pretty good."

I nodded slowly. "And that's the only reason why you're here?"

A flash of guilt came and went in his eyes. Before I could comment, my other church admirer approached, clearly ready to perform his self-appointed protector role.

"Hi, I'm Pax," he said, shoving out his hand to shake Sean's.

They measured up one another, and I nearly rolled my eyes. While they exchanged cordial pleasantries, I scanned the room looking for anybody to save me from the awkwardness.

Coming to my rescue was Jon Roseman once again. "Sean, I'm glad you could make it," he said, clapping him on the shoulder. "Charlotte's told me a lot about you."

He visibly swallowed and then let out a small cough. "Is that right?"

Jon smiled warmly. "All good, I promise. I see you've met Pax and Allie."

I didn't like how he joined our names together, and even Sean glanced between the two of us in question.

I fished for my purse still sitting on the chair. "I hope you guys enjoy the rest of your Sunday, and I'll see you around."

Just a hair faster, Pax reached it first and then made sure to hand it to me.

I didn't lift my eyes to his, instead focusing on the designer bag I'd purchased from the thrift store. I also made a conscious effort to avoid touching Pax as I took it back. "Thanks," I murmured.

As I turned and tried not to immediately bolt from the room, Jon called after me. "Allie, will we see you tonight at Bible study? Sean, my fiancée wanted to invite you as well."

Both Sean and Pax watched me for a response. Charlotte had rejoined her fiancé and seemed to pick up on the tension. She offered an inquiring glance of concern, and I shook my head as I stared longingly toward the exit.

"I, um…I'm not sure," I finally said.

Pax couldn't hide his disappointment and Sean couldn't hide his curiosity.

Meanwhile, all I wanted to do was hide myself.

OTHER WORKS BY ANA WATERS

BEAUTY FOR ASHES SERIES
Book 1: Tabula Rasa: Writing a New Story
Book 2: Ex Nihilo: Learning to Live Again
Book 3: Tikkun Olam: Restoring What Was Lost
Book 4: Lev Tahor: A Heart Redeemed
Book 5: Brit Hadasha: All Things Made New

www.ingramcontent.com/pod-product-compliance
Lightning Source LLC
Chambersburg PA
CBHW070314310726
48976CB00005B/1701